BLACK SUN

The Eclipse of Zulu Power

BLACK SUN

The Eclipse of Zulu Power

Christopher Lloyd King

Copyright © 2024 Christopher Lloyd King

Christopher Lloyd King has asserted his rights under the Copyright, Design and Patents Act 1988 to be identified as the author of this book.

Apart from any fair dealing for the purposes of research or private study, or criticism or review, as permitted under the Copyright, Designs and Patents Act 1988, this publication may only be reproduced, stored or transmitted, in any form or by any means, with the prior permission in writing of the publishers, or in the case of reprographic reproduction in accordance with the terms of licences issued by the Copyright Licensing Agency. Enquiries concerning reproduction outside those terms should be sent to the publishers.

All rights reserved. No part of this publication may be reproduced, stored in a retrieval system, or transmitted in any form or by any means electronic, mechanical, audio, visual or otherwise, without prior permission in writing of the copyright owner. This copyright work may not be circulated in any form of binding or cover other than that in which it is published without similar conditions including this condition being imposed on the subsequent purchaser.

Troubador Publishing Ltd
Unit E2 Airfield Business Park,
Harrison Road, Market Harborough,
Leicestershire. LE16 7UL
Tel: 0116 2792299
Email: books@troubador.co.uk
Web: www.troubador.co.uk

ISBN 978 1805143 093

British Library Cataloguing in Publication Data.
A catalogue record for this book is available from the British Library.

Printed and bound in Great Britain by 4edge Limited
Typeset in 11pt Adobe Garamond Pro by Troubador Publishing Ltd, Leicester, UK

*In memory of my parents,
Tom and Gwenda King*

FOREWORD

This story has its origins in contemporary accounts of events that led up to and beyond the British invasion of Zululand on 11 January 1879. This created the circumstances for a four-year-long war resulting in a permanent change in Zulu fortunes.

The characters involved are historical figures – although different names have been ascribed to some. Certain incidents in the narrative have been fictionalised, but by and large what is described actually happened.

Compared with histories of the Anglo-Zulu conflict from the British perspective, material describing the Zulu point of view is in short supply. Zulu tradition is based on word of mouth. Warriors returning from the battlefields recounted their stories to their relatives, and it is these reports that have been handed down to posterity.

The nearest we have to an authentic first-hand account of the Zulu experience is provided by a young Victorian writer who, immediately after the Zulu defeat, travelled extensively through Zululand and recorded his impressions. Bertram Mitford's *Through the Zulu Country: its Battlefields and People*, originally published in 1883 and reprinted in 1992 by Greenhill

Books, records interviews with warriors who were physically present at the important battles. Mitford describes encounters with both Mehlokazulu and Sihayo and sets down in detail their eyewitness accounts of these events. It is a fascinating and invaluable source of direct personal memory.

The modern edition of *Through Zulu Country* contains an introduction by Ian Knight, and here I'd like to record my indebtedness to this scholar, the foremost authority on the period during the last twenty years. Ian Knight has conducted tours over the Zulu battlefields and published several books covering various aspects of the war. His *Zulu Rising*, published in 2010, was the starting point for *Black Sun*. His vivid descriptions, cutting backwards and forwards between the two embattled sides using a technique cinematic in its scope, left an indelible impression.

As an eighteen-year-old, between leaving school and going to university, I spent a year teaching in Zambia during which I used some holiday time to travel to kwaZulu-Natal. I took photographs that have enabled me, years later, to reawaken memories and impressions of the landscape. While reading *Zulu Rising*, I was able to populate the hills and valleys of kwaZulu with the historical protagonists described by Ian Knight.

Most histories of the Anglo-Zulu conflict written since 1986 refer to Paulina Dlamini's *Servant of Two Kings* (published in 1986 by the Killie Campbell Africana Library and the University of Natal Press). This memoir of the great-granddaughter of Swazi King Sobhuza, covering her years of service in Cetshwayo's *isiGodlo* and her subsequent conversion to Christianity, has been an inspiration throughout the writing of *Black Sun*. Nomguqo, or Paulina (her baptismal name), lived at oNdini during the Anglo-Zulu war and her role as handmaiden to the royal family allowed her a privileged view of Cetshwayo before, during, and after the destruction of his kingdom. Her recollections of life in the royal *umuZi*, its daily routines and important ceremonies, was an invaluable resource.

I'm also indebted to Professor Noleen Turner of the School of isiZulu Studies, University of KwaZulu-Natal, for allowing me access to her monograph 'Scatalogical License: The case of ribald references and sexual insults in the *amaculo omgonqo* (puberty songs)'.

CONTENTS

PART ONE: **ANCESTORS**   1

PART TWO: **THE EYES OF THE ZULU**   123

PART THREE: **THE SUN GROWS DARK**   215

PART FOUR: **TRIUMPH AND DISASTER**   293

PART FIVE: **RESTORATION**   425

PART SIX: **THE DAY THAT I DIE**   477

AFTERWORD   497
ACKNOWLEDGEMENTS   500
GLOSSARY   501
BIBLIOGRAPHY   506

ZULU ROYAL FAMILY

BESIYILE
CETSHWAYO's daughter.

KING CETSHWAYO
Inherited the Zulu throne from his father MPANDE, who ruled after his brothers SHAKA and DINGAAN. Through the systematic and ruthless conquest of neighbouring tribes, SHAKA had created the largest kingdom in southern Africa.

DABULAMANZI
CETSHWAYO's brother and royal prince.

DINUZULU
CETSHWAYO's son and heir.

HAMU
CETSHWAYO's brother, royal prince, senior member of the *ibandla* (royal council), general commanding the uThulwana regiment.

NDABUKO
CETSHWAYO's brother and royal prince.

NOMVIMBI
The *Umfazi Omkhulu* (Great Wife), most senior of CETSHWAYO's wives, and DINUZULU's mother.

USIXIPE#
Royal wife and mother of twins.

ZIBHEBHU
CETSHWAYO's cousin, royal prince and *ibandla* member, a senior army commander.

ZULU ROYAL HOUSEHOLD

DLEPHU NDLOVU
CETSHWAYO's *iNgoma* (witchdoctor).

MEHLOKAZULU
CETSHWAYO's attendant, section commander of the iNgobamakhosi regiment.

MNUKWA
CETSHWAYO's *inceku* (servant).

NOBATHWA#
Guardian of the *eNkatheni* (royal hut containing the *inkatha*, the sacred coil of the Zulu nation).

NOBHODLILE#
An *iQhikiza* (older, menstruating girl). NOMGUQO's hutmate in the *isiGodlo* (the king's private quarters).

NGUYAZE#
An *iQhikiza*. NOMGUQO's hutmate.

NOMGUQO
Great-granddaughter of Swazi King SOBHUZA, given in tribute by her father SIKHUNYANE to serve in the Zulu court.

SIXHWETHU#
NOMGUQO's hutmate, the same age as her.

UMAFUTHA#
An *iQhikiza*. NOMGUQO's hutmate.

ZULU ROYAL COUNCIL (IBANDLA)

DABULAMANZI (see royal family).

HAMU (see royal family).

JANTONI (aka JOHN DUNN)
Trader and hunter of Scottish émigré parentage. CETSHWAYO's consultant in British policy and an *inkosi* (important chief) in his own right.

MAVUMENGWANA
Military general.

MNYAMANA
Prime minister, the most senior of CETSHWAYO's *iziNduna* (counsellors).

NDABUKO (see royal family).

NTSHINGWAYO
Military general, commander in the field.

SIHAYO
MEHLOKAZULU's father, close friend of CETSHWAYO. Minister of state, *inkosi* of the amaQungebeni, protector of the southern frontier with the British-governed province of Natal.

VUMANDABA
Minister of state, diplomat in charge of peace delegation.

ZIBHEBHU (see royal family).

NORWEGIAN MISSIONARIES

GUNDVALL GUNDERSEN (aka GUNISENI)
Pastor of the Norwegian Mission Society based at oNdini.

GUNHILD CHRISTINE
His adopted daughter, Zulu by birth.

JOACHIME
GUNISENI's first wife.

MARTHE
GUNISENI's second wife.

OTHERS

DIBOLI
NOMGUQO's sister.

MATSHANA
Inkosi of the Sithole.

MELIYAM
NOMGUQO's sister.

MaMTSHALI
SIHAYO's wife, MEHLOKAZULU's mother.

MAWENI#
iNgobamakhosi herdboy, SIXHWETHU's *iSoka* (recognised boyfriend).

MBILINI
NOMGUQO's cousin, of Swazi ancestry and *inkosi* of the abaQulusi.

MBULAWA#
iNgobamakhosi warrior, UMAFUTHA's *iSoka*.

MKHUMBIKAZULU
MEHLOKAZULU's younger brother.

QHUDE#
uThulwana warrior.

SHIKASHIKA
iNgobamakhosi herdboy, NOMGUQO's *iSoka*.

SIKHUNYANE
NOMGUQO's father.

PLACE NAMES

BANGANOMO
ZIBHEBHU's *umuZi* (homestead).

HLOBANE
Site of Mbilini's victory.

iSANDLWANA
Site of the first battle of the war.

KHAMBULA
Site of third catastrophic Zulu defeat.

kwaJIM
Rorke's Drift, the trading post at the crossing between Zululand and Natal, named after Irish settler and trader James Rorke.

kwaNKATHA
Execution rock.

kwaNODWENGU
Ikhanda (military barracks) close to oNdini, originally King MPANDE's "Great Place".

kwaSOGEKLE
SIHAYO's homestead on the river Mzinyathi, the southern border with British Natal.

MKHUZE
Homestead of SIKHUNYANE, NOMGUQO's father.

oNDINI
CETSHWAYO's "Great Place".

REGIMENTS (in age-group order, oldest regiment first)

uKhokhoti (age group born 1817-18)
iSangqu (age group born 1828)
uThulwana incorporated with the iNdlondlo (age group born 1830)
uDloko (age group born 1835)
uDududu (age group born 1837)
uMxapho (age group born 1840)
uMbonambi (age group born 1842)
uNokhenke (age group born 1845)
iNdluyengwe (age group born 1847)
uKhandempemvu (age group born 1848)
iNgcugce (female regiment age group born 1853)
iNgobamakhosi (age group born 1853)
uVe (age group born 1855-8)

# Denotes fictional character

PART ONE

ANCESTORS

ONE

oNdini, Zululand

The green snake undulated through the thick stems of the thorn fence, the pulses of its motor muscles propelling it along the ground. From time to time, it lifted its head, flicking out its tongue to scent the air, and with lidless eyes, scanned for the movement of potential prey. Experience told it that wherever human beings congregated rodents and other scavenging creatures would follow. It had no fear of humans since its reptilian brain was programmed only to process messages associated with prey or procreation.

Continuing its progress along the fence, it reached an obstacle, a construction of hard-baked mud. It probed upward in exploration, running the soft skin of its throat against the smooth surface. The scales on its belly found purchase where the thorn bushes protruded through the thick impasto of mud, and as the snake climbed, it followed the contours of an arch until it emerged from the interwoven thorn branches on to a natural platform from which it could observe the activities below. The grey half-light before dawn glinted off its emerald scales. It stopped again, feeling a vibration it couldn't place: the shrill sound of a girl's voice. Struggling to process this unknown sound, it stared unblinking from the gateway to the compound.

Below, a group of ten adolescent Zulu girls was gathered around the entrance to a grassed thatched hut. They were naked apart from the rawhide kirtles around their waists; some wore bead necklaces. Their breath condensed in plumes of vapour in the early morning air. Shuffling their bare feet, they blew on their fingers trying to keep warm. Beside them a collection of empty calabashes waited to be filled.

Sixhwethu, square set with an elaborate adornment of feathers and beads covering her chest, stamped impatiently. With the characteristic clicks of isiZulu, she harangued the unseen resident of the hut, '*Inkosazana*, wake up! If you don't stir yourself, the king will send for the hyena men, and your body will be eaten by wild dogs.'

Inside, jolted from her slumbers, thirteen-year-old Nomguqo peered bleary-eyed around the smoky interior of the hut. She was alarmed to find herself alone, all the adjacent sleeping mats already vacated and stowed away. The embers of the previous night's fire continued to smoulder in the hearth, smoke spiralling up into the thatch. She stared at the dark shape filling the doorway. 'Who's that?' she asked.

'It's your phantom lover, the one you've been dreaming about. Quickly now, there's water to be collected.'

Collecting herself, Nomguqo stood, smoothing her kirtle where it had ridden up in the night. Shamefaced at having overslept, she joined Sixhwethu and the other water carriers. Her sleepy-eyed appearance provoked a chorus of giggles.

'Did your lover give you no rest?' Sixhwethu asked.

'Been riding you all night long?' added Nobhodlile, an *iQhikiza* (older girl).

In view of the celibacy rule for unmarried men and women, a direct edict of King Cetshwayo and enforceable by death, it was hardly surprising that sex should be the sole preoccupation of the young, even ones as young as these. What else was there to talk about? And the cruder and more direct the language, the better.

It was a topic to which Nomguqo was indifferent. Physically she was still a child. Her monthly cycles had yet to start and, though her nipples were beginning to bud, she had retained her boyish hips, and the simple line of her genital cleft remained unblurred by any growth of hair.

Ignoring the taunts, she bent down and picked up the largest of the gourds – though physically she was the least capable of carrying the container full of water. She did so in the hope that the generosity of her gesture might deflect some of the ribaldry.

The green snake stared down at the girls as they filed under the arch.

A couple of warriors stood guard at the entrance to the *isiGodlo* – King Cetshwayo's inner sanctum, which contained the huts of the royal wives. Thick oxhide cloaks covered their shoulders against the morning chill. As Sixhwethu drew level, one of them broke wind, the sound resounding in the still air. It seemed like a calculated insult. Sixhwethu certainly took it as such. She flounced past him, sucking her teeth contemptuously and sneering, 'Filthy pig.'

The warrior yawned indifferently while his companion sniggered and shifted his weight from one foot to the other. Leaning on their spears, they returned to their duty.

'Men,' Sixhwethu grumbled as she and the other girls made their way through the maze of huts that made up the rest of the king's "Great Place", 'no better than animals. And to think I'll have to share a blanket with one when I'm married.'

'*You* fart,' Nobhodlile said.

'No, I don't.'

'Yes, you do, and I should know. I sleep next to you.'

The other girls' giggles earned a reproving look from an early riser emerging from her hut. The woman had a squalling infant on her hip, and the haunted look in her eyes suggested she had passed a sleepless night. Recognising Usixipe, one the king's younger wives, the girls were instantly silenced. They knew better than to upset a member of the king's inner circle.

The rest of the *umuZi* slumbered on. More than ten thousand people lived in the oNdini homestead, the warriors of Cetshwayo's favourite regiments and their families. The girls' conversation continued in whispers.

'Anyway, who'd have you as a wife?' Umafutha scoffed. The oldest girl in the hut, she was also the most senior in rank.

'You wait, I'll be married with a son before the next harvest,' Sihwethu retorted.

'Really? You haven't even got a boyfriend.'

'Oh, haven't I?'

'Have you?'

Sixhwethu gave a mischievous grin. 'Wouldn't you like to know?'

Lengthening her stride, Nomguqo was quickly ahead of the others. She looked back. Her companions were clearly absorbed in their banter, so she could enjoy a temporary moment by herself. Shifting the weight of the calabash on her head, she returned to her thoughts. It wasn't that she chose to be alone; it was just easier that way. If the girls in the *isiGodlo* wanted to treat her as an outsider, that's what she'd be. They called her *inkosazana*, princess, a term of respect to which she was entitled as the great-grand-daughter of a king, but they meant it ironically. They smirked as they said it, intending it to hurt. They even imitated her Swazi accent. She was confident that if her father knew she was being picked on he would intercede with Cetshwayo and ensure the bullies were punished, but by the same token she knew she could never reveal the source of her misery.

His own childhood was an object lesson in how to accept, without complaint, the obstacles that life placed along the way. Captured as a boy by a Zulu raiding party, Sikhunyane found his easy-going existence as a royal prince instantly transformed into a routine of backbreaking servitude. From cockcrow to sundown, he was at the whim of Maboya kaMbundunlwane Buthelezi, an officer in King Dingaan's army and a hard taskmaster. He accepted his lot and, through application and diligence, earned promotion in Maboya's household. After many years of service, he became a trusted advisor and eventually an envoy between the Zulu and Swazi royal courts. The rewards for his service were five wives and a large herd of cattle.

Born after her father's fortunes changed, Nomguqo enjoyed a privileged upbringing. She had no reason to believe it would end. Until the day Sikhunyane broke the news that Maboya had decided she should be given as an *umndlunkulu* (handmaiden) to the recently crowned Zulu King Cetshwayo. The announcement felt like a kick in the stomach. She struggled to understand how he could send her away, his own flesh and blood. He explained, 'Nomguqo, this is a great honour – to you, to our family and, most especially, to Maboya and the rest of the Buthelezi clan. When you kneel before Cetshwayo, you will represent us all.'

She accepted her fate without question and, though broken-hearted at the loss of her family, she never let Sikhunyane see how upset she was. She only gave way to her emotions when she was alone. Then the tears flowed without check. She wept until her cheeks ached.

She was some distance from the *umuZi*, following the path as it meandered through the maize fields. It was the start of the growing season, and on either side of the path, row upon row of green shoots poked through the earth.

As she continued down the track, a single-story building emerged from the gloom. It was in the European style: stone-built with a verandah running along one side. A protective thorn hedge separated the carefully tended grounds from the uncultivated scrubland. Flowers grew in abundance – bougainvillea and flamboyants – but the most distinctive feature of the garden was its orchard. All kinds of fruit trees had been planted: peaches, apricots, guavas, oranges, lemons.

She drew closer, recognising in the half-light the tall rangy figure of a white man collecting peaches for his breakfast. Intent on choosing the ripest fruit, he failed to notice her at first. It was only when he started back to the house that he saw her. He put down the basket and buttoned his black frock coat against the breeze that had started to blow. The lower half of his face was hidden by an imposing beard, but where his white skin was exposed, it had been tanned to a rich brown from his many years of service in the tropics. His pale blue eyes betrayed his Nordic origins. They twinkled in greeting. '*Sawubona*, Nomguqo.'

'*God morgen*, Guniseni.'

As she had to pass by twice a day on her way to the river and frequently found the kindly *umlungu* (white man) in his garden, she had struck up an acquaintance with him. She looked forward to their encounters and, though their conversation hadn't progressed much beyond a greeting, he in isiZulu and she in the only words of Norwegian she knew, she had grown to trust him. She also enjoyed the gifts of fruit he gave her.

She'd learned about his background from the *isiGodlo* gossips. They called him *Guniseni*, but his actual name was Gundvall Gundersen, a pastor belonging to the Norwegian Mission Society. She understood little of what being a missionary entailed but she sensed from her own encounters that he was a kindly man.

The other girls had told her that Cetshwayo was intolerant of the pastor's attempts to convert the amaZulu to Christianity. He'd made it clear he would not welcome any attempts to evangelise his subjects. Consequently, Gundersen relied on inducement rather than the force of argument. The gift of a few oranges or peaches showed his own generosity of spirit and, by extension, that of the Holy Spirit. His kindness had made him a favourite of all the *isiGodlo* girls, and they pestered him constantly for fruit.

'You're an early bird,' he said, offering her one of the peaches.

She shook her head and pointed to the chattering girls dawdling along the path in the distance.

'Oh, don't worry, there's plenty more for them,' he said. 'Go on, take it. It's ready to eat.'

After a moment's hesitation, she took the peach, giving a shy smile of thanks. 'Not so early,' she volunteered. 'I overslept.'

Gundersen tutted in mock rebuke. 'Better not make a habit of it. Your hutmates will make your life misery.'

If only you knew, she thought. 'It was smokey in the hut last night. I was coughing so much I couldn't sleep.'

Gundersen smiled sympathetically. 'We know all about oversleeping in our house. My daughter would stay in bed all day if we let her.'

As though to confound this characterisation, a five-year-old girl appeared in the doorway rubbing her eyes. She ran to join them and held up her arms for her father to pick her up. Tucking her head under his chin, she yawned.

'Still sleepy, Gunhild?' Nomguqo asked.

The girl pressed herself even more tightly into Gundersen's embrace. He kissed the top of her head. The contrast of skin colour between them suggested she was adopted, her biological parents clearly Zulu.

'Are you going to help Daddy with the garden today?' Nomguqo said.

Gunhild opened her eyes wide. 'No, silly, I'm going to play with my dolls.'

'No need to be rude,' Gundersen scolded. Setting her down, he patted her head. 'You run along and tell your mother I'll be in soon with our breakfast.'

Gunhild hurried back to the house.

Still some distance away, Sixhwethu shouted, 'Guniseni! Don't give all your peaches to the *inkosazana*. We're hungry too!'

Adjusting the calabash on her head, Nomguqo quickened her pace towards the river. She bit into the downy skin of the peach, its juice running down the corners of her mouth. The sweetness of its taste contrasted with the bland monotony of her daily diet of mealie porridge and milk curds. It was a wonderful treat.

The beams of the rising sun glinted off the rippling water as she reached the riverbank. Birds were already active, swooping through the shreds of mist hanging over the still water in the shallows where the insects were most numerous. A fish eagle, hungry after the night's vigil, flapped its great wings and plunged into the water, grasping a glittering fish in its talons. Flying to a nearby acacia tree, it used its curved beak to tear the flesh apart.

She knelt by the water's edge, dipping the calabash where the river ran faster. As it filled, she had a sudden pang of homesickness prompted by seeing the little Zulu girl in Pastor Gundersen's arms. The intimacy of the embrace, the gentleness with which he kissed her reminded her of her own father's love and what she'd lost. Her eyes filled with tears, and she breathed deeply, shaking her head to dispel the image. There was no point in dwelling on the past. She knew from experience that any display of weakness would invite mockery from her hutmates, particularly Sixhwethu. As a distraction she looked downstream. The royal cattle were being led down to drink, a long procession of cows and calves, their hooves churning up the riverbanks. She watched as the *iziNdibi* (herdboys) chivvied and chased their charges, ensuring each animal drank its fill. The herd never failed to impress her. Forty thousand magnificent animals. A cacophony accompanied them: the shouts of the *iziNdibi* mingling with the cows' bellowing and plaintive cries of calves searching for their mothers.

TWO

Back at the homestead, the snake's hunger remained unappeased. Securing itself around a thorn branch, it let itself down to the ground. Now fully extended, it revealed itself as of considerable size, over eight feet long and as thick as a man's thigh. It had a dark-brown mark just below its head. Hearing a scuffling in the thorn hedge, it dropped to the earth and slithered into the tangle of thorn.

Its hunting instincts, however, were frustrated. Expecting a rat, the green snake found itself face to face with a brown snake of similar dimensions.

Its reactions were immediate. It collected itself instantly into an aggressive stance, coils gathered under it and head poised ready to strike. Before the brown snake had time to act, it darted forward, pink mouth gaping wide, and fangs exposed in a display of belligerence. It was taking no chances. It struck again, sinking its fangs into the neck of the intruder, and retreated ready for another assault. The brown snake recoiled and reared up, air in its lungs expelled in a loud explosive hiss.

The two snakes faced off, their heads swaying sideways as they probed for weakness. It was a trial to establish whose nerve would break soonest. If the green snake considered that the suddenness of its first attack would intimidate its opponent, it was in for a disappointment. The brown snake matched it for size and aggression.

They lunged forward simultaneously, colliding with bruising force. The dry leaves at the base of the hedge were swept aside as their tails thrashed about seeking an anchor-point. Their necks intertwined as they fought for advantage. Being constrictors, neither had venom in its armoury, relying on weight and strength to gain the upper hand. They wrestled this way and that, neither giving ground.

Beyond the *isiGodlo* gateway, the *iMbongo* (praise singer) made his rounds to remind the sleeping residents of the deeds of the king and all the ancestors. An overweight man in his fifties, his physical bulk was in proportion with the prodigious memory banks on which he called as custodian of Zulu history. The rolls of his belly fat wobbled as he made his way through the royal enclosure. His eulogies were part of the *umuZi*'s daily ritual. They were the first sounds Cetshwayo heard on waking. The rapid-fire commentary, composed in the rhetorical style of classical isiZulu, was delivered without pause. 'Behold the break of day, oh mighty one, son of the great Mpande. May the rising sun illuminate you with its radiance, so that you might reflect its glory onto your humble servants. Your exploits have been innumerable, and your grateful people fervently trust that you will be preserved to accomplish many more. You have vanquished all your foes, brought them to grovel at your feet–'

And he would have continued in this vein had not the commotion in the hedge stopped him in mid flow. The shock of seeing the two snakes entwined in a life-and-death struggle made him drop his ceremonial wand. While the snakes continued to wrestle, each seeking to bury its fangs in the other's neck, he picked up his stick, shuffled to the king's residence and used it to hammer on the door. 'Ndabezitha, pardon my intrusion, but please come quickly!' Receiving no answer, he hammered again.

One by one, the entrances to the royal wives' huts filled with their occupants, stretching and blinking sleep from their eyes.

From the hut of the *umfazi omkhulu* (great wife) Nomvimbi – mother of the king's son and heir – Cetshwayo himself emerged. Brow furrowed in anger, he spoke quietly and deliberately but with menace: 'Who dares interrupt my sleep?'

The king was a formidable presence. His exceptional height of six feet three and heavy build meant that he physically dominated his subjects. He was in peak condition, still capable of leading his *amabutho* (regiments) onto the battlefield.

The praise-giver quaked before the royal wrath. Turning and pointing with his ceremonial wand, he stammered, 'Ndabezitha, look.'

By now the snakes had left the shelter of the thorn hedge. They continued their battle on the open ground in front of the huts. The green snake drew blood every time it sank its fangs into its opponent's neck. Wounds opened in their skin and trickles of blood stained the dusty earth.

Cetshwayo watched, rooted to the spot. He knew instinctively that the presence of these snakes was a bad omen. They must be *amaDlozi*, the spirits of the ancestors in bodily form. Their battle signified something important. He lacked the skill to interpret its meaning and required the advice of his *iNgoma* (witchdoctor). 'Send for Dlephu Ndlovu immediately!'

As though by magic, a small wizened elderly man wearing a full-length cloak of oxhide appeared. Staring intently at the battling snakes with eyes made bloodshot by a long addiction to *gwai* – snuff ground from dried cannabis leaves – he came to a quick conclusion. He leaned towards Cetshwayo, speaking quietly but insistently, 'Ndabezitha, I urge you to leave this place.' Gathering his cloak, the *iNgoma* moved off expecting the king to follow. Cetshwayo stood uncertain as to what to do. Dlephu Ndlovu barked a command, 'Immediately, Your Majesty. You're in danger!'

Tearing his gaze from the snakes, Cetshwayo allowed himself to be led towards a hut standing on its own in the centre of the *isiGodlo*.

'Here you'll be safe,' the witchdoctor added.

It looked no different from all the other huts but, this, the *eNkatheni*, was the most sacred shelter in the whole of the homestead. It was where the *inkatha* was kept, the holy coil containing Cetshwayo's own personal power and that of the entire nation. Here, the *iNgoma* reasoned, Cetshwayo would be protected from harm.

The old woman guarding the *inkatha* looked up in alarm as they entered.

'Leave us, Nobathwa,' Dlephu Ndlovu ordered.

The woman needed no second urging. As she scuttled off, the *iNgoma* indicated the *inkatha*, a thick grass plait sewn into a python skin that lay on a mat. It was large enough to accommodate the king's muscled buttocks. This was the sacred coil of the Zulu nation. Over the years it had been infused with the collected body fluids of all the Zulu kings since Shaka and was therefore potent with the values of the king's ancestors. It would act as a powerful prophylactic against the harmful influence of the snakes.

'Please, Ndabezitha, take your place,' Dlephu Ndlovu said.

Folding his powerful frame into a crouch, the king lowered himself onto the coil. His normally assertive voice carried a note of uncertainty. 'What does this portend?'

The witch doctor knelt beside the king and sat back on his haunches. 'I must consult the other *iziNgoma,* but I suspect that these snakes are here to do you harm. They're the physical embodiment of the ancestors. The green one has a fury and frenzy that reminds me of Shaka the Great. The brown one is possibly your father Mpande. Perhaps "Shaka" is jealous of your achievements and wants to kill you, while "Mpande" is acting as a dutiful parent trying to protect you.'

Cetshwayo collected himself. 'The solution is simple. Kill the green snake. We must take no chances. My father was feeble and ineffectual at the end of his life. It follows therefore that his spirit will be feeble and ineffectual. We must not allow "Mpande" to be defeated.'

'With respect, Ndabezitha, an *iDlozi* cannot be killed. Misfortune will follow otherwise.'

The king fixed his adviser with a belligerent glare. 'What must be done, then?'

'For the moment, nothing. But while you're here, no harm can come to you. I'll ensure the gateway is closed so the *amaDlozi* are not disturbed.' Rocking forward, the witch doctor pushed himself upright. 'Is there anything you require?'

The king settled himself on the coil, resigned to his temporary confinement.

'I'll make my ablutions,' he said. 'Send in my bathwater.'

Gourds of water teetering on their heads, Nomguqo and the other girls milled around the gateway, barred by a section of warriors carrying spears. One of them was the guard whose flatulence had offended Sixhwethu earlier. She stood on tiptoe to peer over his shoulder. 'What's going on?'

'This gateway is closed until further notice. Orders of His Majesty.'

'Why?'

'The ancestors are not to be disturbed.'

'Ancestors?'

Crouching down, the girls peeked through a gap in the thorn bushes. The snakes were still embattled, although the attacks were less violent and had become a war of attrition.

A large crowd was ranged in a semi-circle in front of the huts, held in check by heavily armed warriors. They repeated the familiar salutation to the ancestors: *Bhayede! Bhayede!* – the same cry used by the *impi* (army) when it went into battle.

The guard turned to the girls. 'You can use the western gateway. And you'd better look lively. The king has ordered his ablutions to be prepared.'

Those in charge of the royal bath were waiting at the western gate: four men in their early twenties. All wore their hair long since they hadn't yet been given permission to marry. Apart from the *beshu*, the hide apron covering their buttocks, they were naked. One of them stepped forward: a strongly built youth to whom the others appeared to defer. His piercing eyes, earning him the name Mehlokazulu ("Eyes of the Zulu"), blazed with anger.

'Stupid girls,' he spat. 'Where have you been? His Majesty can't be kept waiting.'

Sixhwethu squared up to him. 'No need to adopt that tone, Mehlokazulu nGobese. His Majesty's bath is your responsibility, not ours.'

'Do *you* want to explain to His Majesty why he can't take his bath when he wishes? Be warned, I'll make sure he learns of your impertinence.'

Sixhwethu's eyes narrowed. 'You don't frighten me. Anyway, if the king needs his bath so urgently, why are you standing here arguing with us?'

The other girls supplied encouraging tongue clicks. Nomguqo stood to one side balancing the gourd on her head. It was unbearably heavy but she no choice but to wait until the power play resolved itself.

Sixhwethu stared the attendant down. It was a dangerous ploy because Mehlokazulu was a known hothead given to ungovernable rages. He was also an intimate of the king through his father Sihayo, an important courtier and adviser. Sixhwethu could easily have bitten off more than she could chew. As it was, Mehlokazulu decided on expediency. 'Follow us!' he ordered, turning in the direction of the *eNkatheni*.

Smirking at her companions, Sixhwethu led them to where a large earthenware pot had been dragged from the sacred hut.

Mehlokazulu could take no chances that the silly *isiGodlo* girls would disturb the king. He recognised that the fighting snakes had created a fragile frame of mind and in that state His Majesty was unpredictable. He stood beside the mixing pot, arms folded, impatiently waiting for the girls to empty their calabashes.

Sixhwethu went first. Fixing Mehlokazulu with a haughty expression, she stepped forward, both hands on the gourd and, with knees bent, tipped the contents into the pot. Her kirtle rode up exposing her dimpled bottom. One of the male attendants took the opportunity to grab a handful of her flesh. Sixhwethu nearly dropped her gourd in shock. The other boys sniggered. She swung around trying to hit her tormentor.

Mehlokazulu hissed at his companions, 'This is no time for stupid games. Act your age.'

One by one the other girls stepped forward to empty their gourds while Sixhwethu, tears of shame and embarrassment running down her cheeks, ran off towards the communal hut.

Nomguqo was last, almost overbalancing with the weight

of her burden. Mehlokazulu had the good grace to lend a hand. She smiled her thanks when he returned the empty calabash. It was unprecedented for a warrior of his standing to help a servant girl and she was anxious to acknowledge it. He gave no sign he'd even noticed, dismissing her with a wave of the hand.

The other girls had already left, so Nomguqo was on her own. An impulse stopped her following them. Lingering beside one of the huts, she pressed herself into the shadows and looked back.

From a tray of dried herbs Mehlokazulu carefully selected some choice sprigs and threw them in, agitating the water until a foam appeared. He called to the unseen king, 'Ndabezitha, by your leave, your bathwater is ready.'

An unseen voice grunted, and the attendants formed a line from the mixing bowl to the doorway.

Nomguqo looked around nervously. Had she been seen? If so, she'd have to explain why she was intruding on this most private of ceremonies, the king's ablutions. Everyone knew the penalty of disturbing the king's privacy.

Curiosity outweighed her fear. Peering into the dark interior of the hut, she could just make out the naked figure of the king standing on a large stone. Mehlokazulu scooped foam onto his broad shoulders and back and kneaded it into his muscles. Her vision was intermittent, masked by Mehlokazulu's movements, but she couldn't stop looking. It wasn't as though the adult male form was unknown to Zulu girls – nudity among adults was commonplace – but this was the first time she'd seen her sovereign without his clothes. The rays of the early morning sun reflecting off the polished floor caught the gleam of moisture on his body. Water dripped down the cleft in his buttocks onto the stone. She was enthralled. Even at her tender age –

although there was no sexual element to her interest – she could appreciate the beauty of the king's body.

Mehlokazulu called for another. Dipping both hands into the bowl, Cetshwayo ladled out a large portion of foam, which he applied to his massive chest and stomach. Rivulets of water cascaded off the ridges of muscle across his abdomen and down into his pubic hair, dripping off the end of his phallus.

Nomguqo's breathing quickened. She knew she should leave immediately but couldn't help herself. She stared. For an organ in such constant use, there was nothing remarkable about the royal penis. She might have expected something in proportion with the rest of the king's enormous frame, but there in its resting state it looked no bigger than his thumb.

A movement in her peripheral vision made her start. The muscles in her throat tightened. Prone to asthma when under stress – and what greater stress could there be than this? – she recognised that an attack was imminent. Concentrating hard on suppressing the tickle that rose from her chest, she clapped her hand over her mouth and spluttered.

She looked around wildly. Had she been heard? If so, her death was guaranteed. No mercy would be shown. The *iziMpisi*, the "hyena men", would be called and she'd be bound in leather thongs and dragged off to the rock beside the river where the executions were carried out. There she'd have her brains beaten from her skull with war clubs. She'd witnessed it many times, even in her short time in oNdini. She retreated further into the shelter of the hut, shocked by her own stupidity.

Suddenly, she saw the *iNgoma* scuttling towards the *eNkatheni*. What did he want? Having used up several of her nine lives, she wasn't prepared to find out. Picking up her empty gourd and, keeping to the shadows, she scurried past the huts of the royal wives.

A group of them teaching a toddler to walk stared curiously as she broke into a coughing fit and struggled to gulp air into her lungs.

Cetshwayo tied his *beshu* around his waist and arranged an *isiNene* to cover his genitals. The witch doctor stepped forward. 'Good news, Ndabethiza. Not only have the *amaDlozi* stopped fighting, but they've disappeared. Nobody saw them go and nobody knows where they've gone.'

Cetshwayo nodded with satisfaction, watching Mehlokazulu and the other attendants use their hands to spread the remaining foamy water across the hut's earthen floor so it could dry ready for polishing. 'We must show our gratitude, then. We'll sacrifice some of the best bulls in the herd.'

'At least six, Your Majesty,' the *iNgoma* advised.

THREE

Nearly a year had passed. It was time for planting again. The bitter wind from the snow-capped uKhahlamba Mountains had been replaced by warmer breezes blown in from the Indian Ocean. Already the signs of the emerging spring were noticeable. The courtship rituals of weaverbirds had already begun, the males vying with each other in their elaborate nest constructions. Aloes sprouted new growth and the Mahlabathini plain beyond the cultivated fields around oNdini was studded with spring flowers. The royal herds took advantage of the new growth of grass, the cows putting on weight and filling their udders with nourishing milk for their new calves. The herdboys, ankle deep in the meadows, urged their charges gently forward, keeping an eye out for predators concealed in the long grass. Since two calves had already been taken by leopards, they were particularly vigilant.

The *isiGodlo* women made full use of the longer days. They burned off the dried stalks left after the harvest of last year's crop and, in long lines strung out over the fields, used their hoes to turn over the soil. Stooping to remove weeds and stones was backbreaking work. They improvised songs to distract them, the rhythm of their singing synchronous with the action of their digging. Here Nomguqo was in her element. She could be alone with her thoughts, removed from the constant banter of the other girls.

Although preoccupied with digging, she registered the activity of the small animals around her. She noticed tiny lizards, disturbed by the blows of her hoe, scurrying in and out of the clods of earth. She watched the birds swooping to pick at the worms and invertebrates exposed by the digging. Perhaps they approached her rather than the other girls because they trusted her more, sensing that she bore no malice to any creature, be it animal or human. With the sun on her back and her animal companions, what more did she need? Bending to free the roots of a weed, she was taken by a sudden pain low down in her belly. The sharpness made her gasp out loud. She looked around, anxious not to draw attention to herself. The other girls continued with their digging unaware she'd stopped.

The pain shot through her belly again, enough to double her over. She dropped the hoe. Through her skin she sensed a pulsing, a rippling of the muscles deep in her core unlike anything she'd ever felt before. She'd had stomach upsets before, a reaction to food that had disagreed with her. But this feeling was more elemental and therefore more unsettling.

She sank to her knees as the next wave of pain pulsed through her, pressing her forearms into her belly to push the cramps away. The action seemed to offer some relief, but soon she became aware of a separate sensation, a trickling high up on her inner thigh. The realisation hit her that her uncomplicated child's life had now ended and that she had joined a sisterhood sharing the same biological function. Beyond the temporary discomfort was the alarming prospect that this was the beginning of a cycle that would repeat itself every twenty-eight days for the foreseeable future.

Taking care not to be observed by the other girls, she reached under her skirt. The blood at the end of her fingers confirmed her suspicion. She already had a firm understanding of menstruation from sharing a hut with other women, observing how they dealt with the practicalities of hygiene. Her immediate dilemma lay in whether to tell them. From experience, she knew she'd find little sympathy. Worse, her admission might invite further teasing. On the other hand, she'd find difficulty concealing the crippling spasms that left her gasping for breath.

The acceptance of discomfort was deeply ingrained in her character. From the earliest age she'd been taught to bear pain without complaint. She recalled her father praising her determination not to cry when she hurt herself. What was so different now?

She decided to make the best of it and carry on with her work. She bent down and picked up the hoe.

'Something wrong?' Sixhwethu shouted from the end of the line.

The other girls paused and looked towards Nomguqo.

'Just catching my breath,' she shouted back before swinging the hoe over her shoulder.

'Well, get on with it. We'll never finish if you keep stopping every two minutes!'

High in the Hlophekhulu hills above oNdini, Mehlokazulu sat cross-legged on a flat rock, his war shield by his side. He fingered the edges of his *iklwa* (stabbing spear), testing its sharpness. Peering more closely at the weapon, he noticed that in places the edges had been indented, notches cut into the smooth surface. He'd to attend to it later on the grindstone.

Alongside his duties as close attendant of the king, Mehlokazulu was a ranking military officer. Experienced in campaigns against the Swazi, he had "washed his spear" in the blood of a dozen men and distinguished himself as a dependable and courageous fighter. Already he had caught the eye of his commanders and been promoted from the ranks. He now commanded an *iviyo* of the iNgobamakhosi regiment, a company of fifty men who followed his orders without question. Within the military hierarchy Mehlokazulu was known as a strict disciplinarian.

At first light he had brought his men up to this secluded place where he could drill them without the distractions of an audience. Here he could give them instruction in the art of close combat knowing he'd be free to correct any mistakes in technique without the commentary of the know-it-alls. With no spectators, the men were less inhibited and more focused. They could give themselves more freely to the exercises he set them. They'd been hard at work all morning. An officer who expected the highest level of fitness both from himself and his men, Mehlokazulu had taken the steep ascent from the plain at a run. Many of the men had found it hard to maintain the pace he set. The last three men to arrive he had sent back down again to repeat the exercise.

Because Mehlokazulu led from the front and was in better condition than any of them, his men were prepared to follow him anywhere. At present he had them practicing the use of the shield as an offensive weapon. A technique developed by King Shaka some forty years earlier, it consisted of hooking the top of the shield under the opponent's and levering upwards to expose the left flank to a thrust from the *iklwa*. Its success in the field depended on timing and the ability to catch the opponent off-guard.

Mehlokazulu watched intently as a pair of warriors feinted and parried, using the contours of the ground to exploit each other's weakness. The rest of the *iviyo* gathered around them.

'That's it, circle him. Find the upper ground, then you can use your weight,' Mehlokazulu said.

Instead of the sharp-pointed metal combat spears, the warriors carried wooden practice weapons. One of them lost his footing as he stepped in a hollow, and with lightning speed his opponent swung his shield between his legs, sending him sprawling on the turf, then followed through in the same movement, thrusting his wooden spear into his chest.

Mehlokazulu clicked his tongue in despair and jumped down to the same level as the fighting pair. Pulling back the victorious warrior, he knelt beside the other man.

'Look, Mbulawa, I know you think you know it all, but you must pay attention. It could save your life. Never look down. Never take your eye off the other man. It only takes that…' he clicked his fingers, '…and you're food for vultures. Understand?'

The warrior nodded.

'Now, get up and do it all again. And this time, I want to see him on the floor, not you. The rest of you,' turning to the other members of the squad, he pointed further up the mountain, 'up to that ridge and back.'

The men threw down their heavy war shields and set off.

'Get back here!' Mehlokazulu ordered. 'Did I say you could leave your shields? I want you carrying them. And at the double!'

Sixhwethu stepped onto the path beside the ground they'd been tilling. Leaning on her hoe, she looked across the field in the manner of a satisfied farmer. The perspiration ran down her cheeks into the folds of her neck. 'Job well done,' she said as the other girls trooped off after her. 'Shows what we can do when we put our minds to it.'

The last remark was directed at Nomguqo as though admonishing her for not pulling her weight. It was unwarranted. Nomguqo had worked as hard as the others and together they'd accomplished a great deal. The field was now ready for sowing: the soil broken down into a fine tilth and all the stones, weeds and dead stalks from last season's growth piled at the margins. Their tired muscles and aching shoulders were evidence they'd done enough for one day. Sowing was a task that would wait until tomorrow.

'I'm boiling,' said Sixhwethu. 'And going straight down to the river to cool off. Coming?'

She didn't wait for the answer, abandoning her hoe to run down the path. The rest of the girls followed – all except Nomguqo.

Now she was alone, she could give way to the pain she'd been suppressing all morning. Sighing with relief, she lowered herself onto her haunches and wrapped her arms around her knees. She watched gratefully as the girls skipped after Sixhwethu. After a moment, when the spasms subsided, Nomguqo looked at the hoes carelessly discarded in front of her. If these were lost, they'd all be punished. Tutting at her companions' thoughtlessness, she gathered them up and tied them into a bundle, which she hoisted onto her shoulder.

The track up to the hills where Mehlokazulu and his men were drilling intersected with the path from the cultivated fields. At certain times of the day, it became congested with teams of porters carrying water from the Mbilane stream to irrigate the fields and to supply the royal household's ever-present need for drinking water.

After the morning's exercises, Mehlokazulu dismissed his men. Their exertions had built up an appetite and they were only too glad to head down the mountain towards the nearest food. Mehlokazulu observed the headlong rush with amused detachment – they hadn't been so keen to head up the mountain earlier. Picking up his shield, he followed them at his own pace.

On the path to the *umuZi*, Nomguqo found the bundle of hoes awkward to manage. The warriors from Mehlokazulu's *iviyo* raced towards her just as she adjusted the weight on her shoulder. She saw they weren't slowing and stepped to one side, but in turning, she swung the bundle of hoes on her shoulder into the path of the leading runner. He thrust out his shield to fend it off. The impact span her around and pitched her into the ditch by the side of the path, the hoes flying in all directions. She ended up face down in a pool of stagnant water.

The warriors laughed as they ran past. None of them offered to help her out. That would have been beneath their dignity. In any case, it was her own fault. As warriors they had right of way; she shouldn't have been on the path in the first place.

She fought hard not to cry, determined not to show them how upset she was. Lifting her face from the mud, she stared after them, their laughter receding as they ran towards the *umuZi*. She swallowed, trying to keep her emotions in check. Shortness of breath told her she was about to develop an asthma attack. She gulped in air and forced herself, through an effort of concentration, to breathe normally.

Crawling out of the ditch, she inspected the damage. Covered in stinking sludge, she couldn't stop the tears rolling down her cheeks, leaving tracks in the mud. She sobbed. Could her day get any worse?

'I saw what they did and, don't worry, I'll make sure they're punished.'

She looked up into Mehlokazulu's stern face. Instinctively she tried to stand, but suddenly felt faint and had to sit back down.

'Are you hurt?' he said.

She shook her head, not daring to look at him. Tears dripped onto her muddy chest.

'I know you, you're one of the *isiGodlo* girls. What's your name?'

'Nom–' Her shortness of breath made her voice stick in her throat.

'I didn't catch that.'

'Nomguqo.'

'Well, Nomguqo, let's get you back to your hut so you can clean up. The royal wives won't want to see you looking like this.'

He laid his shield flat on the path. Stepping into the ditch, he collected the scattered hoes.

'Please, don't trouble yourself,' she stammered. 'I can take care of it.'

'No trouble. It's the least I can do.'

She watched as he gathered the hoes, laying them on the upturned shield.

'Thank you for your kindness,' she said.

His quizzical, slightly protuberant, eyes studied her. Kindness wasn't a virtue ever ascribed to Mehlokazulu. Even his immediate family considered him insufferably arrogant, used to getting his own way and incapable of considering the needs of others. Now he found himself in unchartered waters offering to help a girl whose status was far beneath his own. 'Grab the other end,' he ordered, pointing at the shield with all the hoes neatly stacked on top.

She winced as she stood, cramps gripping her belly. She took hold of the brace in the middle of the shield. Mehlokazulu waited at the other end.

'Ready?'

She nodded. With a combined effort, they lifted the shield and started to carry it towards the *umuZi*, Mehlokazulu leading the way. She was grateful he couldn't see the difficulty she was having. She was dizzy from her fall and, although Mehlokazulu had carefully balanced the load, there was a tendency for the shield to twist in her hands. Shifting her grip, she concentrated on keeping it level.

'All right at the back?' he said, glancing over his shoulder.

'Yes.'

It was sheer effort of will that allowed her to complete the journey. By focusing on the play of muscles in Mehlokazulu's back and shoulders flexing and shifting against each other, she found the pain and discomfort fading into the background. The workings of the human body were so beautiful, she thought, so perfectly demonstrated by the example before her. She gritted her teeth as another spasm seized her belly.

The other *isiGodlo* girls had already arrived back at the hut. They stood goggle-eyed as Mehlokazulu helped Nomguqo stack the hoes against the side of the hut. The task complete, he picked up his shield, turned on his heel and strode off.

They gathered around.

'Well?' demanded Sixhwethu.

'Well, what?'

'You and Mehlokazulu nGobese?'

'Someone had to carry the hoes back and I couldn't do it by myself.'

'And he volunteered?' Sixhwethu shook her head in disbelief. 'Why would he do that? You of all people. It's not as though he'd get anything in return.'

It was on the tip of Nomguqo's tongue to explain the

circumstances, but she was aware she'd be opening herself to further mockery.

'Doesn't change my opinion. Men want only one thing. Him taking pity on you means he thinks you'll lie with him,' Sixhwethu continued.

This was too much. Nomguqo's confidence had been raised by Mehlokazulu's interest. She couldn't help herself – the words came tumbling out. 'Why do you always think so badly of people? Is it because you think so little of yourself? Maybe it's just plain and simple jealousy.'

Sixhwethu scoffed, 'Listen to yourself. The monkeys in the trees make more sense.'

Then one of the girls started giggling. The rest followed suit, pointing at Nomguqo and laughing at her appearance.

'Just look at you!' Nobhodlile said.

She suddenly realised what they were pointing at. Her pleasure at being escorted back to the *umuZi* by such a handsome and distinguished warrior had completely eclipsed the fact she was covered in mud.

With the girls' cruel laughter in her ears, she retreated to the back of the hut where a small area was screened off for ablution purposes. She doused her head and shoulders in the water butt. Using a scoop, she poured water over her chest and legs, rubbing away as much of the offending muck as she could.

'Why are you late? My son is waiting to be fed.'

With her hair still dripping, Nomguqo stood in the doorway of the hut of Nomvimbi, the king's most senior wife. There was no excuse she could reasonably offer. Attendance on any of the royal wives was a big responsibility, particularly so in the case of those with seniority.

Nomvimbi exploited her status to the full. Grossly overweight through an ingrained habit of indolence, she required model service from her attendants. An imperious and short-tempered woman, she was impatient with the most minor fault. To her mind, a lack of punctuality was inexcusable. Nomguqo's fault was aggravated by the demands of the hungry prince. Dinuzulu, nine-years-old, had inherited his mother's temperament and was in a sulk. He repeated loudly, 'I'm hungry!'

'Stop your noise. The girl's here. You'll have your food soon.'

'I'm sorry,' Nomguqo mumbled.

'See it doesn't happen again. Otherwise, the king will get to hear about it.'

Nomguqo swallowed. 'Shall I toast some pumpkin seeds?' she said to the boy. 'I know they're your favourite.'

Dinuzulu sneered, 'What am I – a chicken?'

'We'd better see what you would like to eat, then. You choose.'

She propelled him to the centre of the hut where the cooking fire was smouldering. Beside it were food containers. Dinuzulu went straight up to one of them and thrust his fist deep inside, bringing out fingers dripping with honey. They went into his mouth, smearing his lips and chin, clearly going out of his way to be difficult.

Nomvimbi watched unimpressed. Spreading her copious buttocks into a sitting position on her mat, she started to string beads into a chest ornament.

Kneeling so she was on his eye-level, Nomguqo restrained him from any further assaults on the honey jar. He was already a sticky mess with honey all over his chest and arms. 'I'm going to cook up some porridge. Why don't you have some *amaSi* while you're waiting?' Ladling a portion of milk curds into a bowl, she put it in front of him. Then reached for a cooking pot, half filling it with water to which she added some corn meal, stirring all together. As she stretched to place the cooking pot on the fire, she was overtaken by another spasm. It took her by surprise. For the last couple of hours, the sudden sharp pains had subsided into a constant dull ache, but this pain felt as though someone had knifed her, making her cry out loud. Nomvimbi looked up. Dinuzulu stopped eating and watched as Nomguqo doubled over in pain.

Nomvimbi laid down her beadwork and moved to the fire. 'What is it? Are you hurt?' She knelt beside her. 'Where's the pain?' She noticed a few drops of fresh blood where Nomguqo had been kneeling. She smiled as she understood. 'Have you told anyone about this?'

Nomguqo shook her head.

'Do you know what's happening to you?'

Clenching her jaws to stop herself crying, Nomguqo nodded.

'It's perfectly normal. The other girls will tell you what to do, but I can give you something immediately to help with the cramps.'

Nomvimbi moved to her sleeping mat, rummaged around, and found a few dried leaves. 'Here, chew these, they'll ease the pain. You'll start to feel better by the time the porridge is cooked.'

Dinuzulu reached out and stroked Nomguqo's shoulder. This comforting gesture and her mistress's uncharacteristic kindness brought tears to Nomguqo's eyes.

'And here's something for the blood.' Nomvimbi handed over a handful of leaves softened into an absorbent pad. 'Why haven't you told the other girls yet?'

Nomguqo couldn't confess that her admission would be likely to invite more mockery. She shrugged.

'Well, they'll have to know, since they'll soon become your attendants. Isn't one of you girls about to go into seclusion?'

This was the development Nomguqo had been dreading. It hadn't seemed important when Sixhwethu's initiation ceremony was announced but, realising that her own initiation would have to be shared with the girl who made her life miserable, it took on an entirely new dimension. She, Sixhwethu and the other initiated girls would be locked away in their hut for eight days and nights. They wouldn't be allowed to mix with anyone else – certainly no males for whom it was taboo to see any girl in seclusion. The prospect of living so close to Sixhwethu for such a long time was intolerable. How would she manage it?

FOUR

Her anxieties and the pain of her cramps left her tossing and turning through the night.

Just as dawn broke, she finally drifted off, only to be jolted awake by the proclamations of the royal praise-giver on his rounds.

The hut was deserted. The other girls had already left to start their tasks for the day. Her heart sank. Her failure to wake on time would lead to even more scolding. She wasn't even sure she was capable of working. Her head pounded from lack of sleep, and she was doubled up with abdominal pain. Leaning over the communal drinking bowl, she doused her head with water. However bad she felt, the day's work had to be done. Collecting the only remaining calabash outside the hut, she ran towards the river. A piercing scream brought her up short. Apart from her own breathing and the distant barking of hunting jackals, there was no other sound.

The silence was broken again: an agonised female voice begging for the pain to stop. It was unlike any sound she'd ever heard, alarming in its intensity. Ahead, she could see her route led to the hut from which the screams were coming. She redoubled her pace. A wail ending in a despairing whimper stopped her just outside the entrance.

An old woman emerged. Nomguqo recognised Nobathwa, the guardian of the *eNkatheni* and "wise woman", who acted as midwife to the *umuZi* women. Nobathwa grabbed her arm. 'Run and fetch the pastor's wife. This woman needs powerful *muthi* – way beyond my powers.'

Nomguqo hesitated.

'Go quickly, girl! You don't want to be responsible for the death of one of the king's wives, do you?'

Nomguqo had no alternative. If the wise woman admitted defeat, the king's wife must be in danger. Pastor Gundersen and his wife Joachime provided practical medical assistance to the oNdini community, dispensing European medicines, and performing minor surgery in the clinic attached to the mission station. Joachime was a midwife trained in modern obstetric practices and able therefore to provide the *umuZi* women with help during particularly difficult labours. In general, however, the fear of damaging her own reputation prevented Nobathwa from calling on their services except in extreme circumstances. This was obviously one such occasion.

Spirals of vapour eddied from the mission roof where the heat of the early morning sun evaporated the overnight dew. Out of breath from running, Nomguqo peered over the fence at the silent house. Was the Pastor's family awake? Could she disturb them? The urgency impressed on her by Nobathwa overcame her natural diffidence. She sprinted up the path and, without pausing, barged through the front door. 'Guniseni! Guniseni!'

She held back, clearly interrupting a private moment in their routine. All three were on their knees, hands clasped in prayer. Only Gunhild reacted to the interruption. Dressed in a simple calico frock with her hair braided into cornrows, the little Zulu girl stared solemnly at the intruder as her father completed the prayer: '…Dear Jesus, by your living dying and rising you have changed us all. With your guidance let us change the world. Help us to be committed enough and strong enough, patient enough and wise enough, compassionate enough and forgiving enough, to do something good for others – because of what you have done for us. Amen.'

'Amen,' spoken in unison by all three, was the signal for Nomguqo to speak. Her words came in a rush. 'Guniseni's wife, the old woman Nobathwa asks for you. She says she must come quickly. The king's wife will die if you don't.'

Joachime reacted instantly. Crossing to the sideboard, she opened her medical bag and checked the contents. 'The king's wife is in labour?'

'I think so.'

'Is she conscious?'

'She's been screaming in pain.'

Satisfied she had everything she needed, Joachime closed the bag and moved to the door.

Gunhild grabbed her mother's skirts, her eyes starting to fill with tears. To distract her, the pastor lifted the little girl onto his shoulders. 'Mamma won't be long. You can help me make breakfast.'

The hut's only source of light was the doorway. With Nobathwa at her shoulder, Joachime peered into the murky recesses. It was ominously quiet. 'I need to see what I'm doing,' she said to the midwife. 'Bring me a brand from the fire.' Fumbling for a candle in her medical bag, she entered the hut.

Nomguqo followed. For as long as she could remember, she'd been aware of the process of childbirth, but this was the first time she'd witnessed a complication with such frightening consequences.

Nobathwa touched a flaming torch to the candle and stood back. The flame revealed the inert figure of the king's wife lying on a blanket at the back of the hut. A dark pool of blood between her legs glistened in the flickering light.

'What's her name?'

'Usixipe,' Nobathwa said.

Joachime knelt, holding the candle towards Usixipe's face, her eyes fluttering beneath closed lids and beads of sweat running off her forehead. Needing both hands to perform an examination, Joachime handed the candle to Nomguqo. She checked the pulse at Usixipe's throat, then ran the flat of her hand over her distended belly, pressing her ear to the bump to listen for a foetal heartbeat, all the while firing questions at the midwife: 'When did the contractions start?'

'Six hours ago.'

'This her first pregnancy?'

'Her third.'

'Did you know she's carrying twins?'

The midwife flinched and whispered under her breath, '*Umnyama.*'

'What did you say?'

'It's a bad omen. The ancestors are displeased,' Nobathwa replied.

'The ancestors displeased! It'll be the king who's displeased if his wife dies. Superstitious nonsense.'

The pastor's wife understood only too well that multiple births were regarded as bad omens and the babies unlikely to survive. She put this concern to the back of her mind as she concentrated on their safe delivery.

Crouching between the mother's legs, Joachime gestured for the light to be brought closer. Nomguqo leaned over her shoulder, careful not to drip any hot candlewax. Amid the blood and amniotic fluid oozing from the birth canal, the crown of a baby's head was visible. As the womb contracted, the head protruded further, but there was clearly an obstruction. Joachime reached into her obstetric kit and handed a set of forceps to Nobathwa. 'These must be cleaned. With alcohol ideally, but clean water will do. As much as you can find.'

The old woman stood rooted to the spot.

Joachime barked, 'This woman will die if we don't deliver her babies. She can't do it without our help.'

Yet another contraction contorted the king's wife's body.

Eyes wild with fear, the midwife backed out of the hut and was gone.

With her fingers inside the mother's birth canal, Joachime felt around the baby's head. 'Here's the problem – the cord's wrapped around his neck. It'll strangle him unless we get him out quickly.' Reaching into her kit again, she produced scissors and a length of twine. 'I need you to tie off the ends when I make the cut. Can you do that for me?'

Nomguqo nodded.

Reaching around the baby's head, Joachime withdrew the thick cord swollen with blood vessels. She stretched it into a loop and pointed to where she wanted the ligatures tied.

Nomguqo wrapped the twine around the cord and made two knots. Either the scissors were blunt or the cord particularly tough, but Joachime had to apply force to cut through the cord. She checked the neck pulse again. Nomguqo held her breath, horrified and fascinated in equal measure. The pastor's wife sat back on her heels and, using the back of her forearm, wiped her brow. The tension and concentration had made her perspire. She looked towards her young helper. 'First time you've seen a baby born?'

'First like this.'

'So far so good. *uMvelinqangi* has been kind to us.'

Nomguqo had never heard the word in such a context before. Her father had referred to *uMvelinqangi* when he told her the Zulu story of creation, but he'd meant it in terms of "the First Appearer", the first of the ancestors. The notion of a god who invited communion at a personal level, who might be called up to intercede on an individual basis, was completely foreign to her. Nomguqo couldn't imagine how *uMvelinqangi* would have the slightest interest in their welfare, why He would care one way or another what happened to her, the pastor's wife, or indeed the king's wife. Their fates were entirely determined by blind chance and no amount of prayer or supplication would change that.

Joachime waved a phial in front of Usixipe's face. Miraculously and immediately, the king's wife recovered consciousness, spluttering as the smelling salts took effect. Another contraction left her gasping. Her eyes scanned the hut in panic and finally came to rest on the pastor's wife.

'Breathe deeply,' Joachime urged, stroking her hand soothingly. 'Your babies are safe and about to be born.'

Usixipe ran her tongue over her lips. Nomguqo reacted instantly, offering her water in a beaker. Usixipe drained the contents in a single draft, gasping in pain as a massive contraction gripped her. She grabbed Nomguqo's hand, squeezing hard.

Joachime, on hands and knees, encouraged her, 'That's it. Push. Push!'

Usixipe strained, and the baby's head appeared, face wrinkled and covered in thick white grease.

'Another push and the baby will be here.'

Usixipe grimaced with the effort, her eyes rolling back into her head as she rode another contraction.

Finally, the baby's body slithered into Joachime's hands.

Holding him aloft, Joachime smacked his bottom and provoked a thin, reedy wail. 'A little boy,' she announced. 'He's perfect,' then placed him on his mother's chest.

Usixipe turned her face away, forcing her hands to her side.

A shadow fell across the doorway. The old woman re-entered the hut. She wasn't alone. Behind her, Dlephu Ndlovu appeared.

Usixipe's expression changed immediately, the physical pain of childbirth replaced by abject misery.

Joachime was fully aware of the reason the *iNgoma* had come but clung to the hope that the king's wife's status would protect the babies.

The *iNgoma* spoke, 'If I can be of assistance…' He left the rest of the sentence hanging.

Usixipe knew her babies were doomed. From the moment she'd felt movements in her womb, she sensed she was carrying more than one baby and known therefore that they'd be taken from her and destroyed at birth. It was the only way the *umnyama* could be purged. She'd spent the previous four months preparing herself emotionally for this moment.

The tension in the hut crackled.

Joachime faced the *iNgoma* down. 'It's all perfectly under control here, thank you. We don't need your help.'

Dlephu's expressionless eyes reflected the flickering candlelight. He looked the missionary's wife up and down, sucking his teeth contemptuously.

Nomguqo's heart was her mouth. Was it wise for Joachime to contradict the *iNgoma*? Dlephu's reputation was frightening. Would he pronounce a terrible curse?

Joachime stood her ground. A head and shoulders taller than the *iNgoma*, she dominated him physically. It was a battle of wills she was determined to win.

After a long pause, Dlephu spat on the ground and marched out, followed by the old midwife.

Usixipe gasped in pain as her contractions resumed. With the first baby lying on her chest, she bore down again and delivered the twin into Joachime's hands, who passed him over to Nomguqo so she could deliver the afterbirth.

Nomguqo stared at the tiny infant. His limbs and their extremities were exactly as they should be. Another perfect little boy. His face contorted in a loud wail.

Dlephu Ndlovu reappeared in the doorway and called to the mother, 'The king wishes to see his new sons. Ndabezitha has asked me to convey his wishes for your safe recovery. He'll send for you when it is no longer taboo.'

On his signal, Nobathwa moved forward, knife in hand. Seizing the baby in Nomguqo's arms, she slashed the umbilical cord, then lunged for the first-born lying contentedly on his mother's chest. Usixipe instinctively tried to protect him, but the midwife pushed her hands away, handing both babies to the *iNgoma*. Usixipe, pain and horror etched on her face, watched as Dlephu scuttled to the entrance, the babies cradled in the crook of his arms.

Joachime called, 'I expect you to return the babies once they've been presented to their father.'

'Of course, wife of Guniseni,' Dlephu Ndlovu replied. The knowledge that the infants were being taken straight to their deaths was unspoken. No objections were raised – Joachime because she couldn't jeopardise the future work of the mission, and Usixipe because she couldn't be seen publicly to contradict one of her husband's most influential advisers. Her personal safety was also at risk. To confront the *iNgoma* was to invite his anger, which in turn could lead to an accusation of witchcraft; there were enough precedents. Only Nomguqo, in her innocence, took Dlephu Ndlovu at his word.

He paused in the doorway, gave a perfunctory nod and was gone. Only then did Usixipe give expression to her grief, a single heart-rending howl of anguish.

After the event, when she considered the potential consequences of her reckless action, Nomguqo's whole body stiffened in fear. She had no idea why, but she felt impelled to make sure the *iNgoma* carried out his promise. She whispered to the pastor's wife, 'Do you need me?'

Preoccupied with the needs of the mother, comforting, and cleaning her up, Joachime answered, 'Not if you have other duties. I can manage. Thank you for helping.'

Nomguqo whispered to Uxisipe, '*Sala kahle* (go well),' and hurried after the *iNgoma*.

He was already a distant figure heading towards the king's residence; she could see the little bundles in his arms. Their crying attracted curious glances from other royal children playing in the dirt beside their mothers' huts. One of the wives approached him, but quickly backed away when she saw what he was carrying.

He was now only a couple of paces away from the king's front door. Nomguqo's stomach contracted when she saw that, instead of knocking on the door to announce himself, he headed straight on.

His true purpose became apparent as he hurried, half walking, half running, towards the gate at the rear of the compound. The babies wailed louder, touching a nerve deep inside Nomguqo. Tears pouring down her cheeks, she broke into a run. She must find some way of stopping him.

Normally the rear gate was used exclusively by the king en route to his personal latrine. In this case, special dispensation had clearly been given to the *iNgoma*. The warriors on guard uncrossed their *imikhonto* (throwing spears) and let him through. Then, as Nomguqo approached, crossed them again. This was as far as she could go.

Through the opening, she watched the *iNgoma* disappear over the brow of the hill. The screaming seemed to get louder. Her mind raced. Even if she persuaded the warriors to let her through, what would make the *iNgoma* hand them over? What could she say?

A sudden, awful silence fell as the crying stopped. Assuming the worst, she concentrated hard. Maybe she could alter the outcome by applying her willpower. Maybe, by some miracle, the *iNgoma* would calm them and reappear with them in his arms. This last vestige of hope disappeared when he came back empty-handed. Her stomach heaved. Her hand over her mouth, she ducked out of sight of the warriors and, with back braced against the nearest hut wall, retched uncontrollably.

FIVE

The twins' murder played on Nomguqo's mind throughout the week preceding her seclusion. She felt entirely alone; she had no one with whom she could share the burden. A conspiracy of silence pervaded the *umuZi*. It was as though it had never taken place. In normal circumstances, the birth of a child would be reason for communal rejoicing but in this case the subject was *ukuzila* (taboo), not to be mentioned.

For Nomguqo, it was ever-present. During the day, she was busy preparing the communal hut where she and Sixhwethu were to be confined. There was firewood to be collected and stacked, millet beer to be brewed, food stores to be brought in – activities that distracted her. At night, however, alone with her thoughts, she found herself conjuring up images of the babies' deaths. She saw the *iNgoma* choking them, his hands pressed over their noses and mouths. She saw wild animals – hyenas, and jackals – sniffing the inert corpses, then tearing them limb from limb, chewing on the dismembered body parts. Instead of fading, the images became increasingly vivid and kept her awake. By the time she and Sixhwethu were ready for their week of seclusion, she dreaded the nighttime.

'If you pull back these folds of skin, there's a little button, see?'

Nomguqo and Sixhwethu were being given a basic lesson in female anatomy. Umafutha, the oldest girl in the hut, lay, legs akimbo, her kirtle pulled up, the dark triangle of her pudendum thrust upwards.

'Don't tell me you haven't played with it before.'

Sixhwethu nodded vigorously, but Nomguqo shook her head. Only a few days had passed since she'd helped in the birth of the twins. Thus, she had a detailed knowledge of female genitalia. She found it difficult to reconcile the generative purpose she'd seen demonstrated so recently with the idea of them being a source of pleasure. In the context of the babies' fate, the whole notion of reproduction was horrifying anyway.

'Well, if you lick your fingers and rub it, it'll become wet and then you'll start to feel warm all over.'

The other *amaQhikiza* (older, menstruating girls) were ranged in a semi-circle behind Nomguqo. They sniggered, clearly well versed in the practice.

'Isn't it better if a boy does it lying on top of you?' said Sixhwethu.

Umafutha's knees came together sharply, and she propped herself up on her hands.

'How do you know?'

'Everyone knows that.'

'You haven't let a boy do it to you?'

'Well…' Sixhwethu gave a sly grin.

Umafutha sat upright. 'Tell me you haven't.'

The eyes of all the girls were on Sixhwethu, waiting for her response. The admission of any sexual relations at this stage in her life would be highly problematic. All contact between the sexes was policed by the *amaQhikiza* and could only be undertaken with their approval.

Sixhwethu enjoyed the stir this caused. She kept them waiting, then exploded with laughter. 'Of course, I haven't.'

Umafutha sucked her teeth. 'You obviously know how important it is not to let a boy touch you like that, but maybe Nomguqo doesn't.'

Overcome with tiredness, Nomguqo yawned.

Umafutha leaned forward. 'After your seclusion, when you leave this hut, you'll start to find boys taking an interest. You might even take an interest in them. When you find someone – someone you really like – you must tell us, then we'll let the king know. Only Ndabezitha can make the decision to let you marry. Remember, he must agree on your choice of husband and on the amount of the bride price and he'll choose when it takes place. Be warned – even when you've made your choice, you may not be able to marry immediately…'

As Umafutha repeated the familiar warnings, Nomguqo's mind drifted off to the memory of Mehlokazulu's naked back with the fascinating play of muscles on either side of his spine rhythmically rolling and flexing. In her mind's eye she saw the apron covering his buttocks moving from side to side as he walked ahead of her. But these were idle daydreams. The hard reality was that Mehlokazulu was a warrior of high standing, and she was a lowly servant girl.

Sixhwethu's voice jolted her back to the present. 'Does that mean we can't share our blanket with the boy?'

'Depends on what you want to do.'

The *amaQhikiza* chuckled.

'Heard the expression *ukuHlobonga*?' Umafutha asked.

The initiates shook their heads.

'Means that, once the boy has become your *iSoka*, your

"official lover", you can let him lie with you. He can put his cock between your thighs, and you can let him spend his seed. But under no circumstances can you let him put it inside you. If you fall pregnant, you and he will be disgraced. And believe me, from now on until you're officially married, you'll be regularly examined to see if you've been penetrated.'

The girls digested this revelation in perfect silence. Then a furrow appeared on Sixhwethu's brow. 'Where's the pleasure in that for us girls? We just end up with a mess all over us.'

They burst out laughing.

'Oh, you'd be surprised what we women can get out of it,' Umafutha said. 'Remember the little button I just showed you? Well, you just make sure that your *iSoka* rubs his cock against that. That's guaranteed to make you warm all over.'

'How do you know?' Nomguqo asked. 'Do you have an *iSoka*?'

One of the older girls standing next to Nomguqo answered, 'Didn't you know? It's Mbulawa.'

'That boy from Mehlokazulu's *iviyo*?' Sixhwethu said. 'Why didn't we know about that?'

'It's an open secret,' Umafutha answered. 'We haven't exactly been hiding it. Where do you think I go in the evening after we've completed our duties?'

Sixhwethu clicked her tongue in disbelief. 'You let a friend of that pig rub himself against you. That's disgusting.'

'He's very good at it.' Umafutha stood. She pulled down her kirtle indicating that the conversation was over and marched over to the fire. 'Right, you both need some more ointment where you've rubbed it away.'

The initiates groaned. When they first entered the hut, they'd been smeared from head to toe in red ochre. It proved to be the most disagreeable part of their confinement. It blocked the pores of their skin and made them sweat to release the uncleanliness of their menstruation. In the close confines of the hut, and with the cooking fire being constantly stoked up, it was oppressively hot. A large vat of millet beer stood beside them, from which they frequently helped themselves to stop becoming dehydrated.

'Be glad when this is over,' Sixhwethu muttered as the girls smeared the thick mixture of red pigment and animal fat over her chest.

Waves of pain eddied around Nomguqo's head. As well as broken sleep from nightmares featuring the dead twins, on the previous two nights she'd had no sleep at all, kept awake by the drumming and chanting of the *amaQhikiza*. It was relentless. For hours on end, their hands beat out the rhythm on goatskins stretched over earthenware pots. Reeds attached to the bottom amplified the sound so the girls' seclusion could be broadcast to the far ends of the *umuZi*. The noise was ear-splitting.

The *amaQhikiza*'s purpose was to teach the initiates all they needed to know about the sexual act and what to expect from their prospective husbands. The language of their chants concerned the size and shape of sexual organs and the variety of uses to which they could be put.

Nomguqo was so tired she began to hallucinate. The sound seemed to be coming from inside her own head. The thudding of the drums had the same cadence as her heartbeat. The veins and arteries of her brain pulsed inside her skull, which acted as a sounding board and increased the volume until it became unbearable. She was sure she'd lose her mind if it continued any longer. Willing it to end, she screwed up her eyes.

Suddenly, as though in answer to her prayers, the drumming stopped. She opened her eyes.

Sixhwethu was on her feet marching towards the hut entrance. 'I can't stand any more of this. I'm leaving.'

'Sit back down!' Umafutha ordered. A couple of the other girls grabbed her, pushing her to the floor. Sixhwethu hunched her shoulders in resignation.

Umafutha smiled mischievously. 'Right, some games. Truth or dare.' She directed a couple of girls to clear a space in front of the cooking fire. 'The object is to pick up an ember from the fire with your teeth and carry it from one side of the hut to the other.'

'What!' Sixhwethu protested.

'Drop out or drop the ember and you pay a forfeit. You must tell us a secret.'

'What if we don't want to play?' said Sixhwethu. Either way it was going to be painful. 'What if I say I need the latrine?'

'You'll have to play when you get back.'

There was no way out… until Nomguqo realised they could play the *amaQhikiza* at their own game. 'Why don't you go first, show us how it's done,' she said. 'Truth or dare, right?'

Umafutha's eyes narrowed: Nomguqo was too clever by half. Her hand had been forced. What would she choose: burn her lips on the coals, or divulge a deep and dark secret? 'Truth, then,' she said. 'Remember how it's forbidden to let a boy inside you? Well…' she paused for maximum effect. 'Mbulawa and I were together the other night. I had his cock in my hand. It was very hard. He was touching my button and I could feel I was getting very wet. Then he got on top of me. He put it between my thighs and started rubbing. I began to feel the tingling, and our breathing got faster and faster. Then, I don't know what happened but… it slipped in.' The girls held their breaths. 'Only the tip because I immediately shut my legs and pushed him off. He was angry, but I knew we'd get into trouble if we went all the way. I finished him off with my hand.'

Her audience stared at her in shock. There was a moment's silence, followed by a chorus of protest.

'That's really bad!'

'Did he break the membrane?'

'What's going to happen when you're inspected?'

'Will the king have to be told?'

Umafutha raised her hand to shut them up. 'No, it didn't break the membrane, and no, the king doesn't need to know.'

The girls went into a huddle to discuss the implications. Umafutha clapped her hands. 'I've had my turn. It's yours now. Who's first?'

Sixhwethu approached the fire. At its heart, the charcoal burned white hot but, around the sides where the ends of the wood remained unburned, the heat seemed less intense. On hands and knees, she leaned forward.

The *amaQhikiza* encouraged her with hand claps.

The fierce heat brought out beads of sweat on her forehead. Unafraid, she moved ever closer, sinking onto her haunches. But the heat drove her back.

The *amaQhikiza* groaned with disappointment.

Realising it was cooler at floor level, she tried again. Rolling onto her side, she squirmed forward like a snake, slowly at first then with a sudden darting movement with teeth bared. With the end of a burning stick clamped in her mouth, she quickly retreated, her movement causing the wood to flare. On her feet now, she sprinted across the hut and dropped it at the far side. Sparks scattered over the polished floor. Triumphantly she kicked it with her bare foot back in the direction of the cooking area where it rolled in front of the other girls.

Umafutha enveloped her in a hug. 'That was amazing. None of us would have done it.'

The others gathered around to clap her on the back. Sixhwethu beamed. Then all eyes turned to Nomguqo.

'What will you choose?' Umafutha asked. 'Truth or dare?'

'Sixhwethu was very brave,' Nomguqo replied, 'but I'm certainly not going to try. What if I was burned? You'd be the ones getting into trouble. You're supposed to be looking after us, not torturing us.'

'So, what *are* you going to do?' Sixwethu asked.

'I don't know.'

Umafutha pressed her, 'You must have some deep dark secret.'

'Not really.'

'What do you mean "not really"? Either you do, or you don't.'

'Then, I don't.'

'In which case you'll have to do the dare.'

The *amaQhikiza* pounced and pulled her off her feet. Each grabbed an arm or leg and overpowered her. She squirmed and kicked but they were too strong. They dragged her to the fire and forced her down, pushing her so close she felt the heat burning her cheeks.

'All right, all right,' she conceded. 'If you let me go, I'll tell you something I haven't told anyone else.'

Releasing her, they resumed their position in a circle around the fire.

'I've seen the king naked,' she announced.

The girls' gaped. Umafutha said, 'That's impossible. Only his wives and body servants have seen him naked.'

Now the secret was out, there was no going back. She had to trust they wouldn't betray her. In any case, she realised, Umafutha's confession would be equally incriminating.

'Remember last year, the day the *amaDlozi* snakes were fighting and Mehlokazulu and his friends made a fool of Sixhwethu?'

Sixwethu scowled as she remembered.

'Well, when they were bathing the king, I stayed behind, hid behind the *eNkatheni* hut and watched.'

The *amaQhikiza* reacted immediately:

'Don't believe you.'

'Didn't anyone see you?'

'That was a really stupid thing to do!'

Thrilled by their reaction, Nomguqo elaborated: 'He's very handsome without his clothes. He has a strong body: powerful shoulders and there are these ridges across his belly…'

'Well, that isn't exactly news,' Nobodhlile said.

'Go on, *inkosazana*, don't keep us in suspense. What's it like?'

'Well… it's very small.' She paused. 'Are they always so tiny?'

The more experienced girls sniggered.

'You should see Mbulawa's when it's full of blood,' Umafutha boasted. 'Like a puff adder.'

'Without the markings, I hope,' Nobodhlile said.

'Or bite!' Sixhwethu added, provoking a loud guffaw.

'And?'

'And what?' said Nomguqo.

'Anything else?'

'Well, I haven't seen many to compare it with, but it looked pretty normal to me.'

'Maybe small but it's seen a lot of action,' Umafutha said. 'How many wives has he got now? How many concubines?'

'Shush, you mustn't talk like that about the king. The hyena men will come for you.'

Sixwethu mused, 'Wonder what it's like having the king make love to you.'

'Why would it be any different from any other man?' Nomguqo asked.

'Well, he's the king. He's bound to be better at it. He's had a lot more experience,' Sixhwethu answered. She spoke an obvious truth. The number of women expecting the king to service them totaled over forty.

Nomguqo asked the question that had been bothering her: 'When the king allows you to marry, and you go the whole way, what's the best thing you can do to please your husband?'

No one had an answer. Eventually, Umafutha said, 'My grandma told me that men like it nice and tight. They want it to touch the sides.'

'Your grandmother told you that?' Sixhwethu spluttered.

'She said they're not happy if it waves about like a straw in a storm.'

Sixhwethu retorted, 'Not much we can do about that, is there?'

'There is,' Nobodhlile countered. 'My grandma showed me a plant you can pick that stops you getting wet. So, when your husband puts it inside you it's nice and firm.'

'Isn't there a reason women get wet?' Nomguqo said.

Umafutha shook her head, amazed at her ignorance. 'Well, obviously, to lubricate you and make it easier.' She reached for the water gourd and drank.

'What's the point in drying it up?'

'To make it better for the husband,' Sixhwethu suggested.

'What about the wife?'

'*Inkosazana*, you're very naïve.' Nobodhlile sighed. 'Haven't you learned? A woman's job is to put her husband first.'

Nomguqo frowned. 'Why would it increase the husband's pleasure?'

This was a conversation destined to go nowhere. Umafutha shut it down. 'That's enough of that. I need to pee.'

As she moved towards the hut entrance, Nomguqo caught her arm. 'I need to go, too.'

'Get your blanket, then.'

Since it was taboo for her to be seen in public before the end of her seclusion, she needed to be concealed. The girls threw the blanket over her head and made sure no part of her was visible.

Within the ablution area, the latrine was partitioned by an oxhide curtain. Umafutha squatted over an earthenware pot, while Nomguqo, safe from prying eyes, uncovered her head.

As Nomguqo took her turn, Umafutha said, 'You know it's my duty to supervise any contact you have with boys?'

'Yes.'

'You have an admirer.'

'What?' She burst out laughing at the incongruity of the idea.

'It's true,' Umafutha said. 'One of the *iziNdibi* has been making eyes at you. You must have noticed.'

Nomguqo shook her head.

'And his cousin likes Sixhwethu.'

'I don't believe you.'

'It's true.'

'Which boys?'

'Well, I won't promise they're the best-looking boys in the *umuZi*. The one who likes you is Shikashika; his cousin is Maweni. They belong to the Mazibuko family of the abaQulusi. Now, you must swear not to tell Sixhwethu. You're sensible and can conduct yourself in a modest way. But I don't trust her.

She'll offer herself to the boy and get us all into trouble. You promise?'

Nomguqo nodded. She couldn't put a face to this secret admirer and was desperate for more information. 'Who he is? How does he know me? Where did he see me?'

'Both of them serve the iNgobamakhosi *ibutho* in the emLambongwenya barracks but aren't not old enough to join a regiment themselves.'

'How does he look? Tell me.'

Her impatience made the older girl smile. 'Well, it's only my opinion but I think the cousin's carrying too much weight.'

'No, not him, Shikashika. Is that his name?'

Umafutha decided she'd teased her enough. 'He's tall for his age, long, slim legs, good shoulders. The perfect shape for a warrior. But as I said, he's not without faults. One especially might put some girls off.'

'Which is?'

'His skin, it's not black all over. Looks like someone's splashed him with white paint.'

Nomguqo immediately knew who he was. She'd seen him at the river when she collected water. Even from a distance, the pigmentation of his skin was distinctive. But she hadn't properly registered him, given that their lives were so separate. What she couldn't fathom was why he'd selected her from all the *isiGodlo* girls. 'I'd like to meet him,' she said.

'All in good time. Now, not a word to Sixhwethu.'

Pulling Nomguqo's blanket back into place, Umafutha led her back to the hut.

SIX

'Up you get, lazybones.' Umafutha pinched Sixhwethu's big toe.

She stirred, opened a bleary eye, and peered into the recesses of the dark hut. 'It's still night,' she moaned.

'Move yourself. There's lots to do,' Umafutha snapped.

Nomguqo was already awake. Had been for some time worrying about what lay ahead. This was the day they ended their seclusion and "officially" became women.

Pulling Sixwethu to her feet, the *amaQhikiza* wrapped her blanket around her and pushed her to the door.

The *umuZi* was as quiet as a grave. Not even the praise-giver stirred.

Umafutha led them in a race to the river. A low mist lay across the path, swirling round their ankles as they ran. Sixhwethu struggled to keep up. The additional weight gained from a seven-day diet of heavy porridge left her breathless. Nomguqo was also surprised how much the week of inactivity slowed her down.

They plunged into the bathing pool, gasping in shock at the freezing water. The other girls helped wash the red ochre off their bodies. Soon their skin was restored to its normal appearance.

'Back to the hut.' Sixhwethu ordered.

Before they could appear in public, they had to be prepared. The *amaQhikiza* daubed red and white ochre on their faces, then dressed them in their elaborate costumes: intricate beadwork ornaments around their necks, wrists and ankles, and bands of plaited grass across their backs and breasts. The girls insisted they parade their new outfits in front of them.

Umafutha nodded approvingly. 'Now you look the part.'

The entire oNdini population was gathered in the cattle enclosure. An orchestra of drums and reed flutes worked the crowd into a frenzy.

Cetshwayo took his place under a shelter of leafy screens, his guests, and advisers on either side. The royal wives sat in a separate enclosure. Only Usixipe was absent, considered taboo because she'd so recently given birth. In the absence of shade, Nomvimbi fanned herself vigorously, feeling the effect of the heat.

A place of honour was reserved in the wives' area for Pastor Gundersen and his family. Gunhild Christine was perched on his knee. Her treble voice cut through the drumming and animated conversation. '*Pappa*, what's happening?'

'Shush, you'll see soon enough,' he said.

Her mother whispered, 'Nomguqo and Sixhwethu are soon to become women.'

A roar from the crowd signalled Dlephu Ndlovu's arrival. Into the centre of the cattle enclosure he led a pair of beating goats, selected from the royal herd to serve as sacrifices.

The women trilled in welcome. The sound was so piercing Gunhild stopped her ears with her fingers.

An expectant hush fell as Nomguqo and Sixhwethu appeared at the *isiGodlo* gate, flanked by the *amaQhikiza*.

Gunhild Christine pointed. 'Look, there she is, there's Nomguqo.'

The pace of the drumming accelerated. The crowd whistled and clapped, producing an ear-splitting noise.

Looking across the sea of faces, Nomguqo's pulse raced. Her own sisters' initiation had given her an inkling of what to expect. But she hadn't reckoned on the extreme upheaval of her emotions, the realisation that, from this moment, her carefree life as a child would end and the responsibilities of adulthood would begin.

Her eyes were drawn to the royal enclosure as she saw someone she recognised. Her father Sikhunyane sat next to the king. Her heart skipped a beat. Blood rushed to her head, and she had to use every ounce of self-control to stop herself buckling at the knees. What was he doing there? How had he learned she was to be initiated? And why had nobody told her he was coming?

The king must have sent for him, she realised. Her chest swelled with pride, and she felt weightless as though the burden she'd carried for so long had been lifted.

She noticed her sisters Meliyam and Diboli waving from the wives' enclosure. They'd made the journey too. How she longed to run to them, to throw herself into their arms. But that would have to wait.

A nudge from Sixhwethu reminded her where she was, and they slowly processed to the middle of the cattle enclosure.

The crowd cheered. A knot of adolescent herdboys stood in the front rank. A pudgy youth among them frantically waved his cattle stick to attract their attention. However, it was the boy next to him, motionless but watching intently, who caught Nomguqo's eye. She realised he must be Shikashika, her "admirer". Umafutha's description was accurate. He was tall – head and shoulders above the other boys in the group – and slender, with strange pale blotches covering his chest and arms. For her, his most distinctive features were his eyes, which radiated a reassuringly calm and kind expression. She found herself instantly wanting to find out more about him. But the split-second interaction was over before it began.

Dlephu Ndlovu raised his spear high in the air. His voice cracked and quavered as he delivered the thanksgiving prayers: 'Spirits of our ancestors, we thank you for being with us today. We thank you for your generosity in bringing these two girls...' a junior *iziNgoma* whispered their names in his ear, '...Nomguqo and Sixhwethu into the exalted state of womanhood. May they be a credit to their sex. May they find worthy husbands, and may they be blessed with many healthy children.'

Nomguqo's memory of the *iNgoma*'s sinister presence at the birth of the *umnyama* twins was still raw. It took the shine off her elation.

He approached the sacrificial goats, spear in hand, and slashed their throats. With blood gushing over his hands, he ran the blade up their bellies spilling their entrails onto the earth. Delving amongst the guts, he isolated the caul, the membrane covering the intestines.

He motioned the girls forward. With each in turn he held up the caul and draped it first over their chests, then their shoulders. Nomguqo shuddered with revulsion and fear. He intoned, 'May the taint of blood be removed from these girls, that they may enjoy pure and unpolluted lives.'

The drums starting up again announced the beginning of the dancing. It was the girls' chance to demonstrate their sensuousness and perhaps catch the eye of a potential husband.

His part in the ceremony complete, Dlephu strutted out of the arena. Collecting the bloodied goat corpses, his assistants followed.

In response to the drumming, Sixhwethu undulated her hips and stamped on the ground, using the rattles on her ankles to mark the rhythms of the dance. Her movements were inhibited and increasingly energetic. Sweat poured from her face and ran down her chest. Shouting its approval, the crowd egged her on. The chubby *udibi*'s eyes were on stalks.

'I'm a very fortunate man.' Sikhunyane beamed. 'I have not one, but three beautiful daughters.'

In her father's presence again, Nomguqo found she didn't know how to behave. The spontaneity of childhood had been replaced by a self-consciousness created by their separation and her new status as an adult woman. No longer could she expect the embraces she'd enjoyed as a girl.

She averted her gaze, turning instead to her sisters, hoping they would provide a lead. They also appeared awkward, in their case overawed by their surroundings. Cetshwayo had generously offered the use of his parlour. It was the only place in the whole *umuZi* where they could enjoy some privacy. The sisters had never seen a building in the European style and marvelled at the glass windows and brick construction. Meliyam was sixteen and Diboli fifteen years old, from different mothers, but all three daughters shared their father's physical characteristics. They were tall, slim, with dark complexions.

Nomguqo broke the ice. 'I was so shocked seeing you in the *isibaya* I nearly fainted. You should have told me you were coming.'

'We didn't know ourselves until the last minute,' Diboli said.

'The king's messenger didn't reach us until two days ago,' Meliyam added. 'We set off as soon as we received the invitation.'

Sikhunyane cupped Nomguqo's face. 'What a fine young woman you've become. I'm so proud.'

The blood rushed to her cheeks. 'How long are you staying?'

'Listen to you,' Meliyam chided, tongue in cheek, 'trying to get rid of us already.'

'No,' Nomguqo answered quickly, 'I meant I hope you'll stay for a while.'

Sikhunyane smiled. 'We came a long way to see you. Of course, we'll stay – if Ndabezitha will have us.'

'Tell me about home. I want to know everything.'

'Well, your orphan heifer has calves of her own now. And she's a good mother, gives lots of milk.'

'Naledi?'

'Is that what you named her?'

'Yes. Because of that white mark on her forehead. She was such a lazy little calf.' Nomguqo giggled as she remembered.

'The laziest in the herd,' Diboli agreed. 'Always the last out of the pen in the morning.'

'More. I want to know more. Have any children been born?'

'None,' said Meliyam, 'but our brothers have taken wives.'

'Which brothers?'

'My first wife's sons,' Sikhunyane said. 'They married girls from Myeni.'

'Myeni? Swazi girls? I remember them.' Nomguqo stopped to think. 'But they're not much older than me.'

Sikhunyane nodded, 'Now you're a woman, you'll be able to marry soon.'

Nomguqo looked at him in shock. 'Oh, I don't think Ndabezitha would allow that.'

'He has a high opinion of you…'

She frowned in disbelief.

'...told me so today. When it's time, he'll choose well for you, I'm sure.'

As the visit progressed, Nomguqo reverted to the easy familiarity of family life and reconnected with her past. Since their conversation was based on common experiences and social connections, it wasn't long before they started to anticipate each other's thoughts and complete each other's sentences. Secure in their affection, she knew that, from then on, they'd never seem quite so remote.

All too soon, the time came for them to leave; Sikhunyane had responsibilities to attend to at home. Nomguqo had prepared food for their return journey. Standing at the main gate, she handed over the basket and lectured her sisters, 'Look after our father. He's not as young as he was.'

Sikhuyane tapped his walking stick impatiently on the ground. 'Not in my dotage yet, young lady.'

As they embraced, Nomguqo forced herself not to cry. It was a massive effort of self-control. She touched foreheads with her sisters, lingering to prolong the moment. Finally, they broke away and joined their father.

Nomguqo felt the tears pricking as her family started down the track heading north. She watched until they were out of sight.

Their newfound status as *amaQhikiza* brought new responsibilities for Nomguqo and Sixhwethu. There was no excuse for childish behaviour; but by the same token, they were accorded a new respect. All children, both male and female below their status, were obliged to defer to them. True to form, Sixhwethu exploited her superiority, lording it over the younger members of the community, finding every opportunity to discipline them. This cut very little ice and turned her into a figure of fun. Behind her back, they aped her airs and graces, mocking her high and mighty manner. Their secret nickname for her was *untinginono* (secretary bird).

By contrast, Nomguqo's reliability and modesty persuaded Nomvimbi to choose her as minder to her children: a great distinction. She now spent much of her time tending to the needs of Prince Dinuzulu and the newborn princess. She had infinite patience and the boy responded to her attention. The baby had only just been weaned and at first howled for the comfort of her mother's breast. Nomguqo found the means to distract her, singing soothing lullabies. She taught her to eat solid food and the baby princess soon held out her arms to Nomguqo rather than her mother.

Dinuzulu soon became Nomguqo's shadow, following her everywhere. They played endless games together. Dinuzulu's favourite was "house". Nomguqo draped a blanket over an improvised frame, and he retreated under it, pretending to go to sleep. Then popped his head out to surprise her, convulsing them both in giggles.

The care of the children was all-consuming, but her mind constantly turned to Shikashika. Four weeks had passed since the initiation ceremony, and she hadn't seen him since. He'd evidently returned to his duties at the military barracks. She wondered where and when, or indeed if, she would see him again.

One afternoon, having fed the children their midday meal and put them down for their nap, she approached Nomvimbi who was stretched out on her sleeping mat, fanning herself with a wooden paddle. 'I've completed my duties,' she said. 'The children have been fed and are sleeping now.'

'Did they eat well?'

'The princess certainly likes her food. Two whole bowls of *amaSi* and she's taking it without honey now.'

'Good.' Nomvimbi sank back on her mat, exhausted by the effort of keeping cool.

'If you've no further need of me, may I have your permission to leave the *umuZi*?'

'Where are you going?'

'Nowhere particular. Just need to stretch my legs.'

Nomvimbi rolled onto her back and grunted noncommittally, which Nomguqo took as an approval.

With no specific purpose in mind, she wandered along the well-trodden path to the river. It hadn't rained for weeks, and the compacted earth had cracked and turned to powder. Small dust devils swirled, lifted by currents of air. The grasslands on either side were withered and brown from lack of rain. A heat shimmer distorted her vision. The river would offer relief from the unremitting heat.

Reaching the water, she walked into the shallows, wriggling her toes as the cool water revived her aching feet. A sudden whistle broke into her thoughts. She looked in its direction, but the blinding light reflecting off the water's surface made it difficult for her to distinguish the source. Holding up her hand to shade her eyes, she became aware of a figure approaching from fifty or so yards downstream.

Shikashika jogged towards her, slowing as he came within speaking distance. 'Hello,' he said.

A familiar twinge seized her belly; her pulse raced and the muscles in her legs quivered. She couldn't understand why she felt like this. It wasn't as though she knew the boy; she'd never even spoken to him and had only seen him for a split second.

It was idiotic to be so nervous. She stammered, 'What are you doing here?'

'Same as you, probably. Trying to stay cool.' By this point, he was beside her, the shallow water eddying around his feet. 'Feels wonderful, doesn't it?'

She nodded, self-conscious. For the first time, she was alone with a boy her own age. Fraternisation with the opposite sex was strictly prohibited, she knew that. But where was the harm? Could something so natural be wrong?

'What's your name?' she said, knowing full well the answer.

'Shikashika...' He glanced at her shyly. 'I know yours. It's Nomguqo, isn't it, "the kneeling one"? Why are you called that?'

'It's the name my father gave me. I was also called Khulumani by my mother. Means "speak ye" in isiSwazi.'

'You're Swazi?'

She nodded.

'You're a long way from home.'

She chose not to comment, looking instead across the broad expanse of river; a pair of torpid crocodiles lay sunning themselves on the far bank.

Aware he'd touched a raw nerve, Shikashika stole a secret glance. 'I'm sorry, I didn't mean to pry.'

'It's all right,' she said. 'I was homesick at first, but I've got over that now. What about you? You're not from here either, are you?'

'No, my people are from the north. On the border with Boer territory.'

'My father fought against the Boers. During the reign of King Dingaan...' She broke off, aware he might think she was boasting.

'My father is an uKhokhoti, a regiment raised by Dingaan,' he said.

They smiled in recognition of the shared connection.

'I'm part of the next age group to be formed into a

regiment. My father sent me and my cousin to be *iziNdibi* for the iNgobamakhosi.'

'Mehlokazulu's regiment?'

'You know Mehlokazulu?'

'Who doesn't know Mehlokazulu?'

'A great warrior. A hard man,' he suggested.

'One of my hutmates has had direct experience. She hates him.'

'Why?'

'Oh, she hates everyone. Me particularly.'

'I don't believe that.'

'It's true. She's always making fun of me. Calls me *inkosazana*.'

'Princess? Are you?'

'I suppose I am. My great-grandfather was King Sobhuza, but that was a long time ago. I never knew him.'

Shikashika picked up a smooth pebble from the riverbank and turned it over in his hand. 'I know all about bullying.' He indicated his arms with their distinctive pigmentation. 'People always want to make you feel different. Not my fault I look like this.' He sent the stone skimming across the water.

Instinctively, Nomguqo reached out to touch him. 'We're all the same deep down. Doesn't matter what we look like on the outside.'

He studied her. 'I like you.'

Her cheeks felt hot. 'I like you too.'

'Can I see you again?'

'Don't see why not.'

'Must you tell the *amaQhikiza*?'

'Probably.'

They smiled at each other again in recognition of the formal declaration of their friendship.

SEVEN

The opportunity to become better acquainted came sooner than either of them expected.

The suffocating heat of an early summer night left Nomguqo unable to sleep. Tossing and turning on her sleeping mat, with the rhythmic breathing of her hutmates seeming unbearably loud, she decided to cut her losses and go for a walk.

She emerged from the hut into an impenetrable murk. A storm was brewing, heavy cloud cover suppressing any movement of air. She yawned, stretching her limbs, and gulping what little oxygen there was.

The familiar clicking of horns and shuffling of restless hooves told her the royal cattle weren't far away, penned in the *isibaya*. It was a comforting sound. When the movements became more agitated, however, she realised something was disturbing them.

She set off towards the cattle pen to investigate. As she walked, a welcome breeze dried the perspiration on her forehead. Apart from the restive pawing of the beasts' hooves there was no other sound. Reaching the thorn fence, she peered into the gloom.

The clouds parted temporarily to reveal a sliver of moon, which illuminated the enclosure. It was brief, but enough to reveal two figures fifty paces away kneeling among the shadowy cattle. It wasn't entirely clear what they were doing, but the white patches on his skin immediately identified Shikashika. She guessed his companion was the cousin she'd seen at the initiation ceremony.

Her vision was impeded by animals milling in front of her, but she could plainly see the two boys, each beneath the belly of a cow, faces pressed against an udder sucking avidly on a teat. She watched, half amused, half fearful for their safety. If the cattle were suddenly spooked, they'd easily be trampled underfoot. She called softly to attract their attention.

No reaction. Perhaps her voice hadn't carried, or they were so absorbed they hadn't heard her. She clambered over the fence and, using soothing sounds and patting the heavy beasts gently on their backs, manoeuvered her way through the herd.

Halfway across, a fork of lightning split the sky. The lurid burst of white light lit up the cattle pen. Several of the cows bellowed loudly. Seconds later a peal of thunder shook the ground. The boys reacted as though a gun had gone off. Leaping up, Maweni headed as fast as the cattle would allow towards the main gate; some obstinately refused to budge, and he had to use his weight to shove them out of the way.

Heavy droplets of rain fell, bouncing off the backs of the cattle. This seemed to have a calming influence. They became more tractable, moving to one side to let Nomguqo approach Shikashika.

'Does the king know you're drinking his milk?' she said.

He shrugged sheepishly, a milky dribble running from the corner of his mouth. 'It was Maweni's idea. He said it's what we must do to become warriors.'

'But you must be invited. You can't just help yourselves.' She was repeating her father's description of the recruitment process. All boys when they reached the appropriate age were invited to *kleza*, to drink directly from cows' udders. The enriched diet strengthened them to survive the rigorous training before being formed into *amabutho* (regiments). However, the invitation could only come from the king or a senior army officer. Any individual deciding on his own to *kleza* would, in principle, be regarded as a thief and be punished accordingly. In practice, this seldom happened because the king indulged anyone who sought to act in his service.

Shikashika protested, 'We're old enough.'

'What's your hurry? You'll be a warrior soon enough.' Without expressing it directly, she wanted him out of harm's way.

By now the rain was coming down in sheets. Puddles formed in the hard-packed earth, which the cows' hooves churned into mud. One of them lifted her tail and defecated, splattering copious quantities of liquid manure over the ground. Some of it splashed on Nomguqo. Shikashika looked at her serious expression and burst out laughing. Mixed with the rain, it dripped off her face and shoulders. Eventually, she saw the funny side and joined in.

Activity in the fields around oNdini increased towards the end of *uLwezi* (November). The agricultural cycle had come full circle and now the crops were ready to be gathered in.

Nomguqo had been on the go since daybreak. After carrying water at dawn, she spent the rest of the morning in the mealie fields, stripping back fronds from the swelling cobs so they could ripen in the sun.

Preparation of the royal children's lunch followed. Finally, after putting them down for their afternoon nap, she had some time to herself. Wearily, she pulled aside the ox hide door of the communal hut, flopped onto her bedroll, and closed her eyes.

Stifled crying made her aware she wasn't alone. Umafutha crouched on the far side, covering her head with her hands. Her sniffling gave way to racking sobs.

Scrambling across the sleeping mats, Nomguqo knelt beside her. Umafutha collapsed into her arms, weeping as though her heart would break. Nomguqo held her tightly. 'What is it? Nothing can be that bad.'

Umafutha collected herself. 'It can. And it is. I must leave.'

'Leave oNdini?'

Wiping her nose with the back of her hand, Umafutha nodded.

'Well, that's not the end of the world.'

'You don't understand.' She sat back on her heels and took Nomguqo's hand. 'Ndabezitha has ordered all the girls in my regiment to accept husbands from the uThulwana…'

Nomguqo's jaw dropped. 'The uThulwana? But they're men in their forties.'

'I know.' Tears ran down her cheeks. 'I'm supposed to marry Qhude kaKuhlekonke and he's older than my father.'

'What about Mbulawa?'

'Exactly,' she wailed. 'I don't want anyone else but him.'

'What are you going to do?'

'There's nothing I can do. The king says he will kill any girl who disobeys.'

'He wouldn't do that.'

'Wouldn't he?' Umafutha sobbed. 'Don't you remember what happened to *induna* Mbambisi's daughters?'

Nomguqo swallowed. Their fate was the perfect example of what could happen if the king was crossed. On learning that Mbambisi had been over familiar with the royal wives, Cetshwayo sent the whole family – including the four innocent daughters – to the executioner's rock. She shuddered at what might have happened had she been caught watching the king's ablutions.

Wiping away Umafutha's tears, she said, 'How many?'

'I don't know, a hundred maybe. I don't care about the rest. I just know I'll die if I can't have Mbulawa.'

'Does he know?'

'He's already said he'll make sure Qhude never offers the bride-price.'

'How will he do that?'

Umafutha drew a finger across her throat.

'Murder? But what will that achieve? He'll be condemning himself to the *iziMpisi*.'

'I know, I know!'

Her despairing wail was cut short by Sixhwethu and three other *amaQhikiza*. Breathless with excitement, Sixwethu announced, 'Have you seen? Corpses by the main gate? Two girls. Their heads bashed in so you can't tell who they are. Brains all over the path…'

Umafutha whimpered on her sleeping mat.

Sixhwethu blundered on, 'They're all saying the iNgobamakhosi have been ordered to punish anyone who ignores the king's orders. Does that include Mbulawa?'

Umafutha shrieked, 'Shut up!'

'I'm only saying…'

'You don't think I know? It's why I must marry Qhude.'

Sixhwethu shrugged. 'Better than having your skull bashed in? If you marry Qhude what's the worst that could happen? An older man, more experienced, probably a better lover–'

'Enough!' Nomguqo warned.

'Who asked you, Princess Prissy? Miss "Better than the rest of us"?'

To prevent the row escalating, the other girls grabbed Sixhwethu and manhandled her out of the hut.

Nomguqo gathered the weeping Umafutha into her arms.

The girls soon learned that this scene had been repeated throughout the kingdom. On Cetshwayo's orders, girls of the iNgcugce – early twenties – *ibutho* were paired with older men from the uThulwana, forcing them to abandon their unofficial relationships with boys from their own age group, the iNgobamakhosi. The unhappiness it caused was universal.

Being Swazi, Nomguqo was ignorant of Zulu military tradition. She learned about it in a roundabout way from Dinuzulu. The young prince had taken to using her as an opponent in his playfighting. It was a one-way contest since he had the only weapon, a wooden *iklwa*. It allowed him to practise all the moves he'd seen the warriors make on the training field. During one particularly violent session, he stood over her prone body, the wooden *iklwa* point at her throat. 'Yield or die,' he said triumphantly.

'You're too good for me,' she admitted.

'Well, I'm uThulwana,' he said, as though that explained everything. 'And you're iNgobamakhosi.'

'What do you mean?'

He helped her to her feet. 'The uThulwana are *Ubaba*'s *ibutho*. I couldn't be anything else, could I?'

'And why am I iNgobamakhosi?'

'Because they're mortal enemies.'

Nomvimbi, lying on her sleeping mat with Besiyile at her breast, chipped in, 'The hatred goes back a long way. *Inkosi* Shaka always encouraged rivalry between the regiments, and my husband has followed that tradition. He says, when warriors compete against each other it makes them stronger on the battlefield.'

'But the uThulwana and iNgobamakhosi are comrades, aren't they?'

Dinuzulu smirked at her naïveté.

Nomvimbi explained, 'When they're in their barracks far away from their families, they need to blow off steam, so the *izinduna* set them against each other. It's supposed to create a unity of purpose, to inspire them to protect and defend their comrades and direct them towards a common enemy. Sometimes it goes too far, and blood is spilled. That's what happened with those two regiments. Years ago, a stick fight between them developed into an out and out battle. Several warriors were killed, and they've detested each other ever since.'

Nomguqo thought for a moment. 'In that case, why has Ndabezitha allowed the uThulwana to take brides among the iNgobamakhosi's sweethearts?'

Nomvimbi sat up, shocked. 'You're questioning my husband's decision?'

Nomguqo immediately regretted her outspokenness. 'No, no.'

'In my view, it will end badly,' the great wife continued. 'I tell him so, but he's determined. Says it will test their loyalty.'

Dinuzulu interrupted, 'Can you stop talking so we can get on with the fight?' He offered Nomguqo a concession, 'This time you can be uThulwana.'

After a morning of allowing Dinuzulu to devise ever ingenious ways to kill her, Nomguqo headed back to the hut. She turned the conversation over in her mind. The king's decision seemed destined to irritate an already festering wound. And Nomvimbi's further revelation – that some girls had refused the advances of their older suitors and the furious king had sent iNgobamakhosi warriors to kill them and their lovers and parade their bodies as a warning to everyone else – was an additional reminder of his authority.

A squad of warriors wearing the *isicoco* headring approached her from the opposite direction. In the lead was Qhude kaKuhlekonke. He had a self-satisfied bounce to his step. As they barged her out of the way, she caught sight of Umafutha in the middle, her possessions bundled on top of her head. She offered a smile of encouragement, but Umafutha's eyes were downcast, apparently resigned to her fate.

Sixhwethu commented, 'Don't know why she's complaining. Qhude's a man of property and a fine reputation. She should count her blessings.'

'Don't be so sure,' Nobhodlile said. 'He has six other wives. Umafutha will end up skivvying for all of them.'

Nomguqo watched until the bridal party was out of sight. *This will not end well*, she thought.

umKhosi WokweShwama was a big event in the life of the community. In other circumstances, the harvest festival would be a source of rejoicing throughout the kingdom, but this year was different. The bodies of thirty girls and their lovers left to rot at the crossroads of the busiest thoroughfares gave a clear message. Anyone who resisted the king's will would meet the same fate. The whole population harboured a sense of dread, including the relatives of the executed girls who stayed silent for fear of the royal retribution.

In nearby emLambongwenya barracks, the iNgobamakhosi brooded, angry that their sweethearts were in the arms of other men. Their jealousy made them increasingly short tempered, and fights broke out. Mehlokazulu had his work cut out to maintain discipline. Mbulawa took it particularly badly. He sank into a deep depression and sat for hours at a time staring at the barracks walls.

Apart from the opportunity it offered for feasting and drinking and, most importantly for the *isiGodlo* girls, singing and dancing, the *umKhosi* ceremony had huge symbolic significance. It was when the king reaffirmed and rejuvenated the strength of the nation. Youths were dispatched throughout the kingdom to collect "soul substances" containing the power of the nation to be incorporated into the *inkatha*. These comprised the "body dirt" of the population – especially that of the *amakhosi* (the chiefs). Wisps of grass gathered from well-trodden paths, scrapings from door openings touched by important men, samples taken from cups or plates used by them, all contained potent essences that, gathered into the *inkatha*, provided protection against the nation's enemies.

By tradition, the king kept vigil during the two days of the festival, sitting on the *inkatha* and drawing into himself the strength of the entire Zulu population. It was a time for rejoicing, and despite the gloom cast by the deaths of so many young people, excitement started to bubble. For the girls it was a chance to refurbish their wardrobes and adorn their appearances, to be able to look their best. They used every available moment to prepare new outfits. They cut soft leather skins and stitched them into new kirtles. And laced beads of every imaginable colour into intricate necklaces and headpieces.

Working on an elaborate chest covering, Sixwethu panicked at the thought she might not complete it. 'It's impossible,' she wailed, gathering up the beads she'd spilled in her haste. 'It'll never be finished in time.'

Her whining earned her no sympathy from the others.

During the final few days of preparation vast numbers of people gathered around oNdini. Regiments from military garrisons from as far as the coast and the uKhahlamba Mountains mustered in bivouacs on the Mahlabathini plain. Across the landscape temporary shelters of wattle and reed appeared, and the smoke from numerous cooking fires hung in a dense cloud.

Married men had dispensation to bring their families with them. Wives and children made camp with their husbands. Qhude, in his capacity as an officer in the king's regiment, was allowed to stay inside the *umuZi*. He and his wives were assigned two large huts and joined the general activity within the compound. Except for Umafutha who stayed shut away from the world.

The *isiGodlo* girls looked for her in vain. They had no idea she was living so close.

On the evening before the start of the ceremony, Nomguqo stood with the other girls at the river waiting their turn in the bathing pool. As the population had grown, so the waiting time for the washing facilities increased. Crowds of women lining the riverbanks badgered those ahead to hurry. The sun was sinking fast and with it, the temperature. Those who had already bathed rushed to dry themselves and cover up.

Scanning the crowd, Nomguqo saw Umafutha climb up to the riverbank. She waved frantically trying to attract her attention, but Umafutha turned away, throwing a blanket over her shoulders.

Nomguqo gave an involuntary gasp. She glanced at her fellow hutmates. Had they seen what she'd seen? Even in the half-light, the dark, livid cuts stood out on Umafutha's back. Who could have inflicted such terrible wounds and for what possible reason? Desperate to know the answers, Nomguqo pushed past the women on the riverbank, inviting their reprimands, 'Wait your turn!' 'Get back!'

Eventually she was close enough to call her name.

Giving no reaction, Umafutha continued to dress herself.

'It's me, Nomguqo.'

Again, no reaction. Nomguqo paused, doubting for a moment it was her old hutmate standing only ten yards away. Qhude's other wives formed a shield, preventing Nomguqo from approaching, then, as one, moved towards oNdini.

Umafutha's face was blank, her eyes fixed on the ground as she walked past, giving no sign she knew Nomguqo was there.

She watched them climb towards the *umuZi*, certain as to the author of Umafutha's injuries. Were they the inevitable consequence of being married? If so, she'd remain a maiden. No man would ever hurt her like that.

EIGHT

It began as a murmur, a guttural note that resounded across the cattle enclosure. A swirling, cyclical hum, like the buzzing of bees, but several octaves lower, waves of sound building one on top of the other. In the beginning it was formless, but it gradually coalesced into recognisable human words. In increments it built in volume as two hundred thousand Zulu voices, young and old, male and female, rose in a hymn of praise to their king.

It was a huge gathering. The married regiments of uThulwana, uDloko, uDududu, and uMbonambi were assembled on one side, the head rings denoting their married status gleaming with newly applied mimosa gum. Opposite were the *amabutho* of youths not yet granted the privilege of marriage – the iNdluyengwe, uKhandempemvu, iNgobamakhosi and Uve. In between, the ranks of the female age-related guilds – the amaQwaki, the amaDlundlu, the amaDuku, the iNkwelembe and, youngest of all, the iZijinga. Men and women, boys and girls were adorned in their finest ceremonial attire. Elaborate headdresses of feathers swayed in time with the chanting. Warriors brandished sticks, displaying their armbands and wristlets fashioned from rare animal skins. Women covered in beadwork marked the rhythm by stamping their feet and striking the ground with the ends of long reeds.

These were the preliminaries to the main event: the entrance of the king. The chanting encouraged him to appear, repeated over and over, increasing in volume. The excitement intensified.

In the company of the king's other close attendants, Mehlokazulu stood with the iNgobamakhosi. They competed with the older regiments as to who could sing the loudest; their voices strained with the effort. Normally the rivalry between the *amabutho* was ritualised into challenges where regiments hurled insults and goaded each other into mock attacks. However, the recent enforced marriages of their sweethearts gave this hostility an extra edge.

Mehlokazulu's obedience to the king was absolute, but he shared the grievance suffered by other members of his *ibutho*. He glared at the uThulwana across the parade ground, teeth clenched in anger. He had no girlfriend of his own, so there was no direct reason for his animosity. Nevertheless, his comradeship with Mbulawa made it personal. They shared the grudge against Qhude. Any pretext would be sufficient to settle the score.

A great shout went up as Cetshwayo appeared. His disguise was so heavy that only his immense stature identified him. His face was daubed with three colours: his right cheek white, forehead vermilion, and left cheek pitch black. His body was wrapped in a green covering made of gourd fibre. He looked for all the world like a large, decorated vegetable.

He strode imperiously down the ranks, as each *amabutho* vied with the other to attract his attention. In his right hand he held the only weapon on display: the sacred spear, the *inhlendla*.

Flanked on one side by his praise-giver and Dlephu Ndlovu

on the other, he took his place under the acacia tree at the centre of the cattle enclosure.

Bhayede inkosi! The crowd shouted and waved a forest of ceremonial wands and reeds. The king smiled with pleasure.

Joining the other girls in trilling their tongues, Nomguqo stuck her fingers in her ears to mute the deafening sound. She strained for a sight of the king through the feathers of the girls in front of her and grinned with the thrill of it all.

Cetshwayo raised the *inhlendla* high in the air, the crescent-shaped blade flashing in the midday sun. Then he stamped his foot to initiate the singing of the royal anthem.

Over-enthusiastic, Sixhwethu jumped the gun. Filling her lungs, she bellowed out the words of the *iNgoma*, ahead of everyone else. All the girls of the *isiGodlo* turned to shush her. Then the massed voices took up the song:

It is you, Dlambula
It is you, Mswazi!
We shall overcome them with weapons,
Those that are there,
As vast as the heaven when it thunders.

As the echoes died away, the uThulwana rushed into the open space. They began their regimental song, brandishing their sticks in mock aggression, the white oxtails around their waists swaying from side to side and the ostrich plumes in their headdresses nodding in time with the chanting, words that entreated the king to satisfy their thirst for battle: *You mighty elephant, give us war!*

The uThulwana nearest the younger *amabutho* chose them as targets for their aggression. Qhude kaKuhlekonke urged them forward. The heavy scar across his jaw pulling his mouth into a lopsided rictus, Umafutha's husband made repeated rushes at Mehlokazulu and the iNgobamakhosi. They stopped just short of making contact, but the effect on the iNgobamakhosi was immediate. Only their respect for the king stopped them from joining battle there and then. Mehlokazulu had to grab Mbulawa's arm to prevent him striking his enemy. The two of them stood locked eyeball to eyeball daring each other to make the first move.

Mbulawa spat out his challenge, 'Qhude, you will meet your ancestors very soon.'

Grunting scornfully, the uThulwana thrust his chest forward, knocking the younger man off balance. Suddenly, the song ended, the dancing stopped, and the tension was released.

The uThulwana dispersed towards the food distribution area and another regiment took its place in front of the king. This time it was the turn of the girls.

Nomguqo hoped she would remember the steps of the dance she'd rehearsed so diligently with the others. It was one thing to dance in private, quite another to perform in the presence of His Majesty and two hundred thousand of his subjects. Nerves made her stomach clench and throat muscles tighten up. She was one in a troop of five hundred dancers – the king would never notice whether she made a mistake or not; even so, she wanted to give of her best.

The girls took up position. From where she was standing in the third row, Nomguqo saw the king's painted face beaming.

As lead singer, Sixhwethu began the melody, her pure soprano carrying across the parade ground. This was her moment of glory and the beauty of her singing more than made up for her earlier impetuosity.

You have been treated with disdain
By the nations, O king...

The assembly murmured their approval as the other girls added their counterpoint.

They have treated you meanly.
Lie down;
The famine is bad indeed!

The footwork of the dance was imprinted in Nomguqo's memory. Her eyes shone with pride as her feet followed the steps and her heart soared as her voice joined the others in harmony.

Then, suddenly it was all over. Panting with excitement and the exertions of the dance, the girls stood waiting for the king's approval. Extending the *inhlendla* graciously, he waved it over them as a sign of his pleasure.

The female feeding area was set apart from the male. Still tingling with the thrill of performing, the girls gathered round the tables laden with good things to eat – roasted ox, goat and antelope, bowls of mealie porridge and various vegetables including pumpkin and, Sixhwethu's favourite, *amadube* (lily root). Dropping their reed wands, they grabbed the food and ate as though they hadn't eaten in days, washing it down with drafts of millet beer from large vats.

Huddling with the others, Sixhwethu could hardly contain herself. She licked the foam from her lips and hissed, 'Did you see the way that Mbulawa looked at Qhude? Blood will be spilt before sundown I just know it.'

'Mehlokazulu will defend a warrior from his own *iviyo*, that's for sure. And you wouldn't want to pick a fight with *him*,' said Nobhodlile.

'He's already washed his spear in the blood of twelve Swazi warriors,' Nguyaze agreed.

'But Qhude is twice his age. He must have sent many more to join their ancestors,' said Sixhwethu.

'Yes, but Mehlokazulu is fitter, more agile, the best warrior in his *ibutho*. Even the men in his own company are afraid of him,' Nobhodlile said.

'Well, I hope the arrogant pig gets taught a lesson. Needs to be taken down a peg in my view.' Sixhwethu laid down a challenge. 'Who wants to bet he gets his arse kicked?' She turned to Nomguqo. 'What about you, *inkosazana?*'

Nomguqo's thoughts were elsewhere. She was thinking of Umafutha, the livid wounds on her back, the vacant look on her face. Having witnessed the violent challenges and mock charges in the *isibaya* and Qhude's face contorted in hatred and blood lust, she had no doubt who had caused Umafutha's suffering.

In the context of such pain, Sixhwethu's flippancy suddenly grated. Nomguqo turned on her. 'How is it you make a habit of saying the wrong thing?'

The *umKhosi* feast was the first time in weeks that the oNdini residents had leave to eat their fill. Taking full advantage, the girls stuffed themselves. Their bellies full to bursting and tipsy from all the millet beer they drank, they retired early to their sleeping mats.

Oblivious of the heavy snoring of the girls next to her, but disturbed by the alcohol in her bloodstream, Nomguqo tossed and turned on her mat, her subconscious projecting images of Shikashika into her dreams.

He was on a bull's back, urging it forward.

The bull planted its forefeet into the riverbank and came to an abrupt halt. Shikashika sailed over its withers and landed with a huge splash in midstream.

He emerged from the river water streaming from his shoulders.

Shikashika lay naked in long grass. A miraculous transformation took place. As the water evaporated from the patches of white skin, they reintroduced black pigment. His body turned uniformly black. His youthful limbs and torso assumed the dimensions of an adult male. The muscles in the chest swelled, the sinews standing out like braided cord. The thighs grew in proportion, the phallus expanding as it filled with blood.

Shikashika stood upright, his muscled arms reaching forward. His face bore down, his eyes gleaming with desire. The sound of his breathing developed a rhythm that became faster and faster.

Nomguqo's eyes opened. She was wide awake, senses alert, disappointed that it had been just a dream. But the heavy breathing sound continued.

She peered into the gloom. Moonlight reflecting off the polished floor revealed a shape – or was it two shapes? – in the space where Sixhwethu had her sleeping mat.

She strained to listen. More than one person was breathing. And at different pitches – female and male.

As her eyes grew accustomed to the dark, she could see the two figures, one on top of the other, moving in a concerted rhythm. What should she do? If she announced she was awake, the consequence would be two-fold. First, a shared embarrassment and, if the older girls woke too, an enquiry into Sixhwethu's conduct, followed perhaps by disciplinary action. And if it were proved she was no longer a virgin, even worse. She'd heard that, during Shaka's reign, both girl and boy involved in any unsanctioned sexual relationship were put to death.

As she debated with herself, an unexpected tickle in the back of her throat decided the matter. The effort of holding her breath triggered a bout of uncontrollable wheezing and coughing: the prelude to an asthma attack.

The effect on the other side of the hut was dramatic – grunts and complaints, scuffling and scrambling. Snatching up the blanket, the two figures rushed to the door. Becoming tangled in the cowhide door covering, they tore it from its fixings, prompting a torrent of oaths.

By now, all the residents were awake. Nobhodlile, the nearest, grabbed Sixhwethu. 'Where do you think you're going?'

'Let go of me!' Sixhwethu struggled, but the other girls were too strong. In the chaos, the boy managed to wriggle free.

With Sixhwethu kicking in all directions, the girls forced her to the floor and sat on her legs to restrain her. Eventually she stopped struggling and there was a lull as they all got their breath back.

'Who is he?' said Nobhodlile, now the senior girl in the absence of Umafutha.

Sixhwethu stared sullenly at the floor.

'Tell us,' Nobhodlile insisted, 'it will go badly for you if you don't.'

Sixhwethu muttered, 'Maweni.'

'Maweni? How long have you been seeing Maweni?'

'You'd never have found out if she hadn't started her stupid coughing.' Sixhwethu glowered at Nomguqo who was still trying to control her breathing.

'How long?'

'Does it matter?'

'You're in deep trouble,' Nobhodlile warned.

'It was the first time he's come to the hut.'

'You think we're going to believe that?'

'It's true. The only reason we came in here was because there was nowhere else to go.'

'It wasn't the first time you've been together then?' Nobhodlile turned to Nomguqo. 'Did you see them coupling? I mean, beyond *ukuHlobonga* (sex without penetration)?'

Nomguqo shook her head.

Sixhwethu struggled against the weight of the girls holding her down. 'Let me up. Please.'

Relenting, the *amaQhikiza* released her. Sixhwethu swung

her legs around and levered herself up. Grabbing her blanket, she covered her naked breasts to regain some dignity. 'All right,' she said, 'we've been seeing each other since Umafutha left the hut. I knew she'd have made a fuss if she found out.'

'And we wouldn't?'

'Anyway, I'm only doing what she,' she pointed accusingly towards Nomguqo, 'has been doing for a month or more.'

The attention turned to Nomguqo whose breathing was returning to normal.

'Is this true?' Nobhodlile asked.

'No.'

'Liar! Maweni told me his cousin's been seeing you,' Sixhwethu said.

'It's true I'm friends with Shikashika, but we don't do what you were doing.'

There was a standoff, neither girl willing to admit any more. The older residents looked at each other unsure as to the best course of action.

'Right, we'll work out what to do with you two tomorrow,' Nobhodlile said. 'In the meantime, get back to your beds.'

NINE

Eyes wild with terror, the Nguni bull shivered as warriors wrapped rawhide tethers round his thick neck. He was penned up behind the fence on the perimeter of the main cattle enclosure in a special corral designated for royal cows in calf. For the duration of the first fruits festival these had been moved to another area.

This bull was the strongest and meanest in the king's herd and had been selected to try the strength and courage of the young men yet to be bloodied on the battlefield. His name was Idube (Zebra), a reference to the characteristic striped markings on his hide.

He knew instinctively he was in danger as the young men struggled to hold him still. He tossed his head, and his sharp horns scythed the air, causing the youths to dodge and weave to avoid being gored. Eventually, the tethers were judged to be sufficiently secure, and a particularly brave soul stood in front of the gate and goaded him. This was the *ukuxoxa*, the ritual challenge.

'Idube, you are no match for the boys of the uDududu,' the young warrior shouted. 'You may be a big bull, but you will die like an unmilked heifer.'

He strode up and down defying the beast as the other boys in the *ibutho* grabbed the loose ends of the leather straps and prepared to pull as he was released onto the parade ground. It was a trial of strength. All that prevented him from charging into the crowd were the concerted efforts of the boys gripping the rawhide ropes.

Idube fought back. But the combined strength of the dozen fit young warriors made it an unequal struggle and, though the huge beast succeeded in dragging the youths across the parade ground, their feet scuffing up the dirt and raising a cloud of dust, he eventually tired and stood, tongue lolling and chest heaving. The crowd bayed its encouragement.

The king surveyed the spectacle from a dais erected for the occasion at the top of the *isibaya*. With a retinue of courtiers surrounding him, he was protected from the sun by a shelter of leafy branches. He smiled and remarked to no one in particular, 'That beast comes from a remarkable bloodline. His sire had the same markings, a truly handsome animal – and very brave. If that bull has inherited his father's spirit, it will be an interesting contest.'

Standing to one side of the royal shelter but in the full glare of the sun were the female members of the *isiGodlo* – the wives and their attendants. On public view for the first time was Uxisipe, mother of the twin boys. Having served her time of seclusion, she'd been relieved of the taint of *ukuzila* and reinstated as a royal wife. She provided a focus of interest. Sixhwethu stared openly. Apparently untroubled by the previous night's events, she had slept the sleep of the righteous. Nomguqo, on the other hand, had been awake worrying she'd be banned from seeing Shikashika again. Her eyes searched the crowd hoping to catch sight of him. Finally, she found him among the other herd boys on the far side. She wanted to wave, to attract his attention, but he was too far away, and in the context of the previous night's events, discretion was clearly a better policy.

Nodding towards the king, Sixhwethu whispered, 'You reckon he's taken Uxisipe to his bed yet? I bet he can't keep his hands off her.'

Stupid, thoughtless girl, Nomguqo thought, *what do you know?* Uxisipe's birth pangs and anguish at having her babies wrenched from her arms was all too vivid.

Sixhwethu sniggered. 'One thing's for sure – she'd better not conceive any more twins.'

The other girls burst out laughing. Turning her head sharply, Nomvimbi indicated her disapproval with a furious click of her tongue.

Attention was redirected to the parade ground. Two warriors released their hold on the restraints and ran in on Idube's blind side. He tossed his head in response, and one of his horns caught the nearest in the armpit, tearing the muscle and hooking the ligaments that attached the arm to the shoulder. The upward momentum took the boy off his feet. The crowd gasped collectively as he cartwheeled through the air and landed some yards away. Blood spurted from a severed artery.

Under the royal shelter, the courtiers looked to the king for his reaction. Cetshwayo simply nodded in appreciation of the bull's fighting spirit.

The uDududu boys could do nothing for their stricken comrade as Idube attacked the wounded boy on the ground, kneeling with his full weight on his chest. His ribs splintered and his lungs collapsed. Blood gushing from his mouth pooled in the dust as the great beast pawed the earth.

The warriors now reasserted themselves. One of them took charge, shouting instructions to his fellows. While the bull headbutted the inert body, the team on the far side succeeded in looping their tether over his horns and ran around the back to join the others.

The rest of the action happened in a flash. The team leader signalled, and with a collective shout "*Ji!*", they hauled on the ropes together. The sudden jolt pulled Idube off-balance. Knees buckling, he toppled, landing with a resounding thud on the bloodstained earth.

The warriors pressed home their advantage. They swiftly hobbled the front and back legs, preventing Idube getting back on his feet. The bull kicked and struggled but now he was securely pinioned. Eight of them used their combined weight to hold him down while the remaining three took hold of his head, using the wide span of the horns for purchase. He bucked and rolled, and the warriors struggled to hold him. But with his legs tied, Idube was powerless.

The team leader signalled again. The three at the bull's head yanked, twisting the horns against the weight of the body. The neck vertebrae buckled and dislocated with a loud crack. Idube's body shuddered as his spinal column was severed, sending his central nervous system into spasm. His legs stiffened. It was over, the once great beast reduced to a lifeless carcass.

The warriors sat back on their haunches, rivulets of sweat carving channels down their mud-caked bodies. They were exhausted; the struggle had used up every ounce of their energy. The king brandished the sacred spear to acknowledge their achievement and invited them to receive the applause of the crowd.

People rushed forward from every side. Men and women of all ages danced around the fallen bull and poked him with sticks, everyone taking collective ownership of his death. Even the *isiGodlo* girls joined the scrum, all except Nomguqo who held back, her attention on the dead warrior. She noticed that Joachime Gundersen had broken through the ranks of spectators and was crouched over the prone body. Feeling compelled to join her, she ran across the parade ground past the crowd milling around the dead bull.

The pastor's wife's fingers were at the boy's throat feeling for a pulse. He was beyond all medical help, his features set in a grimace of pain, and his eyes protruding from their sockets. Joachime gently closed them and stepped back as the family gathered around the body.

Nomguqo flinched at their anguished screams. Howling with grief, the distraught mother had to be supported by her daughters. The somber-faced father and brothers arranged the boy's limbs and lifted him high onto their shoulders, carrying him from the parade ground to where they could begin their mourning in private.

The crowd's blood lust and the grief of the dead youth's family presented such a stark contrast. Death was such an everyday occurrence in Zulu society that the bereavement of an individual family was of little consequence. Struggling to understand, Nomguqo stood beside Joachime. From her expression, she clearly had the same difficulty.

The crowd around the bull was replaced by a team of butchers. They set to work, slicing through the thick hide, dissecting the meat, flaying it from the bones with their sharp knives. Using cutting boards, they reduced still further the slabs of flesh into strips, which they piled into woven baskets. Soon the whole area around the bull was trampled into a morass, the butchers' feet churning the blood-soaked earth into a quagmire.

These actions were ritualised by Dlephu Ndlovu. He sprinkled herbs and magic potions over the strips of meat, directing that the baskets containing them should be carried to the king. Any bones and organs remaining from the butchering were set to one side and thrown onto a large fire.

The basket carriers filed past the royal dais. Passing the *inhlendla* over each, Cetshwayo endowed the meat with royal power.

The *amabutho* roared their approval.

As an iNgobamakhosi section commander, Mehlokazulu faced his men, leading the chants and punching the air with his fists to regulate the rhythm.

Dlephu Ndlovu now supervised the roasting of the meat. The strips of flesh were passed through the flames, then gathered again into baskets and hurled high above warriors. Hands reached up to pluck the meat strips from the air.

Anyone lucky enough to catch a piece of meat, put it in his mouth, chewed for a few seconds, then spat it out and passed the masticated meat on to his comrades. Mehlokazulu kept a watchful eye on his men to make sure none of the meat was swallowed.

The meat strips, now impregnated with the collective saliva of the regiment, were collected up and returned to the *iNgoma*. As the distillation of the shared essence of all the warriors in the *amabutho*, they contained enormous *muthi* – medicine with spiritual properties – to protect and invigorate the warriors protecting the king.

The men were fired up, ready for anything, confident they could go against any enemy and return unharmed and victorious. They were amaZulu, the greatest warriors on the continent, inspired with the conviction they could overcome any enemy of their beloved king. Mehlokazulu stood ramrod straight, eyes shining with pride at the display of national unity. If ordered to lead his men into battle there and then, he'd have done so without a moment's hesitation.

TEN

The dry summer weather had reduced the Mfolosi's flow so that, even at its widest, the river was reduced to a width of twenty feet.

Towards the end of the afternoon the oNdini population gathered for the last phase of the *umKhosi* ceremony, the ritual ablution. The sexes were segregated. The women, out of sight of the men, were confined to their pools while the men bathed a mile or so downstream.

A contingent of warriors patrolled along the upper reaches, throwing spears at the ready, making sure the water was safe from the ever-present danger of crocodiles.

The sun was low on the horizon and its golden light reflected off the glistening wet bodies as they plunged into the water. Others took the places of those who, having already cleansed themselves, climbed onto the banks to dry off.

In the female section, Nomguqo waited her turn. The royal wives had priority. They cavorted in the shallows splashing each other and behaving like children. Nomvimbi, her baby on her hip, cupped water in her hands and poured it over her head. Prince Dinuzulu gleefully sprayed around him and made his sister cry by drenching her.

Nomvimbi grabbed him. 'Now look what you've done. Go to the men's pool if you want someone to splash!'

Downstream, long lines of warriors waited to wash the dust and sweat from their bodies, leaning on their sticks, and discussing the events of the day. Mehlokazulu and Mbulawa gathered with a group of iNgobamakhosi hotheads. They'd been brooding ever since the *amabutho* delivered their mock charges before the king. The uThulwana had wound them up tighter than drumskins. It was enough they'd had to swallow the bitter taste of having their sweethearts forcibly married to men against their will. Now the uThulwana were parading their new wives in full view of the oNdini residents. Some had even been seen to caress and cuddle their brides. It was too much to bear. Action needed to be taken to restore their injured pride.

Mbulawa raged. 'I must find that piece of baboon shit and settle it with him.'

'It's bare-faced provocation,' Mehlokazulu's younger brother agreed, 'Bastard needs to be taught a lesson.'

Mehlokazulu advised caution, 'What would that achieve, Bekuzulu? Our brains bashed out on the killing stone. These things can't happen on the spur of the moment. Revenge must be planned.'

'I don't want you involved. This is my quarrel,' Mbulawa said.

'No, Mbulawa, we're all involved. The insult is to the whole *ibutho*. I can think of at least twenty of our girls who were married against their wishes.'

'It's mad to think it would end any other way. What was Ndabezitha thinking?'

The question caused a collective intake of breath.

'Hold your tongue, Mbulawa,' Mehlokazulu warned. 'You know that's treason and traitors end up on the killing stone. We need to be cool-headed about this. I'll talk to our commander.'

'And he'll tell you what any officer will tell you: "leave it alone",' said Mbalawa. 'They want unity in the *amabutho*.'

'Maybe not. Sigcwelegcwele's own sister is an iNgcugce. She was also married against her will. I'll talk to him and work out a plan. But you must promise me, no hasty actions. Is that clear?'

Mbulawa resumed his sullen brooding.

From his customary vantage point in the Hlophekhulu hills, the king indulged his customary pastime – the inspection of his herd. Cetshwayo's Nguni cattle were his pride and joy, the result of years of selective breeding to produce animals of the finest quality. Though the herd contained over forty thousand individual beasts, Cetshwayo prided himself on being able to trace, through the markings on their hides, the bloodline of every single animal.

Perched on a rock beside his close friend Jantoni, one of his senior advisers, he squinted through the rays of the setting sun. In the far distance the herd was being driven towards the safety of the oNdini cattle enclosure. If affairs of state permitted, this was Cetshwayo's daily routine. He derived an aesthetic pleasure in watching his animals, and since they represented his wealth and power, he also found it reassuring. No so tonight; he was beset with worry. 'Lung disease is taking its toll,' he said. 'My men have had to destroy thirty animals this week to stop the infection and isolate all the calving mothers. That's on top of the preparations they had to make for the *umKhosi*.'

Jantoni agreed. 'I sympathise with Your Majesty. I share the same problem. The devil has taken the form of a cattle tick.'

Cetshwayo sighed. 'My inheritance from my father was

over one hundred thousand beasts. That has now dwindled to less than half. It's a bad business, Jantoni. What am I to do?'

He relied on Jantoni's advice. Appointing him counsellor over fifteen years earlier, the king had rewarded him for his service, endowing him with a large tract of land near the coast. By marrying him to two of his own sisters, he'd cemented the alliance. Jantoni as was close as any man to the Zulu king. Yet, for someone speaking perfect isiZulu and living the life of a Zulu chief, Jantoni was not Zulu by birth. John Dunn was his name, the son of Scottish émigrés, brought up in English speaking Natal. His red hair and brick red complexion testified to his British origins.

Dunn pulled his hat down to shade his eyes. The wide brim also served to protect his pale complexion against the fierce tropical rays. As further protection he sported a bushy moustache and beard and was incongruously attired in Scottish tweed. 'Ndabezitha, as I see it, we've no alternative but to live with the ticks. That said, science may yet come to our aid. I hear European cattlemen are developing medicines to inoculate their animals. Perhaps this is the way we can eliminate this scourge. In the meantime, we can only hope that our surviving cattle will develop a resistance to the disease.'

'A forlorn hope, my friend.' The king stared glumly at the evidence of his dwindling fortune. He changed the subject. 'Enough of this. Give me some cheerful news. What of your new son?'

Dunn grinned proudly. 'Mother and baby are fit and well.'

'And who does he resemble?'

'Facially, he's the image of his mother, but he has your build, Ndabezitha.'

Cetshwayo preened at the comparison. 'Good. When will I have a chance to meet him?'

'The journey's too dangerous for a new-born. Besides, your sister needs time to recover. When I return in two months, he should be old enough to accompany me.'

'I look forward to it. Have you decided on a name for him?'

'That's your prerogative, Your Majesty.'

Cetshwayo chuckled. 'We must find a good one, then. I'll consult my *iNgoma*.'

'My household will be honoured by your choice.'

Cetshwayo slapped Dunn on the thigh. 'A man of property, with a growing family, eh?'

'Thanks to you, Ndabezitha.'

'You've given good service over many years, Jantoni. It's only natural I should reward you.'

'And I hope to serve you for many years to come.'

'I hope so, too.' The king's eyes crinkled with amusement. 'You were in a sorry state when you were first brought to me. Do you remember?'

'How could I not?' Removing his hat, Dunn wiped the sweat off his brow, acknowledging privately that he owed his good fortune, and quite probably his life, to the generosity of the Zulu king. He'd first met Cetshwayo at a low point in his life. His father Robert, instrumental in establishing the ivory trade in Natal, had been gored to death by a stampeding bull elephant – poetic justice, some said – leaving his fourteen-year-old son to fend for himself. With no other trade or training, John followed his father's profession. During one of his solo hunting trips across the river Mzinyathi, he became disoriented, and after wandering about in the bush, encountered Zulu warriors who took him, half-starving and with his clothes torn off his back, to Cetshwayo's *umuZi* where their friendship developed. When Cetshwayo succeeded to the throne, he sent for his English ally and made him one of his main advisers. Jantoni thus became an important emissary between Cetshwayo and the government of Natal.

The king steered the conversation around to affairs of state. 'Speak to me of your compatriots. Do they support us in our dispute with the Boers? I want your honest opinion.'

'Your Majesty, you know as well as I do, there is no love lost between the British and the Dutch.'

Cetshwayo flicked away an insect with a fancy giraffe-tail flywhisk – a present from Dunn.

'I'm told the Pietermaritzburg authorities are planning to stop the Dutch trespassing into Zulu lands,' Dunn added.

Cetshwayo's brows knitted. 'Not so much "trespassing" as "stealing". I've complained about this repeatedly for the last three years, and it seems to make no difference – Dutch farmers continue to annex Zulu land. My father was too generous, and the Boers took advantage of him. Now the British have control of the Transvaal, I rely on them to draw a definite boundary line. The Dutch must be kept in their place.'

'As I understand it, a boundary commission has already been established. I've no doubt it will find in our favour.'

'That would be a welcome outcome.' But Cetshwayo remained unconvinced. The farmers of the Afrikaner Republic of Transvaal had long been a thundercloud in the sunny skies over the kingdom. His father Mpande had given the Boers grazing rights over land bordering the Ncome and the Mzinyathi rivers, over which they now claimed absolute title, intruding further and further into Zulu territory. Beyond sending out his *impi* – thereby risking confrontation with his imperial neighbours – the king was at a loss as to how to deal with the problem. A commission sanctioned by the British authorities was a step in the right direction. He was also aware that the recent arrival of a new governor of the Cape Province heralded a significant change in the political climate: a much larger cold front was on its way. Sir Henry Bartle Frere was known to be an aggressive expansionist, dedicated to extending the influence of the British crown wherever he could. It was rumoured that he held ambitions to create a federation of southern African states under British control. An independent Zululand threatened those ambitions. 'Give me one good reason why I should trust the British,' he said. 'They're no friends of ours, that's been obvious for some time. The signs are clear enough – the massing of their troops along our borders for the past few weeks. What's the purpose of that if not to threaten us?'

'Ndabezitha, have you considered that the authorities in Pietermaritzburg are threatened by *you*? You have the largest and most effective force of fighting men in the whole of Southern Africa. Your *amabutho* have proved invincible in battle for over forty years. Do you imagine that the British would risk sending their soldiers onto the battlefield against your warriors?'

'Then what *is* their purpose?'

Dunn turned his hat over in his hand. 'Greater emphasis is being given to the security of British settlers in Natal. Beyond that, however, I suspect Bartle Frere has an ulterior motive.'

'Exactly!' Cetshwayo struck his palm with the flywhisk. 'The man's reputation precedes him. This is not a conciliator, Jantoni. This is a man set on empire building. As the new governor-general, he'll be doing everything in his power to extend British dominance in southern Africa.'

'Well, if that were so, he'd be disobeying his political masters. You have it in writing that the British government wishes to live in harmony with the amaZulu. Believe me, Your Majesty, it would be career suicide for Bartle Frere to ignore the orders of his Foreign Office superior.'

'Then how do I interpret the division of soldiers deployed along the Mzinyathi?'

'As I say, Your Majesty, these are purely defensive tactics.'

Cetshwayo breathed deeply and stared into the distance. The slow, plodding steps of the royal cattle kicked up a cloud of dust that filtered the rays of the setting sun – like the spokes of a giant wheel passing over the Mahlabathini plain.

'I hope you're right, Jantoni, I hope you're right.'

Down by the river, Sihayo's sons joined the throng heading back to take shelter for the night. It was a vast movement of people, following the innumerable tracks leading to the *umuZi*.

Both sexes mingled now as, tired from the exertions of the day, they looked forward to a good night's sleep. Warriors wearing head-rings walked beside their wives, some hand-in-hand, others with arms draped over their shoulders. Children, with inexhaustible energy, chased each other between the adults' legs. Here and there a voice was raised to scold an over-excited child. Against the background hum of the emerging nocturnal insects, the banter was lively and good-natured as they exchanged their impressions of the day.

Suddenly a female scream cut through the hubbub. A flurry of movement ahead stopped Mehlokazulu and Mbulawa in their tracks. Umafutha ran towards them against the general direction of the crowd. She wove frantically in and out of the oncoming people, clearly fleeing from something or somebody. Mbulawa stood in her path and caught her as she ran headlong into his arms. She sobbed with relief. The crowd parted as Mbulawa consoled her.

With a bellow of rage, Qhude charged after her, his staff raised threateningly.

Mehlokazulu stepped forward and used his stick to trip him, sending him sprawling in the dirt.

The uThulwana recovered, twisting in a way that belied his bulk, and struck out at Mehlokazulu's unprotected shins.

Skipping to avoid the blow, Mehlokazulu thrust the butt of his stick into the other's throat, snarling, 'Back off.'

Sensing violence, the crowd formed a circle round them.

Mbulawa elbowed his way past them. 'Leave him to me.'

A sneer contorted Qhude's face. 'You? You're not man enough.'

Mehlokazulu smashed his stick into the ground, missing Qhude's head by inches. With lightning reflexes, Qhude rolled away, springing to his feet with the rage of a mad bull. He launched himself, staff upraised. Sidestepping, Mehlokazulu swung his stick in an arc towards the Qhude's solar plexus. The uThulwana rocked back on his heels and Mehlokazulu's stick whistled harmlessly past his chest. Qhude feinted this way and that, probing Mehlokazulu's weaknesses. Mbulawa, circling around the back, looked for an opportunity to begin his attack.

Other warriors, attracted by shouts from the crowd, broke into the circle, which widened to accommodate them. Soon, over forty warriors from both factions, iNgobamakhosi and uThulwana, squared off against each other.

John Dunn peered intently through a telescope. He struggled to find focus in the fading light. His attention was drawn to movement beyond the line of cattle. A small group of men ran towards the hill where he and Cetshwayo sat.

'There, below us, just to the right.' Dunn offered the telescope to the king.

Cetshwayo had already registered them. Waving the telescope away, he moved swiftly towards the running men, covering the ground with long strides. Dunn had difficulty keeping up. Though heavyset, Cetshwayo was swift on his feet. In his youth there hadn't been many men who could match him for speed. He quickly reached the runners.

'Ndabezitha,' the leader panted, 'you must come immediately. There's an emergency at the *umuZi*.'

'*Must* is not a word to be used to a king,' Dunn warned.

'A thousand pardons, Ndabezitha, but if you don't come, blood will be spilled.'

The others in the group arrived and stood, their chests heaving, waiting for the king to respond.

'What is it that requires my immediate attention?'

'Men of the uThulwana are fighting with the iNgobamakhosi.'

'Where are their commanders? Why have they allowed this to happen?'

'They couldn't stop them!'

Sucking his teeth with irritation, Cetshwayo gestured for their horses to be brought.

Blood had already been spilled. As sunset darkened the sky, the area in front of the oNdini main gate teemed with frightened women and children anxious to escape the violence. Torches held by warriors urging the people through the gate illuminated the terrified expressions on their faces. The suddenness and ferocity of the fighting had taken them all by surprise.

It had spread so quickly. Sticks had been replaced with stabbing spears and what had seemed like harmless posturing had degenerated within minutes into an out-and-out fight to the death.

Hamu, the general commanding the uThulwana and a half-brother to Cetshwayo, outraged by the offence to his regiment's reputation by beardless iNgobamakhosi boys, had ordered his men to arm themselves. Returning with spears, they started an indiscriminate slaughter.

The cultivated fields, mealie stalks still standing after the harvest, were turned into a battleground. Shadows flitted through the lines of corn as hundreds of men chased each other, slashing this way and that.

Mbulawa was one of the first to fall. On the far side of the battlefield and occupied in defending himself, Mehlokazulu was unable to help. Through the frenzy of fighting men, he glimpsed Qhude attacking the boy. It was a one-sided fight. Mbulawa with his stick offered little defence against his much stronger and heavier opponent armed with a spear. Qhude lunged and caught the boy under the rib cage, driving the blade up through his lungs into his heart. Mbulawa shuddered as it flooded with blood and stopped beating. He collapsed to the ground, his life draining from him.

Qhude wrenched the *iklwa* free with a terrible sucking sound and stood over the corpse. 'Boy,' he spat, then turned on his heel looking for a fresh target.

Mehlokazulu saw Mbulawa on the ground just as he too was swept off his feet. The blade of an *iklwa* whistled towards his chest. He had the presence of mind to turn. The blade grazed his skin and buried itself in the ground. Reacting quickly, he scissor-kicked his opponent's legs and toppled him. Then grabbed the haft of the spear, yanked it free, and drove it hard into the man's throat.

He ran over to Mbulawa. Staring into eyes already turning opaque, he knew the boy was dead. Dropping to his knees, he whispered gently in Mbulawa's ear. 'Rest now little brother. I will challenge him – and, when I do, I promise he will suffer.'

Quickly scanning the battlefield, he drew a bead on the direction Qhude had taken and took off after him.

ELEVEN

Night had fallen by the time Cetshwayo and John Dunn covered the mile and a half from their observation point. Now it was pitch-black on the battlefield and the ferocity of the fighting had subsided. However, the widespread groans of the wounded were evidence that an extensive battle had taken place.

Reaching the edge of the mealie field, Cetshwayo dismounted. He stared into the black void and bellowed, 'This is your king speaking! Lay down your weapons!' Men ran from the direction of the *umuZi* carrying flaming torches. Grabbing one, he strode over the trampled maize stalks. Here and there he stooped over a fallen warrior. The savagery of the attack was apparent from the wounds that had been inflicted. Even for someone inured to human suffering – and responsible for much of it himself – Cetshwayo was shocked by what he saw. Youngsters from the iNgobamakhosi were lying with their brains spilling from their shattered skulls, their throats slashed, and terrible wounds in their chests and bellies. The occasional uThulwana corpse was found but, by and large, the casualties were among the younger *ibutho*. It had been an unequal contest: men against boys, metal weapons against sticks. By the time he'd examined a dozen bodies, Cetshwayo had seen enough. He roared, 'I want the men responsible for this outrage!'

John Dunn grabbed a young boy by the arm. 'Run quickly to the missionary. Tell Pastor Gundersen what has happened here. Ask him to bring his medicine box and lots of bandages.'

The *isiGodlo* girls squatted outside their hut, chattering about what they'd just witnessed. Though their retiring time was long past, sleep would be a long time coming. Once the stick fighting started, they'd been ushered into the safety of the royal enclosure and the warriors responsible for the safety of the king's immediate household had posted guard at the entrance to the *isiGodlo*. The girls felt safe enough, but could the same be said of their male counterparts? How many of them would see the dawn?

Sixhwethu bubbled with excitement. 'I knew there'd be fighting. Didn't I tell you?'

Nobhodlile said, 'You think Mehlokazulu got what was coming to him?'

'Let him not be hurt,' Nomguqo said.

Sixhwethu's eyes narrowed. 'What did you say?'

Anticipating the mockery, Nomguqo steeled herself.

Sixhwethu continued, 'What's it to you, *inkosazana*? You going for the older man now? Shikashika not experienced enough for you?'

Nobhodlile joined in, 'Mehlokazulu likes himself too much. I pity his wife if he ever marries.'

'Marry?' Sixhwethu scoffed. 'Who'd have him?'

The arrival of Mnukwa, an officer of the royal household, ended the speculation.

'Ndabezitha requires your presence in his quarters,' he ordered. 'Immediately!'

Cetshwayo paced up and down.

His fleshy half-brother Hamu attempted justify his regiment's actions. 'The dignity of the uThulwana was affronted. Their reputation as fighting men was compromised. I don't blame them at all.'

Others present – John Dunn and four other government advisers: Mnyamana, the king's prime minister, Zibhebhu and Ntshingwayo, military generals, and Sihayo, Mehlokazulu's father – kept their heads down. The argument had to run its course.

The king jabbed his finger at Hamu. 'I know better than you what's good for the uThulwana. This is my regiment, and what happened out there is a stain on our honour. Who gave the order to bring weapons?'

Hamu answered, 'Before you jump to conclusions, hear the other side. Send for the iNgobamakhosi commander. Ask Sigcwelegcwele that question. Once you've interviewed him, we will speak again. Until then, I'll be in my own *umuZi*. Good night to you, Ndabezitha.' Heaving his bulk upright, he turned his back on the king and waddled out of the room.

The ministers held their breath. Such open defiance usually ended violently.

'You're treading a very thin line, Hamu!' the king shouted after him.

The *isiGodlo* girls arrived in time to witness this last exchange. Conscious they were intruding at a sensitive moment, they watched Hamu storm off into the night. They stood at the door unsure what to do next.

Cetshwayo spluttered with frustration. 'I'll have him arrested and charged with treason.'

Mnyamana, a wise counsellor and cool head in moments of constitutional crisis, reminded the king of the realpolitik. 'With the greatest respect, Ndabezitha, that will not be possible. The Northern Territory comes under Hamu's jurisdiction. We can't afford to alienate the man who protects our northern borders.' He noticed the girls standing beyond the door. 'Why don't we take some refreshment and consider what steps we must take to reunite these two factions? It's imperative we present a united front at this time when Your Majesty's kingdom is in the greatest peril.'

The king stared at his prime minister and then at the others. Their expressions told him Mnyamana was right. He gestured to the girls. 'Bring u*Tshwala*.'

The girls scurried away and Cetshwayo took his seat on the soft furnishings on the floor, inviting his ministers to do likewise. 'Wise words, Mnyamana,' he said, then turned to John Dunn. 'Let's hear the white man's perspective.'

Helping himself to the snuff bowl on the table beside him, Dunn used a handkerchief to dust the excess from his nostrils. 'It is vital the integrity of the kingdom is preserved, Ndabezitha. Sihayo holds the land bordering the Mzinyathi and the territory of the British. He knows better than anyone how the redcoat forces have been building up in the last months on the far side of the border…'

Sihayo confirmed this with a nod.

'…and the government in Pietermaritzburg will see any quarrel between you and Hamu as evidence your authority has been compromised. It doesn't take much imagination to see how they'd exploit any internal dispute.'

'That's precisely my concern,' said Cetshwayo. His anger at Hamu was replaced by a fresh anxiety. 'I seek to live in peace with my British neighbours. I have accommodated every single one of their demands. Jantoni, you are my witness that this is so.' He laid his hand on Dunn's shoulder. 'I rely on you, my friend and brother, to keep the peace between the two nations.'

Dunn inclined his head deferentially. 'I'll do my best, Ndabezitha.'

Sixhwethu led the other *isiGodlo* girls in bringing the refreshments. They distributed drinking bowls. Then, with eyes lowered submissively, Nomguqo poured from a large jug of foaming beer.

Sihayo, silent throughout this exchange, voiced his main concern, 'Where are the iNgobamakhosi now? Where are my sons?'

As the senior military man present, Zibhebhu had already gathered the necessary intelligence. 'They've taken to the hills, afraid of retribution from His Majesty.'

Cetshwayo drained his *uKhamba*. 'I suppose we'll see them slinking back tomorrow to face their punishment.'

Sihayo leaped to their defence. 'Ndabezitha, you know Mehlokazulu. He's a proud boy, and I can see how he might have taken offence. But he's loyal to Your Majesty and a good soldier.'

Zibhebhu added his support. 'We need many more of his type in the regiments. He's a good example to both younger and older men. Fearless and with a good military brain.'

Nomguqo was aware how privileged she was to hear matters of such moment being discussed. She also felt an inexplicable sense of pride in the praise being offered to Mehlokazulu. Her feelings surprised her. Did she have a right to take such a personal interest in him? The king held out his drinking vessel to be filled and she duly obliged.

'I trust with all my heart that war can be avoided,' he declared. 'If not, we shall put great responsibility on the shoulders of men like Mehlokazulu. Tomorrow, I shall interview Sigcwelegcwele and discover the iNgobamakhosi version of events. I shall also need a list of all casualties so the relatives can be informed. This was an act of the greatest stupidity. We must not allow it to compromise the morale of our warriors. As Mnyamana says, unity among the *amabutho* must be maintained at all costs.'

The council members of the council digested this in silence, lasting for some moments until John Dunn cleared his throat. 'Ndabezitha, our men's morale will have suffered a terrible blow from tonight's events. Only with the greatest difficulty will unity in the *amabutho* be restored. What's needed is a common purpose, an operation to bring them together…'

The council members sat forward. What did he have in mind?

Dunn continued, 'Ndabezitha, from time to time, you and I have enjoyed the *inqina* (hunt). Indeed, your skill in the field is legendary. I've often seen you bring down game at apparently impossible distances.'

Cetshwayo slapped his thighs. His laugh came from deep in his chest. 'And who taught me to shoot?'

'I taught you very little, Your Majesty,' Dunn replied. 'Your talent is natural.'

The king's eyes twinkled at the flattery. 'But why do you mention hunting?' Then he twigged. 'Jantoni, your judgment is as always faultless. I see exactly what you're proposing.' He clapped his hands. 'It's the perfect plan. We shall organise a hunt on the borders of the Mzinyathi. The cream of the regiments will be involved.'

Zibhebhu agreed, 'It's what we've all been demanding – an opportunity for the men to wash their spears.'

'And demonstrate to the British our battle strength,' Mnyamana added.

The king concluded, 'An *inqina* will draw a line under tonight's fiasco and be a means to unify the regiments. The common purpose will remove any friction and sharpen their instincts for killing. At the same time, it will show our neighbours we're not to be trifled with.' Cetshwayo squeezed John Dunn's thigh. 'Excellent advice, Jantoni. We'll leave it to Ntshingwayo and Mavumengwana to organise the muster.'

The king yawned, and his ministers recognised their cue to withdraw.

A field hospital beside the battlefield had been set up under the supervision of Pastor Gundersen and his wife. Flaming torches illuminated the ghastly scene. Dead bodies lay where they'd fallen. The survivors waited for their wounds to be dressed. Over forty young men held makeshift bandages over their injuries to staunch their blood loss. The task of treating so many injured warriors was beyond the Norwegians' capabilities, so they'd sent for girls from the *isiGodlo* to act as supplementary nurses.

Joachime made a tour of the remaining patients to establish a triage based on the severity of their injuries. Gunhild Christine clung to her mother's skirts. It was long past her bedtime, and she was wide-eyed with fatigue.

Meanwhile, Nomguqo assisted the Pastor. 'That's it,' he said, 'use plenty of water, wash the wound clean, make sure there's no dirt in it, otherwise it will turn bad.'

One of the other girls held up a torch as Nomguqo peered into a hole in a warrior's shoulder. A spear had penetrated deep into the muscle narrowly missing the lungs. The skin was badly torn and oozing blood. The warrior's eyes were wary as Nomguqo irrigated the wound with fresh water infused with herbs. If the astringent lotion caused him pain, he gave no sign of it, staring impassively into the distance.

Gundersen took over, pulling the jagged edges together with needle and thread. Nomguqo watched intently, fascinated by the surgery. Satisfied with his handiwork, Gundersen looked across at his wife already urging the next patient forward. 'It will be a long night,' he said.

The following morning, John Dunn discovered the king had relocated his court to the *umuZi* of his dead father. kwaNodwengu had been transformed into a military barracks with its own garrison of warriors. They provided for all the king's needs.

Dunn was ushered into Cetshwayo's presence. The king sat with his own personal armoury spread out on a table in front of him, a mixture of antiquated Brown Bess flintlocks and muzzle-loading rifles.

Cetshwayo greeted him. 'Jantoni.'

'I called on Your Majesty at oNdini this morning–'

The king interrupted. 'I cannot stay at oNdini while the spirits of the dead warriors remain there. Until the warriors are buried and my *iNgoma* conducts the purification ceremony, there's a danger they could haunt us forever.'

Picking up a rifle, he unwrapped the oil-saturated sacking around it. It was a modern breech-loader, a Martini-Henry, standard issue of the British forces. 'This has yet to be fired.' The king put it to his shoulder, taking a bead towards Dunn's chest. 'Your latest gift to me, Jantoni, remember?'

Dunn stepped quickly out of the firing line.

Cetshwayo laid the rifle down on the table, wiping his oily fingers on the wrapping. He sighed, 'I wish you could lay hands on more of them.'

'Unfortunately, the British army has placed an embargo on their sale. They're too good a weapon to risk putting on the open market.'

Cetshwayo shrugged. 'It's a fine weapon, but as we know a weapon is only as good as the man who wields it.'

Dunn changed the subject. 'Ndabezitha, I've come to ask your permission to return to my own lands. My wives require my presence. I've received word my eldest boy has fallen sick.'

Cetshwayo leaned forward. 'How sick?'

'You know how it is with children – one minute at death's door and the next jumping around. His mother is worried, however.'

'You must go, don't wait a moment longer.'

'Thank you, Ndabezitha.'

The king escorted his friend to the door. 'That was a bad business last night. I've just heard Sigcwelegcwele's side. It's exactly as I thought – Hamu overreacted. However, for the sake of peace keeping, I've banished Sigcwelegcwele to the coast.' He gave a conspiratorial wink. 'I'll let the dust settle, then let him come back. He's too good a man to sit idle.'

'You must take great care to bring Hamu back into the fold,' Dunn warned. 'You cannot afford to alienate him.'

'Yes, yes,' Cetshwayo said. 'Incidentally – another strange event happened after the fight: a baboon came to my hut in oNdindi and left gifts.'

Dunn raised an eyebrow. Although rational in many other ways, Cetshwayo was superstitious about supposed manifestations of the spirit world.

'It was Sigcwelegcwele,' Cetshwayo said. 'Knowing I'd require him to account for the fighting, he sent a wild beast to placate me.'

'A wild beast?'

'Yes, a wild beast.'

'He left gifts, you said. What gifts were they, Ndabezitha?'

'A bunch of bananas.'

Dunn struggled to keep a straight face. 'A rare gift indeed.'

The stench of death hung in the air for several days afterwards. Over sixty dead warriors from both factions needed to be buried.

The pall of sorrow over oNdini was equally thick. The loss of so many young warriors distressed the whole community. Mothers' and sisters' crying echoed round the *umuZi* day and night.

Each family was responsible for its own burial arrangements. For those living within oNdini or its immediate vicinity these could be quickly organised. The purification rites had to be handled with speed. Until they'd taken place normal routine would not be resumed. For those coming from a distance, it was more complicated. Mbulawa's parents and sisters, for instance, had to travel across mountainous country from the Northern Territory beyond the river Phongolo. The journey took nearly three days. In the interim, Mehlokazulu assumed the melancholy responsibility of moving his comrade's body to the iNgobamakhosi military barracks. It was there waiting for them when they arrived.

The female relatives laid out the corpse, shaving and washing it. The father slaughtered an ox and skinned it so the fresh hide could be used as a shroud. As Zulu tradition dictated, the women sewed Mbulawa up inside it. Mehlokazulu and members of the *iviyo* dug a grave in the garrison's cattle enclosure at a spot chosen by the father, who was on hand to make sure the pit was sunk deep enough. Then he and Mehlokazulu gently laid the body in the grave, propping it in an upright position ready to face the ancestors, and covered it with soil. They piled heavy flat stones on top to protect it from jackals and hyenas.

Their duty to their dead comrade discharged, Mehlokazulu and his men started to prepare for the great hunt. They'd been told to expect to spend a week in the field; the days before leaving were therefore spent collecting supplies and checking that their hunting nets and weapons were in good order.

The whole male population of oNdini and its surrounding area was mobilised, with the effect that, on the day of departure, the *umuZi* was suddenly deprived of its menfolk. Every single man, including the king, left to join the hunting party – except the royal bodyguards and servants whose duties kept them inside the *isiGodlo*.

Among the women, nothing much changed in their routine. Fields had to be prepared for the next season, children tended, meals prepared. With the harvest gathered into the granaries, mounds of mealies had to be dried and ground into flour.

Teams of women, organised according to their age groups, busily removed the kernels from corncobs and spread them to dry in the baking summer sun. Others took responsibility for grinding – lifting heavy billets of hard wood and driving them into hollowed out tree stumps – pulverising the corn into meal.

The *amaQhikiza* took their turn. It was physically demanding work, and no allowance was made for their youth. After an hour with the pestle and mortar, their shoulder and arm muscles ached. Sixhwethu conveniently announced a crippling headache. She sat in the shade clutching her forehead while the others toiled in the hot sun.

Sweat poured into Nomguqo's eyes as she pounded the maize. Up and down, she drove the pestle in a seemingly endless repetition. The continuous drumming developed a hypnotic rhythm that distracted her from the discomfort of her tired muscles. Increasingly removed from the present, she entered a trance-like state. Images from the first fruits festival flashed through her mind. She saw the grimaces of faces contorted in pain and heard the cries of the wounded men.

Driving the pestle into the mortar with greater frequency and ferocity, she attempted to dispel the unwelcome images. The present receded even further until she lost all sense of where she was.

A tap on her shoulder jolted her back to reality. Standing at arm's length was Umafutha. Not the full-cheeked, smiley-eyed girl that Nomguqo remembered but a pale shadow of herself. Umafutha had lost weight. She looked awkward, apologetic. Her eyes were sunk into sockets surrounded by dark shadows, her vitality leached away. Shocked by her appearance, Nomguqo took a backward step, then remembered that her friend had just suffered a bereavement. She took Umafutha into her arms. As the two girls held each other, Nomguqo felt the bones of her rib cage under her fingers. She struggled to find words of consolation. 'How wonderful to see you.'

Umafutha gave a sad smile. The other *amaQhikiza* gathered around, taking turns to hug their old hutmate. Sixhwethu made a characteristically blunt observation: 'You're all skin and bone. Why're you not eating?'

Umafutha shook her head: if she couldn't see for herself, what would be the point in explaining? Squeezing Nomguqo's hand, she explained, 'My husband is at the hunt with all the other warriors. Can I–'

Nomguqo completed the sentence, 'Stay with us? Of course, you can.'

The tension drained from Umafutha's features.

'Where else?' said Nobhodlile.

Beaming, Nomguqo announced, 'This is cause for celebration. We must make a feast.'

Eighty or so miles away beside the Mzinyathi river, not far from his father's homestead, Mehlokazulu and his *iviyo* sat around a cooking fire. The day's hunting had been successful. They were about to enjoy what they'd killed.

Mehlokazulu watched Shikashika skinning an antelope. 'You're fast for your age,' he said. Unaccustomed to compliments, Shikashika blushed as Mehlokazulu continued, 'When we flushed that buck from the undergrowth and you took off after him, I'd have bet on the antelope. But you ran him down – and your spear throwing was as accurate as any of ours. We should call you *ingulele* (cheetah).'

The others took up a chant, tapping their spear butts on the ground: '*Ingulele! Ingulele!*'

Turning over choice morsels of heart and liver in the embers of the fire, Maweni scowled.

Shikashika divided the venison into joints and handed them to Mehlokazulu who, while arranging them on the fire, noticed Maweni sneaking a kidney into his mouth. 'On the other hand, we can see where your skills lie, Maweni. Not so much *ingulele*, as *ingulube*.'

The comparison to a pig invited catcalls and the pointing of mocking fingers. Shame-faced, Maweni spat out the contents of his mouth.

'Enjoying yourselves?' Cetshwayo's question immediately brought the jeering to a stop. Having failed to notice his arrival, the warriors leaped to their feet in confusion. He put them at their ease. 'Pardon my intrusion. I wanted to know how the day went for my favourite regiment.' Squatting beside the fire, he indicated the warriors should join him.

Mehlokazulu pointed out Shikashika. 'We were just saying how quick he is.'

Cetshwayo studied the boy. 'Oblige me with your name.'

'Shikashika,' he replied.

'Ah yes. Shikashika. I know your father – uThulwana, isn't he?'

Overcome with shyness, the boy nodded.

'He *kleza*'ed with me and has been beside me in many a scrape. I hope you're as dependable.'

Shikashika swallowed, unable to speak.

The king smiled. The opportunity to engage with individual subjects arrived infrequently and he enjoyed the contact. Noticing the animal corpses lying in a pile. 'So, what was your tally for the day?'

'Two eland, four waterbucks, half a dozen impala… oh, and a bush pig,' said Mehlokazulu.

Maweni, anxious to recover his position, piped up. 'We nearly brought down a buffalo, too. Got three spears into him, but he disappeared into the bush. We thought it was too dangerous to follow him.'

'Quite right,' the king agreed. 'Nothing more dangerous than a wounded buffalo, very unpredictable.' Turning back to Mehlokazulu, 'Tell me, did you catch sight of any British soldiers across the river?'

'No, Ndabezitha,' Mehlokazulu said.

'They were certainly there, garrisoned at kwaJim. We saw their telescopes trained on us. What do you think they learned from watching us today?'

Mehlokazulu sat up straight. 'That the Zulu *impi* are to be feared. We're the bravest and most powerful warriors the world has ever known.'

Cetshwayo laughed, 'Just what I wanted to hear. Enjoy your supper, you've earned it.'

Relaxed in the company of her former hutmates, Umafutha ate and drank her way through a huge meal; it was as though she'd never been away. Swopping stories of shared mishaps and embarrassments, they laughed hysterically. No reference was made to Mbulawa's death, nor Umafutha's marriage.

Full to the brim, the girls' heads started to droop; one by one they retired to their sleeping mats. Nomguqo stretched out in her usual place, with Umafutha beside her. As she drifted off, she became aware of her snuggling in. They lay like spoons, listening to the snoring of the other girls.

'Are you awake?' Umafutha whispered. 'Can we talk?'

Nomguqo turned to face her. They lay, just able to see each other in the glowing embers of the fire. 'I saw the marks on your back,' she said. 'Has Qhude been beating you?'

Umafutha nodded. 'He started the day he married me. When we arrived at his homestead, he raped me in full view of his other wives…'

'What?'

'…and carried on – twice, three times, even four times a day. If I protested, he beat me with his fists. My face swelled up with his blows.'

Nomguqo gasped.

'After a week, I couldn't take any more and left in the middle of the night. I was so bruised I could hardly walk. He came after me of course. His men held me down while he thrashed me with a rhino hide whip until I fainted with the pain. The wounds took ten days to heal.'

Nomguqo reached for her hand and squeezed. 'We must tell Ndabezitha. Qhude must be punished. At the very least, stopped from hurting you.'

'It's too late,' Umafutha pushed Nomguqo's hands onto her belly. 'What do you feel?'

Nomguqo held her spread fingers against her skin. 'Nothing, except you're painfully thin.'

'Can't you feel the bump?'

'You're pregnant?'

Umafutha wailed, 'I can't bear it. The baby should have been Mbulawa's. How can I bring that man's child into the world?'

Nomguqo held her close and whispered, 'Shush, shush.'

There was no comforting her. Her chest heaved with wracking sobs.

Nomguqo knew Umafutha was right. The pregnancy changed everything. All she could do was hold her until the sobs subsided and Umafutha relaxed into sleep.

Nomguqo lay awake, her mind wrestling with the dilemma of how to help her friend. Until she too succumbed to fatigue and fell asleep.

In the early hours, she woke with a start, conscious that Umafutha's arms were no longer around her. She looked to either side. In the dim light she could see the other girls sound asleep on their mats. But no trace of Umafutha. A premonition seized her. Umafutha was in no fit state to be alone. What if she'd hurt herself? Or even worse, taken her own life? Nomguqo had heard stories of people killing themselves. Was Umafutha one of those? She stood and crossed to the entrance.

It was a clear night with not a breath of wind. The stars and moon shone brightly, casting enough light for her to see right across the *umuZi*. She stared in all directions. The compound was still and quiet, no sign of movement anywhere. Where had Umafutha gone? Assuredly not back to her husband's *umuZi* – and that made it doubly worrying.

She wondered what to do. Should she raise the alarm? On what pretext? The suspicion that Umafutha might harm herself? If so, what evidence could she offer?

In any case, nothing would be done until the morning. Only then would it be accepted that Umafutha was missing. Only then would a search party be sent out.

She was overthinking it, she concluded. There had to be a perfectly valid explanation for Umafutha to have left the hut. Shaking her head at her over-active imagination, she returned to her sleeping mat.

The following morning there was still no sign of Umafutha. Or the day after. The rumour that she was missing circulated round the *umuZi*. On the third day a search party was sent out.

Her tracks were eventually picked up on the path to the Hlophekhulu hills, where they were followed all the way to the edge of a precipice. Umafutha's body was found at the bottom.

PART TWO

THE EYES OF THE ZULU

TWELVE

kwaSogekle

'Why do you let her live? She's openly flaunting her adultery,' Mehlokazulu snarled, 'mocking you and making our family a laughingstock. On both sides of the Mzinyathi they're saying how weak you are. Not one, but two of your wives living openly with younger men.'

'What do you propose I do?' Sihayo asked.

'There's only one penalty for an adulteress.'

'She's your mother.'

'Exactly! And that's what gives me the right to demand it. How can I object to people calling my mother a whore when that's what she is?' He spat the words in his father's face. 'You're a cuckold. Have you no shame?'

Mehlokazulu had summoned all senior male members of Sihayo's family to discuss how best to handle the present crisis. They'd come from near and far. Mehlokazulu himself had been forced to ask the king for special dispensation to return to kwaSogekle, *umuZi* of the nGobese clan. The embarrassment and shame he'd felt when he gave the explanation to the king still made him seethe with anger.

The entire male contingent was present – full brothers, half-brothers, and uncles – all sat in a circle in the cattle pen. The debate had been raging for over an hour and the old man had been battered from all sides.

The evidence against his wives was compelling. The "senior wife" MaMtshali and one of the younger wives had taken secret lovers. A whispering campaign mounted by zealous members of the household had finally reached Sihayo's ears but, before the *inkosi* had time to take the necessary action, the two women fled across the river Mzinyathi, which represented the border between Zululand and the British colony of Natal. There, under the protection of the British authorities, the wives imagined they'd be safe from their husband's wrath.

Much as his reputation had been damaged by the defection, Sihayo was enough of a politician to know that a sensitive diplomatic situation had been created requiring careful handling. To bring the women back would involve a trespass onto British territory, which might damage the delicate relationship between the kingdom and its imperial neighbour. Sihayo was responsible for maintaining law and order in the territory bordering Natal. The build-up of British military forces across the Mzinyathi was all too apparent. In his reports to Cetshwayo, Sihayo had made it clear that the situation was volatile. The least provocation could jeopardise the uneasy peace. Yet the defection of his wives was a festering wound that caused him great pain. He had suffered many sleepless nights worrying about what to do.

Stalling for time, he'd chosen to swallow his pride and take no immediate action. He hadn't reckoned with his first-born son's highly developed sense of family honour.

Mehlokazulu squatted in front of Sihayo, using a more deferential tone. 'Father, I owe you the respect due to an *inkosi* and a royal *isikhulu*.' He gestured to the rest of the gathering. 'We all do. Under any other circumstances, I wouldn't contradict your wishes. However, in this case I insist you act to restore our honour.'

Sihayo sighed wearily. 'My son, I accept your argument, but my hands are tied. Had your mother remained here, she would have faced the punishment that Zulu law requires. However, we must deal with the situation as it exists. Until she returns to the kingdom, she remains outside our jurisdiction. We will take no action and I want no further discussion on the subject. Do I make myself clear?'

Sihayo stood, the matter closed. Nodding curtly at the other members of his family, he strode off towards his private quarters.

Mehlokazulu stared after him, muttering to himself, 'If you won't act, I will do it for you.'

That same night, some five miles from kwaSogekle on the far side of the river Mzinyathi, Mehlokazulu's mother squatted to pee, her arms resting on her knees. She looked out towards the stockade that protected the huts from wild animals. Through gaps in the fence, she could see the river. A low-lying mist shrouded the water, but here and there as the breeze swirled around, she could see moonlight glinting off the ripples breaking over the stones in the shallows. With an involuntary shudder, she pulled the blanket more tightly around her shoulders. Staring intently into the impenetrable shadows of the opposite riverbank, she wondered when they would come for her. It was just a matter of time.

For nearly a month she had lived in fear of Sihayo's vengeance. She knew well the consequences of adultery. As a young girl, she'd been made to witness the punishment of an errant wife. Had seen the woman dragged, shaking with fear, into the communal area in front of *inkosi* Xongo's homestead. Had watched the braids of ox sinew wound around her neck. Had heard her screams dwindle to a hoarse gurgling as the garrotte was tightened. Now, some thirty years later, MaMtshali remembered the bulging eyes, the lolling tongue, the twisted limbs soiled where the woman had voided her bowels, and the pitiless expressions of the executioners.

It was the Zulu custom. A man could marry as many wives as he could afford. But a wife who took another man instantly condemned herself to a slow and agonising death. MaMtshali stood and adjusted her *umutsha* – the leopardskin apron that denoted her status as an *inkosi*'s wife. Gathering her blanket, she tucked it into her waistband. She yawned, longing for the temporary peace that sleep would bring. Yet she knew with absolute certainty that, as dawn broke, she'd still be wide-awake. Better to be out in the fresh air than to lie beside her young lover listening to his rhythmic breathing and watching the rise and fall of his chest. It was at night the demons of guilt came to people her dreams and give her no rest.

She'd discussed it endlessly with MaMthethwa, her fellow fugitive. They'd convinced themselves they were beyond Sihayo's reach. Three weeks had passed since fleeing his *umuZi*, stealing away under cover of darkness. So far, nothing. Not even a whisper they were under threat. Having survived three weeks, they concluded they were free of their husband's tyranny.

Also, they were living next to an outpost of British imperial power. The small band of border guards armed with British rifles and wearing British uniforms was a comforting presence in the huts adjacent. And a large garrison of British redcoats was only a day's march away. But MaMtshali could not dispel the fear she would eventually pay with her life for her offence.

She was on the verge of nervous collapse. The initial joy of discovering she still had the power to awaken a man's desire had been replaced by a desperate desire for sleep. Since the birth of her last child eight years earlier, she had not been invited to share her husband's hut. She knew he'd grown tired of her, favouring the toned limbs and firm breasts of his younger wives over a body worn out by twenty years of childbearing. She had reconciled herself to a life without the pleasure of a man's embrace, but when the youth first caressed her and whispered his soft words of seduction, she felt appreciated. She ignored the inner voice that urged caution. The thrill of attracting a boy the same age as Mehlokazulu drove out all thoughts of danger.

MaMtshali followed the path to the water's edge. Apart from the splashing of water in the rapids and the guttural croaking of toads, there was silence.

Standing on the riverbank, she peered upstream. Above the tambookie grass swaying in the breeze, she could make out the roofs of kwaJim, the trading post that marked the Mzinyathi crossing. The drift, a causeway through the shallows, was marked on both sides by ruts caused by heavy oxcart wheels. Here the riverbanks had been eroded by the heavy traffic flowing in both directions. English and Dutch traders from the coast had literally beaten a path to Cetshwayo's court.

Shifting her gaze to the far bank, she searched for any sign of movement. All her senses were alert, her ears straining to pick up any unusual sounds.

She stiffened as she heard a cough. Animal or human? The grasses parted to reveal a leopard and her cub. They padded down to the water, and the cub hunkered down to drink as his mother kept vigil. MaMtshali watched them intently.

His thirst slaked, the cub retreated, and his mother escorted him back into the all-enveloping tambookie grass.

MaMtshali resumed her scanning. The chill in the air made her shiver uncontrollably. She thought of the warm body she'd left in the hut, the embers of the fire still glowing. Lying on the sleeping mat drowsy from their evening meal, she'd reached for him and felt him grow big between her fingers. His hands caressed her flanks and between her legs, his fingers parting the soft folds of her flesh. Wrapping her legs around him, she arched her hips to receive him. They climaxed together, her grunts of pleasure urging him to more vigorous thrusts. In such encounters with her husband, she was never considered an equal partner, merely a receptacle into which he spent himself. They fell asleep with him still inside her. Waking sometime later, she extricated herself from his embrace and lay beside him, watching him sleep as his seed drained from her, congealing on the warmth of her inner thigh.

The memory of their lovemaking reassured her. Tonight, she was safe. She could return to his embrace convinced they wouldn't come for her yet awhile.

On his sleeping mat at kwaSogekle, Sihayo cleared his nasal passages with a loud snort and, collecting the phlegm on his tongue, projected it into the fire. It sizzled as it struck the embers. Reaching for the earthenware jug beside his sleeping mat, he lifted it to his lips and took a copious draft of gin. He swilled the liquid round his teeth and gums to rid himself of the foul taste in his mouth. Swallowing, he stared at the hissing gobbet as it was consumed by the heat.

Like MaMtshali, the *inkosi* was prey to nocturnal demons, but his demons were those of anger. However much he justified his inaction to his sons, his wives' defection rankled with him. Their continued existence was an insult to his dignity and a challenge to his authority.

MaMtshali had long ceased to be of value to him. She'd served her purpose by bearing him four sons who had, in turn, increased his power and influence. But she was one of over twenty wives. One less, what was the difference?

He looked down at the young wife peacefully asleep beside him. Nobuhle, *the beautiful one*, was aptly named. Still virtually a child, her face was untroubled by bad thoughts or petty jealousies, her belly and breasts so far undistorted by the rigours of childbearing. This wife was well brought up, a credit to her parents: respectful, compliant, and eager to please. He'd paid six of his best cattle for her, and for good measure had included a rifle sold to him by the Dutch trader during his last visit. Nobuhle was all a wife should be. Why couldn't they all be like her?

The knot of anger in his belly tightened, bringing bile into his mouth. For four weeks he hadn't been able to digest his food properly. The constant sour taste on his tongue made him irritable, his temper unpredictable. Like a mamba, he struck out at the slightest provocation.

Spitting into the fire again, he reflected on his predicament. Were it as simple as punishing the adulteresses, he'd have had no compunction whatever: MaMtshali and MaMthethwa would have paid with their lives, and his honour would have been satisfied. But there were complications, the scale of which dwarfed his domestic problems.

Adjusting the blanket around Nobuhle's shoulders, he struggled to his feet. His muscles ached; his head was muzzy through lack of sleep. Tonight, Sihayo felt every one of his sixty-three years.

Pushing aside the oxhide curtain over the entrance, he emerged into the still night air. He stretched his back and tightened his muscles to ease the pain in his joints and limped over to his cattle pen. Beyond the fence of thorn branches, he heard the clicking of horns and restless stamping of hooves. Leaning his elbows on the fence, he contemplated the moving mass of beasts that stretched across to the far side. There were over three thousand animals. Alongside the king's, his was one of the most coveted herds in the kingdom. In normal circumstances, he'd be smiling with pleasure at the sight of his beloved beasts, but tonight he was beset with racking self-doubt and uncertainty.

The turmoil in his household was merely one of his concerns. The threat to the kingdom was far more important. The Zulu homeland was potentially at war with its imperial neighbour, and Sihayo's future, indeed the future of all amaZulu, was under serious threat.

The informal discussion on the night of the first fruits festival had become the agenda for a full *ibandla* (royal council meeting) only four weeks ago.

John Dunn repeated his warning about the British threat. He reported further belligerent declarations from the British administration in Durban. It was now clear that British policy towards the amaZulu involved the annexation of their kingdom to include it within the British dominions.

Sihayo reflected on Jantoni's influence over the king – Cetshwayo seemed to accept without question the Englishman's advice – but Sihayo wondered where Jantoni's true allegiances lay. He didn't trust Dunn, and neither did the others in the king's council. *Elephants should herd with elephants, antelope with antelope.* The plain fact was that Jantoni wasn't Zulu. It would have been treason to suggest the king had misplaced his friendship and trust, therefore Sihayo and the other *iziNduna* kept their opinions to themselves, reluctantly tolerating Dunn although some of his conclusions about the British intentions were patently absurd. When he declared that the Natal government was planning to capture Cetshwayo to demonstrate the greater power of the *indlovukazi etikwemanti* ("the queen across the water"), the council members found it hard not to laugh out loud. But the king had taken the warning seriously and insisted on a policy of non-aggression. Nothing must be allowed to compromise the state of peace existing between the two nations.

Sihayo sighed in resignation. His personal problems would remain a low priority.

THIRTEEN

Mzinyathi

In the half-light just before dawn, a small herd of springbok stooped to drink in the shallows of the Mzinyathi, lifting their heads periodically to scent the air for danger. They trod warily, their hooves churning up the mud at the water's edge.

Spooked by a sudden intrusive sound, they scattered in an explosion of movement. Leaping high in the air, they jumped from one mud flat to the next, and disappeared into the undergrowth on the far bank.

Peace was restored. The only sounds were the water splashing over the rocks and the croaking of toads as they resumed their chorus.

Yet the antelopes' heightened senses and keen hearing had not been mistaken – they'd recognised a genuine threat. The tambookie grass rustled, then moved, and its fronds parted to reveal a horse's head.

Jaws working the iron bit in its mouth, the horse jibbed against its bridle. A hand reached down to soothe it, stroking the muscles of its neck. Bent over its withers, the rider whispered reassuringly in its ear, then urged it forward into the shallows at the river's edge. Pulling back gently on the reins, he brought it to a stop.

Mehlokazulu's impassive stare was directed across the water towards the grass-roofed huts. His eyes were alert, searching for any sign of movement. The "Eyes of the Zulu" was on a mission.

He wasn't alone. Thirty warriors moved forward, trampling the grass. Grey light from the coming dawn gleamed off their spearheads. They stood, flanking him, their breath and warm bodies raising a cloud of steam.

From behind, three additional horsemen approached, two youths and an older man, his head shaved except for his *isicoco*. Reining in, he followed Mehlokazulu's gaze.

'A good time for killing, Zuluhlenga?' Mehlokazulu said.

'It must take place on this side of the river,' the older man replied. 'And her blood must not be shed. As my brother's wife she has that right.'

The distinction between killing and bloodshed was a fine one. Tradition decreed that the rebellious wives of *izikhulu* (Zulu aristocrats) could be punished only by strangling; killing them by any other means was *ukuzila*. Mehlokazulu was aware that, though he was in breach of his father's orders, he must not compound his offence by spilling blood. There would be no expiation of that crime; for all eternity he'd be *inxweleha* (wet with yesterday's blood), with no opportunity to cleanse himself of the taint of her death. Mehlokazulu reassured him. 'Don't concern yourself, uncle. My brothers and I guarantee it will be done correctly,'

Turning to them, he could see second thoughts in the face of the youngest. His cheeks were wet with tears, and he averted his eyes for fear of appearing weak.

Mehlokazulu reassured him, 'Don't think of her as our mother, Tshekwane. She has forfeited that privilege. We must do this to preserve the law.'

Zuluhlenga picked out a group of men and gestured with his spear. 'I'll take the left flank.'

Mehlokazulu gave his other brother an order. 'Mkhumbikazulu, take your men and cut off any escape from the rear. Tshekwane, you come with me.'

The party split into three. With Zuluhlenga leading, a dozen warriors moved upstream on foot, while a similar body paddled obliquely through the shallows into the mainstream of the river, the water up to their waists. They carried their heavy oxhide shields high above their heads and their spears at the ready. The current was strong and the snowmelt bitterly cold. They struggled to maintain their footing against the force of the water. Mkumbizulu urged them on from the comparative security of his horse's back.

Transferring his muzzle-loader into the crook of his right arm, Mehlokazulu kicked his horse on, in a direct line to the huts.

Having finally succumbed to her weariness, MaMtshali snuggled into the warmth of the youth's recumbent form. The boy's slow rhythmic breathing lulled her to a restless sleep. Her eyes fluttered as a stream of images crowded into her dreams, memories of her beautiful sons. She pictured Mehlokazulu, always unsmiling, always determined on his own course of action. The other wives considered him wilful, but she loved him for his independent spirit.

He had never openly shown her affection in the way his younger brothers had. He was too serious by half. On the other hand, he'd never been disrespectful or dishonest. Sometimes she'd needed to discipline his brothers for stealing the milk they collected while milking the cows, the telltale white residue around their guilty mouths. Mehlokazulu had never been naughty like this. In so many ways he was a model son.

Mehlokazulu was first across the stream. Swinging his leg over the horse's back, he dismounted, allowing it to shake the water from its sodden coat. Droplets showered him as he stretched to encourage some blood into his cramped muscles. Turning back to the river, he waited for the others.

The warriors from both flanks jogged towards him. They ran in formation, in single file. He smiled with pleasure at the sight of men in battle order. There was an aesthetic element to the discipline of well-drilled warriors, fit men with a common purpose. Here he felt most at home, among the men of his *ibutho*, men on whom he depended and they on him. And his cause was justified. Nothing could deflect him from his mission.

There was no movement from the huts, the inhabitants still apparently dead to the world.

The warriors gathered around Mehlokazulu, their breathing laboured from the effort of the crossing. They jumped up and down to restore the circulation to their limbs and waited for the signal to move off.

The riverbank was some thirty yards distant from the settlement, up the well-trodden path walked earlier by MaMtshali. Mehlokazulu, leading his horse by the rein, quickly covered the ground. Close behind him were his brothers and uncle. Together, they spread out in a semi-circle in front of the stockade.

A bleary-eyed figure emerged from the largest of the three huts pulling on the jacket of the uniform that identified him as a border guard of Her Imperial Majesty Queen Victoria. It didn't take him long to register the armed men on the far side of the fence. Faced with such an overwhelming show of force, he dithered, unsure what to do. The matter was taken out of his hands as the gate was thrown open and the war party swarmed into the open area in front of him. He swallowed nervously. 'What's your business here?'

Mehlokazulu stepped forward. 'You know who I am?'

The guard replied, 'Son of Sihayo, *inkosi* of the amaQungebeni. Your deeds are known on both sides of the Mzinyathi.'

'And you are Mswagele, lackey of the white man. Do not dare to question my business.'

Mswagele's wife, baby on her back and clutching the hand of a wide-eyed toddler, appeared in the doorway behind him. Her eyes darted fearfully towards the heavily armed men.

From the nearest hut, two other guards appeared, throwing spears at the ready.

Mehlokazulu warned, 'Your next move could be your last.' To reinforce the threat, he cocked the hammer on his muzzle-loader. 'It will end badly for you unless you stand aside.'

Mswagele gestured to his fellows to lay down their spears.

From that moment, events followed each other in quick succession. Zuluhlenga led six men to the furthest of the huts. They burst through the doorway, wrenching aside the cowhide curtain. Alerted by the commotion and raised voices outside, MaMtshali and her lover were already on their feet. They stood, paralysed with shock and fear. Zuluhlenga aimed his gun directly at the boy's chest. 'Our quarrel is with the woman,' he said. 'Stay still and you will come to no harm.'

In his terror, the boy lost control of his bladder. He turned away in shame.

MaMtshali stared at him. Now she knew she was utterly alone.

The warriors moved quickly. Pulling her off her feet, they tethered her like a steer about to have its throat slit. Strips of oxhide were thrown around her shoulders and legs, and she was dragged out of the hut. She resisted, bucking from side to side, but the warriors were too powerful. They pulled her into the area in front of Mswagele's hut. At the sight of her sons, her behaviour changed: she became instantly subdued. Searching desperately for an ally, she noted the border guards sitting dejectedly, a phalanx of warriors surrounding them. And Mswagele's daughter beside her mother, mouth open in shock. The memory of herself as a child witnessing the execution of the adulteress provoked an impulse of anger. 'I'm your MOTHER!' she shouted at Mehlokazulu.

'No mother of mine, you whore!'

He swung his warclub and connected with MaMtshali's mouth, splintering her front teeth. Whimpering with pain, she spat out the pieces of broken tooth and looked up at her son, baring her bloody stumps in open defiance.

Careful to avoid her accusing eyes, the younger brothers uncoiled a long strip of rawhide and wound it around their mother's torso, tying it off securely under her armpits. Handing the free end to their elder brother, they stood back.

He attached the rawhide to the horse's withers, fastening it with a series of knots, then urged it forward until it strained against MaMtshali's weight.

Mswagele had no choice but to watch, helpless, as the warriors started to chant, beating the hafts of their spears against their shields. This was the *iNgomane*, the ritual challenge to Zulu enemies, and Mswagele knew the inevitable outcome was the death of the woman writhing on the ground. He recognised the words from the days of the great King Shaka: *Thou hast made an end of the tribes! Where wilt thou make a raid now?*

Mehlokazulu waved the muzzle-loader. The war party moved off, still chanting, and followed the horse dragging MaMtshali towards the river. She'd stopped struggling and was now an inert baggage resigned to her fate.

There was no dignity in this. The friction of the rough ground removed most of her clothes. Blood appeared as her legs were lacerated by sharp stones on the path.

As they reached the water's edge, Mehlokazulu didn't hesitate and drove the horse into the icy current. Buoyed up by the water, MaMtshali's body turned over and over. She tried to keep her shattered mouth above the surface but in vain. Water was everywhere – her mouth, her nostrils, her lungs. She was close to drowning. By the time they reached the far bank she was barely conscious.

Mehlokazulu was determined the punishment would be administered at kwaSogekle, to be witnessed by all the amaQungebeni. By his reckoning it would take at least an hour to reach. Would she last that long? Reining in the horse, he squatted to examine her. She was in a pitiable state. Her mouth was a gaping wound, her lips swollen. She was still choking from the river water and the cuts on her legs oozed blood. However, the spark of life blazed in her eyes as she stared him down.

Beyond his self-righteousness, Mehlokazulu was aware of a contradictory emotion. He took pride in his mother's courage. Whatever she was suffering she was stoical in the acceptance of her fate. She was a whore, yes; she had betrayed his father and compromised the honour of the family. Yet she was brave as a Zulu woman should be. This was to be admired.

But there was no place for sentiment. He knew it, and from the expression in her eyes, so did she. Dismissing any thought of compassion, he slapped the horse on its rump.

With the width of the river between them, Mswagele and the other border guards kept pace with the war party. They watched helpless as Mehlokazulu's horse picked its way between the boulders along the riverbank, dragging MaMtshali over the gravel and stones.

The relatively flat terrain through which the river flowed gave way to rockier ground. Great boulders disturbed the stream, forcing it into foaming cascades as it sluiced through the narrow gaps in the rocks.

A tributary joined the main river. Here Mehlokazulu halted, pulling back on his horse's reins. Relieved of its burden, it stood, flanks heaving. Mehlokazulu looked down at his mother, her face unrecognisable through the swelling and contusions, her limbs and torso a bloody mess of cuts and bruises. Mercifully, she'd lost consciousness when her head collided with a large rock.

Dismounting, Zuluhlenga and the younger sons joined the warriors gathered around the broken body. Tshekwane forced himself to look at her distorted features. This would be the last memory he'd have of her. Whatever she'd done to insult the family's honour, this was unacceptably cruel. But he was too deeply involved and too intimidated by his oldest brother to protest.

Mehlokazulu had already decided. It was time: she wouldn't survive until they reached kwaSogekle. He unwrapped the rawhide rope from the horse's neck while the brothers lifted their mother up to release it from her shoulders. Tshekwane's tears flowed freely. They sat her forward on her knees, propping her up on either side. Forming a noose with the rope, Mehlokazulu slipped it over her head. The brothers each took hold of the free ends and pulled it taut so that MaMtshali's weight was suspended between them.

Mswagele and the guards on the other side of the river watched as two warriors stepped forward, warclubs in their hands.

Mehlokazulu knelt before MaMtshali, her head lolling on her chest. Grabbing her hair, he yanked back her head so he could gaze into her eyes one last time. Her eyelids flickered as she regained consciousness – considering her ordeal, it was amazing she'd lasted this long. He stepped back, satisfied she'd be aware of her punishment. This was required in Zulu custom.

The two younger brothers took the strain as the warriors lifted their warclubs high above their heads. In unison they swung the heavy clubs onto the outstretched rawhide, producing a sudden jerk on the garrotte, which dislocated MaMtshali's vertebrae and severed her spinal cord. An involuntary spasm contracted her limbs into a strangely poignant foetal shape. It was over.

From the other side of the gorge, Mswagele watched as the younger brothers released the rawhide rope and MaMtshali's lifeless body pitched forward. Thirty voices were raised in a shout of triumph. The Zulu royalist war-cry *uSuthu! uSuthu!* was reflected from the rock faces on either side of the river, echoing as the warriors shook their spears and discharged their guns in grim celebration.

FOURTEEN

oNdini

The seasons had come full circle, and in that time, Nomguqo's status within the *isiGodlo* had changed dramatically. As well as her other duties – looking after the needs of the royal children – she had been appointed guardian of the *eNkatheni*. This involved polishing the floor, keeping the hut free of insect infestation, and making sure the sacred coil itself was in good order. To be entrusted with such an important job proved how well regarded she was by the court hierarchy. Nomvimbi reported to His Majesty that Nomguqo had become an indispensable member of her personal household. Dinuzulu and the baby were completely besotted with their minder, refusing to leave her side for a moment. In recognition, the king made her responsible for the *eNkatheni*, a duty that carried enormous prestige.

She had risen early, collected water from the river and made the children their breakfast. Now she was sweeping the *eNkatheni* and buffing up the shine on the floor.

As she tidied her cloths, the *inceku* Mnukwa put his head

through the door and announced, 'Ndabezitha requires your immediate presence.'

Her heart skipped a beat. Had she done something to offend the king? Was she being summoned for punishment? What could this possibly mean? Flustered, she dropped everything and hurried after the servant.

Maybe the *amaQhikiza* had blabbed about her friendship with Shikashika. Certainly, everything had changed since her discovery of Sixhwethu and Maweni together. Sixhwethu's virginity test had proved inconclusive, so she avoided a more severe punishment. Nevertheless, heavy restrictions were placed on any further contact with the herdboys: any requests for meetings had to be sanctioned by the *amaQhikiza*. Since then, Nomguqo and Shikashika's sole contact – apart from passing each other at the river – had been a disaster. Desperate to see him, she agreed to a rendezvous by the cattle pen at milking time. Chaperoned by the *amaQhikiza,* who stood in a circle around them, she was so inhibited she became completely tongue-tied.

Sixhwethu suffered the same constraints, and she expressed her frustration by persecuting Nomguqo even more, leaving her lonelier than ever. Only by burying herself in her work could she escape Sixhwethu's sarcasm and backbiting. To stay out of the way, she volunteered to help tend the vegetables, in addition to her childminding and domestic duties in the *isiGodlo*, the cleaning and endless polishing of the floors of the royal huts. After the evening meal, while the other girls worked on their bead jewellery, Nomguqo went to work in the gardens. As the sun disappeared behind the hills, she weeded and watered the plants, taking pleasure in seeing them grow. It also allowed her to spend time with the animals she'd adopted as companions. The lizards and geckos catching the last rays of the setting sun were her surrogate friends. They listened when she opened her heart, paid attention when she shared her confidences, her deepest secrets.

Because it provoked Sixhwethu's jealousy, the king's patronage was an added burden. She was surprised the king even registered her existence; she imagined her shyness made her invisible. This was a man with responsibilities as leader of over a third of a million people; how could he spare the time to acknowledge her? And yet, he went out of his way to speak to her and, on occasion, bring her news of her father. Once, she suffered an asthma attack in his presence and he'd been so concerned he insisted that his personal physician prepare a medicine for her. Was there no end to his kindness?

Hamu pointed an accusing finger at Sihayo, his jowls wobbling with indignation. 'That man and his cursed progeny will bring about the destruction of our homeland, our legacy from our wise and mighty forefathers.'

In recognition that the killing of his wives had far-reaching consequences, the Qungebeni *inkosi* sat by himself, fully exposed to the heat of the noon sun. It seemed like an act of penance. Other members of the royal council were shaded by the *isibaya* acacia tree. Hamu, Mnyamana, Zibhebhu, Ntshingwayo, Vumandaba, head of the king's diplomatic mission, and other minor *iziNduna* formed a circle around the king. With their grey blankets around their shoulders, they had the appearance of a flock of aging and overfed vultures. The council had been hurriedly convened to deal with the crisis provoked by Mehlokazulu taking the law into his own hands. Cetshwayo sat grim-faced, flicking his flywhisk periodically to discourage unwelcome insects. John Dunn was beside him, hat pulled over his eyes.

Hamu continued his rant, 'Mark my words, Cetshwayo, this will be the ruin of everything you inherited from our father. And Sihayo's family is responsible. May I remind the council, this is not the first time we've had to discuss the excesses of Mehlokazulu and his brothers. The last time he nearly caused a civil war.'

Sihayo leapt off his seat in a fury of self-justification. 'And you take no responsibility for that? How much blood is on your hands?'

'My men defended themselves and the honour of their regiment!' Hamu retaliated.

The *ibandla* degenerated into a free-for-all, each member shouting the others down, speaking in support or condemnation of Mehlokazulu.

'Gentlemen! Brothers!' Cetshwayo's voice cut through the commotion. 'We will get nowhere by airing old grievances. The past is the past; let it remain there. I'd remind you that an amicable resolution was found then and I'm certain we can find one for the present situation. What are the facts? Sihayo's wives were adulteresses. As *inkosi*, he had every right under Zulu law to bring them to justice. Mehlokazulu and his brothers were merely acting in their father's interests. We are a sovereign country. The British government can make no objection when we administer our own laws. We don't interfere with the running of their country. Why should they interfere with ours?'

Reluctant to let the matter rest, Hamu replied, 'You're missing the point. The trespass onto British soil is what will give offence and what will be used as the pretext for war.'

The king nonchalantly flicked away another fly.

Hamu shook his head in frustration. 'Why do you insist on ignoring the danger signs? Only last week an eagle was attacked and driven off by four hawks right here where we're sitting. A sure sign the states surrounding your kingdom are combining to destroy it – your own *iNgoma* told you so. I need not remind you of Shaka's dying words: *Sons of my father, you will not rule when I am gone, for the land will see the white locusts come.*'

Cetshwayo sighed, 'My brother is prone to hyperbole. I hardly imagine that two countries will go to war on such a slender pretext.'

'Then you're a bigger fool than I took you for.'

The other counsellors shifted in their seats. Nobody addressed the king so disrespectfully, particularly in such a public arena. They looked to him for his reaction, expecting him to call for the *iziMpisi*. Cetshwayo bristled but stayed seated.

John Dunn stood. For him, this was a critical moment. The challenge to the king's authority would have one of two consequences, each equally disastrous. Either Hamu would exploit the king's perceived weakness and encroach on his authority, or the king would overreact and order Hamu's execution; the latter would alienate a large part of the kingdom. It required him to choose his words very carefully. 'May I offer an observation? With due respect to other council members, I'd argue that, as an *umlungu*, I can offer a particular insight in this matter, one perhaps that they lack. I know my people. I know how they think.' Smoothing his moustaches, he looked around.

The chiefs stared at him impassively.

'I'm aware that some of you consider my loyalty lies with the British, that I'm bound, because of the colour of my skin, to represent their interests rather than those of my friends the amaZulu. I'm also aware that some of you regard me with such hostility that you would have me killed. I know who my enemies are…'

Again, no reaction.

'…and I know where my allegiances lie. Ndabezitha, you took me in when I was destitute. You made me your brother, gave me land, and took me into your confidence. I owe you much, but most of all, I owe you the advice of a loyal subject and friend.'

Cetshwayo smiled.

'The British have demanded that Sihayo's sons and brother be delivered to their jurisdiction in Pietermaritzburg. The renegade Mbilini's continued attacks on white-owned farms is an additional thorn in their side. They request that he too be surrendered.' Pulling a letter from his jacket pocket, he held it aloft. 'This is from the Lieutenant Governor Sir Henry Bulwer. It contains a list of these demands.' He lowered his voice as if taking them into his confidence. 'Here's where my knowledge of my people might be useful: I believe they'll require a much more substantial pretext to mobilise against you. Were a gesture of reconciliation to be offered, acknowledging the fault of the young men, and perhaps adding a financial recompense, there's no doubt it would calm matters down.' He resumed his seat as the other council members went into a huddle.

Cetshwayo got to his feet. 'We'll discuss this further. In the meantime, I wish to consult with Jantoni in private.' He strode off towards his quarters.

Dunn followed, pausing at the gate to listen to the counsellors' reaction. Within earshot, he heard Mnyamana remark, 'The *umlungu* is nothing in this country. When his influence with the king wanes – as it surely will – his days will be numbered.'

Nomguqo's heart thudded as she waited for Mnukwa to announce her. 'Ndabezitha, the girl Nomguqo is here.'

'Send her in.'

Pushing her through the door to the king's private residence, the *inceku* withdrew.

She stood uncertainly on the threshold.

'Come in child.' The king beckoned her forward. 'You know Jantoni, of course.'

She nodded shyly, aware of the *umlungu* ever since her first days at court. The *isiGodlo* girls always looked forward to his visits because of his generous gifts. He always arrived with cartloads of coffee, salt, sugar, bananas and, most important of all, guns. The royal wives and the *isiGodlo* girls were remembered, too. Bolts of cloth and jewellery were shared among them; no-one was forgotten. She marvelled at the whiteness of his skin, wondering about the country of his birth where clearly the sun shone so infrequently. 'How can I serve you, Ndabezitha?' she asked.

'Refreshments, child.' He indicated the drinking vessels on the table.

She poured the beer, aware of Jantoni's eyes on her, then withdrew to a corner of the room where she squatted quietly awaiting further instruction.

The king drank deeply. 'You saw how they're at each other's throats, Jantoni. It's vital we restore peace. Some are actively seeking war with the British – most, I'd say – paying too much attention to hotheads like Mehlokazulu…'

As he listened, Dunn fanned himself with his hat. In the confined space of the king's brick house, the heat was overpowering.

Cetshwayo continued, 'To placate the British I'm tempted to accede to their demands. Sihayo's domestic issues have become a liability. Delivering Mehlokazulu and his brothers to British jurisdiction would solve that problem.' He took another draught. 'However, I take issue with being dictated to by a remote functionary of the Queen overseas. It's intolerable!' His anger erupted without warning. Nomguqo flinched as his fist came crashing down on the table, upsetting the drinking vessels. 'This is a Zulu matter, nothing to do with the *abelungu*. Justice was administered on the Zulu side of the Mzinyathi. No blood was spilt on British soil.'

Dunn returned the cups to an upright position. 'That may be so, Ndabezitha but, as Hamu pointed out, the issue is the trespass onto British soil. That's the offence.'

'Then it's a trifling matter.'

'On the contrary, Your Majesty, it could potentially grow out of all proportion. Like a weed, it will invade the whole vegetable patch unless it's uprooted at once.'

Nomguqo, waiting for an opportunity to wipe up the split beer, noted the use of a horticultural metaphor. She was impressed by his command both of idiomatic and classical isiZulu.

'What's to be done, then?'

'As I suggested, a gesture in the right direction, perhaps the payment of a fine, a symbolic offering. That may very well smooth the ruffled feathers.'

'I will not part with my cattle,' said the king.

'Then perhaps a cash offering?'

'If that will resolve the matter, so be it.' He got to his feet. 'No more than fifty pounds, though.'

John Dunn smiled. The king's penny-pinching was well known. He might be generous at a personal level, offering wives and land, but when it came to distributing money or cattle, Cetshwayo was as tight as a clam.

Picking up his hat, Dunn joined the king at the door. He glanced casually towards Nomguqo. 'I've not seen this young lady before, Ndabezitha. She's fine addition to your *isiGodlo*.'

The implication wasn't lost on her: he'd assumed she was one of the youngest concubines. It wasn't her place to disabuse him, but she was delighted when the king set the record straight.

'Nomguqo is of the Swazi royal house and her presence in my *isiGodlo* does me great honour. She's a credit to her family, and when the time is right, I shall arrange a good marriage for her.'

The king smiled benevolently as he left the room with Dunn at his heels.

Her heart sang. *Her presence did the king great honour.* She scrubbed and polished the table with renewed vigour, then started on the rest of the room, determined that the king's praise would be deserved.

The sun had set by the time she emerged. Excitement still bubbling, she knew she'd be incapable of sleep. Besides which, she had no one to share it with. How could she confide her reason to any of the others? With no concrete plan, she walked through the main gate towards the vegetable gardens. There she'd be alone to commune with her thoughts.

As the light faded, the hills around the homestead changed from violet to deep purple. The air, scented by the fresh smell of new growth, started to cool. She passed rows of young maize on either side of the path, their growing tips waving in the gentle breeze. Then came to an open space on the edge of a pumpkin field planted with geometric precision.

Ahead of her on the path, and so completely absorbed in what she was doing that she failed to notice Nomguqo's presence, was Pastor Gundersen's daughter. Her eyes were fixed on something lying on the dusty path, with which she seemed to be deep in conversation.

Not wishing to alarm the child, Nomguqo called out softly, 'Good evening, daughter of Guniseni.'

The six-year-old nodded noncommittally.

'It's late for you to be out here by yourself,' Nomguqo said.

She could now see whom Gunhild Christine had been addressing. With its bifurcated toes gripped firmly around a maize stalk, a bright emerald chameleon stared at her, eyes slowly swivelling in their sockets.

'This is *Unwabu*,' Gunhild announced.

Nomguqo knelt beside her. 'Do your mother and father know where you are?'

'I told them I was taking him for a walk.'

Well versed in Zulu lore, Nomguqo knew that chameleons were regarded as *umnyama*; it was bad luck to have anything to do with them.

When she was a child, her father told her the story. *Unkhulunkhulu*, the Great One, sent *Unwabu* to the people on earth, promising them eternal life, having already dispatched *Intulo* (the salamander) to tell them they were destined to die. Fickle *Unkhulunkhulu* changed his mind and instructed the faster *Intulo* to overtake the chameleon and command that mankind should die after all. The naturally slower chameleon was distracted by a particularly delicious fruit bush and failed to deliver the good news in time. So, the salamander delivered the sentence of death. The consequence was that both reptiles were regarded with great suspicion by the amaZulu.

'You know about *Unkhulunkhulu* and *Unwabu*?' Nomguqo asked.

The chameleon rotated its scaly eye towards her.

Gunhild frowned. 'My father says I shouldn't listen to old wives' tales.'

Nomguqo laughed. 'I don't believe them either.'

'It's a silly story, anyway. How can a chameleon speak, let alone speak our language?'

'You're right.'

'In any case, my father says that, if men accept Jesus as their saviour, they won't die. They'll sit at the right hand of God for all eternity.'

'What does that mean?'

Gunhild recited Pastor Gundersen's teaching: 'God sent his only begotten son to save us. We have only to believe in Him to be washed clean of all our sins.'

'Do you believe in God?'

Gunhild hesitated, unsure whether this was a test of her loyalty to her adopted father. 'Yes, I think so.'

'Who is this Jesus with so much power?' Nomguqo asked.

'A tall *umlungu* with a long beard and blue eyes.' Gunhild's image of Christ was drawn from a picture-book her father showed her in a bible study class.

'And can this Jesus also save the amaZulu?'

'Yes,' the little girl replied.

Nomguqo reached out to stroke the chameleon, turning the thought over in her mind.

'So, he could save me?'

'I don't see why not.'

'I don't think I need saving, though.'

'Everyone needs saving – that's what my father says!' Gunhild jumped up, suddenly bored with talk of redemption. 'My mother's going to have a baby.'

'Really?' said Nomguqo. 'That's wonderful news. When will it come?'

'On Jesus's birthday, she says.'

'If it's a boy, they can call it Jesus,' Nomguqo suggested.

Unaware she was being teased, Gunhild replied, 'No, I don't think that would be a good idea.'

'Why?'

'Because there is only one Jesus.' This was the end of the conversation. Looking around at the gathering gloom, Gunhild suddenly became aware of how late it was. She reached down and picked up the maize stalk with the chameleon clinging to it. 'I must go. My dinner will be waiting.'

While they'd been talking, the light had faded. Now the dusky blue haze over the mountains pervaded the vegetable fields as well. They both shivered as a chilly breeze started to blow. Nomguqo scrambled to her feet. 'Shall I walk you home?'

'That's all right, I can manage.' Carefully clutching the chameleon, Gunhild skipped down the path towards the mission station.

Nomguqo watched her for a few moments then headed back to the *umuZi*.

FIFTEEN

Cetshwayo jabbed his finger into the chest of Mbilini kaMswati, a small man in his mid-twenties. They stood toe to toe in the king's parlour. 'This has to stop!' he commanded. 'Either you desist, or I hand you over to the British. Which is it to be?'

Mbilini was the son of the amaSwazi king, and through a common bloodline, a relative of Nomguqo. In physical appearance, Mblini resembled her – dark complexion and slender, wiry physique. The genial expression on his unlined face belied his true nature. Superficially, he appeared perfectly affable but in truth he was ruthless, with a reputation for uncompromising cruelty.

Mbilini shrugged, offering no opinion either way.

Cetshwayo clicked his tongue. He'd tolerated Mbilini's insubordination for long enough. His patience was all but exhausted.

Complaints about Mehlokazulu and Mbilini had continued to be issued by the lieutenant governor of Natal's office. Cetshwayo had taken matters into his own hands, hoping that the recompense he offered for Mehlokazulu's trespass would be accepted and forestall any British military action. The additional demand for Mblini to surrender had brought forward an action Cetshwayo had deferred for too long.

For the last few years, Mbilini had rustled cattle from Afrikaner farmers in the neighbouring Republic of Transvaal, murdering the farmers and their families when they defended their herds. Warnings were sent to the Zulu king in his capacity as Mbilini's overlord.

Cetshwayo had been patient with Mbilini because he recognised some of his own character in the younger man. Their personal histories had many similarities. Just as Cetshwayo had struggled with his brother for the right of succession, so had Mbilini with his brothers. And, like the Zulu king, Mbilini had been ruthless in dispatching his rivals. In his case, his father Mswati intervened to avoid further bloodshed and banished his eldest son. As an outcast in Zululand, Mbilini was forced to pledge his allegiance to Cetshwayo, who in turn gave permission for the Swazi prince to settle in the northern territory of his kingdom. It was a decision based on political expedience. It gave Cetshwayo the opportunity to exploit Mbilini's resentment towards his own tribe. By appointing him titular head of the abaQulusi, a tribe fiercely loyal to the Zulu royal family, he further allied him to the Zulu cause.

Had Mbilini confined himself to attacking Swazi homesteads, Cetshwayo would have turned a blind eye. But these raids on white-owned farms compromised the good relations the Zulu king was desperate to maintain. They had to stop. His forefinger drove home the argument. 'Five times in as many months I've received reports of you attacking Dutch farms. Because of you, my position on the border is untenable. How can I persuade the authorities our intentions are peaceful when you carry on killing Dutchmen and driving off their cattle?'

Mbilini's eyes narrowed. 'Ndabezitha, whoever's been spreading these libels is making mischief.'

'You're telling me your hands are clean?'

Mbilini's smaller stature put him at a disadvantage. 'Ndebezitha–'

Cetshwayo cut him off, 'Don't waste your breath, I already know the answer.' He drew himself to his full height and let his bulk intimidate the Swazi prince. 'You should know this: I've already informed the Dutch that I approve whatever measures they take to defend their property. If this means shooting you like the mad dog you are, then so be it.' He stared down at him, willing him to make a protest. Had he seen any sign of rebellion, he would have had no hesitation in calling for the *iziMpisi*.

'Now, get out of my sight!'

Mbilini left without a backward look.

Cetshwayo watched him go. In his heart of hearts, he approved the attacks against the Boer farmers. They had it coming. As he saw it, the Dutch were sneak thieves who'd already stolen vast tracts of Zulu land and were moving ever westwards to consume more and more Zulu territory. He'd described them to John Dunn as "toads who keep hopping and hopping – until they hop right into the middle of your house" – a description that pleased him so much he repeated in numerous other conversations.

It hadn't rained in Zululand for several months and the effects of the drought were visible in the fields around oNdini. The mealie crop on which the residents depended was half its normal size, and where the cobs had developed, they were thin, puny specimens, desperately in need of water.

Nomguqo and the other girls were on irrigation duty. In the burning heat of the midday sun, they traipsed backwards and forwards to the river, heavy calabashes of water on their heads. It was exhausting work: back and forth, carrying the water, tipping it into the irrigation channels, then back to the river again, in an apparently endless cycle. Tempers started to fray.

Dipping her gourd into one of the pools left by the retreating stream, Sixhwethu complained, 'I'm not a beast of burden. Why don't they use the oxen?'

Nomguqo muttered, 'Always something to moan about.' Glancing up, she noticed a change in the light. It had become appreciably darker. Threatening black clouds were massing in the sky.

'What did you say?' Sixhwethu snapped.

Lifting her calabash onto her head, Nomguqo sighed. Would this constant carping never end? What she would give to have Sixhwethu out of her life.

'Ndabezitha's favourite obviously thinks she's too good for us–'

A huge flash of lightning split the clouds that had been gathering. It shut her up instantly. A roll of thunder followed, and the clouds opened, discharging their burden of water. Large raindrops fell, stinging the girls' skin. With a scream of joy, they started to dance, faces upturned to catch the rain in their mouths. They jumped about in the pool, kicking up the water, celebrating the end of their labours. Sixhwethu lay on her back waving her arms and legs in the air.

To begin with, the rain disappeared into the parched earth but, very soon, as the ground became saturated, water collected into rivulets and, following the undulations of the riverbank, poured into the pools. It didn't take long before the river was restored to its normal flow.

With levels rising, it became dangerous to stay in the water. Nomguqo scrambled onto the bank, its sides already collapsing as water poured over them, scouring channels through the soft earth. She shouted to the other girls to follow.

The landscape became transformed in a short space of time. Streams cascaded down pathways through the tilled fields, overfilling the irrigation channels.

Lighting zigzagged across the dark sky, casting an unearthly light over the huts of the *umuZi*. The girls ran for cover as thunder crashed over their heads.

Standing by the main gate, staring at the deluge, was the *iNgoma* Dlephu Ndlovu. Surrounded by a small crowd of onlookers, he seemed totally dumbstruck.

On the way to their huts, the girls passed him and saw the expression on his face. When they were out of earshot, they started to giggle; by the time they reached the *isiGodlo*, they were in fits.

'Did you see it?' Sixhwethu snorted: 'the look on his face…'

Nguyaze completed the thought, 'Taking credit for the rain!'

'And all those gullible fools encouraging him,' Sixhwethu added.

'What a fraud.' Nguyaze agreed.

'Stop it, you'll get us into trouble. He's the king's *iNgoma*,' Nobhodlile warned.

'But all those stupid things he did,' Sixhwethu replied. 'All the messing about with sticks and tar.' She pointed to the roof of one of the huts, over which an impromptu construction of saplings had been erected, their tar-dipped ends dug into the ground. 'As if that's responsible for making it rain!'

This set off another explosion of giggles.

They looked back to the gate. By now, the crowd around the *iNgoma* had grown even further; he basked in the attention.

'He can fool most of the people most of the time,' said Sixhwethu, 'but he doesn't fool me. Come on, let's dry ourselves.'

Laughing, the girls skipped into the hut.

Nomguqo was left outside, peering through the rain at the witch doctor. For her, he was far from a figure of fun. The memory of his presence at the birth of the king's twin sons had stayed with her. Her flesh crawled every time she was near him.

Cetshwayo listened with satisfaction to the rain bouncing off his roof. From the entrance he watched the *isiGodlo* residents scurrying to take cover. A cluster of his children stamped about in the puddles. Cloaks over their heads, their mothers scolded them and shooed them inside. The king spoke to an unseen companion.

'Children and puddles, eh?' He turned back into the room. 'I'm sure you were the same at that age. Always into mischief…'

Mehlokazulu's expression gave nothing away.

The king took a seat. 'And a leopard never changes its spots. What are we to do with you, Mehlokazulu? My ministers are telling me to send you to the British. What do you think?'

Mehlokazulu picked at a hangnail on his thumb. 'Whatever you think best, Ndabezitha. I shall obey you and follow whatever course of action you decide to take.'

'Obey? Obedience and Mehlokazulu live in separate huts. Isn't that's what your father would say?'

'I honour my father, as I do all my elders.'

'Ah yes, "honour" – a much overused word. Also, its opposite. "Dishonour" is the starting point for many an ill-considered action, wouldn't you agree?' He searched Mehlokazulu's inscrutable expression. 'However, what's past is past. No need to remind ourselves, except to teach us how to behave in the future. You take my meaning?'

Mehlokazulu nodded.

'This is what I've decided. You will leave oNdini and put as much distance between you and the British as you can. You will travel with Mbilini to the Transvaal borders and wait until the crisis you provoked has passed. I'm sure Mbilini will find a way to put your services to good use. I'll send for you when it's practical. Go now. When I hear of you again, I expect it to be of the great deeds you've performed. I have high expectations of you.'

'I won't disappoint you, Ndabezitha.' Mehlokazulu slung his oxhide cloak around his shoulders and, with eyes lowered deferentially, retreated towards the door. He paused at the threshold, then marched resolutely into the curtain of rain.

Cetshwayo watched the retreating figure. That problem shelved for the time being, he turned his attention to the next. Since the delivery of his fifty-pound gesture of appeasement, there'd been an ominous silence from Pietermaritzburg. He had no way of knowing whether the British authorities had accepted the fine and therefore whether the threat had been averted. It was a matter of some concern. He looked pensively at the rain.

Cetshwayo wasn't alone in watching Mehlokazulu leave. In the middle of preparing the royal children's meal in Nomvimbi's hut, Nomguqo popped outside to collect water. Sheltering in the doorway, she saw Mehlokazulu striding in her direction. She caught herself wondering what manner of man could put his own mother to death. What could ever justify such a disregard of filial devotion? Her hutmates said it was an honour killing, justified by MaMtshali having disgraced the family name. Sixhwethu, despite her loathing of Mehlokazulu, found his action totally understandable. It was beyond Nomguqo's understanding.

The rain bounced off Mehlokazulu's shoulders as he came level with Nomvimbi's hut. He glanced sideways and caught sight of Nomguqo in the doorway. He checked his stride as she held his gaze, then flicked his oxhide cloak and continued his march towards the gate.

SIXTEEN

'I said to John Shepstone, *you're planning to destroy Zululand for the sake of two foolish children?*'

Cetshwayo listened intently. 'What was his reply?'

'He made no reply, Your Majesty.' The speaker, Vumandaba, a courtly man in his mid-fifties, commanded the uKhandempemvu *ibutho* and was the most senior of the delegation sent by the king to hear the conclusions of the boundary commission. Cetshwayo considered the meeting to be of sufficient importance to have sent his highest ranked diplomats, including John Dunn. Convened two days earlier on the Natal side of the Mzinyathi, it was attended by the Zulu delegation and representatives from the Pietermaritzburg government. He continued, 'A battery of field guns was trained on us throughout the meeting. The message was clear: force would be used to impose their demands.'

Other council members gathered in the *isibaya* bristled with anger.

John Dunn reminded them, 'History proves the Shepstone brothers are hostile to Zulu interests. What happened to the Sithole tells us all we need to know.'

These events were fresh in the memories of the *izikhulu*. Theophilus, the older of the two brothers, ran the office of Native Affairs for the government of Natal and was therefore responsible for administering justice. Ten years earlier he'd sent John, also a government official, under a flag of truce, to negotiate with Matshana, chief of the Sithole people, allies of the amaZulu. The true motive was to arrest Matshana for murder, but the meeting had turned into a bloodbath when Matshana, suspecting treachery, made to leave and Shepstone turned his guns on him and his followers. Though Matshana made his escape, several of the Sithole chiefs were shot down.

A clue to the Shepstone's attitudes lay in their forenames: Theophilus ("God loving") and John Wesley. Firm believers in the civilising power of Christian teaching, they came from devout Methodist stock. Their Wesleyan minister father left his native Bristol to settle in southern Africa. Both boys were brought up to speak Xhosa and isiZulu but showed contempt for what they considered to be the tribes' barbaric and degenerate cultures. Their presence at this meeting did not bode well.

'I have some *good* news,' Vumandaba announced. 'I can report that the boundary commission has found in our favour. It has been decided – I'm paraphrasing from the document read out to us – that the Dutch farmers' claims of title to land within the Zulu kingdom have no basis.' Though illiterate, Vumandaba's recall of the detail of argument and discourse was faultless, which made him such a valuable envoy.

The counsellors murmured their approval – they'd expected no less. Vumandaba pointed to the thick document in John Dunn's hands. 'That's the commission's report – Jantoni will read it out later. But matters of greater urgency require your attention. It's become clear that these findings are being used to impose unacceptable conditions.'

Cetshwayo shifted in his seat. 'Which are?'

'In brief, they involve the dismantling of the *amabutho*.'

The very idea triggered gasps of disbelief.

Dunn explained, 'They claim the *amabutho* system damages British interests. They see the existence of a large standing army as a threat to settlers farming any territory that borders ours.'

The king spluttered. 'That's preposterous. My warriors have never committed a single hostile action. Indeed, we've gone out of our way to keep on good terms with the settlers. You yourself Jantoni, have welcomed them with open arms.'

'I couldn't agree more, Ndabezitha,' said Dunn. 'Unfortunately, the authorities see it differently. They referred to your coronation, where you accepted British support, and promised to disband your armies. They say you've broken that promise. They expressed the British government's disappointment and told us that the present situation is intolerable. Zulu warriors are a clear and present threat to British interests, but they claim there's no evidence the British military represents a reciprocal threat.'

'Outrageous!' shouted Mnyamana. 'Five thousand redcoats are camped on our boundaries.'

'Exactly,' Hamu said.

'Hypocrites,' Sihayo said.

Cetshwayo cut across them, 'Go on, I want to hear the rest of this.'

Vumandaba continued, 'The subject of Sihayo's sons' trespass into Natal and their abduction of his wives came up. John Shepstone reminded us of the lieutenant-governor's request to deliver the perpetrators to the Natal authorities for punishment. He said the king has ignored it and, to add insult to injury, offered a derisory recompense of fifty pounds. This has been refused.'

The *isikhulu* fidgeted. They also deemed the fifty-pound offer inadequate.

'They require us to surrender Mehlokazulu, Mkhumbikazulu, Tshekwane, and Sihayo's brother, Zuluhlenga. They must be delivered to the Natal authorities within twenty days of receipt of this demand. Not only that, but his Majesty is also required to pay a fine of five hundred cattle, to be sent within the same timescale.'

'That's ridiculous!' Mnyamana said.

Cetshwayo sat with a face like thunder. 'Twenty days! Even if I agreed – which I have no intention of doing – that timescale is impossible.'

'There's more…' Vumandaba cleared his throat nervously. 'A further list of demands…'

'Demands?' Hamu grunted. 'They place demands on the king of a sovereign country. Under what compulsion?'

'Five thousand armed soldiers on our borders,' Cetshwayo replied grim-faced. 'What demands?'

Vumandaba listed them: 'One, the indiscriminate shedding of blood shall cease. Two, no Zulu shall be condemned without trial, with automatic right of appeal to the king. Three, no Zulu's life shall be taken without previous knowledge and consent of the king. And four, for minor crimes, the loss of property shall be substituted for the punishment of death.'

Cetshwayo shrugged. That wasn't worth arguing about.

'The fifth condition, however, is the sticking point. This involves the disbandment of the *amabutho*. I'm quoting Shepstone directly here: *For what purpose does the king maintain such a large army? Its presence is dangerous to the peace of all the countries adjoining Zululand, and it is hurtful to the Zulu people itself. The British government cannot allow it to continue.*'

'They're driving us into a corner, Ndabezitha. These demands are non-negotiable,' said Mnyamana.

'It does seem they're determined to force the issue. As I see it, there is no alternative to war,' Cetshwayo concluded.

From that moment oNdini was on a war footing.

For two weeks after the deputation's return, all people could talk about was the expected British invasion – when and how it would come. The general view was that it would be sooner rather than later.

The order went out to collect the harvest as quickly as possible. If the warriors were to march into battle, they'd require extra rations. The entire female population were sent to the fields to collect mealies and bring them back to dry in the sun.

Empty spaces were piled high with corn cobs. Women sat in clusters, stripping grains from husks. The children helped, carrying off the empty cobs and stacking them for fuel. No one was exempt. Even the royal wives did their bit, working alongside ordinary folk. It wasn't long before the grain stores were full.

The menfolk, meanwhile, performed military exercises on the Mahlabathini plain. They practised drills that would be used on real battlefields. Older regiments acted as the enemy to allow younger untried warriors to be trained in the classic Zulu tactic of *impondo zankhomo* (horns of the buffalo), a tactic Shaka employed to encircle his enemies and close off their retreat. The main body advanced towards the enemy, while the two flanks – ideally invisible through careful choice of battleground – moved around from the rear and surrounded them, creating a killing-ground from which there was no escape.

Hand-to-hand combat was drilled into them. Now, instead of competition between the *amabutho*, veterans shared their experience with the youngsters. Over and over, they repeated the exercises until they became second nature. They took pride in their battle-honours. Against neighbouring tribes, they were undefeated, but how would they perform against the more sophisticated weaponry of the British army?

It wasn't that the amaZulu lacked firearms. Traders such as John Dunn had seen to that, importing thousands of guns into Zululand. But most were antiquated muzzle-loaders he'd bought at discount prices.

Superiority in arms gave the British a clear advantage. Their standard-issue Martini-Henry carbines were modern weapons, breech-loaders that allowed a much greater frequency of fire. Four bullets could be fired in the time it took to load a musket. This obvious disadvantage needed addressing.

Cetshwayo summoned his generals to discuss tactics. 'We can't rely on our men's trust in the power of *ithonya*,' he said. 'Gone are the days the medicine men could anoint them with *muthi* and send them off to war believing they're invincible. Battles are now decided by how good our weapons are.' He looked from one to the other. 'And in that regard the British have a massive advantage. Our warriors may be second to none in hand-to-hand combat, but we can't ask them to advance against Martini-Henry rifles: they'll be annihilated. We must drill them in avoidance tactics.'

Ntshingwayo, appointed field commander, nodded. 'With respect, Ndabezitha, we've already considered this. Mynanama and I have some proposals to make.' He turned to his superior in age and rank, the army chief of staff.

'A simple solution is to space the men at greater distances,' Mnyanama advised. 'In their usual formations they present too easy a target.'

Ntshingwayo elaborated, 'We've observed that the redcoats are trained to fire their weapons in volleys. We can turn this to our advantage. In the time it takes for the redcoats to reload, our men can make ground and overwhelm them.'

Cetshwayo stroked his chin. 'That's exactly my thinking.'

Mnyanama continued, 'Also, we mustn't underestimate our other natural advantage. The *abelungu* will be crossing territory unknown to them but familiar to us. We must use our knowledge of the ground, the contours, the gullies, and clumps of vegetation to set up ambushes and pick them off. The cumulative effect of losing men in this way will drain their morale.'

Cetshwayo folded his arms. If it came to war, the future of his kingdom was in good hands.

SEVENTEEN

The backbreaking work in the fields became routine for the *isiGodlo* girls. Up before sunrise, they didn't return until long after the sun had set. The effort of transporting heavy baskets of ripe corn all day left their muscles tired and aching. By nightfall, they were so weary they fell asleep as soon as they hit their bedrolls.

Towards the end of the harvest, Nomguqo woke in the early hours needing to empty her bladder. It was still night. The other girls' heavy breathing indicated they were fast asleep. With her stiff joints protesting, she pushed herself upright and limped to the door.

The crescent moon was low on the horizon as she squatted in the latrine. The shadow of a human figure passed across it. Recognising Sixhwethu, she gave a low whistle.

Sixhwethu turned sharply. 'Who's there?'

Nomguqo rearranged her kirtle. 'What are you doing up so early?'

'Nothing.'

'Why are you looking so guilty then?'

'Don't know what you mean.'

'You've been off to see Maweni, haven't you?'

'Keep your voice down,' Sixhwethu hissed. 'What if I have?'

'Don't you care if you're found out?'

'Doesn't matter one way or another. Whatever anyone says, I'm going with him when the *amabutho* march. Nobody's going to keep us apart.' She stared Nomguqo down. 'You're jealous, aren't you? Because I'm doing what you'd like to, except you're too much of a coward. And let me tell you, there is nothing sweeter than wrapping your legs around a boy, feeling his hands on you.'

Nomguqo swallowed. Between imagination and reality there was a huge gulf.

'What's the worst that could happen?' Sixhwethu said. 'Being confined to the hut? Well, I can tell you that's not going to happen because none of us can be spared. The harvest must be brought in. The boys will be off to war in a few days. Who's going to worry about taboos and stupid rules then? Do yourself a favour, Nomguqo, go and taste some of that sweetness yourself. Shikashika is down by the river right now.'

'How do you know?'

'It's where I've just been, stupid. The herdboys are bivouacked with their *iviyo*. Maweni and I sneaked off to be alone. If you're careful, nobody'll see you.' She pointed at the moon. 'There's at least three hours before the sun comes up. Lots of time to get there and back before the others wake.'

The seed of independent action took root. 'Where are they camped?'

'You know the male bathing pool? They're just upstream of that. Not hard to find. Theirs is the shelter nearest the river. Go on, you won't regret it.'

'How did you get past the guards at the gate?'

'The gate? I never use the gate. Remember where we saw the

snakes fighting? Just where the *isiGodlo* joins the main fence, there's a hole right at the bottom just big enough to crawl through.'

Nomguqo needed no further persuading.

The gap in the fence was exactly as Sixhwethu described it – except it was so small she couldn't see how she got through it. Liberated by her newly acquired daring, she flew towards the riverbank where the temporary shelters had been built. One was set apart from the rest with two sleeping figures inside. Heart pounding, she saw the familiar white patches on the face of the nearest. Hovering over him, she blew air gently onto his eyelids. His eyes opened and he made to speak, but she pressed her fingers against his lips. Taking his hand, she pulled him from his sleeping mat and guided him from the bivouac.

By the time they'd moved a hundred yards upstream, out of earshot of the sleeping warriors, her self-confidence deserted her. Tongue-tied, she sat on the riverbank dabbling her toes in the water.

Reaching for her hand, he kissed her fingertips. 'You have some nerve,' he said. 'What if someone had seen you?'

'Shouldn't I have come?' she whispered. 'Are you angry?'

He squeezed her hand. 'Of course I'm not angry. Did you hear the good news? Maweni and I have been selected to carry the bedrolls for Mehlokazulu's *iviyo*. It means we'll march with them, maybe even get as far as the battlefield.'

She frowned. 'That's not good news at all. You might get hurt.'

'No chance of that. Herdboys never get near the fighting. In any case, it'll be over very quickly. Always is with our *amabutho*. We're invincible.'

Tears brimmed onto her cheeks as she imagined the worst.

'There's nothing to cry about.' The tears wet his lips as he kissed them away.

Responding, she lifted her mouth to join his and wrapped her arms around his shoulders. They clung to each other.

During the ensuing days, the officers continued the drilling. To develop aggression and competitiveness, they encouraged the warriors to challenge each other to stick fights. No quarter was given, and many fights ended with spilt blood and broken bones.

To increase their endurance for the long march to the battlefield, they were sent on cross-country runs, and to sharpen the speed of their attacks, inter-regimental sprint competitions were held.

Mehlokazulu's *iviyo* trained particularly hard. They wanted to impress their absentee commander when he returned. The *iziNdibi* were included in the training. No one came near Shikashika's speed, and he won every race he entered.

Ntshingwayo made his inspection on horseback. He had words for every group – encouragement here, and criticism there – coaxing them to the highest level of physical fitness.

Observing from the high ground above oNdini, Mynamana was pleased with the progress. The sheer number of men below him showed how successful the muster had been. The plain was covered. A carpet of fighting men, as many as thirty thousand. From villages throughout the kingdom, they'd responded to the call-up, and were now fully trained, waiting only for the orders of the king.

On the far side of the *umuZi*, away from the crowded main gates, John Dunn set up a rifle range and gave instruction in the loading and firing of muzzle-loaders. His students were the *isiGodlo* girls, but he also had an audience of royal children who found the guns' flashes and bangs endlessly entertaining. Dunn demonstrated by pouring a measure of black powder into a musket barrel, then pushing a lead bullet packed with wadding into the barrel, ramming it home with a thrust of the ramrod. He primed the pan, then settled the stock into his shoulder. Flash! Bang! The children cheered as the shot found its target – a large drinking pot – shattering it into hundreds of pieces.

'Jantoni, let us fire the gun. Let us!' they shouted.

Dunn beckoned to the girls. Sixhwethu pushed herself to the front. He singled her out. 'If you're so keen, young lady, you'd better show us what you can do.'

Thinking she knew it all, she brushed aside his offer to help. Grabbing the musket, she followed the steps she'd observed – all but one, the most important.

'Haven't you forgotten something?' said Dunn, pointing to the ramrod.

Glaring because she hated to be shown up, she thrust the rod into the barrel and tamped energetically. Then took aim.

Dunn could see she hadn't seated the stock tightly enough into her shoulder. Before he had time to point it out, she pulled the trigger. The recoil took her by surprise and bowled her over. She fell backwards, landing in an inelegant heap in front of him.

The audience howled.

He helped her to her feet. 'We'd better not depend on you to protect his Majesty.'

She slunk to the back of the group where Nomguqo tried hard not to smile. 'If you find it so funny, *inkosazana*,' she snapped, 'you show us how it's done.'

Nomguqo hated being the centre of attention, but a challenge had been made and in public. If she refused, she'd be accused of cowardice and Sixhwethu would never let her hear the last of it. Another factor was at work. Since kissing

Shikashika, she'd developed a new confidence. Now she had an *iSoka* – a special friend who found her attractive – Sixhwethu's sneers and insults had no effect. All she cared about was Shikashika and the next time she could enjoy his caresses. With head held high, she walked forward.

Dunn remembered her from his audiences with Cetshwayo. *Pretty girl*, he thought, *would make a fine addition to my household*. He smiled. 'Let's hope you remember more than your hut mate.'

She followed the loading process meticulously, measuring the correct quantity of powder, expertly ramming home the ball. Then looked for a target.

'Over there, the rock sitting on the boulder,' said Dunn. 'See it?'

She pushed the musket stock tight into her shoulder, squinted along the barrel and, taking a deep breath, squeezed the trigger.

As the smoke from the exploding powder cleared, she saw the stone had disappeared. She couldn't believe her eyes. Handing the gun to Dunn, she ran over to the boulder to make sure. Its fragments were scattered over the rock.

'If you're as brave as you're skilful with that gun, I shall have to recruit you into my bodyguard.'

She turned. Cetshwayo stood on raised ground behind her. Where had he come from? Then she remembered. His frock coat reminded her he was returning from the latrine. Her pulse raced. *He must think I was showing off. What's he going to say?*

'You learned your lesson well,' said the king.

She blushed. 'I'm here to serve Ndabezitha as he wishes.'

'We must find many more like you,' he added. 'The *abelungu* won't dare attack if they know we're protected by girls like you.' He raised his voice to include the others, 'Please, carry on with your practice. Nomguqo, instruct the other girls while I speak with Jantoni.'

He crooked a finger and Dunn fell into step with him.

They returned to the *umuZi* through the crowded enclosure. The king's subjects respectfully stepped aside as they passed.

Cetshwayo drew a document from an inside pocket and handed it to Dunn. 'A messenger has just arrived from Pietermaritzburg with this,' he said. 'Please read this to me.'

The crest of the Secretary for Native Affairs was clearly visible on the envelope. Breaking the seal, Dunn scanned the contents. 'This is from John Shepstone in response to the letter I wrote on your behalf last week,' he said. 'He writes, *I am directed to express the satisfaction of the high commissioner at the receipt of your letter, and to inform you that the word of the government, as already given, cannot be altered. Unless the prisoners and cattle are given up within the time specified Her Majesty's troops will advance; but, in consideration of the disposition expressed in your letter to comply with the demands of the government, the troops will be halted at convenient posts within the Zulu border and will await the expiration of the term of thirty days, without in the meantime taking any hostile action, unless it is provoked by the Zulus.*' Replacing the letter in its envelope, he returned it to the king.

Deflated, Cetshwayo searched for somewhere to sit. Dunn pointed out a bench beside a nearby hut, and the king sank onto it, resting his hands on his knees and staring into space. After a long pause he spoke, 'I've sent word to Sihayo to collect the cattle…'

Dunn said nothing. This wasn't the time to offer an opinion.

'I will not, however, deliver his family. I will not be punished twice over!' His head sank onto his shoulders. 'War seems inevitable. I see no alternative.' He patted Dunn's knee. 'Jantoni, my friend, it's with great sadness that I must send you away. When the fighting starts, you must stand aside, return to your own territory, collect your family, and find a neutral place where you can protect them.' He smiled weakly. 'When our cause is vindicated, I will recall you and we will sit together to celebrate our victory. It will be a time for great rejoicing. We will eat heartily and drink deeply. Until then, my friend, we must tread separate paths.'

Dunn hadn't expected this. He had a great deal invested in maintaining his relationship with Cetshwayo. He protested, 'Ndabezitha, I may have a white skin, but I am Zulu through and through. I am of your flesh and blood. My wives are of your family, my children likewise. Please do not send me away.'

Cetshwayo shook his head. 'In the days to come, you'll be forced to make a choice. Please don't assume our friendship obliges you to stand with the amaZulu against your own people. And by the same token, I hope you won't be persuaded to join them against us.'

'What do you advise, Ndabezitha?'

'Retire to your lands and stay out of the way.'

Losing interest in their artillery practice, the girls soon drifted away to find other distractions. Nomguqo was left to gather up the discarded guns. They looked so innocuous lying on the buckboard but, having seen how the bullet had pulverised the pebble, she shuddered at what it might do to human flesh and bone. She had a fleeting, but horrifying, vision of Shikashika with a gaping wound in his chest.

Having stowed the guns, she returned to the *umuZi*. Reaching the gateway, she felt a stinging sensation on her arm, followed by another on the crown of her head. Hailstones bounced off the ground around her.

Residents caught out in the open quickly took cover as

the volume and frequency increased. A summer hailstorm wasn't an unusual occurrence, but the damage inflicted on the ripening crops made it especially unwelcome; some of the individual stones were as large as hen's eggs. She ducked into the doorway of the nearest hut, head and shoulders protected by the overhanging thatch, to wait out the storm.

As it weakened, she saw Dlephu Ndlovu scuttling towards the *isiGodlo*, closely followed by Nobathwa. The wise woman carried the missionaries' daughter on her back. Their hurried manner and apparent indifference to the hailstorm indicated they were responding to an emergency. Intrigued, Nomguqo followed them.

Standing outside Cetshwayo's residence, the *iNgoma* hammered insistently on the door, which opened eventually to reveal the king.

Gunhild Christine spoke first, 'My mother is sick…'

The witchdoctor added a clarification, 'The pastor's wife has miscarried, and lost a lot of blood.'

'And how does this concern me?' Cetshwayo had no interest in the missionaries' welfare. He tolerated rather than welcomed them.

Dlephu Ndlovu's bloodshot eyes narrowed, weighing up what to say. Were the pastor's wife to die, it might reflect on Nobathwa's powers, and he was determined to maintain their unholy alliance; each knew where their respective bodies were buried. 'Ndabezitha, the woman is gravely sick. Nobathwa and I have applied poltices and administered potions, but the blood continues to flow. Pastor Gundersen entreats Your Majesty's indulgence for the girl Nomguqo to attend his wife.'

'Why not? Send her if you think it will help.' He waved them away and turned back into his residence, irritated by the intrusion.

A carpet of ice covered the path to the mission station. Nomguqo trod carefully. At the verandah steps, an anguished cry brought her up short. Through the open door she saw the pastor on his knees in front of his wife's body laid out on a bench. His back was to the door, forehead resting on Joachime's hand, and shoulders heaving with wracking sobs.

Nomguqo's natural reserve held her back. She could find no words of consolation. A small hand slipped into hers. Gunhild Christine stared dry-eyed at her father and dead mother.

Pastor Gundersen, now clean-shaven to mark his mourning, stood at the head of his wife's grave. The stark whiteness of his beardless chin stood in contrast to his sunburned cheeks and black Geneva gown. The long bands of his clerical collar fluttered as the breeze took them. Beside him, Gunhild Christine clutched Nomguqo's hand.

The grave lay in a corner of the orchard, shaded by a large peach tree laden with fruit. A congregation of mourners was gathered. Some stood in the immediate vicinity of the grave, but most were positioned respectfully outside the orchard along the boundary fence. All women – those who'd benefitted from Joachime's obstetric and gynecological care. Among them was Usixipe, mother of the murdered twins.

Gundersen read from his Bible, open at the Book of Psalms: *'My days are like a shadow that declineth; and I am withered like grass. But thou, O Lord, shalt endure forever, and thy remembrance unto all generations. Thou shalt arise and have mercy upon Zion: for the time to favour her, yea, the set time, is come. For thy servants take pleasure in her stones and favour the dust thereof.'*

Though she found it difficult to accept the idea of a God who would take interest in her personally, Nomguqo was entranced by the sounds and rhythms of the poetry translated into isiZulu.

'So, the heathen shall fear the name of the Lord, and all the kings of the earth thy glory.'

The word *kings* caught her attention. She doubted that Cetshwayo – the only model she had of a king – would fear anything or anyone? Perhaps it was treasonous even to consider it.

'They shall perish, but thou shalt endure; yea, all of them shall wax old like a garment; as a vesture shalt thou change them, and they shall be changed: But thou art the same, and thy years shall have no end. The children of thy servants shall continue, and their seed shall be established before thee.'

Closing his Bible, he took one last look at the coffin, then nodded to the gravediggers to fill the grave.

Gunhild Christine buried her head in the skirts of his gown.

Addressing the mourners, he said, 'My daughter and I must leave you now. Your king has advised that it is not safe for us here. I want you to know that we shall return as soon as we can...' Faltering at the sound of soil hitting the coffin lid, he fought to control his emotion. 'As you can see, my heart lies here. In the meantime, I wish you all safe deliverance from the hostilities I fear will engulf this kingdom.' He closed his eyes and clasped his hands in prayer, 'Abide with us, O Lord, in Thy grace and mercy, in holy word and sacrament, in Thy comfort and Thy blessing. Abide with us in the night of distress and fear, in the night of doubt and temptation, in the night of bitter death, when these shall overtake us. Abide with us and all Thy faithful ones, 0 Lord, in time and eternity.' Then, with the sign of the cross, he delivered the blessing, 'The peace of God, which passes all understanding, keep your hearts and minds in the knowledge and love of God, and of His Son, Jesus Christ our Lord. And the blessing of God Almighty, the Father, the Son, and the Holy Spirit be amongst you, and remain with you always. Amen.'

Nomguqo, without realising she was doing so, repeated the "amen".

The pastor led Gunhild Christine to the front gate where a horse and four-wheeled cart waited, laden with necessities for their journey. The women crowded around as Gundersen lifted Gunhild Christine onto the running board.

'Where will you go, Guniseni?' Usixipe called.

Gundersen smiled. 'Don't worry, we won't be far away.' Gathering the reins, he urged the horse forward. The gravediggers tamped down the earth and placed heavy flat stones over the grave.

The crowd dispersed, but Nomguqo stayed behind watching the cart make its way to the river crossing. She reached up and plucked a ripe peach. As she lifted it to her mouth, a maggot's head bulged from a hole in the skin. With a sickening sense of dread, she let it fall to the ground.

EIGHTEEN

The military preparations accelerated. Now, the whole Zulu nation was mobilised to serve the war effort.

The warriors who had stayed behind to bring in their own harvests arrived to swell those gathered on the Mahlabathini plain. They announced their arrival by singing war songs and beating their war shields with their spears. The sound echoed around the adjoining hills.

The iron foundries were recommissioned; blacksmiths set to work to make new spear blades. Thousands of the refurbished weapons were stacked into bundles ready for distribution when the time came.

War shields were removed from their storerooms. Any necessary repairs were made and, for those irreparably damaged by termite infestation, replacements prepared. Ox and cowhides, chosen specifically for the markings that represented the various *amabutho*, were cut into shape and wooden handles attached.

It was a factory line created to produce sufficient weapons to keep thirty thousand warriors in the field. The scale had not been seen since the days of Shaka. In fact, during the five years of Cetshwayo's reign, there'd been no military action to speak of.

The warriors' psychological preparation ran in parallel with their physical training. Of greatest importance was their ritual cleansing, the *ukuhlanza* (vomiting). Here, Dlephu Ndlovu took charge. The army had to be purged of *umnyama,* spiritual impurity, be bound together in a unified body and, above all, be protected from harm in the forthcoming battles.

The *iNgoma* instructed his herbalists to prepare vast quantities of *muthi* – an operation on the grand scale. He designated a place beside the Ntukwini stream where it intersected with the White Mfolosi as the location for the ceremony. Teams of men prepared the ground, digging thirty narrow pits, two feet wide and six feet deep. He sent out the order for the men to fast. For two days beforehand no one took solid food, merely water. On the appointed day the army was mustered and ordered to take up position on the surrounding hillsides. Lines of men, arranged according to their regiment, sat patiently waiting.

Each *ibutho* in turn was directed to come forward and line up beside the pits. Here, the *iziNyanga* administered the medicine, two herbalists for each pit. They gave out doses, which the men were required to down in one swallow. The effect was immediate, the bitter emetic reacting violently on their digestions. They vomited copiously, directing their stomach contents into the pits.

Some foolhardy souls tried to avoid the ordeal by pretending to drink, but the sharp-eyed *iziNyanga* spotted them, dragged them out of line and thrashed them to jeers from their comrades. Now disgraced, they were forced to complete the process.

Already the stench was overpowering. The warriors needed supreme self-control to avoid retching as they approached the pits. When each man reached the herbalists, he tipped his head back, gagging as the bitter potion was poured down his throat, but determined not to show any weakness.

It took the whole day to doctor the regiments. Soon the pits were overflowing with the stomach contents of thirty thousand men. A foul miasma hung in the air.

By the end of the day, the *muthi* was no longer necessary. Proximity to the vomit pits alone produced the emetic effect: many warriors spewed involuntarily. It wasn't long before their feet and their spilled vomit churned the margins of the pits into a stinking bog.

The company commanders toured the hillsides inspecting their men. For some, weak with hunger from the fast and with their stomachs purged, the experience proved too much. They collapsed unconscious and had to be carried by their comrades back to their mustering point. But, because the fast was continued to the following day, there was no prospect of relief.

Peering into each pit, Dlephu Ndlovu pronounced the operation a success. He directed his *iziNyanga* to twist bundles of grass into knots, dip them into the vomit pits and collect them in a basket. These formed the essence of the *impi* and were integrated into the *inkatha*, to act as a protective talisman when they went into battle.

Having completed their "cleansing", the warriors of uVe – the youngest regiment – marched to the derelict homestead kwaNodwengu. As king Mpande's *umuZi* and burial place, it radiated symbolic power and spiritual significance. The dead king's ancestral spirit offered a potent benign influence.

Six young bulls were penned up in the kwaNodwengu *isibaya* – great black beasts in their prime, shoulders and necks thick with muscle and needle-sharp horns.

The uVe youths lined up along the *isibaya* perimeter. With nervous anticipation they assessed their forthcoming ordeal. As at the first fruits festival, they were required to wrestle the bulls and kill them with their bare hands. If they survived, they'd become *abaqawe* (heroes). It was asking a great deal since the two-day fast had weakened them, but it was a trial designed to replicate the conditions of the battlefield. If they overcame the challenge of the bulls with their energies so far depleted, they would be ready to face any test. They would prove they could overcome any adversity and therefore have nothing to fear.

'Who'll be first to prove his manhood?' The *iziNyanga* sent out the challenge, their voices echoing around the deserted homestead.

The youths, barely into their twenties, eyed each other anxiously. They knew the dangers. Each of them had witnessed the deaths of men tossed on bulls' horns. The task ahead was, if anything, more dangerous than its equivalent at the harvest festival. Admittedly, these bulls were younger with less muscle mass but, being lighter, they were faster and much more agile.

'Six volunteers to lead six teams,' an *iNyanga* called.

The boldest youths stepped forward and, in turn, called out the names of those they wanted by their side. Six teams of six boys each were now ready to face their test. They moved to the fence, each team collecting around their leader. As they huddled, they discussed tactics. It was simple. They knew they had to be faster than the bull.

More daring than the others, one team climbed over the barrier. The bulls immediately turned towards them, treading the ground, and flicking their sharp horns.

Four of the boys fanned out, leaving two to face their target. On a given signal, the front two jogged forward. One of the bulls peeled away and broke into a run. As he charged, the four other boys converged from the side. Timing was all. If they couldn't reach the bull before he finished his charge, the front-runners would end up on the horns.

The other uVe warriors watched in awe as their comrades reacted to the challenge. As the bull reached them, the two front runners fell to the floor, rolling to distract him. Confused, the bull turned this way and that, giving the side runners the opportunity to vault onto his back. Their combined weight was enough to stop him in his tracks. His hooves skidded and knees buckled as the momentum carried him forward. In the split second while he was off-balance, one of the boys transferred his hold to the horns. Using them as a lever, he gave a violent twist and dislocated the vertebrae. The bull dropped, instantly paralysed, all four legs suddenly unable to bear its weight. The team leader ran to the fence and grabbed an *iklwa*. Plunging it into the stricken bull's neck, the warrior stood back as blood fountained. The bull's eyes glazed as its body stopped twitching.

Sticks rattling the fence signalled the regiment's approval.

During these ceremonies, Cetshwayo convened a council of war – the largest assembly of dignitaries since the start of his reign. The royal princes, Hamu, Zibhebhu, Dabulamanzi, Ndabuko and Sikhotha representing the outlying Zulu provinces, the ministers of state, Mnyamana, Vumandaba, Sihayo, and the military generals Ntshingwayo and Mavumengwana – not to mention the minor *iziNduna* and the attendants brought by each official – all sat in the oNdini cattle pen. No excuses for absence were accepted. Over a hundred officials were present.

The *isiGodlo* girls were kept busy attending to their needs. Nomguqo had a large pitcher of *uTshwala*, which she used to refill their drinking vessels.

Cetshwayo held the floor, wearing his full ceremonial regal robes and carrying the sacred spear. This was a meeting of some importance. He raised his voice so it could be heard at the back. 'The deadline approaches. All our entreaties to the British authorities have been ignored. We can only assume the attack is imminent. We have little time to plan our strategy.'

Hamu leaned forward. 'It's not too late, Ndabezitha. War can be avoided. All it requires is for Sihayo to behave like a responsible, honourable man and surrender his sons.'

The king clicked his tongue irritably. 'We've heard this before, Hamu, and we won't waste time hearing it again. We're here to discuss strategy, not repeat an argument that's already been aired and resolved. We must talk of practicalities now, where we expect the invasion to start, therefore where best to deploy our *impi*. I wish to hear from our commander-in-chief.'

Nomguqo stole a glance at the prince. From her previous observations, she knew Hamu had the potential to defy his brother. Would his snub of Cetshwayo be the straw that broke the camel's back? She held her breath.

Hamu sat back, jaws working in anger. He looked around him. The council members avoided his gaze. There was obviously no point in pressing the point further and, in view of the impending crisis, every reason to support a unified policy. He decided to remain silent.

Mnyamana stood to give his report. In contrast with the overweight Hamu, the chief minister and commander-in-chief was as slim at seventy as he had been during Shaka's reign. The longest serving of Cetshwayo's ministers, he had the authority of experience. Stroking his wispy grey beard, he gazed over the gathering. 'According to our information, the British are massing in three places – beside the Thukela at the Middle Drift, across the Mzinyathi at kwaJim, and on the coast, where many troop ships have been arriving. Apparently, the enemy intends to invade at these three points, then march on oNdini. To meet the threat in these sectors, I suggest we should also divide our forces into three. But keep back a sizeable reserve to protect you, Ndabezitha. Your security is our highest priority.'

'That seems to make sense,' said the king.

Mnyamana resumed his seat.

'I take it there are no objections?'

Not one of them raised his hand.

'In which case, let us pass on to the details of the deployment. Ntshingwayo, tell us what you propose.'

The war council deliberated until late afternoon, then adjourned to kwaNodwengu for the purification ceremony climax. Tradition decreed that all council members attend. The king led the way to their horses.

Meanwhile Nomguqo and the other *isiGodlo* girls tidied up, collecting drinking vessels and picking up the *iziNduna*'s blankets.

Ever keen to air her views, Sixwethu said, 'If they're going to war, I wish they'd be quick about it. The sooner they're gone, the sooner they'll be back. I'm getting very lonely without Maweni. I haven't seen him for days.'

Her complaint struck a chord with Nomguqo. She had also lost contact with her *isoka*. Nearly two weeks had passed since they'd kissed and that was her last sight of him. Throughout the preparations for war, contact between the sexes was suspended. During training, the warriors were billeted in their barracks, out of sight of the women. For them to retain their virile power and preserve the mystical union of the regiment, they had to remain celibate.

'Anyway, I've decided that, if they ask for volunteers to march with the *amabutho*, I shall put my hand up,' Sixhwethu said.

'What makes you think you'd be picked?' Nomguqo asked.

'Someone must carry the food and blankets for the

warriors and I'm as strong as any of the *iziNdibi*. Besides, Maweni will be going. I shall walk with him during the day, and at night—'

Before she could finish the sentence, the other girls threw the dregs of the drinking cups over her. Beer dripped off her face and chest.

Nomguqo joined in the laughter, then was struck by the thought that she could volunteer in the same way. The opportunity to be with Shikashika was tempting – long days, and nights, together. There were bound to be complications, however. The girls would be separated from the boys – they always were. Also, and more importantly, she would risk the king's displeasure if she left him when he'd singled her out so publicly. Her inner voice of caution prevailed, and she decided to stay. There'd be time enough for her and Shikashika when the *amabutho* returned victorious from the war.

A large fire blazed in the kwaNodwengu cattle pen. The carcasses of the six bulls slaughtered in the afternoon had already been prepared by the *iziNyanga* – the hides stripped, the flesh flayed off the bones, and the meat carved into long strips, then roasted in the embers.

During the preparations, the regiments arrived from the vomit pits. They formed a concentric circle – the *umkhumbi* – many ranks deep, around the fire. Thirty thousand men waited, dizzy from hunger and thirst. The occasional warrior collapsed and had to be propped up by his comrades.

Just as the sun set, the king and his court appeared. The great orb sank onto the horizon, silhouetting the king against the golden light. The effect was awesome, turning him into a figure of myth and supernatural power.

The army greeted him. The sound reverberated around the

hills: *Bhayede! Bhayede!* Then they began a war chant, which followed the rhythm generated by spears drumming against shields. Their feet stamping in unison raised a cloud of dust, and the ground shook with the impact.

Raising the *inhlendla*, Cetshwayo shook it vigorously, encouraging the warriors to sing ever more loudly. There were no words, no descriptions of past heroic deeds, merely the repetition in close harmony of the sounds *Ha! O! Ji! Ha! O! Ji! Ha! O! Ji! Ha! O! Ji!* until it developed a hypnotic rhythm.

Beside the fire, the herbalists completed their preparations. They removed the roasted meat strips from the ashes of the fire, infused them with *muthi* and placed them in baskets; carried them to the inner circumference of the *umkhumbi*, and swept the baskets in great arcs, tossing the meat pieces high above the heads of the warriors. A forest of hands rose to catch them.

Then suddenly, it degenerated into a free-for-all. Warriors trampled over each other to grab the meat, sucking on it rather than swallowing, then throwing it back into the air. Dust filled the atmosphere and many warriors struggled with their breathing. Anyone unlucky to fall was helpless and ended up being trampled on.

Eventually, every man of the thirty thousand was judged to have ingested enough of the precious protective essence to face the enemy safe from harm.

NINETEEN

The following day dawned bright; by mid-morning the temperature was stifling. Gasping in the heat, the *isiGodlo* girls found themselves with time on their hands. Because the male members of the court had moved from oNdini, their duties were lighter. They sat listlessly outside their hut wondering how to spend the rest of the day.

Mnukwa, head of the royal household, settled their dilemma. He stood over them, his staff of authority in his hand. 'As you know, Ndabezitha and the *izikhulu* are at kwaNodwengu for the doctoring of the *impi*, so once you've finished preparing the midday meal your duties will be complete; you can have the rest of the day to yourselves. Use the time profitably and don't get into mischief.' Turning on his heel, he strode back to the king's residence.

'Mischief, us?' Nobhodlile giggled.

'I know exactly what I'm going to do,' Sixhwethu said. 'I'm off to the bathing pool. I'm not spending a minute longer in this heat.'

'Good idea,' Nobhodlile agreed. 'I'll join you. Anyone else?'

A line of girls, including Nomguqo, walked along the path to the river. Just past Pastor Gundersen's abandoned mission station the path divided, one track continuing down to the bathing pool, the other leading to higher ground.

Sixhwethu, several steps ahead of the group, suddenly stopped and looked up at the hills. 'I've a better idea,' she said. 'Who wants to come with me?'

'Where?'

'How many women have seen the doctoring ceremony?'

The girls looked at her as if she had taken leave of her senses. 'No one. And for a very good reason,' Nobhodlile said.

'Well, I'm going to be the first,' Sixhwethu announced and set off up the track. 'Anyway, it'll be as cool up there as in the river. Come on. No one will see us from that distance. It'll be our secret – something to tell the grandchildren.'

The other girls looked dubiously at one another and then, collectively and without discussion, trooped after her.

Cetshwayo's voice rang out, 'Kumpega Qwabe of the uKhandempemvu!'

A well-muscled man in his mid-thirties stepped from the ranks, a wooden practice spear in his hand. He faced his uKhandempemvu comrades. They acclaimed him as their champion, the one chosen to carry their honour in the *ukuxoxa*, the climax of their preparation. The purpose of this ritual challenge was to sharpen their appetite for battle, to put fire in their bellies. Individual warriors were selected from each *ibutho*, paired against one another, then invited to challenge each other, thereby building aggression in the individual and solidarity within the regiments. Cetshwayo was wise enough to remember the bad blood between the uThulwana and the iNgobamakhosi and took care not to match pairs from those regiments.

'Mangwanana Mchunu of the uVe,' the king called, 'Come and prove yourself!'

A tall, lithe twenty-year old strutted into the circle. He too carried a stick, which he used to feint and parry in practice moves. His supporters shouted and whistled, trying their best to outdo their rivals.

Kumpega Quabe harangued his opponent, fifteen years his junior, 'Listen to me, Mangwanana Mchunu. My deeds will be greater than yours. If you kill a white man before me, you may take my cattle; you may take my sister.'

His uKhandempemvu comrades roared their support and drubbed their sticks against their shields in the *iNgomane*, the ritual encouragement. All weapons had been surrendered beforehand. No one wanted a repetition of the *umKhosi* bloodbath.

Kumpega Quabe threw himself into his *giya*, dancing from one foot to the other, and brandishing his stick and ceremonial shield with naked hostility. He leaped high in the air and then ran at Mangwanana, tongue out and grimacing fiercely. His eyes glared ferociously as his comrades beat out the iNgomane at deafening volume.

Anyone with less composure might have been intimidated. But Mangwanana was brimful of confidence. He issued his own challenge: 'If you outdo me on the battlefield, Kumpega Qwabe, you can have *my* sister.' Face contorted into a mask of fury he began his own dance. Younger and more agile, his movements and contortions were even more extreme. He circled Kumpega Quabe, hurling insults and waving his stick so wildly that at times he nearly hit him.

Kumpega Quabe stood his ground, sneering at the elaborate performance.

Banging their shields, the uVe shouted their support. Then a single voice sang the words of a praise song, which the others took up. The noise produced by a thousand throats and shields was huge, much louder than the uKhandempemvu equivalent.

Sitting among his generals, Cetshwayo waved the *inhlendla* to end the challenge. The two warriors stood in front of him, panting and wild-eyed. 'I commend you both,' he said. 'You're a credit to your respective *ibutho*.'

The regiments cheered their champions. Then, as the *inhlendla* hovered between them, they held their breath. Who would the king choose?

Wavering first one way, then the other, Cetshwayo ratcheted up the tension. At last, he settled on Mangwanana, indicating that he had displayed the greater ferocity. The uVe went wild. Sweeping their champion off his feet, they carried him off the parade ground, ecstatic at his triumph.

Meanwhile, Cetshwayo called for champions of the uMbonambi and the uNokhenke to show themselves.

The *ukuxoxa* lasted all day. At the end the warriors were at such a frenzy they would have gone into battle there and then.

Up in the hills above kwaNodwengu, Nomguqo looked directly down into the parade ground. She was so far away that the warriors were indistinguishable as individuals, but she could hear their voices clearly enough, with the challenges and counter challenges rebounding off the cliff faces below.

Sixhwethu pointed excitedly, 'There he is, right there.'

'Who?'

'Maweni, of course. Standing next to Shikashika.'

Nomguqo whispered, worried they could be heard even at that distance, 'Since none of us can see Shikashika, we'll have to take your word for it.'

Under pain of death, women were forbidden to witness the *amabutho* being prepared for war. They were taking a huge risk.

However confident and independent she'd become, Nomguqo wondered whether the flouting of the rules was worth risking their lives.

Holding their breath with excitement, the girls peered into the distance. This was what they'd come to see – the pride of the nation's manhood preparing to fight for king and country. It sent shivers down their spines.

During the *ukuxoxa*, Dlephu Ndlodvu and his herbalists prepared a medicine for the final purification procedure, concocted with ingredients chosen for their power as symbols of virility and masculinity.

They carried a cauldron of the steaming liquid to the middle of the *umkhumbi* and placed it on the fire to continue simmering. Its odour wafted across the front row. The warriors wrinkled their noses in disgust. It was the rancid smell of rotting human flesh – trophies from enemies killed in battle – body parts including the penis, skin from the right (*iklwa*-bearing) arm, flayed beard skin: ingredients suffused with the attributes of manhood.

The *iziNyanga* called each regiment in turn to file before them. As the warriors doubled past, the *iziNyanga* dipped cows' tails into the liquid and flicked the *muthi* into the air. Passing through curtains of spray, the men were drenched from head to toe.

The setting sun reddened the horizon as the last warrior filed past. Cetshwayo and his court had long ago left the parade ground. The girls, on the other hand, had stayed to the very end. Now it was over, and the warriors were leaving to bed down for the night, it was time to return to the *umuZi*. It wouldn't be long before the main gate was shut.

Sixhwethu headed down the mountain. 'Last one back cooks supper,' she called. The others followed, running pell-mell down the path.

With her mind on what she'd witnessed, Nomguqo was slow to react. Before she knew it, she was alone on top of the hill. She followed the sound of their laughter, which seemed quite close to begin with. But, as the light faded, forcing her to pick her way more carefully, it grew fainter. In the time it took her to reach the bottom, thick cloud cover blotted out the sky and plunged her into darkness.

With a growing sense of panic, she stopped beside a large rock to reorient herself. It was big enough to act as a landmark; she must have seen it on the way up. But it was unfamiliar. Whichever angle she tried she couldn't convince herself she'd seen it before. She listened for the girls. Nothing. Silence, apart from her own breathing and the blood racing in her ears.

She had to choose a direction, but which? The *umuZi* curfew would sound very soon. What if her absence was noticed? The girls might cover for her, but she couldn't be sure. Her belly contracted with fear when she thought of the consequences.

Having made several circuits of the rock, she convinced herself she recognised the path. She walked a few steps along it, and satisfied she was headed in the right direction, started to quicken her pace.

As she ran, her mind turned to Shikashika. She sensed him running with her, urging her on, his long stride covering the ground. With him beside her there was nothing to fear.

A distant splashing reached her from below. She stopped to listen. No doubt about it, water was breaking over rocks – the river must be nearby. Once she found that, she would easily find her way back to oNdini.

Reaching the riverbank, she looked in both directions. Was oNdini upstream or downstream? There were no landmarks to guide her. On the horizon, the clouds parted to reveal the rising moon, which lightened the sky. Picking her way carefully over the stones at the water's edge, she made her way instinctively upstream. Her progress was much slower now, impeded by the rough ground.

An odour reached her, which became stronger with each step she took – a deeply unpleasant smell that she recognised as rotting flesh.

The ground rose slightly at a bend on the river. Suddenly she found herself walking over much larger stones. She climbed from one to the other and eventually reached a large flat rock suspended on a platform of other rocks. Now the smell was overpowering. To stop herself retching, she placed her hand over her mouth and nose.

Clambering onto the flat rock, she gingerly placed one foot in front of another. It took twelve paces to cover the distance from one side to the other. A rock of such dimensions was exceptional. There was one she knew about but only by reputation. Horror-struck, she realised she was standing on the *kwaNkatha* – the execution rock – and in the same instant understood that the appalling smell on the far side of the rock was coming from the corpses of execution victims.

The moon on the horizon cast a faint, eerie light over the landscape. Gripping her nose and mouth tightly and trying not to gag, she peered over the side of the rock.

It was a sight beyond anything she could ever have imagined. A tangle of bodies lay in various states of putrefaction – piles of them as far as she could see, their limbs entwined in ghastly embrace.

Backing away, she retraced her footsteps to level ground.

Absorbing the full horror of what she'd just witnessed, she couldn't prevent her stomach rebelling. She heaved until there was nothing left.

Now she faced the problem of finding her way out. Wherever she trod, there was a body; she couldn't understand how she'd avoided them in the first place. The whole area around the *kwaNkatha* was littered with human remains. Long dead skeletons lay under relatively fresh corpses. Scavengers – hyenas, jackals, and vultures – had torn the bodies apart, scattering limbs indiscriminately, leaving half-eaten legs and arms and heads picked clean of their brains. She tripped over a torso, falling headlong into a jumble of bones, where she saw the terrible injuries inflicted on the skulls – massive holes from the impact of the war clubs.

She had no idea which way to turn. All she knew was she had to find her way out of the nightmare. Mercifully, most of the bodies were piled on the far side of the rock, so it didn't take long to negotiate a path out of the graveyard.

By now the moon had risen far enough for her to see spirals of smoke from the oNdini cooking fires silhouetted against the sky. She ran towards them as though her life depended on it.

Climbing up the final slope, she stumbled against an object on the ground. Bending to identify it, she saw she had trodden on a tiny skull. Another lay beside it. Picking them up, she turned them over in her hand. Unmistakably human and baby-sized, they were what remained of the murdered twins.

TWENTY

kwaSogekle

Mkhumbikazulu, Sihayo's second son, looked down from the Ngedla heights overlooking the Mzinyathi. Far below, past the precipitous gorges through which the waters of the river boiled, towards where it widened out, lay the crossing-point between Zululand and Natal, marked by kwaJim's outpost. Preparations for the invasion were well under way – rope hawsers slung across the stream attached to pontoons. Provisions and equipment were being ferried across. Soldiers, their redcoats visible through the mist, lined the riverbank waiting to cross. The distance diminished the scale, so they appeared like an army of soldier ants, too small to offer a threat. The fog swirling up from the river reinforced the air of unreality.

Mkhumbikazulu was reminded that kwaJim was where he and his brothers had executed their mother. The scene was still fresh in his mind. MaMtshali's battered face and her struggles as they administered her punishment were as vivid as if they happened yesterday. He was proud she died a Zulu's death, stoically and without complaint. But she was his mother, the woman who had suckled and cradled him; she deserved better. Mehlokazulu, on the other hand, had showed complete indifference. Did he genuinely not care? Or had he suppressed his natural feelings? Perhaps he was merely following the Zulu way. Mkhumbikazulu hoped he could live up to his older brother's example. Now he was responsible for defending the family *umuZi*, he would need to be equally single-minded.

After the call to arms went out, the king ordered him to organise the kwaSogekle defences. With Mehlokazulu cooling his heels up on the northern frontier and Sihayo discharging his duties as a general in the field, it fell to him as the second in line. He accepted the challenge with pride; he wouldn't let his father down.

As the first redcoats climbed onto the pontoon, he turned his horse and urged it down the slope. He estimated they would reach kwaSogekle by the time the sun reached its zenith. He didn't have long.

Anticipating this moment, he had already ordered the evacuation of the homestead. The Qungebeni women, children, and men too old for the muster, were hidden in a series of caves high in the cliffs that gave kwaSogekle its name – Cock's Comb.

The broad floor of the Batshe valley, where the Qungebeni herds normally grazed, was also deserted. He had taken the precaution the previous day of driving the cattle into the caves, following the plan Sihayo had devised for such a contingency.

He crossed the pasture at a gallop, making for the head of the valley, with its formidable horseshoe of cliffs. Wisps of low-lying cloud obscured the rocks at the bottom, so it seemed as though he was riding towards a vertical wall. Reaching the point where the ground began to climb, giant boulders appeared out of the mist, covered with thick vines and scrub to create an impenetrable barrier.

Dismounting, he led his horse towards a narrow path between the large blocks of stone, whistling to signal his approach. An answering shout came from the makeshift barricade in front of him. Half a dozen elderly men appeared brandishing their guns. He picked his way towards them. 'Everything in order?'

'As you left it,' one replied, gesturing towards the top of the rock fall. 'Women and children in one set of caves, cattle in the other. The *abelungu* will find it hard to dig us out.'

'They're coming in big numbers,' Mkhumbikazulu warned. 'I didn't stop to count them, but they mean business.' Handing over the reins of his horse, he proceeded up the cliff face.

The earlier drizzle gave way to more persistent rain. Sheltering in one of the spacious caverns, Mkhumbikazulu watched the British forces mustering on the level ground below. Officers chivvied the native levies of the Natal Native Contingent into the front rank. Carrying the traditional Zulu weapons of shield and stabbing spear, they were indistinguishable from the amaQungebeni except for the piece of red rag they wore around their foreheads. So far, the defenders hadn't revealed themselves, but now a chorus of insults came from high on the hillside:

'Traitors, you dare to come against us!'

'amaQungebeni are invincible!'

'Prepare to die, lackeys of the white man!'

Intermittent fire from their ancient muskets accompanied the taunts. For the most part the shots were inaccurate, but they succeeded in breaking up the NNC ranks below, scattering them in all directions. One unfortunate clutched his leg as a stray bullet shattered his thighbone. He groaned in agony as his fellows dragged him to the shelter of the boulders. While the defenders reloaded, the NNC officers ran among their men and urged them up the hillside, resorting to kicks and blows from rifle butts when they resisted.

The amaQungebeni fared badly in the initial encounters. Many of those manning the lower barricades surrendered their positions and were shot as they retreated up the cliff.

A fiercer resistance was met further up. Twenty defenders countered the attack by driving a small herd of cattle down the slope. The frightened beasts formed a temporary obstruction as they tossed their horns, but the NNC took the long way around and stampeded them to the valley below. Regrouping, they swarmed up the hill.

The resulting skirmish was bloody. Men fought each other hand-to-hand. No quarter was given. The amaQungebeni were battle-hardened veterans whose experience and knowledge of the terrain gave them the initial advantage, parrying with their shields the spear thrusts of the NNC who struggled to keep their footing on the uneven ground. Tripping over a stone, an NNC warrior flung out his shield arm to retain his balance, leaving his left flank unprotected. The deathblow came almost immediately – a spear thrust through his ribcage directly into his heart. The weight of the falling body twisted the weapon from his assailant's hand. A nearby white officer fired three shots in quick succession into the Qungebeni's chest.

Higher up, where the slopes on either side of the path became steeper and narrowed into a gorge, a defender was on his knees, trying desperately to shove his intestines back into the gaping hole in his belly. Diluted by the heavy rain, blood coursed down the rocks.

Having swept aside the resistance lower down, the attackers streamed towards the cave where the women and children were sheltering.

Higher still, Mkhumbikazulu, alongside the main body of fighting men, watched the NNC overrunning those left to defend the cave. Outnumbered and outgunned, Mkhumbikazulu was powerless to help. Several of his men started back down the slope, but he pulled them back. 'It's all up with them. We must look to ourselves.' He turned to consider the almost perpendicular rock-face above. 'Our only hope is up there. If we can reach the top, we'll circle around and attack them from the rear. Are you with me?'

The warriors watched the NNC escort their womenfolk and children down the mountain to an uncertain fate. They had no choice.

It was a punishing climb. Slinging their shields over their backs, they picked their way up the cliff. When the slope became particularly steep and they risked losing their footing, they grabbed hold of the vines growing from crevices in the rocks to pull themselves up. Sheets of water cascaded off their shields and it became increasingly difficult to find a safe route. Sharp rocks shredded their bare feet. Missing his step, one of them trapped his foot between two boulders, twisting his leg until his shinbone snapped. Unable to move, he waved his comrades on and turned to face the enemy. Saluting his bravery, Mkhumbikazulu continued to climb.

By the time they reached the top, they were spent. Chests heaving, they collected themselves below an overhang. From here it was a short climb to the level ground above. Despite their exhaustion, they grinned triumphantly. They had done it, completed a difficult climb in almost impossible conditions.

Mkhumbikazulu was first to the top. On his belly, he lent over the precipice to haul the others over the last few feet. Flopping onto the level ground, they sucked air into their tortured lungs. There was no recovery time, however. It became immediately obvious they had been outflanked. Riding towards them at a canter was a squadron of cavalry. At the onset of the skirmish, this had been sent along the ridge to join up with two companies of infantry, which had worked their way up the steep spurs of the gorge. Mkhumbikazulu and his men were caught in a pincer movement.

They scattered, every man for himself. Fifteen made for rising ground along the ridgeline and ran straight into one of the redcoat companies, already in a firing position. The volley from the Martini-Henrys was devastating – all fifteen were mown down.

Mkhumbikazulu and the rest ran in the opposite direction away from the guns. They tried desperately to outrun the horses but were quickly overtaken, tripping on the uneven ground and ridden down by the galloping hooves and cut to pieces by the horsemen's sabres.

The fastest runner, Mkhumbikazulu, was the last to fall. Lungs burning and legs pumping, he ran along the lip of the precipice he'd just climbed. Far below, plumes of smoke drifted up from kwaSogekle, put to the torch by the British forces.

With the pounding of the horse's hooves in his ears, he turned and saw the raised sabre. His last reserves of strength faded, and he stumbled to his knees as the blade slashed across his unprotected neck.

The news of kwaSogekle's fall reached the royal *umuZi* before the end of the day. The signal horns, echoing from valley to valley, announced the catastrophe. Not only had Zulu sovereignty been violated but the fortress defending its southern boundaries had been destroyed and its garrison defeated.

Throughout oNdini, groups of anxious women discussed the implications. If Sihayo's stronghold could fall, where next?

All the men were now garrisoned with their respective *amabutho*, either in their military *amakhanda* or in bivouacs built specifically for the purpose. Of the male population normally resident at oNdini, only the king's council and his *isikhulu* remained, assembled in the largest room of the king's personal quarters, sitting informally on cushions laid on the floor. Sihayo was bowed down with grief, hunched in a corner with a blanket over his head, Mnyamana, Vumandaba, Ntshingwayo and Mavumengwana struggled to find words of consolation.

Cetshwayo spoke for them, 'My friend, your loss concerns us all. We all feel your pain. Nothing will ever compensate for the destruction of your *umuZi*, the theft of your cattle…' he paused, knowing this was the least of it, '…the death of your son. To lose a child is to lose part of ourselves. It's what every parent dreads.' The others murmured in sympathy. 'We will all understand if you choose to stand aside from your duties to the council. You need time to grieve.'

Reaching for the beaker of gin at his side, Sihayo drained it in a single gulp. His cheeks were hollow and eye sockets sunken: he had aged appreciably since the last *ibandla*. When he spoke, his voice quavered with emotion. 'As you say, Ndabezitha, our children are precious; it is why we indulge them.' He smiled thinly. 'I'm forced to consider my own responsibility in this. My sons' actions led directly to today's events. My *umuZi* lies in ruins, my cattle looted, my people turned out of their homes. Who can I blame? Only myself.'

Cetshwayo patted his old friend on the knee. 'If you're guilty of indulging your children, then so are we all.'

Taking a deep breath, Sihayo addressed each counsellor in turn. 'I'll make whatever sacrifice is necessary to avert the disaster that threatens to overwhelm our nation. My family is at your disposal. Recall my sons and surrender them to the British authorities.'

Cetshwayo shook his head. 'It is too late for that. In any case, our action was based on a joint decision. Your sons weren't the issue. The British were determined on war from the start. We have sued for peace, offered reparation, but our entreaties have been ignored. Today's attack on kwaSogekle shows they're bent on unjustified aggression. We've no choice now but to defend ourselves, and we have right on our side.'

Ntshingwayo stood. 'You have only to give the word, Ndabezitha. Our warriors are desperate to wash their spears.'

Mavumengwana joined him. 'Let it be so, Ndabezitha. We will push the invaders back to the ocean. They will drown in their own blood.'

The king now had a renewed purpose in his voice: 'My trusted friends, you will lead our *amabutho* from here. On your shoulders will rest the sacred duty of defending our nation. I know the decisions you take will be wise ones. I counsel only this – even at the point of engagement when the armies are facing each other, send emissaries to the British. Implore them to lay aside their weapons and leave Zululand in peace. I do not wish to have the bodies of our warriors returned on their shields. If these entreaties fail, then and only then send your men to sweep the *abelungu* aside.'

TWENTY-ONE

kwaNodwengu

'My children, you are setting forth on a great enterprise – nothing less than the defence of your homeland…' Cetshwayo stood on raised ground before the *impi*. His formidable stature and elevated position made him visible to every warrior assembled in the kwaNodwengu *isibaya*. The whole space was covered with fighting men. Never in the nation's history had so many men been sent out to defend it.

Bhayede! Bhayede! The warriors stood in ranks according to their respective regiments. They were stripped for action, their elaborate body adornments set aside. They all carried shields, the colour of the hides distinguishing the various regiments. Each man carried his offensive weapons, his *iklwa* and *umkhonto* (throwing spear), razor-sharp from hours on the grindstone.

All eyes were on Cetshwayo. He was in his full regalia. A magnificent oxhide covered his broad shoulders. This carried a symbolic significance. The bull ox from which it had been taken was the progenitor of the bloodline of the royal herd. Cetshwayo wore this cloak with immense pride. Around his waist hung a kirtle of lambs' tails that swung to and fro as he moved. His right hand held the sacred spear, which he shook for emphasis. This was his final address before the army took to the field.

'Five days ago, the invader's armies crossed onto our lands. We have taken every measure to avoid war, but the aggressor has refused all requests for peace. We have no quarrel with the *abelungu*, but when he threatens our beloved country, we have no choice but to resist. It is our sacred duty. While the aggressors remain on Zulu soil, the spirits of our ancestors are and will remain displeased.'

The warriors murmured angrily.

The king changed tack, adopting an aggrieved tone. 'Have I travelled overseas to attack them?'

A resounding 'No!' echoed back at him.

'Completely unprovoked, they have invaded us. It would be no surprise if they stole our wives and cattle, our crops, and our land. What shall we do?'

The warriors bellowed their reply: 'Leave it to us!'

'What will you do?' the king shouted.

They roared back, 'We will eat up the *abelungu*! We will finish them off! They will not take you while we are here! They will have to take us first!'

Cetshwayo flourished the sacred spear. 'Go, my children. Honour our forefathers by driving the invader back across our borders. Our cause is just; we have right on our side. And make no mistake, there is no army standing that will match the skill and bravery of my *amabutho*!'

The acclamation was thunderous.

'You are commanded by fearless warriors…'

Ntshingwayo and Mavumengwana stepped forward. The warriors drummed an *iNgomane* on their shields, sounding like a locust swarm had landed.

Cetshwayo shouted to make himself heard, '...Their knowledge and tactical ability are second to none. Trust in them. They will lead you to victory. My orders to them are simple. Number one, march slowly to meet the enemy – it is vital you conserve your energy for the battle. Two, under no circumstances trespass onto British territory.'

The *iNgomane* increased in tempo and volume. Raising the *inhlendla*, he called for silence. 'I've no doubt you want to know who I've chosen to "drink the dew".'

Thirty thousand voices shouted as one: 'Tell us, *inkosi*, tell us!'

'Because they proved their valour in the *isibaya*, the honour of leading our *impi* to meet the enemy falls to…' he paused for maximum effect, '…the uVe!'

The effect of his announcement was dramatic. The uVe comprised the youngest warriors, scarcely out of their teens. Their excited cheers drowned out the groans of disappointment from the other regiments. Jumping up and down, they waved their spears repeatedly in the air and wouldn't settle for several minutes.

The king smiled benevolently as the uproar continued. Again, he called for silence. 'When you march from here, I shall retire to the *eNkatheni*, from where the nation's power will be transmitted to you. There will be only one day of fighting – that is all it will take. Then you will return to us victorious; and each of you will have earned the right to wear the heroes' necklace. Go now, my children.' Climbing down from the dais, he joined them.

Bhayede! Bhayede! Thirty thousand spears reached into the sky. Ntshingwayo and Mavumengwana accompanied him down the length of the parade ground. On the way, he stopped periodically for a private word with old comrades-in-arms. Beside the main gate, the iNgobamakhosi waited with their colonel-in-chief. 'Which *iviyo* is without its commander?' Cetshwayo asked.

Sigcwelegcwele singled out Mehlokazulu's section.

The king addressed them, 'You will not go into battle without your commanding officer. I have sent word to Mehlokazulu. He will join you in the time it takes you to reach the *abelungu*.'

The army took the rest of the morning to file through the gates. The thousand uVe youths proudly led the way onto the Mahlabathini plain. Untried in battle and ignorant of the dangers ahead, they chattered away excitedly, looking forward to the great adventure. Many would not return, but for the moment they were immortal; the medicine men had assured them so.

Behind them was Mehlokazulu's regiment. A decade older, the iNgobamakhosi had already washed their spears. They knew what to expect; they had seen the horrors of hand-to-hand combat, experienced both the giving, and receiving, of spear thrusts. Some bore the scars on their legs and arms (warriors with chest and belly wounds seldom survived). For them, the excitement was tempered by a fear this might be their last view of their homes and loved ones. They would never admit it to their comrades but deep down they feared they might not return.

Older regiments waited their turn. Grizzled uThulwana and uDloko veterans ragged each other. They had seen it all before, survived countless battles. Since Shaka's time fifty years earlier they had not been beaten. Individuals might perish, but they were convinced the *impi* would triumph and bring victory to their king.

As each *ibutho* received the order to move off, its commander marked time by leading his men in the regimental war-chant.

Sigcwelegcwele, colonel of the iNgombakhosi, shouted *Hohho! Hohho! Hohho!* which was then taken up by a thousand voices.

A voice from the uThulwana led his comrades in their chant: *Mina! Mina! Mina!* (Me! Me! Me!)

The regiments' attempts to drown each other out created an ear-splitting din. Now they shared a common cause; their mission was clear. They would resist the invaders or die in the attempt.

In the pastures out on the plain, five hundred well-muscled bullocks grazed under the watchful eyes of the *iziNdibi*, the fattest and healthiest of the royal herd. The king had said only the best was good enough for his boys.

As the *amabutho* emerged onto the plain, the herdboys abandoned their cattle and rushed forward. They jostled each other for a good view. Shikashika and Maweni secured a position in the front. They watched proudly as the warriors filed past. The uVe were only five or six years their senior, but they seemed so much older – heavily muscled bodies toned from long days of training, and skin glowing with good health. The two warriors whose bedrolls and personal equipment they would carry winked as they passed.

Also watching the parade, but on the other side, were the female porters. Sixhwethu had achieved her wish and was going with them. She expected to exploit the opportunity to be with Maweni. She'd been told that, once the fighting started, they'd be pulled back out of harm's way, but until then she would be with her beloved night and day.

When her selection was announced, her behaviour became intolerable. She drove her hutmates mad with her boasting: 'I'm going to fight the British', 'I'm going to come back a war-hero', and 'I'm going to be with Maweni without you breathing down my neck!' For three days and nights, her bragging continued, until Nomguqo reached the end of her tether: 'Will you shut up!'

'You're just jealous,' Sixhwethu retorted. 'While you're cold and miserable on your lonely bedroll I'll be nice and warm in Maweni's arms.'

The girls breathed a sigh of relief when the departure time arrived.

Standing with the other porters, Sixhwethu wore a sulky frown. It wasn't what she'd expected. For a start, she was segregated from the boys, and if she couldn't be with Maweni, what was the point in going? Also, the reality of the task ahead had begun to sink in. The night before the army assembled, she reported to the military quartermaster responsible for dividing up the loads. Sacks of cornmeal and millet were piled on her shoulders: it would be the load she would carry while the army was on the move. Then she was told that, at midday and in the evening when the warriors made camp, she'd be responsible for lighting campfires and cooking porridge. Prolonged physical effort wasn't her strong suit. With such heavy loads on her back, how could she be expected to keep up with fit soldiers? As she saw it, she'd be spending long days slogging up hills with sacks of mealie flour on her head, with no consolatory cuddle from Maweni at the end of the day.

Past the line of marching warriors, she caught Maweni grinning at her. All doubts immediately evaporated. She would use every means at her disposal to be with him.

The royal wives and concubines watched at the oNdini gate. Way in the distance, through a heat haze, they could see the warriors streaming out of kwaNodwengu. The women, Nomvimbi and Nomguqo among them, wore their most precious body adornments to mark this significant moment. They shook their beads and trilled their tongues.

The sound carried to the distant marching men. Turning towards oNdini, they saluted with their spears.

Nomguqo strained to see Shikashika. Through the dust cloud raised by the marching feet, she caught a momentary glimpse before he disappeared into the teeming mass of bodies. She felt her stomach tighten. The discovery of the tiny infants' skulls had awakened a sense of outrage. Why should men lose their lives to defend a regime that perpetrated such horrors? But as her doubts took form, she dismissed them. Such heresy was dangerous. Also, her loyalty to the king was absolute. As for Shikashika, she convinced herself that he would be sufficiently level-headed to stay out of trouble.

Across her field of view, from kwaNodwengu up to the Mfolosi, the land was dark with marching men. At the front, the uVe – from her perspective, tiny figures dwarfed by the landscape – were already wading through the water. The warriors continued to stream through the kwaNodwengu gate. For mile after mile, the procession was unbroken. It took until lunchtime for the last stragglers to cross the river. Nomguqo watched until they were out of sight. From her elevated position, she could see where the army had marched. A swathe of trampled grassland hundreds of yards wide looked as though a giant log had rolled over it.

# PART THREE

THE SUN GROWS DARK

TWENTY-TWO

oNdini

The sun had risen and set twice since the army marched from oNdini. The *umuZi* was empty of men – apart from Cetshwayo's bodyguard. The remaining women and children had enjoyed little sleep, worrying about the outcome of the forthcoming battles and whether their menfolk would return.

An eerie quiet pervaded the settlement, interrupted by the voice of the king's praise singer on his rounds. Though still early, the summer's heat radiated from the ground. Mopping the sweat running down his neck, the *imBongo* improvised an addition to his standard delivery, 'May the spears of our warriors cut deep into the chests of the invaders and may their generals be forced to grovel in the dust before His gracious Majesty.'

Normally, he would have had a captive audience, but the place was deserted – not a living soul. Puzzled, he peered into the empty huts. Where were they all? Concluding they must have risen early, he decided to cut his losses and retreat to his own hut.

For the girls of the *isiGodlo* the day had begun two hours earlier. In the absence of the herdboys, the feeding and watering of the royal cattle had become their responsibility. They were beyond the main gate, driving cows and their calves along the path to the river.

The royal wives had also been forced to accept a change in routine. With no servants to attend them – prepare their meals, clean their huts, and look after their children – they were obliged to fend for themselves. Fully occupied, they had no time, or indeed inclination, to indulge their usual practice of sitting around and gossiping. At that moment they were collecting drinking water from the Mbilane stream.

Because of her special position in Cetshwayo's household, Nomguqo was excused cattle duties and was on hands and knees polishing the floor of his residence. The task was repetitive, and as she worked on the area around the large flat stone by the door, her mind drifted. She saw the king bathing, water cascading off his chest, running onto the stone. The memory triggered another image – the play of muscles in Mehlokazulu's back as he helped her carry hoes from the fields. Her stomach fluttered as she heard his voice. But this wasn't a memory; it was Mehlokazulu talking. Blood rushed to her cheeks, a sensation she had come to associate with Shikashika, and it took her by surprise. Why would the sound of Mehlokazulu's voice be so disturbing?

'Come in,' said the king, pushing open the door. He entered, followed by Mehlokazulu, an antiquated musket over his shoulder. She quickly withdrew to a corner of the room, conscious of his eyes on her. The king eased himself into a chair beside the table.

She moved towards the exit, murmuring, 'If you don't need me, Ndabezitha…'

'On the contrary,' Cetshwayo replied. 'Bring us gin to celebrate Mehlokazulu's return.' He gestured to a display cabinet stacked with bottles. Each bore the same label: gin distilled and bottled especially for the king. She chose one, and picking up a couple of beakers, carried them to the table. She turned to leave. 'Stay, child. Mehlokazulu has something to tell you. He has news of your family.'

She looked at Mehlokazulu, then back at the king. 'How can that be?'

'He's been in the north with your kinsman Mbilini.'

'We visited your father's *umuZi* five days ago,' Mehlokazulu said.

She couldn't help herself. The idea he'd had such recent contact with her family unlocked her tongue. 'How are they? Is my father well? Is he still working too hard? Have any babies been born?'

'Slowly,' Cetshwayo said. 'One question at a time.' Pouring generous measures from the bottle, he invited Mehlokazulu to sit.

She was on tenterhooks. Since the kingdom had been placed on a war footing, she'd had concerns about her family's safety. What would become of them if British soldiers occupied that part of the country?

'Your family is well,' Mehlokazulu reported. 'They send their greetings. Your father hopes you are working hard and serving the king well.'

Cetshwayo beamed.

'Your sister Diboli hopes you're behaving yourself,' Mehlokazulu continued, 'And your father tells you not to worry; they'll make sure they stay safe.'

She shuffled her feet with embarrassment and pleasure. 'Thank you, thank you.'

Cetshwayo changed the subject. 'Ready to join your men?'

'As soon as Your Majesty commands,' Mehlokazulu replied.

The king gestured to an ornate cabinet. 'Nomguqo, in the bottom drawer you'll find something I wish to give this brave young man. It will help him in the battles to come.'

The cabinet drawer revealed a package wrapped in oilcloth. She lifted it out and carried it to the table. The king unpacked it. John Dunn's gift, the brand-new Martini-Henry rifle, lay there unused and unmarked. Indicating Mehlokazulu's battered muzzle-loader, he said, 'No doubt that musket of yours has given you fine service but look at this.' He held up a sample cartridge. 'See, charge and bullet in one. No more fumbling with ramrods. Imagine how many you can fire in the time you take to load your musket.' He demonstrated the gun's bolt action.

Mehlokazulu was impressed. 'If we had all weapons like these, Ndabezitha, the war would be over in no time.'

'Nothing I would wish for more. Unfortunately, that isn't possible. We must rely on our superior fighting skills.' He put the rifle into Mehlokazulu's hands. 'Please, carry this for me.'

Mehlokazulu examined the firing mechanism, then squinted down the barrel. 'With this, Ndabezitha, I will send many of the invaders to their deaths.'

'I'm sure you will, *iqawe*. I'm sure you will.'

While they were speaking, Nomguqo wondered how she might thank Mehlokazulu for bringing her family's messages. It occurred to her that Mkhumbikazulu's death might be weighing on his mind. Words of condolence came tumbling from her mouth. 'I hope you won't think me impertinent, but I want to say how sorry I am for your loss.' She waited for a reaction. All she received was the ghost of a smile.

The king raised an eyebrow. It was unheard of for a girl of her station to express an opinion in male company. Yet her tone and the expression were so sincere that the lack of decorum was excusable. 'Kind words indeed, child. Now, we mustn't keep this man from his duty.' He laid his hand on Mehlokazulu's shoulder. 'You're a day behind the *amabutho*. Go, make a name for yourself.'

Lowering his head, Mehlokazulu backed respectfully through the open door.

Watching him leave, Nomguqo tried to reconcile this impression of a considerate, kind man with the hard-faced warrior of her memory, the man who had not hesitated in garrotting his adulterous mother. It didn't make sense.

The warmth of the rising sun burned off the mist and spilled across the Zulu bivouacs. It cast long shadows from the warriors standing guard. The army was encamped in emaKhosini, the valley of the ancestors, beside a tributary of the Mfolosi. Here they would pray to the spirits of their forebears to look kindly on their enterprise.

The warriors took most of the previous day to gather. By late afternoon the camp was laid out in order of regiment, each *iviyo* designated its own space. Provisions in the form of meat and mealies were distributed and firewood collected, a responsibility given to the *iziNdibi*. By the time they had collected sufficient fuel, the surrounding hillsides were denuded, and, as night fell, the light from six hundred campfires flickered across the valley.

Sixhwethu and the other female porters were quartered apart from the men: their presence was thought likely to damage the warriors' fighting spirit and cancel the special powers instilled by the medicine men. Sixhwethu saw this as a minor obstacle. Nothing would stop her from sleeping with Maweni. She waited until the evening meal was finished, and the others were fast asleep, then crept off to find him. He was with the other herdboys taking turns to guard to cattle. They spent the night with their limbs wrapped around each other, waking just before the sun rose. She sneaked back in the half-light, her blanket over her head to conceal her identity.

Smoke from the cooking fires curled into the still morning air. Warriors yawned and stretched their muscles, stiff from sleeping on the rough ground. The officers patrolled their companies, kicking awake the late risers and mustering them into formation.

Council members Ntshingwayo, Mavumengwana, Vumandaba and Sihayo, along with Cetshwayo's brothers Dabulamanzi and Ndabuko and cousin Zibhebhu, pulled their blankets over their shoulders to ward off the chill of dawn and prepared themselves for this important ceremony.

EmaKhosini was a holy place – the graveyard of all the Zulu kings – where the ancestors' spirits could be invoked to support missions of national importance. There was none greater than the present crisis. The grave of Senzangakhona, father to three Zulu kings – Shaka, Dingaan and Mpande, and therefore progenitor of the whole royal family – lay on raised ground surrounded by clumps of thorn bush, the "tree of kings" or *uhlalankhosi*, whose thorns were believed to hold fast the spirits of the *amaDlozi*. Each bush was impregnated with a holy presence.

Sunlight tipping over the Mthonjaneni hills imparted a golden glow over the valley. It illuminated the generals as they led the way to stand reverentially around the grave. Warriors faced them in ranks all the way down to the river. Ntshingwayo summoned the praise giver, an elderly uKhokhoti warrior who had served under king Dingaan. His many years of service earned him the right to lead the prayers. His deep bass voice echoed from the surrounding rock faces. 'Oh, great Senzangakhona, father of our nation, we stand before you, humble supplicants of your favour. You, whose deeds brought great distinction to your people and will ever be remembered, bestow on us your blessings…'

The warriors responded with a deep gutteral, *O ye, iye he yiya! Ha! O ha yiyi! Ha! O ho hu. Oye iye! Iya! Ha O, Hi I ya! Ihi.*

'…We, your children, are about to embark on a mission on which our survival as a nation depends. May your spirit stand with us, offering an example of courage and daring to the warriors who will go into battle on our behalf. May your glory shine on them and inspire them to overcome our enemy.'

The echoes died away. For a moment, absolute silence reigned as the army absorbed the importance of the message. Then a single voice shouted out the battle cry. The whole army joined in, stamping their feet in time with the chant. This continued for several minutes as each regiment competed with the others to shout the loudest.

Ntshingwayo called for silence. Making sure he was visible to the whole army, he shouted, 'Our king commands it. Our ancestors command it. We have the weapons to execute it. What am I referring to?'

The answer came thundering back: 'The destruction of our enemies!'

Heading south, Mehlokazulu waded across the Mfolosi drift, the bundle containing his rolled-up shield and weapons held high above his head.

Reaching the far side, he broke into a rhythmic loping run. It was obvious the direction he should follow. Forty thousand feet had already beaten down the path.

Marching slowly as the king had ordered, the army made slow progress. He caught up with it just as the stragglers were leaving the emaKhosini valley and found his father on horseback, picking his way up the precipitous track leading towards the high ridges above the Mfolosi. The horse stumbled on loose stones. Reaching for the bridle to steady it, he greeted him, '*Ubaba* (Father).'

Sihayo looked at him without expression.

Mehlokazulu was shocked at the change. In the three weeks since he'd last seen him, his father had aged. The destruction of the kwaSogekle family home and his brother's death had taken their toll. Seeking to reassure him, he said, 'I will rebuild kwaSogekle for you, *Ubaba*, I promise. Once again you will sit among your cattle in the *isibaya*.'

Sihayo shook his head. 'Whatever you do, you cannot bring back your brother.'

There was nothing more to say. Leaving his father to his grief, he quickened his pace up the mountain.

The older regiments at the back struggled for breath on the steep path. Supremely fit, Mehlokazulu maintained his speed and easily overtook them. He passed Qhude kaKuhlekonke making heavy weather of the climb. 'Maybe your warriors should carry you, old man,' he sneered.

Qhude scowled but hadn't the energy to reply.

It wasn't long before Mehlokazulu joined his own men. The iNgobamakhosi, along with the uVe, were still at the head of the column. He fell into step with one of them. 'Did you miss me?'

The warrior laughed. 'As a dog misses its fleas.'

The rest of the regiment welcomed him with a loud cheer.

He responded with the regimental war cry: *Hohho! Hohho! Hohho!*

The climb was brutal and unrelenting. Through the rest of the day, the army toiled up the steep slopes of the Mthonjaneni heights. The livestock, used to grazing on flat pasture, rebelled at being driven up the rocky path. The herdboys, including Shikashika and Maweni, did what they could to move them along. They chivvied and cajoled, even hit them with their sticks. Maweni's excess weight made him puff and pant but, determined not to show weakness in front of Sixhwethu, he suffered in silence.

She, on the other hand, found reasons to complain from the moment they started climbing. All morning she moaned about the size of her burden, how it hurt her neck, how her muscles ached. Then at midday, with the sun was at its highest, she stopped. 'I'm so thirsty I can't go any further,' she said. Tipping forward the load on her head, she caught it in her arms; lashed to the pack was a gourd of drinking water. She found a convenient nearby rock to sit on and gulped it down, failing to notice a large cobra sunning itself on the ground beside her, camouflaged against the dry, dusty earth. It immediately coiled itself to attack and would have struck had it not been for Maweni.

Grabbing a throwing spear from a passing warrior, he hurled it with unerring accuracy. The blade caught the snake below its spread hood and severed its head, leaving its body to writhe in its death throes.

Sixhwethu was so shocked she burst into tears. Maweni sat with his arms around her, awkwardly trying to comfort her.

Draping the cobra's dead body over his stick, Shikashika laid it in front of her to demonstrate how close a call it had been.

'Why don't we skin it?' Maweni suggested. 'You can wear it as a good-luck charm. Save you from future snakebites.'

Wiping away her tears, she watched him slit the snake along its length and pull the pelt cleanly from its body. He tossed the bloody carcass over his shoulder. The vultures circling above took immediate notice.

With her new charm around her wrist, she rewarded her rescuer with a kiss.

As the gradient grew steeper, tempers frayed. The *iziNdibi* lost patience with the animals that refused to go any further. They slaughtered and butchered them on the spot. It was a last resort because they then had to carry the meat. Bent double under huge loads, they pressed on. Nothing could slow the progress of the march.

The vultures transferred their interest from the snake to the leftovers of the butchery. Swooping down, they squabbled and bickered in a full-blown feeding frenzy.

High on the mountain summit, Ntshingwayo and Mavumengwana scouted a suitable area for the night's bivouac. Finding level ground wide enough for every warrior to stretch out, they gave the order to pitch camp.

Sixhwethu's shoulders ached. Her feet were bruised and cut from the sharp rocks. Only Maweni's company kept her going. Since the cobra encounter, she stayed glued to his side. They took their minds off their pain by enumerating the members of their respective families – sisters and brothers from their father's other wives, first and second cousins, uncles and aunts, grandparents. In each case, there were over forty individuals. It passed the time so effectively they were surprised when they reached the end of the climb. Warriors had already gathered into groups to make camp on the flat ground. Sixhwethu took it as a cue to throw down her load. Flopping onto a nearby rock, she massaged her neck. 'That's it, not another step. We'll sleep here.'

Maweni shook his head. 'I must find the *ibutho*. My man will want his bedroll.' He peered into the distance. Men settling down for the night stretched across the plateau. The iNgobamakhosi were one thousand among twenty thousand. Even in good light it would take a while. Dark shadows were already creeping up from the valley below. 'Come if you want to, but I'm going now.' He offered his hand. With a resigned sigh, she took it and hauled herself up. She wasn't prepared to let him out of her sight. During the long and difficult day, she'd committed herself to him. He had no choice in the matter – she'd have him whether he wanted her or not.

A command post was set up on high ground from which the commanders could view the *impi*. The vast assembly of men was concentrated into a relatively small space. Younger regiments were billeted cheek by jowl with veterans and had to put aside their historical rivalries to satisfy a hunger sharpened by the long day's march.

The sharing of the evening meal was the perfect opportunity to bring the officers together for a briefing. Ntshingwayo, Mavumengwana, Sihayo and Cetshwayo's blood relatives sat cross-legged with a circle of their officers around them. Female porters distributed platters of meat and roasted mealies.

Mavumengwana was first to speak: 'It's been a gruelling day, but our men have proved their fitness. I'm proud to lead an army in such condition. You, their commanders, must take credit for that. I congratulate you.'

The officers smiled, pleased to have their efforts publicly recognised.

'We'll come on to tactics later, but first, some matters of discipline. Ntshingwayo, over to you.'

'We're within two days march of the Mzinyathi,' said Ntshingwayo. 'By tomorrow night, we shall be within striking distance of the enemy. From now on, it's essential we keep hidden the size of our force. Surprise is our big advantage;

that, and our knowledge of the ground. Our enemy is crossing territory it has never crossed before, whereas we know every blade of grass. Using the lie of the land, we shall hide our *amabutho* until the last moment, then spring the trap.'

His audience applauded by slapping the ground.

'From tomorrow the *amabutho* will split into two columns. I will march with the left, which will include the uKhandempemvu, the uNokhenke, the uDududu, the iSangqu and the uMxapho. Mavumengwana will lead the iNgobamakhosi, the uVe, the uMbonambi, the iNdlondlo, the uDloko and the uThulwana on the right. We shall march within sight of each other, using the land to screen our forces. To begin with, we'll be marching through Sithole country, but we're unsure at this point where their loyalty lies. Zibhebhu will explain.'

Cetshwayo's cousin took his place. 'The Sithole *inkosi* is Matshana kaMondise…' he began.

Officers from the older regiments grunted at the mention of the name.

'…For the benefit of the younger officers, Matshana is *khafula* (outcast). His clan has never offered allegiance to the House of Shaka. Yet he has reason to hate the British. Over twenty years ago, the Shepstones mounted a campaign against him and nearly succeeded in killing him. He sought the protection of our king who, generous as always, offered two of his sisters in marriage. By rights he should make common cause with us, but he has a history of currying favour with the British. In my opinion he is not to be trusted.'

'We must know one way or another whether it's safe to lead our army across Sithole land,' Mavumengwana insisted.

Zibhebhu replied, 'I'll take out a scouting party at first light tomorrow.'

Mehlokazulu's eyes lit up. That was exactly the sort of mission he would enjoy.

Ntshingwayo spoke again, 'Assuming no problem with the Sithole, the following day will take us into Qungebeni country – where we know we'll be safe. Our friends Sihayo and Mehlokazulu will be on hand to guide us. They know these lands like the back of their hands.'

'My son and I are at your disposal,' said Sihayo. 'However, I should point out that we'll be crossing my brother Gamdana's lands. Normally we would expect him to help us. But…' the words stuck in his throat, '…according to intelligence we received today, Gamdana has surrendered to the British.'

This was greeted by a chorus of disapproval. 'Shame!' 'Traitor!' 'A decision he'll live to regret.'

Sihayo continued, 'I'm aware my family has much to answer for in this matter, and I assure you, Gamdana will be made to suffer for his disloyalty.'

'That he will, Sihayo,' Mavumengwana agreed.

Several senior officers glared at Mehlokazulu, clearly assuming he was responsible for the present situation. He, by contrast, showed his indifference by picking meat fibres from his teeth.

'Thank you, Sihayo,' Ntshingwayo said. 'We can assume the British will send out scouting parties. We have already received reports that mounted redcoats have been seen as far west as Hlazakazi. I say again – and cannot stress forcefully enough – we must keep the full extent of our numbers concealed. From now on, rations will be eaten raw to avoid smoke from our cooking fires alerting the enemy. Please pass this order on to your men. It will save them the bother of finding firewood.'

The officers chuckled.

'So, hoping you all enjoy a good sleep and awake refreshed

for the march tomorrow, the rest of the night is your own.'

They clambered to their feet.

'One last matter,' Ntshingwayo added. 'In three days, it will be a new moon. Under no circumstances will we engage with the *abelungu* on that day. It would be *umnyama* and go badly for us.'

The officers dispersed in the direction of their individual commands. Mehlokazulu sought out Zibhebhu. 'If you're looking for volunteers for the reconnaissance party, look no further than me.'

Zibhebhu scoffed, 'You're a hothead, Mehlokazulu. Who's going to trust you on such a delicate operation?'

Mehlokazulu bridled. 'Let me prove myself.'

'You're a brave fighter, I'll give you that. But for this expedition I need more than bravery. I'm looking for men with the initiative to act on their own, but with level heads. You do not meet that criterion.' With curt nod of dismissal, he turned his back.

Fuming, Mehlokazulu stamped off to rejoin his men.

TWENTY-THREE

Hlazakazi

The reconnaissance patrol left while it was still dark. The waning moon provided just enough light for the dozen men to move safely across the rugged landscape. Mounted on small Basuto ponies chosen for their agility and stamina, they picked their way past huge boulders down to the valley floor.

In view of Zibhebhu's dismissal, Mehlokazulu was astonished to receive a tap on his shoulder in the early hours. There was no explanation, just the order to be ready to leave immediately. He knew he was on trial and shouldn't put a foot wrong, but it was an opportunity to break the monotony of the march and perhaps earn the respect of the king's cousin.

What he didn't know was that Zibhebhu had discussed the matter with Ntshingwayo and been persuaded that Mehlokazulu's qualities outweighed his natural tendency to act first and think second. Besides which, his local knowledge was an asset. Zibhebhu admitted he had only the vaguest idea where he would find Matshana and his people.

It took two days to track them down. Spooked by accounts of British brutality from refugees from kwaSogekle, Matshana had deserted his *umuZi* deep within the gorges east of kwaSogekle and was holed up in caves on the lower slopes of the Qhudeni mountain. It was less than ideal. Two thousand men, women, and children, living hand-to-mouth, not knowing from one minute to the next when and from where the British attack would come. When they found him, Matshana showed his relief by declaring a deep and lasting devotion to the royal cause: 'I'm Cetshwayo's man. Always have been,' he said.

Zibhebhu sucked his teeth. Determined to conclude business and be on his way, he confined his remarks to the bare minimum. 'We have your permission to cross your land, then?'

Matshana answered, 'Whatever I can do to help. My warriors are at your disposal; use them as you see fit.'

'How many?'

'Eight hundred. All with weapons.'

'Ready to move off immediately?'

Matshana looked uncertain.

'Are they or are they not?'

Mehlokazulu suggested, 'Maybe he's concerned there'll be no one to protect the womenfolk.'

Zibhebhu shot him a look. *Keep your nose out of it.* 'If that's the case, keep some behind. A hundred men should be enough.'

Matshana was still not convinced. 'One hundred and fifty, and I'll stay to lead them.'

'This is no time for negotiation!' Zibhebhu thundered. 'Either you help, or you don't. Which is it to be?'

With the recce party in the lead, six hundred and fifty Sithole picked their way up the last few feet to the summit of the Hlazakazi plateau.

Light faded as the sun set over the Malakata hills. Reaching level ground, they congratulated themselves on achieving their goal. They'd added six hundred and fifty extra men, and the way was clear for the army to continue its march.

The day had been long and hard, and they looked forward to a well-earned rest. Mehlokazulu looked down with satisfaction at the ground they'd covered. Even he, in the peak of physical fitness and on horseback, had struggled. Easing the Martini-Henry off his shoulder, he watched the Sithole tramping towards him. Beyond, the deepening gloom obscured the ridges and deep chasms that led down to the Mzinyathi. Suddenly, a flash on a distant hillside caught his eye. He called to Zibhebhu, 'There's something down there,' indicating the direction. The reflection off a piece of glass, binoculars perhaps? Whoever or whatever it was, if he could see them, they certainly could see him silhouetted on the ridge. Dismounting quickly, he pulled his horse down. The others followed suit.

Pulling a telescope from his saddlebag, Zibhebhu followed Mehlokazulu's pointing arm. Through the scope, he saw a squadron of cavalry making their way towards the high ground, about thirty strong. In the fading light it was difficult to pick them out against the monochrome grey background, but he could identify navy-blue uniforms, their contrasting white facings clearly visible.

'An advance party?' Mehlokazulu suggested.

'If it is, the main force won't be far behind them.'

'Have they seen us?'

Zibhebhu squinted into his spyglass. 'Doesn't appear so.'

'What shall we do?'

Zibhebhu gave a wry smile. 'There are enough of us. Let's give them the fright of their lives.'

'Are you sure? There's hardly enough light.'

Zibhebhu glared. 'What did I say this morning about obeying orders?'

'Yes, *inkosi*,' Mehlokazulu replied.

The Sithole warriors had also noticed the mounted soldiers. Lying flat to the ground, they waited for orders.

Zibhebhu muttered to Mehlokazulu, 'We'll have to use the element of surprise. Wait until they're nearly upon us, then use the horns of the buffalo.' Using his hands, he divided the force into two groups. 'You can command the left flank. I'm putting faith in you, so don't let me down.'

Tying his horse's bridle to a rock, Mehlokazulu crept on hands and knees to the three hundred warriors designated as the left flank. 'Where are your *iziNduna*?' he said.

Half a dozen officers showed themselves.

'Pass the word. On the order we'll head that way,' he pointed, 'and join our comrades from the other side. The killing ground will be in the middle.'

Appearing on the ridge line, the British cavalry trotted forward in formation. When they were a quarter of a mile away, Zibhebhu shouted, 'Now!'

Screaming the battle cry *uSuthu!* six hundred and fifty warriors formed into four lines across the plateau, eager to close with the enemy as quickly as possible. There was no time for "doctoring". The Sithole were driven by the desire to return to their homes, Mehlokazulu to avenge the death of his brother and the destruction of his family's property. He led the charge, splitting his men from Zibhebhu's as they raced forward. In the fading light, they were an awesome sight. Their feet thudded on the ground and the deep resonance of their war cry reverberated across the plateau.

The cavalry immediately pulled up, wheeling their horses away from the threat. They twisted in their saddles to gauge the situation. Which direction should they take? It was hard to tell in the dark. Horses blundered into each other. Their riders fought to keep their seats. They were hopelessly outnumbered, and the enemy was barely a hundred yards away.

The warriors on the outside accelerated and began to turn inwards, closing the gap between the two horns of the buffalo.

The blood sang in Mehlokazulu's ears. The enemy was at their mercy. Soon there'd be bloodletting.

Now they were within range. The Sithole pulled back their arms to launch their throwing spears. Then faltered as they heard a shout. Mehlokazulu continued, not trusting what he'd heard.

The shout came again: 'Halt!'

The Sithole warriors stopped, uncertain what to do.

Zibhebhu signalled the withdrawal.

Mehlokazulu watched the British horsemen some thirty yards away, equally dumbfounded by the order. He saw the relief on their faces, knowing how close to death they had come. They plunged down the hillside in disorderly retreat.

Peering into the dark chasm, Mehlokazulu could just about make out the white facings on their tunics as they rode to safety. 'They were there for the taking!' he fumed.

'Strategy, son of Sihayo, strategy,' Zibhebhu replied. 'Killing thirty British soldiers would have accomplished… precisely that. But only that: thirty less to face us in the coming battle. However, now they've seen us – nearly a full *ibutho* – what do you think they'll do?'

'Return to their base camp?'

'I don't think so. Like us, they were sent out to gather intelligence – in their case, about the size of our force. Now they've seen us, they'll think we're an advance unit of the main army and…'

Mehlokazulu smiled as he understood. '…send for reinforcements.'

'Exactly. By tomorrow, thirty men will have become three hundred. And what will that accomplish?'

'Their forces will be divided and weakened.'

Zibhebhu nodded. 'Which is how we will win the battle.'

'You're right,' Mehlokazulu admitted. 'Of course, I see that now.'

'So, what now?'

Mehlokazulu thought for a moment. 'We light fires over as wide an area as possible. And then withdraw. They'll think we're still holding the ground…'

'And we can be wherever we want to be.' said Zibhebhu. 'Now you're beginning to think like a commander. Strategy, Mehlokazulu, strategy.'

Mehlokazulu's eyes glinted. He'd learned a useful lesson.

Over the next few hours, he acted like a commander, supervising the collection of brushwood and lighting campfires every thirty feet. Zibhebhu watched with the amused expression of an indulgent parent.

From a distance, the twinkling of the fires gave the impression of a large encampment of warriors.

A low mist wreathed the encampment of the main Zulu force. In anticipation of a favourable report from Zibhebhu's recce party, Ntshingwayo had moved the *amabutho* down from the Mthonjaneni plateau. They passed a miserable night, bivouacked on the eastern slopes of the Babanango Mountain on the way to isiPhezi. A steady drizzle began just after midnight and, as the wind picked up, it drove gusts of rain across the camp. The warriors were forced to seek what shelter they could. Forbidden from lighting fires, they had no relief from the penetrating cold apart from their thin blankets. Each warrior used his shield as protection. Turned against the wind, he crouched under it, and water ran off the thick oxhide.

Sixhwethu and the herdboys were denied the luxury of such shelters. They took their chances in the open along with the cattle. Shikashika improvised some protection by tucking himself close to the belly of one of the bullocks in the lee of the wind. The animal's body radiated warmth and didn't object to Shikashika sharing its space.

Soaked and shivering with cold, Sixhwethu was utterly miserable. With no more than a skimpy cloak to cover her shoulders, she pressed herself tight to Maweni, moaning, 'It's not fair. Our last night together and it rains like this.'

She had started complaining when they learned that she and the other female porters were to be sent back to oNdini. Their role was now taken by the *iziNdibi*. Since so much of the herd had been butchered and eaten, the army was now expected to forage where it could. The herdboys had become the porters for the warriors, carrying their equipment and sleeping rolls. The girls had become redundant.

Sixhwethu stared disconsolately at the remaining bullocks chewing the cud in the wet grass. Water ran down her back. There was no other target for her resentment, so Maweni bore the brunt of it. He had already lost patience with her. 'Please stop moaning Sixhwethu,' he pleaded. 'Try to get some sleep.'

'You don't care,' she whined. 'In a few hours, I'll have to go back. I may never see you again.'

'What makes you think that?'

'A stray bullet might hit you.'

'And the sun might turn black,' he muttered.

She dug her elbow into his ribs. 'I'm serious. You could end up getting killed.'

'I don't think so. The *iziNdibi* will be miles behind the

front line. We won't get anywhere near the fighting. Isn't that so, Shikashika?'

Shikashika grunted.

'Anyway, I want you to wear this.' She unwrapped the cobra skin amulet from her wrist. 'As you protected me from harm, so will this keep you safe.' She twisted it around his arm, then clung tightly to him, convinced he would not make old bones.

The march back to the rendezvous point took all night. With fog swirling around them, Zibhebhu and Mehlokazulu led the recce party, the Sithole advance guard following on behind. They passed sentries on picket duty who whistled to alert the rest of the camp.

Ntshingwayo and Mavumengwana, swathed in thick cloaks, greeted them. 'We were beginning to think you'd been swallowed by the mist,' said Ntshingwayo.

Zibhebhu replied, 'Matshana kaMondise greets you,' and pointed to the Sithole contingent. 'He puts these warriors at your disposal and offers every assistance he can. The way forward is clear.'

Ntshingwayo nodded perfunctorily. 'And the British?'

'We left them something to warm their imaginations,' Zibhebhu replied. 'We think their centre of operations is east of kwaJim behind the Hlazakazi range. It would seem the most likely location. We had contact with one of their scouting parties coming from that direction.'

'Casualties?' Mavumengwana asked.

Mehlokazulu jumped in, 'We decided not to engage—'

Zibhebhu cut him off, unwilling to let the cub steal the lion's prey, 'Instead, I ordered campfires to be lit. A strategy to split their forces.'

'Excellent,' said Ntshingwayo. 'By my calculations, that puts them two days' march away.' He turned to his adjutants. 'Assemble the men. I want the army on the move within the hour.'

Mavumengwana elaborated, 'We shall march in two columns from now on. When you parade the *amabutho*, make sure they've been separated into the appropriate section.'

'To your duties, then,' Ntshingwayo ordered.

Setting off to join their regiments, Zibhebhu hissed at Mehlokazulu, 'If you want to keep your friends, don't take credit for their ideas.'

'But…' Mehlokazulu began, then realised he was on a hiding to nothing.

They found their men beside the stream, flailing their limbs to restore their circulation. Some were on their knees scooping up water to wash down their uncooked breakfasts – the picture of misery.

Among them were Mehlokazulu's comrades. He whistled a greeting and received a half-hearted wave in return. He shouted, 'Pass the word. We're on the move.'

In the cattle pen, five hundred herdboys leapt to their feet.

'That's it. Quickly now,' Zibhebhu shouted. 'Muster as soon as you can.'

The *iziNdibi* moved among the cattle prodding them to their feet. Sixhwethu tried to make herself scarce among the milling animals.

Zibhebhu immediately picked her out. 'What are you doing there?'

Sixhwethu swallowed. 'Just helping Maweni.'

'Well, you can help him by allowing him to do his job. In any case, all girls should be heading back to oNdini now.'

Unwilling to leave, she lingered. 'What are you waiting for?'

Her eyes filled as she realised that she wouldn't have a chance to say goodbye properly. She looked for him, but he was already lost among the press of boys directing the herd towards the stream. Dragging her feet and looking forlornly over her shoulder, she headed to where the other girls had assembled.

Zibhebhu shook his head irritably. 'Females are what men need least now; they're nothing but a nuisance and a distraction.'

Mehlokazulu's mind was elsewhere. Watching the herdboys drive the cattle had given him an idea. Maybe it would be a way to restore Zibhebhu's good opinion of him. 'Now the herd is smaller, do we need so many boys to handle them?' he said. 'What do you say to recruiting some as scouts?'

Zibhebhu stroked his chin. It wasn't the worst idea in the world. They'd be less conspicuous than grown men and would get much closer to enemy positions. He nodded. 'Strategy, eh? You're learning fast.'

Mehlokazulu whistled to attract their attention. The whole group came running and gathered expectantly around the officers.

'We're looking for volunteers to act as scouts,' Zibhebhu announced, 'to collect information about the enemy, the strength of its regiments, and where they're assembled. You'll need to get as close as you can to their position. Our eventual success will depend in large part on the accuracy of the intelligence you bring back.'

'It'll be dangerous work,' said Mehlokazulu. 'You'll be on your own and a long way from the protection of the *amabutho*.'

Zibhebhu corrected him, 'Your youth will be your protection. The enemy is less likely to take notice of you. We're looking for boys with stamina who can run fast…'

'…And who are not scared,' Mehlokazulu added.

'Who thinks they qualify?' Zibhebhu asked.

All the boys stuck up their hands. Mehlokazulu wasn't surprised: they'd been trained to be fearless. Now, he and Zibhebhu were faced with a problem – how to make a choice at such short notice. Inevitably, there would be an element of chance.

As they made their assessment, the candidates vied for attention, gesticulating, and shouting each other down. Those selected were tapped on the shoulder and invited to stand to one side.

Mehlokazulu noticed that Shikashika kept his arms firmly by his side, standing quietly as the officers passed. 'You don't want to be considered?'

The boy replied, 'I thought you'd notice me more if I didn't wave my arms about.'

Mehlokazulu laughed. 'Full marks for initiative. Quiet and observant – exactly the qualities we need. Go and stand over there.'

Maweni, who'd been waving more wildly than anyone, was crestfallen. 'You can't take him and not me,' he said.

'Why's that?'

'Because I'm his cousin – the clever one. He can't do anything without me.'

Mehlokazulu looked him up and down. Perhaps not the finest physical specimen on view, but he was confident enough to speak out. He deliberated for a moment. 'All right, then. Go, stand next to your cousin.'

Grinning from ear to ear, Maweni joined Shikashika and the others.

Zibhebhu addressed the rejects, 'The rest of you will have an opportunity to prove yourselves later. Now, off you go, back to the cattle.'

Casting envious glances at the lucky dozen, they headed back to the river to prepare the cattle for leaving.

'Well done, all of you,' said Zibhebhu, turning back to the recruits. 'This an important mission, dangerous perhaps. There are some important points to remember. First, you'll be going in pairs; each couple will have a specific direction to follow. In that way, you'll be scouting every inch of the country. Once you're in the field, it's vital you stay hidden. You can use the contours of the land to do this – the dips and gullies. Make sure you stay below the ridgeline. If you don't, you'll be seen by anyone below. If anyone challenges you, tell him you're looking for stray cattle. Now, the army will continue towards that mountain over there.' He pointed towards the huge grey bulk of isiPhezi fifteen miles away. 'On the other side is where we think the *abelungu* are camped – a place called iSandlwana. The army will travel along this valley in two columns, and I expect we will bivouac tonight at the foot of the mountain. I want you all to rendezvous there before nightfall. And I don't want to send out a search party. Is that clear?'

They nodded.

'Anything you want to add, Mehlokazulu?'

'Just that you should travel light. Whatever you're carrying now can be distributed among the others.'

'Any questions?' Zibhebhu asked.

The boys looked at each other. The orders were clear enough. Now they had to carry them out.

Fanning out across the mountainside, the scouts quickly lost sight of each other.

Shikashika and Maweni were on their own in the landscape. Half running half walking, Shikashika's long legs quickly covered the ground. Maweni trailed him by some distance. 'Slow down,' he called. They had maintained the same pace for over two hours, and he was finding it hard to keep up. The terrain was particularly unforgiving – long climbs and steep descents. 'In any case, how do you know we're going in the right direction?' It was a reference to their earlier panic when they lost their bearings and walked around in circles.

'As long as we keep our shadows behind us, we'll know we're on the right path,' Shikashika replied.

'But the sun's overhead.'

Scrambling up the last few feet of the gully, Shikashika shaded his eyes against the sun's glare. He was rewarded with a view to a strange rocky outcrop far in the distance. It jutted out of the landscape like a crouching giant, its peak and shoulders towering above the rest of the formation. It was the most significant geological feature in the area. He recognised it immediately. Zibhebhu had called it iSandlwana, using the local Qungebeni word to describe the shape of a cow's stomach.

As Maweni landed beside him, he pointed it out. 'There – iSandlwana.'

Maweni grunted, more interested in quenching his thirst. He drank greedily from the gourd. 'Can we rest and have something to eat?'

Retrieving some sundried beef from the pouches around their shoulders, they perched on a nearby flat rock.

Maweni chewed. 'What now?'

'We haven't seen anything yet. I suppose we carry on.'

'Can I shut my eyes for a moment? I had no sleep last night.'

'Didn't Sixhwethu keep you warm?'

'It wasn't that. She didn't stop talking.'

There was no advance warning. Appearing out of nowhere, horsemen thundered towards them. White men. Maweni swallowed. What could they say? How would they explain their presence?

Reining in beside them, the officer in charge studied the frightened youths from under his wide-brimmed hat. He barked in isiZulu, his moustaches bristling, 'Who are you? What *umuZi* are you from?'

The words stuck in the boys' throats.

'Couple of dumb ones here,' the officer said. 'Either that or they're stupid. See what you can get out of them.' One of his men dismounted and pointed his carbine at Shikashika's head.

Maweni immediately started gabbling. 'Please, *inkosi*, we're Qungebeni herdboys from down in the valley. Sihayo is our *inkosi*. We've been sent to look for stray cattle.'

'Well, you won't find any of Sihayo's herd up here.'

'Why?'

The officer guffawed. 'Because we've taken them all.' Vaulting from his saddle, he sauntered over. 'There are *amabutho* near here. Many, many men.' He crouched; his voice was menacingly low. 'You'd tell us if you'd seen them, wouldn't you?'

'We've seen no one,' Shikashika answered.

'No one,' Maweni echoed.

The officer studied them, searching for any sign they weren't telling the truth. They stared back with blank expressions. Satisfied, he stood. 'If we see you up here again, it will be the worse for you,' he warned.

Remounting, he spurred his horse into a gallop. The rest of his troop followed kicking up a cloud of dust.

Two hours later, the two boys reached the iNyoni escarpment and looked directly down into the British camp half a mile away to the south-west. It said much for their bravery that, after the encounter with the horsemen, they didn't turn tail and return to the security of the great Zulu army. After their initial fright, they concluded they could bluff their way out of trouble. They also understood that this was a great opportunity for them to make their mark, to do something heroic to help the cause.

The sun dipped behind the range of hills to their right and shadows lengthened across the landscape. Remembering Zibhebhu's advice not to show themselves against the skyline, they lay on their bellies watching the activity below. Tents were pitched in orderly lines stretching across the hillside right up to the steep slope of the mountain. On the right a track led down to a stream. Oxen strained as they pulled wagons laden with supplies up the slope. Carts that had already arrived were unloaded, their oxen unyoked and turned out to pasture on the long grass behind the tents. Two large artillery pieces were brought up, the wheels of the gun carriages bouncing on the uneven track and the oxen straining against the heavy load.

Maweni was glued. Shikashika, more wary, scanned the landscape on either side.

Suddenly, Maweni dug his cousin in the ribs. 'Look.'

Below, eight redcoated men led their horses from the camp, one with more elaborate decoration on his uniform. They mounted up and, at a stately pace, headed down the hill. They watched as the horsemen changed direction and headed in a straight line towards them. Though half a mile away, it wouldn't be long before they were discovered. Maweni panicked. 'What are we going to do?'

'Head back. We're well overdue as it is.'

Rolling back from the ridgeline, Shikashika scrambled to his feet. The sun had now set and colour leached from the landscape. Zibhebhu's deadline had passed. Recognising they wouldn't be able to rejoin the main force before nightfall, they had to deal with a more immediate problem: how to put distance between them and the redcoats. With no thought to where they were headed, they threw themselves down the hillside.

A large boulder appeared out of the gloom – a convenient pretext to check on their pursuers. Tucking in behind the rock, they looked back. Their hearts jumped into their throats as the redcoats crested the ridge.

'What shall we do?' Maweni whispered.

'Shush! Just wait.' Shikashika peeped out. The redcoats were still there but not coming on. 'Maybe they haven't noticed us.'

Or were interested in something else. The braided officer had a telescope to his eye, and it was trained, not downwards, but towards a distant object on the opposite escarpment. A group of mounted amaZulu had appeared, but too far away for Shikashika to identify any individuals.

'Are they ours?'

'Hard to tell at this distance.'

The redcoats spurred their horses in the opposite direction and the boys breathed again.

Mehlokazulu wheeled his mount to face the boys as they scrambled towards him. 'We've just spent precious time hunting for you. The other scouts arrived at the rendezvous on time. Where were you? Off on some adventure of your own, your own little war. What if those redcoats had ridden you down? Did you think of that? What if you'd been captured and made to talk? And, believe me, they'd have made you talk. By now they'd know where our army is. You can count yourselves lucky it's me, and not Zibhebhu. He'd have sent you packing along with the girls – which is where you belong.'

Maweni said, 'We know where the *abelungu* are camped.'

'Under iSandlwana mountain, just as Zibhebhu said,' Shikashika added.

Mehlokazulu absorbed the information. 'Numbers?'

'Many. White men and black,' said Shikashika.

'Red coats and blue,' Maweni said.

'How many?'

'Perhaps one *ibutho*,' Shikashika replied.

'A thousand men?'

'Maybe.'

'We saw them hauling up two big guns,' Maweni said.

'How big?'

The boy stretched his arms wide.

Mehlokazulu nodded. 'Cannon.' Though he'd never seen the weapon in action, he had a sense of its firepower. Guns of that calibre would cause devastation. The battle plan would have to be adjusted to take account of them. 'Good,' he nodded curtly at the two scouts, 'Maybe Zibhebhu will keep you after all.'

TWENTY-FOUR

Ngwebeni

Hearing Mehlokazulu's report, Ntshingwayo snorted with derision, 'Herdboys? What a ridiculous idea, sending children out with cattle-sticks.'

Mavumengwana disagreed. 'Effective, though. We would never have known about the cannon without them. It was a good plan. I salute whoever thought it up.'

Zibhebhu took full credit. 'We've also learned the British have no idea of our numbers and our whereabouts – which has achieved your objective so far, Ntshingwayo.'

'And, more importantly,' said Mehlokazulu, 'from what the scouts saw, we know they're sending out large patrols and leaving their garrison weakened.'

'This must be the moment to attack.' Zibhebhu said.

'Well, it certainly won't be today,' Ntshingwayo said. 'Not with the moon in its present phase.'

Mavumengwana explained, 'We've consulted the *iziNgoma* and they tell us that misfortune will follow if we ignore this. We must avoid any element of risk in case *umnyama* unleashes spiritual forces to spoil our chances.'

'What do we do, then? Just sit and wait?' Zibhebhu snapped.

'We know what you think, Zibhebhu, and I warn you not to voice your opinions outside the present company. Our warriors must go into battle believing they're invincible. You understand me?' said Mavumengwana.

Ntshingwayo added, 'We'll use the next twenty-four hours to move the *amabutho* forward, so we're in place when the new moon appears. This will be the most favourable time.'

Later, under cover of darkness, the warriors moved up the valley of the Ngwebeni stream, where they pitched camp and waited.

When the army was settled, Ntshingwayo called a war council. It included every *iNduna* of every *ibutho,* all the way down to the *iviyo* commanders. Over a hundred officers sat cross-legged in a circle around the generals. Ntshingwayo was first to speak. 'Our king advised that we should avoid armed conflict with the *abelungu*–'

'We're beyond that now,' a voice interrupted.

Ignoring the heckle, Ntshingwayo continued, 'Cetshwayo's words are wise, and we must take them seriously. I ask you to consider the following: if we're forced onto the battlefield and we prevail – of which there is no doubt…'

uSuthu! The battle cry interrupted him again.

'…and a peace agreement is drawn up, who will be considered the aggressor?' He studied the faces around him.

Mehlokazulu said, 'What does it matter? We will have driven the invaders from our land.'

'That may be so,' Ntshingwayo said, 'but do you imagine they won't attack again? Their hunger for land – and the precious metals beneath it – is insatiable. From their dealings with the Dutch, we know the British rely on their treaties to steal the lands of others. Therefore, we must ensure, when we come to sign a peace settlement, that it is on our terms.'

'Our men are primed for battle,' Mehlokazulu said. 'They've been doctored. Now they must wash their spears.' He looked for support from his brother officers.

'I hear you, Mehlokazulu,' Ntshingwayo conceded. 'You are a brave warrior and I've no doubt, when it comes to it, you will inspire your men to great deeds. However, it hasn't come to it yet.' He pointed up to the sky, covered with the thinnest layer of cloud. 'When we see the new moon, then we will doctor the men for battle. Until then, keep them in readiness. To your stations, eat and drink your fill, and try to get some rest.'

But no one slept. How could they? With the enemy so close – just beyond the Nquthu plateau, an hour's march away at the most – they were wound up as tight as drums. Some used *gwai*, ground-up hemp, to calm them. They filled the time discussing the forthcoming battle, the deeds of valour they would perform. The company commanders encouraged the competitive boasting. It distracted them from any misgivings they might be feeling. The entire army was bivouacked in the valley, floor and sides teeming with warriors, all ranged according to their regiment. Even the herdboys were included. Shikashika and Maweni sat close to Mehlokazulu's company, spellbound by the tales of heroism, past and future.

Their commander was away from his men. He and three senior iNgobamakhosi were on a reconnaissance mission at the highest point of the iNyoni ridge. Though they had a direct view into the British camp, they could see very little. Clouds covered the sky, blotting out what light the stars provided, so they had to rely on their hearing. In the middle of the night, when it was pitch black, they were alerted to the movement of horses, saddles creaking and tack clinking. The stillness of the night amplified the sounds, bringing them very close. However, as their eyes were unable to confirm what they could hear, they ignored it.

As the approaching dawn lightened the sky, the camp started to wake. Mehlokazulu saw soldiers emerge from their tents and attend to their breakfasts. Auxiliaries brought the oxen down from the pasture at the rear of the tents. Others prepared the harnesses, ready to yoke the oxen to the wagons. He concluded they'd be heading down to bring up more supplies.

Just before sunrise, a dense fog collected by the stream. It billowed up and enveloped the whole valley. Visibility deteriorated rapidly. The lucky warriors who had managed to sleep started to stir, stretching muscles seized by cold and discomfort. Others, sleep deprived, revived themselves in the stream, plunging their bodies into the cold water. They moved through the fog like ghostly apparitions.

Mehlokazulu's recce party returned to camp and immediately reported to the generals. 'Nothing unusual from what we could see,' he said.

Ntshingwayo folded his arms. 'So, we wait. In the meantime, send for the *iziNduna*. We should update them.' He dispatched messengers through the camp.

Mavumengwana addressed the assembled officers, 'Ntshingwayo and I have discussed last night's arguments. We're aware of the consensus among you, so…' He paused for effect. 'We've decided to mobilise first thing tomorrow morning.'

The announcement prompted angry mutterings. That would mean another day and night spent in the open.

'Yes, we know how impatient you are to engage, but think of it as an opportunity for the men to build up their strength.

We've sent out foragers to collect meat and mealies, so the men will start the day with a good meal.'

The dissenters calmed down.

'Now, I come to the battle order. We may have to revise this later today, but the following is how the *amabutho* will engage. The "horns" will be in the same formation as on the march and with the same leadership. The "chest" will comprise the uMbonambi and the uKhandempemvu. And certain *amabutho* will be held in reserve: specifically, the iNdlondlo, the iNdluyengwe, the uDloko and the uThulwana–'

Qhude of the uThulwana leapt up. 'Why us? We've earned the right to fight.'

Ntshingwayo shouted him down. 'You'll obey the order or face the consequences.'

Scowling, Qhude resumed his seat.

Nothing pleased Mehlokazulu more than seeing his enemy slapped down. His hostility to the uThulwana still rankled. Too many of his comrades had lost their lives in the first fruits battle for him to forget – or forgive.

A crackle of distant shots brought the officers to their feet. They listened, trying to gauge its direction. It seemed to be from above them, not from iSandlwana. Whatever it was, it needed to be investigated. Some broke the circle and moved to higher ground.

Mehlokazulu checked on his men. There was no reaction. *Why would there be*, he told himself. The iNgobamakhosi were well disciplined; they obeyed orders. They'd been told there would be no action today, thus assumed the shots were not their concern.

Higher up the valley, it was a different story. Because the *amabutho* were spread throughout the twisting Ngwebeni gorge, they had no direct line of sight of each other. On hearing the shots, the uKhandempemvu assumed one of their rivals were already engaged. Not to be outdone, they ran to the valley head, weapons at the ready, which in turn encouraged the uNokhenke to join them. In vain their officers tried to hold them back. Four thousand warriors streamed onto level ground and across the plateau towards iSandlwana. The initial headlong rush faltered as they realised it was a false alarm. Word passed down the line and they stopped, bewildered. They saw that no one had followed; they were on their own. Another volley of shots came from a different direction. Anxious to restore some discipline, their officers encouraged them back to the bivouac. Their kneejerk reaction had already compromised the element of surprise on which Ntshingwayo's strategy depended.

As the uKhandempemvu and uNokhenke slunk back to their stations, jeers from rival regiments accompanied them. Their impulsive behaviour had upset the entire army's composure. Warriors were now on edge, keyed up but uncertain when they would have to fight.

It was still early. Most had no food in their bellies, which increased their agitation. But the foragers Ntshingwayo had sent out started to appear laden with meat and mealies collected from neighbouring fields and farmsteads. As the warriors wolfed down their breakfast, a sense of order was restored.

A new volley of shots rang out, this time very close. From the high ground across the width of the valley, two British cavalry troops fired into the *amabutho*. The effect was instant. The regiments nearest the head of the valley – the uKhandempemvu and the uNokhenke, smarting from their earlier humiliation – immediately swarmed up the hillside, a dense mass of warriors shouting their battle cries and brandishing their weapons. Some returned fire with their muzzle-loaders, missing by a wide margin.

The excitement spread like wildfire. The iNgobamakhosi, a quarter of a mile deeper into the valley, reacted a split second later. A shout went up, 'This is the king's day!' Snatching up their weapons, the warriors ran forward. This was no false alarm. This time, they were going into battle. Soon, the whole hillside streamed with long lines of men.

Ntshingwayo and Mavumengwana tried to maintain order. 'Wait for your officers! Keep your formation!' They might just as well have ordered the river to flow uphill.

Not all the *amabutho* committed themselves in those first few heady moments. Those bivouacked furthest away – the older regiments designated as the "reserve" – remained seated as their younger counterparts swarmed forward.

Qhude took matters into his own hands. 'I'm not sitting here while the younger regiments seize all the glory.' He goaded his fellow uThulwana, 'Are you cowards, or are you with me?' A hundred and fifty of them followed the stampede to iSandlwana.

The herdboys, who had spent the night with the older warriors, were on the horns of a dilemma. They had received no specific orders. And, as the warriors grabbed their weapons, they were ignored, abandoned in the general rush. They didn't even have time to wish them a safe return. Should they wait in the valley for the men to return? Or retrace their steps to oNdini?

Maweni didn't hesitate. As the warriors disappeared over the ridge, he followed. Shikshika called after him, 'You'll get us into trouble.'

'Do what you like,' Maweni shouted back. 'I'm not going to miss this.'

TWENTY-FIVE

iSandlwana

With his men stretched out in a line on either side of him, Mehlokazulu climbed at an easy pace. Once again, nervous energy surged through him. His heart pounded, not with fear but the desire to shed blood. He shivered at the prospect of plunging his spear into his enemy's soft belly, imagining the death rattle and the eyes clouding over in death. No sensation came close, even making love. There was no greater intimacy than taking another man's life. He was invincible. And he knew his battle-hardened men felt the same. It was a foregone conclusion they would carry the day.

Reaching the highest point on the Nquthu plateau, the *iviyo* paused. Thousands of warriors milled in confusion while their commanders reorganised them into their battle formations. They ran among them barking orders and waving in the direction they wanted them to redeploy. The sheer numbers involved made their task particularly difficult. When they'd poured out of the valley, the regiments had become displaced – right and left "horns" reversed and regiments from the "chest" out on the flanks.

That they imposed order so quickly was a measure of their skill and authority. Soon the regiments were in their correct positions and stood in line to receive the all-important *muthi*. Some took the opportunity to snort quantities of *gwai* from their snuff horns. Fired up and "doctored", they were ready for battle.

Two hundred yards away, redcoat horsemen dismounted and watched with appalled fascination.

The *impi* began a low-pitched hum, like bees about to swarm. The mounted *iziNduna* in the "chest" signalled the warriors on the furthest extremities to advance. Shields held aloft, the "horns" moved forward.

The kneeling redcoats levelled their carbines and puffs of smoke appeared, followed seconds later by the crack of the gunfire echoing across the hillside. Two bullets found their mark in the uKhandempemvu "chest" – superficial wounds to the shoulder and thigh. Other rounds ricochetted harmlessly off rocks. Remounting, the redcoats spurred their horses and retreated.

Mehlokazulu unshouldered the Martini-Henry, excited to be using it for the first time in earnest. Silently dedicating the shot to Cetshwayo, he took careful aim and loosed off the round, watching with satisfaction as his target tumbled off his horse. His comrades cheered. He set off again, covering the ground in an easy, methodical stride. To his left, the younger Uve broke into a trot. Being the youngest and fittest, they and their uDududu counterparts on the right had been chosen to cover the greater distances required of the flanking regiments.

At the far end of the plateau the land dropped steeply away revealing iSandlwana looking for all the world like a massive sleeping beast. The *impi* advanced towards the escarpment bringing into view the British force deployed across it.

To his right, Mehlokazulu watched the formations of the "chest" moving steadily forward and, in the far distance, the long straggling line of the uDududu right "horn" disappearing over the ridge. A tide of warriors swept over the landscape, each man with the shared purpose of *eating up the enemy* and driving it across the Mzinyathi. But gaps started to appear in the Zulu ranks. The retreating soldiers stopped every so often to fire into the advancing Zulu "chest". Although three hundred yards away, they achieved some success.

uSuthu! uSuthu! uSuthu! The battle cry reached the herdboys from their position high above the Ngwebeni valley. The warriors were so far away they looked like soldier ants marching over the grassland, but the sound of their massed voices made them seem so much closer. Maweni was so excited he couldn't contain himself. 'I want to be with them,' he said. 'Imagine what it's like.'

'To be hit by a bullet?'

Maweni clicked his teeth with disdain. 'You'll never be a warrior. You'll spend the rest of your days looking after cattle.'

'At least I'll have some days to spend.'

'Coward.'

'Maybe. But not stupid.'

Mehlokazulu led his *iviyo* up and over the iNyoni ridge. iSandlwana was now in direct line of sight. In the distance a detachment of British cavalry was visible – a hundred horsemen wearing khaki tunics. At their head was an officer distinguished by heavy side-whiskers and moustaches, riding with one arm strapped across his chest. They followed the course of a riverbed rising towards higher ground. Mehlokazulu noticed the men in the khaki uniforms were all black Africans. 'Sotho scum,' he sneered. 'We'll enjoy making your blood run.'

A movement in his peripheral vision made him turn. Youths from the uVe streamed off the ridge and headed towards the horsemen. Among them were Qhude and his uThulwana. Mehlokazulu's rage bubbled up. This was a direct provocation; he couldn't allow Qhude to attack the enemy first. Choosing the quickest route – even though it meant crossing ground broken by dried up streams – he sprinted towards the cavalry. His men followed but were more cautious in picking their way through the broken terrain.

A loud unearthly noise screamed over their heads, followed by a shower of sparks. Instinctively dropping to the ground, they took cover in the long grass. Another rocket, blown off course, squealed past them, shedding burning fuel over one of the warriors. Flailing, he managed to beat the flames off his skin and sustained only superficial burns. They waited until the danger was past, then continued their race across the plain.

Qhude and the uVe made rapid progress along the Nxibongo stream, but were no match for Mehlokazulu and his iNgobamakhosi, who were as sure-footed as mountain goats. They were scarcely eight hundred yards away when a volley of shots made them dive for cover. They sheltered behind the rocks as bullets pinged around them. When the firing stopped, the horsemen remounted and headed back towards the camp, with Mehlokazulu and his men behind them.

Every twenty yards, the same pattern repeated itself – a volley of shots and then another retreat. But as each manoeuvre required time to perform, the distance between horsemen and their pursuers shortened, and in inverse proportion, the accuracy of shots increased. Casualties began to appear among the uVe.

From a safe position behind a boulder, Mehlokazulu saw a young lad take a bullet full in the face, the impact carrying away his jaw and leaving his tongue and throat exposed. The boy sank to his knees, eyes wide with shock and pain.

The horsemen veered right towards the rocket emplacement. Making the necessary adjustment, Mehlokazulu crossed the plain towards a conical hill named amaTutshane. Qhude's uThulwana and the uVe followed, but at half a mile distance.

The higher ground allowed Mehlokazulu and his *iviyo* to see the main body of the iNgobamakhosi overwhelm the soldiers manning the rocket battery. Mules used to transport the rocket launchers stampeded from the marauding warriors, and blue-coated auxiliaries retreated as fast as they could. The commanding officer tried to rally his troops from horseback, but a well-aimed shot pitched him from his saddle. The iNgobamakhosi gave no quarter to the survivors sheltering in a ravine. Shots from both sides crackled in the still morning air. A lone voice cut through the rifle and musket fire, mocking the paltry effect of the rockets compared with the overwhelming force of the amaZulu. It was taken up by all three thousand iNgobamakhosi. *Lightning, lightning of heaven, it glitters and shines. The sun of the amaZulu, it consumes all.*

Mehlokazulu repeated it to encourage his men. Now chanting their new battle cry, they set off again.

From their vantage point, Maweni and Shikashika had a clear view of the skirmishing. They saw the *impi*'s left and right flanks fanning across the plain and the main body marching towards the mounted British soldiers.

Acrid clouds of gun smoke drifted past, which intermittently obscured their field of view, but they could plainly see that the *amabutho* were taking casualties. Warriors dropped out of the battle formation. The distance made it difficult to understand that men were dying in front of them, that the high-velocity bullets were shattering bodies, tearing off limbs and blowing skulls into pieces. Their instinct for self-preservation rooted them to the spot. While bullets were flying, it seemed foolish to risk getting any closer. Even so, Maweni was itching to move forward. Shikashika's eyes were on what was happening behind them.

Deep in the Ngwebeni valley, still sheltered in the lee of the steep slope, the senior *amabutho* sat with their backs to the hillside, waiting patiently for their orders. Much nearer was a group of officers on horseback – including Ntshingwayo and Mavumengwana – on their way up to the ridge. They were nearly at the top.

Grabbing Maweni's arm, Shikashika pulled him down. They pressed themselves to the ground, holding their breath as the horses passed.

From a position close by, the general staff dismounted and tethered their mounts. Then they set up a command post to monitor the battle.

Shikashika and Maweni could not have been better placed. Through a cleft in the rocks, they saw the generals watching through binoculars.

Ntshingwayo spoke. 'There, the uDududu are on their way,' then swung the binoculars to the British forces in the centre, 'and haven't been spotted yet.' The uDuduDu accelerated in a wide arc towards the high ground of Mkwene.

Heavy casualties were being inflicted on the "chest". Mavumengwana watched with increasing alarm. 'The uKhandempemvu are being cut to ribbons. We should send reinforcements.'

Ntshingwayo shook his head. 'A temporary setback. Their fortunes will change once the "horns" circle around. We are many and the *abelungu* are few.'

From their hiding place, Maweni nudged Shikashika. The excitement was almost too much.

Reaching the foot of amaTutshane, Mehlokazulu and his men stopped to catch their breath, gulping air into their tortured lungs. Sweat poured off their naked chests. A combination of their exertions and the hot summer sun now at its midday zenith had left them severely dehydrated. With his tongue sticking to the roof of his mouth, Mehlokazulu drank greedily from his water gourd. Then checked on his men. Apart from one, who'd tripped on a rock by the Nxibongo stream and sprained his ankle, they had survived unscathed.

The fighting on the extreme right, where the other "horn" was moving into position, was obscured by the lie of the land, but they could clearly hear the gunfire.

Boom! Boom! A new sound started up – loud explosions one after another at ninety second intervals. 'That must be the cannon the scouts saw,' Mehlokazulu said. Though they couldn't see the guns, they certainly saw their effects. Shells burst on their immediate right, throwing clods of earth high in the air. None of them landed anywhere near the Zulu lines. 'Haven't found the range yet,' he added. 'But the uKhandempemvu will know it once they do. They must find a way to neutralise them.' He drew attention to another sound. 'Listen.' Above the crackle of small arms and the intermittent reports of the seven-pounders came the rhythmic chanting of the uKhandempemvu. He nodded with grim satisfaction. 'Still in good voice. Right, got your breath back?'

Leading off, he headed towards the main body of iNgobamakhosi, which had collected in a direct line to the encampment. To their right, the uMbonambi were also massing.

The grey mass of iSandlwana rose behind the tents. The ground was strewn with boulders dislodged from the high cliffs above. Streams of water pouring off the slopes had scoured *dongas* (deep ravines), which provided cover for the retreating British from where they discharged volleys of rifle fire into the Zulu "chest". Because it hadn't yet come within range of the guns it was a waste of shot.

Mehlokazulu fizzed with anticipation. They were less than a mile from their objective; it wouldn't be long before they were washing their spears. He switched his attention to the left. The one-armed officer and his hundred horsemen appeared from behind amaTutshane. Three thousand uVe boys, fuelled by blood lust, threatened to overwhelm them. Suddenly, the horsemen disappeared into a dry riverbed, and moments later a hail of gunfire cut swathes through the ranks of the young warriors.

The ground around the donga was flat, devoid of dips and gullies. Apart from long grass, parched and withered by the sun, it offered precious little cover. The British on the other hand had the ravine sides to protect them. Having driven their horses into the gully, forcing them onto their bellies to keep them out of the firing line, the soldiers were spaced in a wide arc stretching over a hundred yards: a hundred marksmen with superior weapons and ammunition to spare.

The uVe youths were totally unprepared for the ferocity of the onslaught. This was their first experience of war and the effect on their morale was devastating. Their trust in the power of *muthi* to deflect the bullets was instantly destroyed. Those with enough sense prostrated themselves, grovelling in the dirt as the bullets whizzed around them. Those left standing were shot to pieces, limbs flying in every direction. Attempts to rush the British position were quickly repulsed – any youth brave, or foolhardy, enough to run at the guns was cut down. Three hundred were slaughtered in the first volley. Spattered with the brains and blood of their comrades, the survivors crawled on their bellies to the long grass. There at least they wouldn't present a target.

Mehlokazulu could see what the consequence would be. If the left horn was held up, the whole battle plan would fail. It was vital they clear the way so they could surround the camp. If they didn't, the *abelungu* would have an escape route.

'Who's with me?' he shouted, and encouraging them with the iNgobamakhosi battle cry, made a beeline for the riverbed. His mind worked overtime. The uVe had to be rallied behind a definite strategy with officers to carry it out. But where were they? Where indeed were Qhude and his uThulwana? This was when a veteran's experience was needed.

He signalled his men to crouch. So far, surprise was on their side: the British hadn't yet seen them. Maybe he could lead a flanking movement and get in behind them.

The British guns blazed away. Watching the pattern of fire, he realised there was a weakness he could exploit: as each soldier popped up above the parapet to take aim, his red hatband presented a perfect target. But there was a more immediate problem: the British now had their range. Shots whizzed past. The warrior nearest him writhed on the ground, clutching a shattered collarbone. They couldn't stay where they were.

Keeping low, he zigzagged towards the donga, making it more difficult for the marksmen to draw a bead. Spread out on either side, the *iviyo* followed. Spaces started to appear in their line, but they pressed on regardless. Within fifty yards, thirty out of the fifty who had started at the foot of amaTutshane were out of action, some killed outright, some with crippling injuries.

Mehlokazulu reached the uVe, crawling forward on his hands and knees, past corpses with their heads blown apart, blood and brains congealing in the heat; past youngsters lying face up, eyes staring sightlessly at the sun; torsos with arms ripped away; a tangle of dismembered limbs littering the grassland. He came across a boy sat bent forward, hands pressing into the wound in his belly trying to staunch the blood pouring between his fingers, a bewildered look in his eyes. Mehlokazulu stroked his neck and murmured soothing words.

A cold fury seized him. He wanted revenge. Moving forward, he peered through the long grass at the riverbed. Here and there the red hatbands popped up. Unshouldering his Martini-Henry, he waited, finger tightening on the trigger. Suddenly he had a target. He fired, and the head disintegrated in a bloody mess.

Rolling to another position, he found himself next to his mortal enemy. Qhude was still with the uVe and in the same predicament – adversity made strange bedfellows. They stared at each other as bullets whined and whistled overhead.

Qhude shouted over the din, 'What do you suggest?'

It was obvious they must find a way out of this death trap. Men were dying with increasing frequency.

'We won't get far pinned down like this,' Mehlokazulu answered. 'If we can work our way to the left, there's some lower ground that will give us protection.'

'Lead the way then.' Qhude said.

Mehlokazulu looked at him twice. Had he misheard? Of all people Qhude was the last he expected to defer to him. He gave an instruction to be passed on through the ranks of the uVe. 'Do not, repeat, do not, advance towards the guns. Use whatever cover you can to retreat. We'll regroup on the left.' Hitching his shield over his back, he scrambled through the tall grass.

The uVe survivors and his remaining men followed. The gunfire continued, targeting any disturbance in the vegetation, and causing more casualties. Those who successfully covered the hundred yards gathered around Mehlokazulu. A head count confirmed what Mehlokazulu suspected – most of the uVe officers were missing, mown down in the first attack on the British position. Leaderless and traumatised by what they'd just experienced, the boys needed reassurance.

'You are all *abaqawe*,' Mehlokazulu told them. 'That was as fierce as I've ever seen it. The king will reward you for your courage. When you return to oNdini you will carve your heroes' necklace.'

The generals moved their command post. After the initial skirmishing and the redcoat retreat from the Nquthu plateau, they galloped to a vantage point beside the Mkwene rocky outcrop around which the uDududu right "horn" had pivoted. On the edge of this sheer cliff face they watched events unfold.

Through the pall of gun-smoke, they had a clear sight of the uKhandempemvu below. The "chest" was in trouble. Mehlokazulu's assumption that the artillery fire would hinder their progress was correct. Shell after shell burst among them as they crouched for cover in the network of gullies and ravines at the foot of the escarpment.

Voicing his concerns out loud, Ntshingwayo remarked, 'Brave though they are, they need encouragement. If the "chest" doesn't advance there'll be little chance of success.'

One of the staff officers, an uKhandempemvu commander, took the hint. Conspicuous in his ceremonial regalia, he scrambled down the cliff and joined his embattled regiment. Disregarding the bullets flying around him, he strode up and down before them, his voice carrying above the noise of the gunfire: 'Cetshwayo, the little branch of leaves that extinguishes the great fire kindled by the white men, gave no such order as this.'

His words had a dramatic effect. To a man, the uKhandempemvu left their hiding places and rushed forward, shields held high, apparently contemptuous of the rifle fire. The dead soon piled up, but the charge proved irresistible. A notable casualty was the officer who had shamed them. Continuing their attack, his warriors streamed past his dead body.

When the danger of discovery passed, the herdboys left their hiding place above Ngwebeni and took the route of the left "horn". Determined to get close to the action, Maweni ran as fast as his legs would carry him.

Reluctantly Shikashika kept him company, complaining all the while, 'You're out of your mind. What will you use to defend yourself? Your cattle stick?'

Maweni's mind was on one thing only, ignoring the fact that they were heading, completely defenceless, directly towards a battlefield.

On the point of launching an attack, Mehlokazulu noticed warriors from the uMbonambi, gripping their distinctive black and white shields, assembling in an abandoned *umuZi* on the righthand side. With them was a herd of cattle. The noise of the guns made the animals mad with fear. Bellowing loudly, they jostled each other looking for a way to escape. The heavier beasts lent their weight against the sturdy thorn bush enclosure testing for weaknesses. Given half a chance they'd stampede.

He indicated them to his men, 'Over there, see – a pincer movement from the uMbonambi. We'll wait until they make their move.'

As though on cue, and as if anticipating the danger to the one-armed officer and his cavalry, the British artillery began a bombardment. Both guns fired shrapnel shells, which burst in the ranks of the uMbonambi, causing devastation. Shards of red-hot metal tore through them, decapitating some, eviscerating others. The shrapnel scythed into the cattle, turning the enclosure into an abattoir. The barrage, however, was only temporary, because the guns were suddenly deployed to forestall the uKhandempemvu advance.

The uMbonambi took full advantage to mount their attack, effectively separating the cavalry in the ravine from the rest of the British force. Two battles now raged and, with the bulk of British fire directed towards the Zulu "chest", the uMbonambi could see an open field directly towards the tents. They would receive the accolade of being the first in the camp.

Mehlokazulu gave the order and deployed his warriors in an ever-decreasing arc, tightening towards the back of the ravine. The fusillades became less frequent as ammunition reserves started to dwindle. The young warriors of the uVe, with their courage restored, grew bolder and pushed forward.

Suddenly, horsemen exploded out of the ravine, galloping hell-for-leather away from the oncoming warriors and taking them by surprise. Mehlokazulu dropped to one knee and took careful aim. He picked off one of the horsemen, the shot throwing the man out of his saddle. With his boot trapped in the stirrup, the man was dragged along the riverbed, his head bumping over the rocks. Another horseman fell in the same way. The one-armed officer displayed considerable horsemanship, using his knees to control his mount while he blazed away with his handgun.

Mehlokazulu and the uVe also had a clear route toward the tents.

Struggling to the top of the amaTutshane hill, Maweni and Shikashika collapsed. They'd been running hard for over twenty minutes and needed to get their breath back. Gulping air into their lungs, they stared at the scene below. It was beyond anything they could have imagined. Thick white clouds of gunsmoke cleared periodically to allow glimpses of the horror. The uMbonambi had released the cattle and the maddened beasts stampeded towards the camp, making short shrift of anyone in their way. Several soldiers in blue tunics were tossed high in the air, impaled on the sharp horns. Behind them the warriors raced forward, their stabbing spears flashing in the sun. They quickly outran the stragglers, knots of warriors gathering round each soldier hacking and thrusting with their *amaklwa*. The screams of the dying men, the bellowing of the frantic beasts and the continuing volleys of gunfire combined to create a deafening noise. The air reeked with the smell of cordite. The boys gaped in reaction to what they were seeing.

Through the din they could hear the incongruous sound of a British bugler sounding the retreat. Miraculously, the guns stopped firing. The British troops – redcoats and auxiliaries in blue tunics alike – began to withdraw. The respite was temporary, however. The artillery pieces opened up again to block the renewed attack from the "chest". Several rounds of grapeshot were fired into the oncoming uKhamdempemvu. Thirty men were felled by each round and gaps appeared in their formation. From Maweni and Shikashika's perspective it was as though an unseen presence had thrown a ball into skittles, knocking them over. But the advance remained unchecked as warriors surged over their fallen comrades.

The "chest" now threatened to overwhelm the guns. Suddenly, mules were brought forward and harnessed to the gun carriages. The herdboys strained to see through the thick smoke. The gunners desperately laid on their whips to encourage the mules to pull the guns clear. Eventually the limbers bumped their way across the rough terrain, the wheels bouncing over the rocks. But it was too late. They were quickly overrun. Men and animals disappeared under an avalanche of warriors.

Mehlokazulu ran towards the camp, his mind occupied by a single purpose: to kill as many of the enemy as he could. During the slaughter of the uVe, he had felt a crippling impotence. Boys were dying in their hundreds, and he was powerless to prevent it. From his own *iviyo*, he alone had survived. Now the tables were turned. The white man was in full flight and the *amabutho* had the upper hand.

Ahead of him, the uMbonambi followed the frenzied stampede of the cattle and reached the tents. A line of kneeling redcoats fired a volley into them, then tried desperately to reload. There was no time. The cattle overran them, scattering soldiers in every direction. The uMbonambi used the confusion to isolate individuals and engaged them in hand-to-hand combat.

Initially the soldiers had the advantage. The bayonets attached to their rifles provided a longer reach than the stabbing spears. Some warriors learned the hard way, finding themselves pierced through the throat or chest. Others adopted a different tactic. Several of them surrounded each soldier. One feinted with his spear, deflecting the bayonet's parry on his shield, while the others slipped under his guard and stabbed him in the side. They then took collective responsibility for the death by taking turns to finish him off. As a precaution against the dead man haunting them, they released his spirit by ripping open his belly and disembowelling him. Many soldiers died in this way, and very soon the ground became slippery with blood and spilled intestines.

Stampeding beasts tangled themselves in the tents' guy-ropes, and further increased their panic by tearing out the pegs and wrapping themselves in the canvas. They charged through the camp, dragging tents, and overturning the soldiers' personal kit. They created havoc in the mess-tent, charging this way and that, upsetting food-stores and upending billycans and cooking pots.

Mehlokazulu's quarry was the one-armed officer responsible for the carnage at the Ngoyane ravine. He had a score to settle and the deaths of his comrades to avenge. It was a personal matter. As to weapons, he realised his rifle was redundant now – any fighting would be with his *iklwa*. He set down the precious Martini Henry and marked the spot. If he survived, he'd return for it once victory was secured.

In the tangled mass of struggling bodies – in which first uMbonambi warriors, then uKhandempemvu, grappled with the redcoats, twisting and turning, pushing and pulling, wounded men falling and being trampled underfoot, blood and guts spilling out of the terrible wounds – it was hard to distinguish any single individual. But through the mêlée, Mehlokazulu caught sight of the one-armed officer leading a group of horsemen. Cavalry swords drawn, they cleared a path through the camp, slashing this way and that, cutting down the guy-ropes and freeing the obstacles to allow the soldiers in the front line to retreat. Their direction was the track leading down to the river Mzinyathi. It was a measure of British desperation. Escape seemed their only option.

Still taking their lead from Mehlokazulu, the uVe followed as he circled around to attack the officer from the side. As they closed in, they were aware of warriors from the right "horn" – the uDududu and Nokhenke – pouring into the camp from the opposite direction.

Pressed on both sides, the one-handed officer and his men dismounted and drove their horses directly towards the warriors advancing on them. The uDududu ranks opened to avoid injury from their hooves but the warriors slashed at them as they passed, severing tendons in their legs, bringing them down. They slaughtered them as they fell, driving their spears into their bellies. The screams of the stricken animals now joined those of the dying men on the field.

The horsemen formed a square around the one-armed officer, standing back-to-back, pistols and swords in their hands.

At that moment, an unearthly transformation occurred, as though a celestial hand had drawn a curtain. Colour drained away and a dark shadow passed over the landscape. The change happened gradually and imperceptibly. Initially, the combatants refused to acknowledge it and continued their bloody struggles.

Soon the dimming of the light became so obvious it could not be ignored. Feeling the effect of the cooling on his skin, Mehlokazulu looked up at the sky. Shading his eyes against the glare, he had the distinct impression the sun was disappearing. He checked on his men. They stood open-mouthed. Nothing in their experience had prepared them for this.

TWENTY-SIX

oNdini

Nomguqo sat beside the bathing-spot used by the royal wives, attending Nomvimbi while she performed her ablutions. The great wife was submerged, her arms cradling her baby as she floated her on the water. The toddler gurgled with pleasure, vigorously splashing her arms and legs.

Prince Dinuzulu dangled his feet in the water next to Nomguqo. The first to notice the fading light, he screwed his fists into his eyes to check he wasn't imagining it. No, it was real enough. 'Why is it so dark?' he asked.

Preoccupied with her own concerns, specifically for Shikashika's safety, Nomguqo was jolted back to the present. She looked up. Dinuzulu was right. The light was fading. She stood, scanning the sky. There were no clouds to explain what was happening.

It grew increasingly darker.

By squinting and using her peripheral vision, Nomguqo sensed what was happening. She instinctively knew she would damage her eyes if she looked at it directly, but she had the impression that the great orb was missing a large chunk, as though a giant had bitten into it.

Nomvimbi also noticed the strange effect. Pulling the baby out of the water, she waded to the bank. 'What's happening?' she said, offering the baby to Nomguqo so she could climb up the bank.

The little princess began to grizzle because her fun had been interrupted. Soon the protests turned into full-blown wails.

Nomguqo quelled her own fear to avoid panicking the children, stroking the baby's head, and shushing her. But Besiyile would not be comforted.

The great wife took her back, put her to the breast, and the howls instantly subsided into a contented sucking.

An unnerving stillness settled over them. Apart from the splashing of the river breaking over distant stones, there was total silence. No birdsong. No sound from the insects. Grasshoppers stopped their sawing, bees their buzzing, as if responding to a supernatural order to suspend all activity.

Dinuzulu's voice broke the silence. 'I'm frightened.' Nomguqo squeezed his hand.

'Don't be,' her mother reassured him. 'There's bound to be an explanation. I'm sure Dlephu Ndlovu and the *iziNgoma* will know why it's happening.'

But Dlephu Ndlovu was as much in the dark – literally – as everyone else. He searched his memory for the last time this had happened. The sun had dimmed once before when he was boy, but not on this scale. As the king's *iNgoma* he knew he would be expected to find a reason for the strange phenomenon. All celestial movements, the phases of sun and moon, might be expressions of *umnyama*. But with the fate of the kingdom in the balance, he was duty bound to find an interpretation that favoured the king's fortunes.

Hurrying around to Cetshwayo's quarters, he found the king outside the *eNkatheni* staring up at the sky. Some of his wives and his father Mpande's widows were with him, tongues clicking with alarm. Dlephu presented himself.

'Well?' Cetshwayo demanded.

'Ndabezitha, you'll observe that the brightness of the sun has dimmed and is taking all the colour from the land.'

'Yes,' the king replied testily, 'tell me something I don't know.'

'Ndabezitha, this is a *good* omen,' said Dlephu. 'The light is fading for the *abelungu* who dared to invade Your Majesty's kingdom.'

'Yes, but it is fading for us, too,' the king countered.

Dlephu was temporarily stumped. Then his bloodshot eyes blinked as he found a formula to confound the sceptics. 'Your Majesty's *amabutho* are illuminated by the righteousness of their cause. They have no need of the sun's rays to guide their weapons. Even in the darkest hour they will find their target.'

The king mulled this over, apparently persuaded by the explanation. 'So, when the light returns, we'll know that we're victorious?'

Dlephu's lips stretched in a toothless grin. 'Exactly so, Ndabezitha.'

'In which case, we must assist our warriors in every way we can. We must strengthen their resolve by taking our place on the *inkatha*.'

The wives and widows trilled their approval.

Cetshwayo laid his hand on Dlephu's bony shoulder. 'You will accompany me.'

'It will be my honour, Ndabezitha.'

The darkness deepened. At the river, the great wife became increasingly anxious. Feeling exposed to all manner of supernatural forces, she gathered her children together and, as quickly as her bulk would allow, hurried towards the *umuZi*.

Clenching Dinuzulu's hand, Nomguqo led the way. The path wound through maize fields, the dried stalks still standing after the harvest. Half hidden among them, a white face was watching. Her stomach turned over in shock. Was her perception starting to warp? Was it a trick of the fading light or a product of her imagination? She blinked to make sure she wasn't seeing things. But there was another one. And another. On either side of the path, bearded white faces stared out at her. All versions of the same face. Expressionless, the eyes followed her as she ran.

Her fear mounted. Was this really happening? Were there actual men standing in the maize fields? It contradicted the rules of nature. Dinuzulu couldn't see them, Nomguqo had already checked. *No*, Nomguqo thought. *It's me; I'm losing my mind.* Her chest was suddenly constricted by an asthma attack. She stopped, fighting for breath. Dinuzulu peered at her, concerned.

Nomvimbi, also out of breath but with the effort of carrying the baby, followed up. 'What's wrong? Why have you stopped?'

'My breathing…' Nomguqo wheezed. 'Please… just leave me. Take the prince… I'll come in a minute…'

Nomvimbi didn't hesitate. Grabbing Dinuzulu, she ushered him up the track. 'I'll send someone for you,' she called back.

Nomguqo closed her eyes. She'd experienced enough of these attacks to know what steps to take. Forcing her shoulders down, she tried to calm herself. She knew the best antidote was relaxation. She sat on her heels in the middle of the path and concentrated. Her being alone helped – she didn't need to worry about other people worrying. Filling her lungs was all that mattered. Sitting with eyes firmly shut, she focused on the pattern of her breathing. Little by little she relaxed and settled into a more regular rhythm.

The concentrated effort induced in her a state akin to dreaming, and what she "saw" in those few moments left her in a state of even greater terror.

Slowed down so she could see every detail, Maweni ran from his hiding-place at the bottom of the iNyoni escarpment. A shell exploded at his feet, blowing his body into pieces.

Shikashika's face contorted in a scream as he watched from behind a parapet. The blast was deflected by the stone wall, but razor-sharp shell fragments showered over him.

Caught out in the open, Maweni took the full force of the explosion. Detached from his body, his head tumbled through the air.

Shikashika's eyes widened with horror as it landed as his feet.

'Are you alright?'

Immediately recognising Sixhwethu's voice, Nomguqo kept her eyes tight shut, profoundly shaken by what she had just witnessed. How could she admit to Sixhwethu that the boy she had set her heart on would never return from the battlefield? Her vision of Maweni's death was undoubtedly a premonition. The detail made her suspect it might be prophetic. It was as though she had been there as it happened.

Sixhwethu said, 'The great wife sent me to check on you.'

Blinking, Nomguqo immediately shaded her eyes. Now that the shadow had passed, the sun's glare was blinding.

'Come on, get up.'

It took a while for her eyes to adjust, which gave her an opportunity to consider what to do next. What was to be gained by telling Sixhwethu? If she confessed to "seeing" Maweni's death, it was possible she would be denounced as a witch, and that had terrifying consequences. Deciding to stay silent, she allowed Sixhwethu to help her up. 'I'm fine now,' she said. 'I just panicked when it went dark.'

'Well, I thought it was the end of the world,' said Sixhethu. 'What do you think it meant?'

Nomguqo shook her head, banishing the horrifying image in her mind's eye. 'No idea. It better not happen again.'

TWENTY-SEVEN

iSandlwana

Shikashika trembled uncontrollably. What he had just witnessed was beyond the realm of nightmares. He had no way of knowing it, but it was exactly what Nomguqo had seen. Every detail, including the decapitation. His cousin's head as it tumbled through the air and landed at his feet, eyes open in surprise, would haunt him for the rest of his days.

A battlefield was no place for him. Forcing himself to stop the shaking in his legs, he started to run. He didn't dare look back and focused on closing his ears to the sounds of battle – the crackle of gunfire and screams of wounded men. They and the desire to put as much distance between him and this vision of hell drove him on. It didn't take him long to scramble onto the iNyoni escarpment. Once on flat ground, he didn't stop until he reached oNdini some eight hours later.

The air was thick with dust raised by the feet of the struggling men and the hooves of animals frantically looking for a way to escape.

The one-armed officer stood with the corpses of his men piled high around him. The thirty survivors stood shoulder to shoulder, using every means at their disposal to repel their attackers. Their ammunition was now spent, so they thrust with their bayonets, then reversed their rifles to use as clubs. Some even used their fists.

Taking careful aim with his pistol and making every bullet count, the officer led by example. Hopelessly outnumbered, they were picked off one by one. Eventually, the officer was alone, the hammer of his pistol clicking uselessly against an empty chamber. In desperation, he unsheathed his sword.

Mehlokazulu stepped forward, tripping over the bodies of dead and wounded men – warriors and soldiers alike. The rest of his men held back, giving their commander the honour of finishing him.

Raising his cavalry sword, the officer made his move. Mehlokazulu used his shield to parry the thrust, deflecting the tip upwards, and throwing him off-balance. In the same movement, he lunged with his spear. The blade struck bone and Mehlokazulu withdrew it to make a second pass.

The officer fought to stay upright, his boots sliding over the loose stones. As his torso twisted, the hand of his injured arm tethered in his tunic came free and flopped uselessly by his side. Wounded, though not fatally, he attacked again, gritting his teeth against the pain. This time the sword tip caught in the thick oxhide of the shield and was held fast.

Using all his strength to flip the shield, Mehlokazulu levered the sword from the officer's grasp. His comrades chanted *uSuthu! uSuthu!* as he struck. With great force, he brought the *iklwa* down into the officer's chest, the point entering in the space between the left collarbone and the ribcage. To prevent the spear being ripped from his hand,

Mehlokazulu wrenched it free, gripping the bulbous end of the shaft.

The officer sank to his knees, blood from his punctured lung flooding into his throat. He coughed, an involuntary action to stop him drowning. His head fell forward, exposing his neck and shoulders. Mehlokazulu delivered the deathblow, burying the spear deep in the officer's back. Then stood back, watching the body twitch spasmodically until it was still.

Drivers and cooks – the camp's support staff – streamed towards the track that followed the Manzimnyama stream, which offered an escape route. Waiting for them were transport wagons already yoked to their oxen. An ambulance full of wounded men struggled to make progress with the press of men clogging the path. Pandemonium set in.

Anyone lucky enough to be mounted spurred his horse around the obstruction. The rest were exposed to a new, and even greater, threat. The *impondo zankhomo* was finally completed. The regiments on the right – the iSangqu and the uDududu – joined the battle, attacking from the rear and stabbing at random anything that moved, man and beast alike.

Leaving the rout, Mehlokazulu led his iNgobamakhosi up to high ground to the left of the tents. From here, a deep and wide *donga* led to a tributary of the Mzinyathi. This too had turned into an escape route. Horsemen and foot soldiers poured over the ridge and down the ravine. Normally dry in the summer, late rains had filled the chasm and water cascaded down the rocky hillsides. It was a treacherous place for anyone on foot. For horses it was virtually impassable. Soldiers on horseback dismounted and led their horses carefully down the steep slopes. Despite their precautions, some horses missed their footing and floundered among the rocks, helplessly kicking their broken legs, whinnying in their distress.

Mehlokazulu's instinct was to ensure that no enemy survived. Total domination was the code by which he fought. He gave no quarter, offered no mercy, destroyed everything in his path.

Like mountain goats, he and his men leaped from rock to rock and plunged over the lip of the *donga*, their hardened feet, greater agility, and knowledge of the terrain giving them a huge advantage. They bore down on the fugitives, overwhelming them with their sheer momentum. The soldiers had no ammunition, and therefore offered no resistance beyond their bare hands. They died where they stood.

In the oNdini *umuZi*, quiet expectation replaced the usual chatter and banter. When the sun turned black, Cetshwayo retired to the *eNkatheni*. Throughout the *isiGodlo*, the womenfolk kept their conversation to a whisper and confined their children indoors. While the king was sitting on the sacred coil all measures had to be taken to keep him transmitting the nation's strength and power to the army.

The few men left behind – the royal servants – patrolled, whispering *ungathinti* (do not disturb) to reinforce the message.

The *isiGodlo* girls performed their duties in absolute silence. Assigned her normal task of preparing the royal children's afternoon meal, Nomguqo was out of immediate contact with Sixhwethu. The relief would be only temporary, however. Once messengers arrived with news of the battle and the casualties sustained, Maweni's death would become common knowledge. She was terrified she would be held responsible. Her fear was irrational, she knew, but it didn't stop her believing she had somehow colluded in the boy's death. Was her wish for

Shikashika's safe return attached to a compensatory requirement for Maweni to die? If so, her guilt was undeniable.

'Feeling better now?' Dinuzulu's voice broke into her thoughts. The prince watched her mixing the maize meal into porridge.

'Oh yes, I'm fine.'

'I was frightened when the sun turned black.'

'Yes, so was I.'

Nomvimbi chimed in, 'I think we all were.'

Something else was bothering him. 'Why does your breathing stop like that?' he asked.

'It doesn't stop,' she replied. 'If it did, I'd be dead.'

He thought it over. 'You're not dead.'

'No, because I'm still breathing.'

The syllogism was beyond him, so Dinuzulu changed the subject. 'I want honey with my porridge.'

Cetshwayo's junior wives and Mpande's widows guarded the *eNkatheni* door, making sure he stayed put. Too much was at stake to let the source of supernatural power be diverted. In the heat of the afternoon sun, they wafted their flywhisks to keep away the persistent insects. None of them dared breathe a word.

A loud voice from inside the hut made them jump. The unseen king shouted, 'I can't sit here all day. I need air.'

'But Ndabezitha…' Dlephu Ndlovu protested.

'No "buts". I'm going to stretch my legs.' Cetshwayo emerged, bending his tall frame to exit the narrow doorway. 'I can't stand this any longer. Is there no news?' He took a step forward throwing his arms wide to fill his lungs, the *inhlendla* waving dangerously.

One of Mpande's widows, Nomadada, flinched as the blade

whistled past her head. As though speaking to a naughty child, she commanded, 'Get back inside!'

His head shot around. Who dared to speak to him like that? When he saw who it was, his expression changed. The Queen Mother's word was law. Also, when it came to a fight with his wives, he knew he'd come off second best.

'When there's news we will tell you,' Nomadada said. 'In the meantime, do your duty and resume your seat on the *inkatha*.'

The orgy of killing along the Manzimnyama continued. The stream was choked with the corpses of men and animals, showing the direction the fleeing British troops had taken.

Finally released by their officers, the older *amabutho*, held in reserve in the Ngwebeni valley, joined the butchery. The veterans resented that the younger regiments had taken the glory of the first attack. The iNdlondlo, the iNdluyengwe, the uDloko and the remainder of the uThulwana – those who hadn't joined Qhude – were fresh and eager to prove themselves. At the start, once the main body of the army was engaged, the king's cousin Zibhebhu and Dabulamanzi, Cetshwayo's younger brother, had taken the initiative to move their regiments down to the Mzinyathi, anticipating that any survivors would head for the safety of kwaJim. Their assumption was correct.

Whooping with delight, they formed a gauntlet all the way down to the river, gleefully stabbing anything that moved – men, horses, and mules.

Mehlokazulu, also involved, registered that Qhude had rejoined his regiment, announcing his presence with a bloodcurdling war cry. The frenzied blood lust in his eyes was alarming even for one as battle-hardened as Mehlokazulu.

So far, the action was all on the Zulu side of the river. For the fleeing redcoats, it was a short distance to the safety of

British Natal: merely the width of the river. But the warriors now lining both banks confounded all hopes of staying alive. For those avoiding the spear thrusts, the river presented an equally frightening prospect. Above kwaJim, the water tumbled through narrow chasms, with terrifying drops to the swirling pools that gathered between the waterfalls. Already the pools were full of men and animals drowning in the turbulent water. A couple of tenacious survivors braved the torrent and climbed the steep rocky banks on the far side. Spears and rifle shots struck the rocks around them.

Mehlokazulu paused to watch Qhude take a flying leap across the chasm – he'd found the narrowest, and safest, place to cross. Soon he was joined by scores of warriors to harry those who had managed not to drown.

Above the deafening noise of the surging water and the shrieks of drowning men, Mehlokazulu heard an angry voice.

Vumandaba, the commander of the uKhandempemvu, called for the men to return to Zulu territory. 'Has Cetshwayo told you to cross? We are not invading. We are defending the land of the amaZulu. Come back!'

Ignoring him, uThulwana warriors, combined with other reserve regiments, poured across the river.

For a moment, Mehlokazulu wondered whether his own men would follow suit, but they were too disciplined. They signalled their obedience to the king's instruction by leaning against their shields with their backs to the river. He nodded with satisfaction. Let Qhude and the other hotheads face Cetshwayo's wrath. Surveying the devastation on either side of the stream, he suddenly felt tired. The job was complete. The day was theirs.

He climbed back to the camp. Now the blood had stopped singing in his ears, the power in his muscles had drained and every step was an effort. All he wanted to do was sit.

The devastation took his breath away. While in the thick of the fighting, he hadn't noticed the chaos. Bodies covered every inch of the ground. He had to pick his way carefully to avoid stepping on them. Redcoats and warriors lay together in the embrace of death.

A systematic search for survivors was under way. Groans from the wounded gave away their position, and their agonies were ended with a spear thrust. The *qaqa* ritual was conducted across the whole battlefield, the dead disembowelled to release their spirits.

Finding the practice repugnant, Mehlokazulu's nostrils flared. He acknowledged that it had a hygienic purpose, to prevent the corpses swelling in the heat, but surely the priority was to get them into the ground as quickly as possible. The dead were dead. Let the burial parties take care of them. Everything else was superstitious nonsense.

Wherever a dead soldier was found, he was stripped of his red tunic. Warriors wearing incongruous British uniform swarmed over the camp.

Clouds of flies, ever-faithful attendants of fresh corpses, were already collecting, attracted by the metallic odour of fresh blood and the stink of slashed intestines.

Amid the tangle of ropes and torn canvas Mehlokazulu found a campstool to sit on. Around him warriors rampaged through the wreckage seeking valuables. Only feet away an uMbonambi rifled through the pockets of a dead redcoat. He pulled out a pocket watch and held it up triumphantly.

Younger warriors searched desperately for liquor. Some found bottles of rum and whisky and gulped the contents. Then, reverting to their basest instincts, tortured any wounded soldier they found.

Mehlokazulu frowned. This was a serious lapse of discipline.

However, he reflected, it was only natural for those who had seen their comrades blown to bits to want revenge. He considered how well they'd fought, not flinching against the greater firepower of the British guns. Even as their comrades were mown down by bullets and grapeshot, they'd continued their charge. And, at the end, when the fighting was hand-to-hand, their skill with their weapons demonstrated how well they'd been trained. These men were heroes, every one of them.

As he watched them plunder baubles and trinkets, he realised there was much more important salvage. Hundreds of Martini-Henrys, the rifles that had caused so much devastation, were lying all over the camp. These needed to be gathered and taken back to oNdini. These and any remaining ammunition were worthy spoils to be laid at the feet of the king. They'd be useful in future battles.

Mehlokazulu barked an order to the looting warriors, 'Stop wasting your time and start collecting rifles.' He demonstrated by picking up the rifle at his feet. Releasing the bolt, he ejected the spent cartridge. It was still serviceable. 'Put any damaged ones to one side. They'll be useful for spare parts.'

A few yards away was a covered wagon, the canvas of its awning in shreds, obviously used to distribute ammunition. Wooden boxes lay upended, unused cartridges still scattered on the ground. 'There's still ammunition over here,' he shouted. 'Make sure you collect it all.'

Suddenly he remembered his own weapon. Retracing his steps to where he'd left it, he marvelled that barely a bare hour previously he'd been fighting for his life. With every step he was reminded of how ferocious the battle had been. Bodies of the uVe – who had taken such massive casualties – were everywhere. The boys lay in heaps, blood from their terrible wounds staining the beaten grass: faces shot away, heads with no backs to them, chests torn open. Already in the heat of the sun the stench of death was overpowering. He stopped to check the lie of the land. The rifle had to be somewhere nearby. Sure enough, he found it on the ground with the hand of a dead uVe clutching the trigger guard. Murmuring, 'I hope you put it to good use,' he disengaged the boy's fingers.

He turned the weapon over in his hands. The stock was badly scratched, but that would polish out. The firing mechanism seemed to be in good order. Putting it up to his shoulder, he squinted down the sight. That too seemed fine. Shouldering it, he headed back to his men.

On the highest points between the battlefield and oNdini, heralds, chosen for the power of their voices, were stationed to relay messages from the battlefield to the royal *umuZi*. In the still air of the summer afternoon, the voices echoed across the mountains, from isiPhezi and Babanango, finally reaching the Mthonjaneni heights above oNdini. Receiving the momentous news of the victory, the last man in the relay raced down the mountain. It wasn't long before he stood panting in front of the king.

Word quickly spread through the *umuZi*. The whole population streamed up to the gates of the *isiGodlo* and waited expectantly.

'Ndabezitha,' the messenger announced, 'no more will the *abelungu* threaten your kingdom.'

The king stared, not quite believing what he'd just heard.

'They've been vanquished. The whole redcoat army has been "eaten up".'

Cetshwayo's face relaxed into a smile.

The whole royal household – wives and servants alike – jumped up and down, trilling in sheer relief and joy.

The *isiGodlo* girls were beside themselves. Sixhwethu threw herself into frenzied celebration. The others produced a drum and improvised a victory dance. Even the reticent Nomguqo joined in.

Sixhwethu was full of it. 'When do you think they'll get back? I can't wait to find out what happened.'

'We'll never get to hear,' Nobhodlile replied. 'We never do. The secrets of the battlefield stay on the battlefield. Men always keep them to themselves.'

'My Maweni will tell me. I'll get it out of him. I'm very persuasive,' she giggled.

'Anyway, what makes you think he got anywhere near the battlefield?'

'He told me that's what he was going to do,' Sixhwethu said, then seeing the look of disbelief on the other girls' faces: 'I know. I did warn him he'd get his head shot off, but there was no stopping him. He's not a milksop like some.'

Nomguqo refused to rise to the bait, frightened to admit she already knew Maweni would not be coming back.

Sixhwethu boasted, 'My Maweni is Zulu through and through. His skin is black all over.'

Nguyaze decided the bullying had gone far enough. 'Stop it, Sixhwethu. There's no need for this. If it comes to personal remarks, you're not without fault yourself.'

Nobodhlile added, 'Oh no, you're wrong. Sixhwethu is perfect in every way.'

The girls sniggered at her sarcasm.

Sixhwethu sniffed scornfully, realising the tables had been turned. She flounced off to sulk in the hut.

The others resumed their singing and dancing. Sixhwethu wasn't going to spoil their fun.

The momentous day was almost over. The sun, which only eight hours previously had ominously and unexpectedly turned black now followed its usual diurnal pattern by setting over the Hlophekhulu heights.

Along the banks of the Mfolosi, the king's cattle cast long shadows as they slaked their thirst before being driven back to oNdini. Nomguqo stood ankle-deep in the water ensuring that every animal drank its fill, prodding the adult cows at the front to make way for their calves.

With night about to fall, it was time to head back. Whistling and cajoling the cattle away from the water, she failed to register the tall slim figure on the far bank. It was only when she heard her name that she looked over and saw Shikashika. Her heart jumped into her mouth as he collapsed and sank to his knees.

The summer sun had exposed much of the riverbed and the water trickled sluggishly between isolated pools. Sprinting, she reached him in time to stop him toppling into the stream. He fell unconscious into her arms.

She held his dead weight until he started to stir. Then, as his senses returned, she helped him sit upright. His eyes flickered open, but they were unfocused. She could see he was completely spent.

'We need get you to the *umuZi*,' she said, thinking out loud. 'But how?' She looked up. The other girls stood gawping on the far bank. 'Don't just stand there!' she shouted. 'Give me a hand.'

He summoned his remaining energy to stagger to his feet.

Draping his arm over her shoulders, she invited him to lean on her. She whispered, 'I'm so relieved you're here.'

He croaked, 'Maweni...' but couldn't complete the sentence.

'Take your time,' she whispered, putting her arm around his waist, and pulling him tight.

Once safely across the river, she and the other girls propped his back against the bank, with handfuls of grass bundled together to make a pillow.

She asked the girls, 'Can you run and get him something to eat?'

They hesitated, reluctant to leave while there was a chance they could hear about the battle.

'Please!' she implored.

Nguyaze finally gave in and dragged herself away.

Shikashika trembled uncontrollably. As his tension was released, every muscle shivered in response to the ordeal he'd suffered. Not only had he witnessed the most extreme savagery, but he had also run himself into the ground, covering the fifty miles from the battlefield without stopping to rest.

Nomguqo wrapped her arms around him to stop the shaking.

When Nguyaze returned with food, she was accompanied, not only by the rest of the *isiGodlo* girls, but many of the warriors' wives, sisters, and daughters. The news that an eyewitness to the battle had returned spread like wildfire. They were desperate to know whether their menfolk had survived. Nomguqo fed him *amaSi* and pieces of roast meat from the bowl. 'There's no hurry,' she said.

A latecomer arrived in a panic. Pushing through the crowd, Sixhwethu crouched in front of Shikashika. 'Where's Maweni? Why isn't he here?'

'Let him eat,' Nomguqo suggested gently.

'Keep your nose out of it,' Sixhwethu snapped. 'I want to know where my Maweni is.'

Shikashika paused between mouthfuls. 'He's not coming back.'

The onlookers gasped. Nomguqo turned away, unable to watch the inevitable response.

'What do you mean?' Sixhwethu's voice faltered.

'He was killed… by a big gun… It blew him to pieces.'

Sixhwethu reacted unexpectedly. Instead of screaming, she stood and, without saying a word, walked back towards oNdini. When she was sure she was alone and unobserved, she gave vent to a howl of pure anguish that echoed all the way back from the Hlopekhulu mountain.

PART FOUR

TRIUMPH AND DISASTER

TWENTY-EIGHT

oNdini

As news of the victory's true cost filtered through, the mood in the *umuZi* changed from optimism to fear. Although the British forces had been routed at iSandlwana, the threat remained; indeed, had increased. The *amabutho* on the other battlefields had suffered massive losses. Near the coastal settlement of Nyezane, a further fifth of the entire Zulu force had been lost. Their commander Godide, Mavumengwana's elder brother, ignoring the king's instructions to avoid fortified positions, exposed his men to Gatling guns and heavy artillery. The result was carnage. And reports were coming back that the senior regiments held in reserve at iSandlwana had launched an attack on the kwaJim garrison. Led by Zibhebhu and Dabulamanzi, they mounted a series of assaults on the tiny, but well-armed, British force. Disregarding another Zulu code – only to fight during daylight hours – they continued to attack well into the night and were eventually forced to withdraw, leaving the ground littered with Zulu corpses. Across all the battlefields the body count was dispiritingly high.

The king was beyond anger. He stormed up and down his quarters in the *isiGodlo* ranting at his *iziNduna*. 'Isn't there one of my commanders I can trust? My orders have been systematically flouted, and now we're in greater peril than ever. Make no mistake, the generals responsible will be punished.'

His black mood had not been helped by criticism he received from senior women in his household. The Queen Mother berated him, 'It's entirely your fault this happened. We warned you what would happen if you left the *eNkatheni*. But you insisted. This is on your head.'

He had no defence. He alone was responsible for breaking the *inkatha*'s power.

Sixhwethu remained in seclusion. For two days and nights she wept, rocking backwards and forwards on her sleeping mat. The other girls tried to console her, but she rebuffed every gesture of comfort and rejected any food she was offered. The constant weeping left her face puffy and eyes bloodshot.

When the warriors finally returned, a generalised grief engulfed the *umuZi*. It took nearly a week for the first to appear. Anyone expecting proud heroes to march in formation back to oNdini was shocked by their appearance. Gaunt with hunger and exhaustion, they dragged their feet, their heads and shoulders bowed, haunted by the horror of their experience.

The walking wounded limped on improvised crutches or leant on their comrades' shoulders; the more seriously injured were carried on their shields. Some displayed wounds beyond the skills of the medicine men. Even the able-bodied seemed damaged, psychologically scarred by the devastating losses in their ranks.

Shocked silence greeted them as they filed through the gates. The first casualties of mechanised warfare – spears against modern rifles and artillery – their missing limbs and horrific chest and abdominal wounds were injuries never witnessed before.

Anguished screams rose as women learned their men would not be coming home. Mothers, wives, sisters, and daughters prostrated themselves. For every family the loss of the man of the household was a personal disaster, leaving children without a father, and mothers to shoulder the responsibility of bringing up children on their own. It would take months, even years, for them to make the adjustment.

The scale of the losses became apparent. The thousand men left on the iSandlwana battlefield, added to those killed at kwaJim and Nyezane, meant that well over two thousand families faced an empty place at the family hearth.

Determined to understand why casualties were so high, Cetshwayo called a meeting of his *ibandla*, including his generals. Top of his agenda was the insubordination that led to the disastrous kwaJim assault. His businesslike tone masked a cold fury. 'Zibhebhu sends word his own people require his presence, thereby avoiding the necessity to account for his actions. Are we surprised?'

The generals shuffled their feet, reluctant to answer.

'Well, I can assure you, he will answer for his part in the kwaJim attack. But he wasn't alone…' He turned to Dabulamanzi, who stared impassively into space. 'Perhaps my brother will explain why he ignored my orders.'

'Ndabezitha, I make no apology for what was done at kwaJim,' Dabulamanzi replied. 'It was a legitimate target. My men were fresh and eager to complete the work so ably and valiantly begun at iSandlwana.' He acknowledged Ntshingwayo and Mavumengwana. 'My congratulations to these great generals on their victory–'

The evasion sparked an angry interruption from the king: 'Yes, we'll come to that later. What I want to know is why you embarked on such a foolish and ill-conceived venture. Didn't you consider why I ordered you not to cross into Natal?' He shouted the answer to his rhetorical question, 'It was so we should not be seen as the *aggressor*!'

Dabulamanzi bristled. 'With respect, Ndabezitha, had we carried the day at kwaJim, the British would have been sent packing all the way to the coast.'

'The point is you didn't carry the day. Your folly has lost us many men, and the British are confident we can be beaten. I'm not able to see into the future, but this much I know – what happened at iSandlwana is just the beginning. The British will not rest until they have overrun our kingdom. Understand this, brother – that miscalculation of yours was your last. You will take no further part in our defences. Your command will fall to others better able to understand strategy.'

Eyes blazing at this public humiliation, Dabulamanzi stood, and without so much as a nod in his brother's direction, marched out of the *isibaya*.

Turning back to his counsellors, Cetshwayo started pacing. 'I've received word from our friend Jantoni. He congratulates us on our great victory and advises that we should send our *impi* to the coast. The British have put a large garrison there. Should our army overcome them, they will be finished.' He paused while they digested this. 'Evidently his letter was written before the disaster at Nyezane – which has completely changed the situation. However, it's good to know that at least one white man remains our friend.' He stopped in front of Ntshingwayo and Mavumengwana. 'Dabulamanzi was right to praise you. Your leadership has given us a notable victory. However, I fail to understand why so many families have lost their menfolk. On a personal level, I'm shocked by the losses in my own *ibutho* – men I grew up with. Explain.'

Clearing his throat, Ntshingwayo glanced at Mavumengwana. Neither was prepared to stick his neck out.

'I'll give you my explanation,' said the king. 'It was ill-discipline pure and simple. You lost control of your men and sent them into battle without administering any protective *muthi*. An army's discipline is the generals' responsibility. Occasionally the commander's orders are ignored – my brother is an obvious example. Then it is the duty of those in charge to reimpose their authority. I leave it to your discretion to punish the hotheads who broke ranks.'

'Ndabezitha, you have our word it won't happen again,' Ntshingwayo promised.

Cetshwayo continued, 'On another matter, why were no prisoners taken? Their soldiers, particularly their officers, might have given us some idea of their tactics.'

Vumandaba said, 'The *abelungu* fought to the last man – no one was left standing. Besides which, it was our first engagement with them. Our men couldn't tell the officers from the men.'

'Officers carry swords – any fool knows that!' Cetshwayo shook his head in disbelief. 'So, now we've lost the opportunity to know how the British intend to continue this war.'

The generals accepted the rebuke in silence.

The king gestured at the plunder taken from the battlefield – an enormous pile of weapons: rifles, pistols, and boxes of ammunition. 'Where are the heavy guns that killed so many of our men?'

Ntshingwayo hesitated before replying, 'Still on the battlefield, Ndabezitha,'

Cetshwayo prodded him in the chest. 'Well, I suggest you send men back to iSandlwana and bring them back.'

Shikashika's behaviour worried Nomguqo. Since his return he'd retreated into a world of brooding silence. It didn't seem normal. He sat for hours, arms around his knees, rocking backwards and forwards. And refused to answer her questions or touch any of the food she gave him.

What could she do to reach him? Who could she confide in? Certainly not the other *isiGodlo* girls, not without admitting her feelings for him and inviting their censure.

One evening, while cleaning the great wife's hut, she blurted out her concerns.

In response Nomvimbi quizzed her: 'What is this boy to you?'

Nomguqo stammered, 'Just someone I know.'

'Then why are you worried about him?'

'His cousin was killed in a horrible way right in front of him.'

'When your friend becomes a warrior, he'll see many such sights.'

'Yes, but he's still very young.'

It was a flimsy argument. From infancy Zulu boys were taught to tolerate pain, both physical and emotional. Any sign of weakness was rigorously suppressed. Also, they were inured to sights of brutality through the punishments meted out to criminals.

'And?' said the great wife.

'I think he needs to talk to someone. He just sits staring into space.'

'Where is his family?'

'Over two days away, at Hlobane.'

'Well, you'd better look after him.' Nomvimbi grabbed the cleaning cloth. 'I'll see to this. Go, see to your boy.'

Smiling gratefully, Nomguqo skipped out of the hut. She knew exactly where to take him: a place of beauty where they could be alone, where the healing process could begin. Realising that Shikashika's dreams were haunted by what he had seen, she had to eliminate anything that might trigger them. She gathered food into a basket and led him from the *umuZi*. He didn't resist or question where they were going.

Sixhwethu's grief subsided, and she started to eat again – a sure sign she was on the mend.

When her initial all-consuming despair receded, she became aware that Nomguqo was regularly absent from the hut. She asked the other girls where she was. Their guarded reply aroused her suspicions. She suspected that Nomguqo was enjoying what henceforward she would be denied. Her jealousy developed a focus. Obsessively she hunted through the *umuZi* with the purpose of denouncing them when she found them. Nomguqo would feel the shame she had felt when she and Maweni were discovered making love. If she couldn't have a lover, then neither would Nomguqo.

She went from hut to hut, demanding to know whether anyone had seen them together. She searched the obvious places – the cattle-enclosure and the grain store. She went into the fields, frantically combing through the rows of corn. As the herds were taken out to pasture, she ran among the cattle hoping she would find them hiding there. At the end of the third day, she was still looking.

The knot of jealousy in her chest was so tight it prevented her from sleeping. In the early hours, she rose and left the hut. In the light of the moon, she roamed the *umuZi*. At the point of giving up, she noticed the water detail leaving the royal quarters on their way up to Hlophekhulu.

That's where they are, she suddenly thought. The place she'd used with Maweni was the only place they could be.

She ran ahead of the attendants, dodging in and out of the huts so they wouldn't see her. The guard on the gate looked at her sleepily as she demanded to be let out, his question about her destination ignored as she ran towards the hills.

Nomguqo slept in Shikashika's arms, a blanket pulled over them to ward off the night chill. They were camped in a hollow, a few yards from the stream, sheltered from the breezes that blew from higher ground. They had built a fire; the remnants of their meal were scattered in the glowing embers. She stirred and snuggled closer into his embrace. Then, as the dawn broke on the far horizon, she opened her eyes.

Disentangling herself from his arms, she set about rekindling the fire. She blew on the embers, adding some small twigs. Eventually, they flared, and she added bigger pieces of wood. Soon the fire was burning brightly. She sat back and warmed her hands.

A sudden crack of dry wood from thirty feet away made her turn. Her senses attuned to danger, she listened. Up on the mountain, leopard attack was always a possibility. Picking up a brand from the fire, she waved it in front of her.

From her hiding place, Sixhwethu watched, eyes narrow with hatred, her suspicions confirmed by what she had seen. A painful lump rose in her throat. It was only ten days since she'd lain in Maweni's arms just like that.

Having completed their purification, the warriors were fit to parade before the king. It was customary to receive his commendation or condemnation for their actions on the battlefield. Those who had fought bravely were invited to carve a necklace of willow-wood to distinguish them publicly as *abaqawe*, heroes or warriors of renown. The cowards were vilified and humiliated – and, during Shaka's reign, even worse. The Great King had insisted they suffer the "cowards' death" of holding their left arm up while a razor-sharp spear was slowly pushed through their armpit into their ribcage.

The parade was also an opportunity for individual warriors to comment on the conduct of their comrades. This often degenerated into a slanging match as tempers flared and scores were settled.

In preparation, Cetshwayo's body was anointed with strong medicine, and, to give him the wisdom to pass the necessary judgments, he spent many hours communing with the *amaDlozi*.

As for all important ceremonies, the warriors were grouped by regiment in the cattle enclosure. A rollcall was taken. The contrast in numbers was striking: a fraction of those who'd marched away so proudly a week earlier were present. Some were registered as dead, but many warriors from the regiments shamed by the defeat at kwaJim had stayed away, unwilling to face the king's anger.

From the *isiGodlo* gate Cetshwayo strode into the cattle pen, *inhlendla* in hand.

The *amabutho* saluted him: *Bhayede! Bhayede!*

He strode through the ranks with a face like thunder. No one dared to meet his gaze. He inspected them, taking note of those who had attended despite their wounds. He viewed the uThulwana last. Searching the ranks of his own regiment for familiar faces, he was shocked at the absences. Qhude, now their most senior officer, stood at the head.

'Where is the rest?' the king asked.

Qhude looked away, unwilling to speak the self-evident truth. The silence was deafening.

Cetshwayo moved to the middle and took his seat under

the acacia tree, his key officials grouped around him.

The praise-singer led the chorus: *Bhayede! You are the elephant. You who devour men. Black lion.*

The *amabutho* shouted their response.

Silencing them with the *inhlendla*, the king called, 'Describe what happened.'

An uMbonambi *iNduna* ran forward, the willow wand in his hand indicating he should be given bragging rights as the first to draw blood. He raised the stick in a mock charge against the king. Stopping at the last minute, he handed over the stick. 'That is how the uMbonambi killed the white men,' he said.

His men waved their willow wands in support.

An iNgobamakhosi scorned the boast: 'The uMbonambi were not in the front rank.'

'We were the first to stab the *abelungu*,' the uMbonambi protested.

Cetshwayo silenced them and turned to the generals. 'Who is telling the truth? Which *ibutho* drew blood first?'

Ntshingwayo equivocated, knowing how much was at stake. 'From our position it was difficult to see who was the first into the camp. All three *amabutho* – uMbonambi, iNgobamakhosi and uKhandempemvu – were in a line.'

'That is not true,' Mehlokazulu shouted. 'It's as exactly as Ntuzwa kaNhlaka described. The uMbonambi were first into the camp. My men and the uVe were on their left flank chasing the one-armed officer. The uKhandempemvu were held back by the big guns. The uMbonambi had open ground, which they exploited.'

The uMbonambi warriors demanded that the king find in their favour.

Cetshwayo exploited the drama to the full by weighing the stick in his hand and pretending to throw it to each of the regiments in turn. Each responded with a loud *Ji!* He kept them further in suspense by consulting the generals again. Eventually, he hurled the stick in the direction of the uMbonambi. The ecstatic victors mocked their rivals.

Beyond this settling of accounts, the issue of Qhude's behaviour remained. It certainly was no way for an officer to conduct himself, but Mehlokazulu suspected he would get nowhere by making an issue of it. It would be his word against Qhude's. But the reckless insubordination on two separate occasions could not be ignored. Mehlokazulu had witnessed both instances – and in the company of others. Here was an opportunity to avenge Mbulawa. His voice rang out across the parade ground. 'I accuse Qhude kaKuhlekonke of insubordination.'

Cetshwayo sat forward, 'And your evidence?'

'Before the battle, the uThulwana were told they were to be kept in reserve. And ordered to stay in the Ngwebeni valley. The generals will verify this.'

Ntshingwayo nodded.

'When the first attack came, the regiments at the head of the valley immediately engaged, including Qhude and his men. Is that not so?'

Ntshingwayo nodded once more.

'Many brave warriors lost their lives because of that man's recklessness.'

If loyalty to their officer demanded the uThulwana refute the accusation, their silence spoke volumes. And sympathetic murmurs grew among the other regiments.

Mehlokazulu continued, 'There was worse. When we overran the camp and pursued the survivors to the Mzinyathi, Vumandaba stood on the banks and ordered us to stay on the Zulu side of the river. Qhude flagrantly disregarded him and leaped to the Natal bank. It was categorically against orders. Your orders, Ndabezitha.'

He was so carried away that he failed to notice his enemy running towards him. Launching himself, Qhude took Mehlokazulu to the ground, hands around his neck. Kicking and squirming, he struggled to break the chokehold. They wrestled, neither able to secure the upper hand. Then strong hands pulled them apart. With warriors on either side pulling them back, they glared at each other, the scar on Qhude's jaw twisting his face into a mask of loathing.

Cetshwayo marched down the parade ground. 'I should have you both taken to the execution rock!' He swung the *inhlendla* to within inches of Qhude's face. 'By your own actions you condemn yourself. What I have just witnessed is proof that Mehlokazulu's accusations are correct. Get out of my sight before I desecrate the sacred spear with your blood.'

TWENTY-NINE

Sixhwethu's jealousy developed into a full-blown obsession. It occupied every single waking thought. Even asleep, her dreams were of Shikashika and Nomguqo embracing passionately, their limbs intertwined, and their lips pressed together in lascivious kisses. The images became increasingly lurid, to the point that she imagined them making love, Nomguqo's legs splayed and Shikashika thrusting vigorously between them. Regularly she'd wake to find the cries of ecstasy in her dreams were her own and the imagined pleasure of their lovemaking the effect of her own fingers between her thighs. It gave her a physical release but had no effect on the gaping emptiness she felt in her heart. She ached for Maweni.

Her disrupted sleep drained her energies. It became an effort to drag herself off her mat in the morning, and altogether too much trouble to wash herself and attend to her personal hygiene. Inevitably, the other girls in the hut started to notice her body odour. They became increasingly intolerant of her lethargy, forced to cover for her and do her work. They'd discover her curled up asleep when she was supposed to be sweeping the hut or hunched over her hoe while they were tending the vegetable garden.

She couldn't help it. She was hollow-eyed with fatigue, literally incapable of keeping her eyes open, falling asleep on the slightest pretext.

In the heat of the midday sun, the girls took a break from planting pumpkin seeds to quench their thirst. Sixhwethu was missing. At first no one noticed. Nomguqo was also absent. In her case for a legitimate reason: she had the royal children's meal to prepare.

'Here she is,' Nobodhlile said, pointing to a prickly pear bush. Sure enough, Sixhwethu was fast asleep in its shade.

'She must be sick,' Nguyaze said. 'We should call the herbalist…'

'No, she's grieving for Maweni,' Nobhodlile said. 'Don't you remember how Umafutha was when her boy died? Didn't sleep for days.'

'She's obviously bewitched. Someone must have cast a spell on her. It's the only explanation I can think of,' Nguyaze said.

'We must wake her,' said Nobhodlile. 'We can't leave her like this.'

'You can if you want. I'm going back to work,' Nguyaze said.

'It's not fair, her sleeping while we're working.'

'Oh, leave her be. It's her affair if she doesn't pull her weight. She'll have to answer to the king.' Nguyaze led the girls back to the area they were planting.

Sixhwethu shifted to make herself more comfortable. Her eyes half open, she smiled. She'd heard every word. One in particular started her thinking. The assumption she was bewitched planted a seed that soon sprouted into a very ugly weed.

The *iNgoma* Dlephu Ndlovu sat cross-legged at his hut entrance digesting his midday meal. Standing in front of him, Sixhwethu blocked the sun. 'May I ask a question?'

The old witchdoctor replied testily, 'I'm resting, child. Can't it wait?'

Sixhwethu got right to the point. 'Do you think a witch could have cast a spell on me?'

He considered her with blood-shot eyes, then waved away a couple of flies. There was a weighty pause before he spoke. 'What makes you think you're bewitched?'

'I can't stay awake during the day.'

He shrugged. 'Many of our people have the sleeping sickness. You too may have been bitten by the cattle fly.'

'No, it's not that.'

He stroked the sparse hairs on his chin. 'This is a serious accusation. What other evidence can you produce?'

She replied, 'Two herdboys went to iSandlwana and only one came back. My *iSoka* was the one who died.'

'Many wives lost their husbands in that battle.'

'Hers came back, mine didn't. She must have cast a spell.'

'That is circumstantial. If you think witchcraft was involved, you must provide solid proof.'

'Witches have familiars, don't they? Well, I've seen her talking to *iziNtulo*.'

Dlephu sat forward. This information put a different slant on the matter. The *iNtulo*, or salamander, was universally feared because it contained the spirit of the agent of death.

'You've seen someone communing with salamanders?'

Sixhwethu nodded.

He peered into her face. 'Then you must name her.'

She swallowed. Such an accusation would have dire consequences. The penalty for witchcraft was severe. Anyone identified as a witch would be put to death in the most painful way imaginable. He or she would have foot-long skewers pushed up the rectum and be driven out into the bush to suffer an agonising and lingering death. She shuddered at the prospect, but her hatred of Nomguqo was now ungovernable. She would stop at nothing to pay Nomguqo back for the pain she caused her.

'Before you identify this individual, I must warn you the penalty for bearing false witness is equally extreme. The perjurer suffers the same fate as the subject of the accusation. I'd advise you to think most carefully before you point the finger. Do you understand?'

With no further hesitation, Sixhwethu blurted out the name: 'Nomguqo.'

Dlephu blinked. This made no sense. He'd heard nothing but glowing reports of the shy girl's virtues. Could such an indispensable member of the royal household be considered an *umThakathi* (a witch)? It was out of the question. But now the accusation was out in the open, he had no choice but to follow procedure and announce a "smelling out" ceremony.

Scuttling through the homestead in search of the king, he found him in the *isibaya* contemplating his prize cattle. Dlephu knew better than to interrupt – it was obvious he was engaged in important business. A group of *iziNdibi*, including Shikashika, was drinking directly from the cows' udders. Shikashika's age group had been given special dispensation to *kleza* before being inducted into a regiment. So many men had been lost that the king had reduced the minimum age of fighting warriors. Now, boys of sixteen were expected to go to war.

The *iNgoma* announced his presence with a polite cough. 'Ndabezitha, I need your judgment in a delicate matter.'

'What is it?'

'Well…' Dlephu paused, nervous to involve the king. 'One of Your Majesty's subjects has been accused of witchcraft.'

Irritated to be bothered with such a triviality, Cetshwayo snapped, 'Who?'

'Who?'

'Yes, who! Who is the supposed witch and who is her accuser?'

Dlephu hedged, 'I know it's improbable, but the girl Sixhwethu is saying that Nomguqo has cast a spell on her.'

Cetshwayo exploded. 'It's a joke. Tell me it's a joke.'

'I'm afraid not, Your Majesty. Sixhwethu is convinced. I warned her of the penalties of perjury, but she's sticking to her story.'

'And the evidence?'

'Well, there are undeniable symptoms. Sixhwethu's life force is weak. She has turned night into day, awake when she should be asleep and asleep when she should be working.'

Cetshwayo's face darkened. 'Maybe she's just lazy? It wouldn't be the first time. What's your proof that Nomguqo is responsible?'

'Apparently she communes with wild beasts.' The old man dropped his voice. 'She's been observed talking to *iziNtulo*.'

'And what if she does? Does a conversation with lizards condemn her as a witch?'

It was a rhetorical question for which the *iNgoma* had no answer.

'It's ridiculous,' said the king. 'Nomguqo is the ablest girl in the *isiGodlo*. The royal wives choose her above all the others. My own children dote on her. And I consider her as one my own daughters. Sixhwethu, on the other hand, has always been disruptive. She's idle and disobedient. And, I imagine, jealous of her more industrious hutmate. My advice is to nip it in the bud. To continue would be unwarranted and cruel. Whatever verdict is reached it's bound to be divisive. Be warned.'

Taking a moment to compose himself, Dlephu Ndlovu insisted. 'I will, of course, defer to Your Majesty but if I don't pursue this allegation, I'll be ignoring a sacred tradition established by the great Shaka himself; it will set a dangerous precedent. Even the suspicion of an *umThakathi* in our community will be enough to panic our people. In the light of the recent losses on the battlefield, they're looking for good omens. What could be more appropriate than to "smell out" the evil influence that has caused so many of our warriors to die? We are at a critical point in our history, and we must ensure the unity of the Zulu nation remains in service of its king.'

Turning his back on the *iNgoma*, Cetshwayo indicated the conversation was at an end.

Still sensitive to the fact that his senior wives blamed him for the military setbacks, the king opted for Uxisipe's less challenging company. Ignoring the danger that he might create disharmony in the *isiGodlo* by favouring one wife over the others, he visited her every night. She pleased him with her undemanding ways. Her beauty and youth were undeniably appealing; also, she was an enthusiastic and imaginative lover. He conveniently forgot that she had borne him twins, thereby attracting the potential for misfortune to his household. He now trusted her so completely that he ate her cooking without insisting it be tasted beforehand.

That evening, he came to her as usual and enjoyed the meal she prepared. Sated, they lay on her sleeping mat. Nestling in the crook of his arm, she untied his *isiNene*, the square of hide covering his genitals. Accustomed to an instant reaction, she was surprised to find that the royal penis remained inert.

'Have I failed to please you, Ndabezitha?'

She ran her fingers down his belly and into the tendrils of his pubic hair. He reached down and laid his hand on hers to prevent it straying further. Grunting noncommittally, he stared at the smoke spiralling through the thatch opening.

Since his conversation with Dlephu Ndlovu, he'd been weighing up the ramifications. He couldn't accept that his favourite might be an *umThakathi*, that she might have malicious motives. A key member of his household for three years, she had not put a foot wrong. Diligent and modest, she was worthy of her royal lineage.

In any case, he reasoned, what time would she have had to learn the practice of witchcraft? She could never have gathered the necessary knowledge. A lifetime's study was needed to understand the effects of secret herbs and poisons. No, it was out of the question.

At the same time, Dlephu Ndlovu's argument had merit. The future of the amaZulu was at stake. What was the worth of a single life when weighed against the survival of the nation? It was a question of *realpolitik*. Perhaps a sacrifice needed to be made for the greater good. The *ukunuka umThakathi* ("smelling out") of a witch and removal of her evil influence would immediately pre-empt anyone objecting to the war's continuation. The sacrifice of an innocent girl made him sick at heart, but he accepted its expedience. Strictly speaking, he had no choice – the "smelling out" process would have to take its course. Had he paid heed to Pastor Gundersen's bible stories – specifically the description of Christ's examination by Pontius Pilate – he would have recognised that he was *washing his hands* of the matter.

Brushing aside Uxisipe's wandering hand, he sprang to his feet, grabbed his cloak, crossed to the entrance, and without so much as a backward glance, headed into the night.

He was nothing if not a pragmatist. In the pursuit of his ambitions, he had no scruples about shedding blood. Even as a young prince, in the war of succession against his brother Mbuyazi, he had not thought twice about slaughtering two thousand Mbuyazi supporters on the banks of the river Thukela; their bodies provided food for crocodiles for months after. Further claims on the throne by other family members led to further bloodletting. Challenges to Cetshwayo's authority were fraught with danger.

Dlephu Ndlovu's appearance in the cattle-pen the following day was truly terrifying. His face, arms and legs were streaked with alternating stripes of red and white limewash. Dried, inflated bladders and viper skins with their fangs bared were interwoven into his *isicoco* head ring. He wore a necklace with leopards' claws and teeth strung alongside a dangling baboon's skull. He brandished a small stick in his right hand with a wildebeeste tail attached. This was his *iShoba*, the instrument he would use to point out the witch. Bags of small pebbles were tied around his ankles, which rattled as he moved.

He wasn't alone. A group of lesser ranked but similarly attired *iziNgoma* flanked him. The crowd gasped. The appearance of these men would have horrific consequences for someone. As with every important ceremony in oNdini, the entire population was obliged to attend the *ukunuka umThakathi*. No excuses would be accepted. Absentees would find themselves marched to the execution rock.

The *iziNgoma*, led by Dlephu, processed across the parade ground to the king's ceremonial chair. Cetshwayo was already in position, *inhlendla* in hand. As they reached him, the crowd's expectant hum died down. Dlephu gave the royal salute, accompanied by a series of high-pitched shrieks and cries from his attendants.

The king shifted uneasily as the formalities were completed. He might justify it politically, but he was complicit in subjecting an innocent girl to unimaginable suffering.

The ritual began. Dlephu craned his neck, sniffing the air as a hunting dog would search for the smell of its prey on the wind. The other *iziNgoma* formed into a circle facing the crowd. Following Dlephu's lead, they chanted: 'We smell evil here. Evil that will harm His Majesty. Evil that will damage our nation. There is a witch amongst us. Make no mistake, we shall smell her out. She cannot hide from us.'

Standing with the other *isiGodlo* girls, Sixwethu shivered involuntarily – she had released the spirit of revenge and it could not be recalled. She glanced at her intended victim. Nomguqo's innocence was plain to see. Nothing in her body language indicated she knew what was to come. She stared at the *iziNgoma* with terror, not for herself but for whomever would receive the hideous punishment. Unable to quell a pang of remorse, Sixwethu looked away.

Breaking into two groups, the "witchfinders" ran up and down the lines of people. Occasionally they crouched, sniffing the air, and hissing like snakes. Dlephu was in his element. Having conducted the ritual many times, he relished the power it exerted. Every detail of the event was stage-managed to induce the maximum terror, so the crowd, rather than objecting to the cruelty, was relieved they hadn't been chosen.

A gang of "hyena men" followed five paces behind, heavy war clubs in one hand, and impaling skewers in the other.

Mehlokazulu stamped his feet impatiently. He was convinced

there was always a personal or political motive to the choice of the "witch". Dissidents and rabble-rousers were often denounced as witches. It was the perfect way to discredit and remove them and was nothing more than a piece of theatre whose protagonists were pre-selected and final act preordained. Also, he had more important matters in consider – the training of the new recruits for a start. iSandlwana had cut swathes through the regiments, the iNgobamakhosi particularly. The recently *kleza*'ed herdboys had been recruited to plug the gaps in the ranks. As a section commander it had fallen to him to supervise their drill. He was itching to get back to the training ground.

Cetshwayo watched Nomguqo among the *isiGodlo* girls, her eyes fixed on the approaching *iziNgoma*. She seemed utterly unaware of what was coming. He shook his head sadly.

On all fours, Dlephu scuttled like a crab, stopping randomly at a potential victim. Starting at the feet, he smelled upwards and ended by staring into the victim's eyes. Very few could hold the *iNgoma*'s penetrating gaze for long. These preliminary "smellings-out" made the rooting out of evil appear haphazard – whereas it was entirely deliberate.

All the while, the other *iziNgoma* delivered a rhythmic chant, their voices increasing in volume as Dlephu neared his intended target. They already knew who she was.

Reaching the *isiGodlo* group, Dlephu shuffled across the front rank, bending this way and that, making it seem he was close to picking her out.

Sixhwethu could not stop her legs shaking. The reality had now sunk in. Nomguqo was about to die. Was it too late to retract her accusation? Her instinct for self-preservation, however, made her hold her tongue.

The rest of the crowd gaped. Surely not – a witch among the king's closest attendants?

The *iziNgoma's* chants grew in volume.

Dlephu stopped, and with his *iShoba*, pointed past the *isiGodlo's* first and second ranks directly towards Nomguqo. The girls on either side moved away, leaving her isolated.

As the *iNgoma* approached, she lost control of her bladder. Urine ran down the inside of her thighs. Swiping downwards with his wand, he struck her across the face, the hairs of the wildebeeste tail brushing her cheek. Her knees buckled, and two executioners ran forward and grabbed her arms to stop her collapsing to the ground. Separating her from the others, the *iziMpisi* half carried, half dragged her, her feet drawing tracks in the dust. Instinctively, the *isiGodlo* girls detected Sixhwethu's hand in it and distanced themselves from her.

The royal wives formed a huddle, whispering in disbelief.

An angry buzz circulated the arena. Taking steps to quell the growing protests, Dlephu pointed his wand at the unconscious Nomguqo, now propped up on either side by the executioners. 'Behold the witch!' he shouted. 'The one who plots against the king. We've smelt her out as we will smell out all who are tainted with witchcraft. How should she be punished?'

A deathly hush descended. Nobody dared speak, until a lone woman's voice rang out: 'Death to the witch!'

Others joined her, and soon the *isibaya* rang with demands for Nomguqo's death.

The commotion brought her to her senses. As the full horror of her situation became clear, she searched the crowd for a compassionate face. She chanced upon Sixhwethu, who refused to meet her gaze. This told her unequivocally who her accuser was.

A male voice cut through the babble: 'This girl is no witch!' Mehlokazulu strode from the ranks of his *ibutho*. 'I know her. If she is a witch, then so am I. Take me to *kwaNkatha*.'

Cetshwayo frowned. This presented him with a diplomatic quandary. Choosing political necessity over compassion was hard enough, but Mehlokazulu now challenged that decision. It was not the first time. His last act of disobedience had led the nation's present perilous position. How many more times could he excuse his favourite's behaviour? Sooner or later the rebellious streak in his character would have to be curbed. 'This is not your concern, Mehlokazulu. Resume your place,' he said.

Mehlokazulu wasn't to be moved. 'A miscarriage of justice is everyone's concern, Ndabezitha.'

'You try my patience, young man.'

'Your Majesty, I beg you to reconsider. Nomguqo does not have the guile to be a witch. If she has offended, it will be at the personal level. Someone here has a personal grievance. It's guaranteed.'

That Mehlokazulu should speak like that on her behalf. Nomguqo felt the strength returning to her legs. Grateful tears started in her eyes.

The king was in a bind. Though his authority was being openly flouted – a crime with only one outcome – it would be foolish to call for the executioners. His demoralised regiments needed strong leadership and he could ill afford to lose one of his best military commanders. He handed the matter to Dlephu Ndlovu. 'I won't encroach on my *iNgoma*'s jurisdiction. He must make the judgment here.'

The old man's eyes shifted nervously. If the king couldn't make up his mind, who was he, a mere servant, to insist on Nomguqo's death? He couldn't immediately call to mind a precedent, but past *iziNgoma* must occasionally have admitted their fallibility without losing status. At the same time, the integrity of the "smelling out" ceremony had to be maintained, otherwise his credibility would be destroyed. Making his decision, he marched to the *isiGodlo* girls, grabbed Sixhwethu by the wrist, and dragged her out into the open. 'This is the accuser,' he said. 'She made the complaint.'

Sixhwethu tried to pull away, but the witchdoctor held her firm.

Mehlokazulu spoke again, 'Before iSandlwana this girl was with the *iziNdibi*. She was sent back because she was intimate with one of them. Maweni was his name, killed by a shell in the battle. After chasing the soldiers down to the Mzinyathi I returned to the camp and found his body blown to pieces. This was wound around his wrist.' He held up Sixhwethu's snakeskin talisman. 'Even this couldn't protect him. His death was nothing to do with witchcraft. His time had come.'

Sixhwethu stayed silent. She couldn't dispute what Mehlokazulu said. Nor could she deny that her intentions towards Nomguqo were malicious, motivated by jealousy. Apparently resigned to her fate, she waited quietly.

Dlephu Ndlovu nodded to the executioners. Releasing Nomguqo, they marched to her accuser. The sight of the grim-faced hyena men brought home the reality of her situation. She let out a piercing scream of terror and started to run. But there was no escape; the crowd surrounded her on every side. They moved closer to tighten the circle. She darted this way and that, and eventually ran directly into the path of the *iziMpisi*, who pulled her off her feet and held her down.

Trussed like a sacrificial animal, she lay whimpering with fear. An ominous quiet settled on the crowd, interrupted only by Sixhwethu's cries.

'Ndabezitha, please let her live.' Nomguqo stood in front of the royal dais.

Cetshwayo levered himself from his throne and leaned

towards her, whispering so only she could hear: 'Don't be afraid, Nomguqo, your ordeal is over.'

Nomguqo whispered in reply, 'Your Majesty, Sixhwethu is tormented with grief. She didn't know what she was doing. Please spare her.'

Cetshwayo's grim expression softened. He stood to his full height and addressed her in front of the assembly. 'You have a big heart, young woman. Your accuser should learn from your example. Some will say your request shows weakness, but I believe it expresses a character of great strength. I will grant your plea for mercy.' He gestured with the sacred spear, 'Release her.' Then led his entourage across the cattle pen to the *isiGodlo*.

The *iziMpisi* untied Sixhwethu's bonds. She scrambled to her feet, rubbing her wrists.

The witchdoctor seethed, his anger unmistakable, 'Never make an accusation you cannot prove.' He wagged a warning finger. 'Next time you will not be so lucky.'

THIRTY

'Nomguqo?' The voice was so soft she could barely hear it above the other girls' heavy breathing. 'Are you awake?'

Sixhwethu's voice made every fibre of Nomguqo's body stiffen with fear. Knowing her hutmate was capable of such treachery had already persuaded her to keep her distance and minimise all contact. She froze, hoping Sixhwethu would think she was asleep. In fact, she had been awake since she first laid down. It wasn't for want of trying, but the welcome oblivion of sleep had eluded her. Whenever she shut her eyes, Dlephu Ndlovu and his grotesque attendants paraded before her. The stench of the *iNgoma*'s foul breath clung to her nostrils; imprints of the executioners' rough hands remained on her arms, their fingers digging into her flesh. Sleep was a long way off.

She replayed the events over and over in her mind. Why had she intervened? Why had she asked the king to grant mercy to her accuser? She could have said nothing and Sixhwethu's death would have brought an end to the bullying. She had no idea why she had spoken out, beyond knowing she could not have stood by and let her suffer such a hideous death.

'I know you're awake,' Sixwhethu insisted. 'Can I come and sit with you?' There was a catch in her voice, which implied she'd been crying.

Nomguqo held her breath. Rustling from the far side indicated she was already on her way. Clenching her eyelids, she concentrated on pretending to be asleep. Even when Sixwhethu perched at the foot of her blanket, she lay perfectly still. Eventually, she could maintain the pretence no longer. Propping herself on her elbows, she said, 'What is it?' In the moonlight she could see the silver tear tracks on Sixwhethu's cheeks.

'Were you scared?' said Sixwhethu.

'What do you think?'

'I was so frightened I wet myself. I thought I was going to die.' She reached for Nomguqo's hand.

Nomguqo recoiled. The gesture of appeasement was physically repugnant.

'Do you forgive me?'

'No.'

Sixwhethu started to sob. Gulping through her tears, she said, 'I did a terrible thing.'

'Yes, you did.'

Wiping her cheeks, Sixwhethu sniffed, 'I couldn't bear to see you with Shikashika.'

At the end of her tether, Nomguqo snapped, 'The middle of the night is not the time to discuss this. If you can't sleep, go for a walk.'

Nobhodlile's sleepy voice broke in, 'Will you two shut up? None of us will get any sleep if you carry on like this.'

In the half-light, Nomguqo saw Sixwhethu's desolation and contrition. But whatever sympathy she felt, she certainly wasn't going to let her off the hook. She lay back on her headrest, closing off any further conversation.

The night sky was bright with stars when she emerged from the hut. Across the compound the eastern horizon started to lighten – dawn would not be long in coming. She stretched and filled her lungs, grateful to be out in the fresh air. She'd waited for this all night long.

Finally accepting that her overtures were not welcome, Siwhwethu returned to her sleeping mat and started snoring almost immediately. No such luck for Nomguqo. The "smelling out" nightmare continued. Every time she relaxed and drifted off, the image of the *iNgoma* sweeping the wildebeeste tail across her face jolted her back into wakefulness. All night long it haunted her. Now, with the coming of day the curfew was about to end, and she could legitimately pass through the *isiGodlo* gate.

The muscles in her legs twitched from inactivity. She broke into a trot, her stride lengthening as she moved towards the gate. The three warriors on duty at the entrance were hunched under their hide cloaks. They failed to register her as she passed. *Asleep on guard*, she thought, *what punishment does that deserve?*

She had no idea which direction her feet would take her, but soon found herself on the path leading to the Hlophekhulu mountain, where she'd taken Shikashika to recover from his nightmares. As she ran, she realised it was a refuge for her too, a place where she would feel safe.

She settled into an easy pace, her footfalls and breathing developing a pattern that distracted her from negative thoughts. She thought of Shikashika. What would the future hold for him? Since his return, he had recovered some of his old spirit, but it was guaranteed he would soon be sent to rejoin the *amabutho*. Other battles would be fought; and many warriors would march away, perhaps never to return. She considered his gentleness, his unsuitability for the brutality of war. He had trembled and wept in her arms. How would someone so sensitive be ruthless enough to take life even in defence of his own? She suspected the killer instinct was entirely absent from his makeup. But that was what had attracted her to him in the first place.

The path started to climb, and she had to slow her pace, negotiating large boulders, and reducing her steps against the steeper gradient. The darkness lifted and dawn light began to streak the sky.

The track zigzagged up the hillside ahead of her. Her breath shortened as she climbed. Turning a corner, she faltered as she caught sight of a someone sitting on a flat rock above the track. From his position, he must have been watching her all the way up the mountain.

She stopped, unsure whether to stay put or move up to where he sat.

'*Sawubona*, little witch,' Mehlokazulu called.

Little witch? Did he think that was funny?

Making her decision, she carried on. He had offered his own life to defend her and that, to her mind, was the action of a hero. Coming up to his level, she greeted him, '*Iqawe* (hero).'

He made room for her on the rock. 'Come and sit.'

Her heart skipped a beat. It was difficult enough for an unmarried girl to be alone with a man of rank and reputation. To be invited to sit so close to him made matters even worse. Calming herself, she settled beside him.

'Isn't it early for you to be collecting water?' he said.

'I'm not collecting water. As you can see, I'm not carrying a calabash.'

'What are you doing up here then?'

She hesitated, unwilling to confess she was on the way to the place she shared with Shikashika. Which prompted her to wonder why she couldn't admit her feelings for Shikashika. Was it because she didn't want to get them into trouble or because, at a much deeper level, she harboured feelings for Mehlokazulu? It was confusing.

'I often come up here to clear my head,' she replied.

He laughed. 'So do I.'

'Also, I couldn't sleep.'

'That's not surprising after yesterday. You were very brave.'

'I don't think so.'

'Pleading for someone who wanted you dead – believe me, that was very brave… or very foolish.'

'Maybe it was foolish. It would have been easier if I'd kept quiet.'

'Easier?'

'Yes.' She changed the subject. 'Anyway, if it had not been for you, there would have been a very different ending. You saved my life.'

He shrugged. 'I was not going to let you die when you were so obviously innocent. In any case, I have no time for the *iNgoma*'s mumbo-jumbo. Witches are denounced because someone wants them out of the way.' He looked into her eyes. 'Why did that girl denounce you?'

'She thinks I was responsible for her *iSoka*'s death.'

'Because?'

She hesitated. Knowing the danger of admitting her prophetic powers, but trusting Mehlokazulu, she admitted, 'I "saw" Maweni die.'

'Saw?'

'In my mind's eye. Just as Shikashika described it.'

'You told Sixhwethu this?'

'No, but she knows I "see" things.'

He chuckled. 'Shall I tell you what I think?'

She frowned. 'What?'

'Your "vision" of Maweni's death is a complete coincidence, but you feel guilty about it.'

'No.' She shook her head.

'Then you are a little witch.'

'You're making fun of me.'

'Not at all. In any case, having "visions" doesn't qualify you to be sent to the execution rock. I still don't understand why you spoke up for Sixhwethu. You should have remained silent. She deserved her punishment.'

'Deserved?'

'She and the rest of her family.'

Intrigued, she shifted her position. Sixhwethu's family background was a complete mystery. Whenever it came up in conversation with the other *isiGodlo* girls, they were equally ignorant. 'The rest of her family?'

He explained, 'Her father was Mphikeleli; her mother Thandekile, of the amaQungebeni. They were subjects of my father and lived in our *umuZi*. In those days we knew them as a family without honour. Though she bore his name, Sixhwethu was not Mphikeleli's child. Thandekile bore her to another man and dishonoured her own husband. The blood father, whose name was Mbambisi Nala, was an evil man who subsequently hired an *iNyanga* to poison Mphikeleli and Thandekile. My father had no choice but to execute him, which meant that Sixhwethu had no family to support her. Through his friendship with the king, Sihayo arranged for her to join the royal *isiGodlo*.'

Her eyes widened. It all made sense. Sixhwethu kept her family background secret because she was ashamed of being an orphan.

'But it seems that Thandekile's child is a liar and a cheat.

The whole bloodline is cursed, and it's a shame it wasn't ended yesterday.'

She digested the information. It explained so much about Sixhwethu: why she had chosen Nomguqo as a victim, why she was jealous she'd been favoured by the king and, more importantly, why she resented that she had a loving family. It wasn't immediately apparent why Mehlokazulu was so hostile towards her, until she was reminded of the parallels in his own family background. His mother was also an adulteress and had been put to death for her crime. In that light it wasn't hard to understand why he had such intense opinions. She wanted to probe more deeply but felt a direct question would intrude on his privacy.

To her surprise, he volunteered, 'I had to punish my mother for the same crime.' He waited for her to react. 'You're shocked?'

What did he want from her? Understanding? Sympathy? Absolution for his matricide? She thought long and hard before answering. 'Frankly, yes,' she said.

'My mother was a whore who brought disgrace to my father, to me and my brothers.'

'And you killed her.'

'Given the choice, I would do it again. A woman who accepts another man's seed deserves to die. It's the Zulu way…' Adding a further self-justification, 'It's also nature's way. Male lions destroy their rival's cubs. It's the same with us. If my mother had conceived her lover's child, it also would have been destroyed. I prevented it happening.'

The words rose unbidden into her mouth, 'Doesn't every child born have a right to life?'

'Not if the family's honour is at stake!'

His statement stopped the conversation dead. She glanced at him, his jaw working with anger, and decided it would be prudent to remain silent.

Brows furrowed, he stared into the distance, then stood, and without another word, strode down the mountain. She kept him in sight until he reached level ground.

During the time they'd been talking the light had lifted and the rising sun appeared over the horizon. Sunlight spilled across the Mahlabathini plain. The concentric circles of the oNdini huts came into sharp relief. She could see the open gates of the "Great Place" and the royal cattle being driven down to pasture beside the Mfolosi.

'*Ungathinti!*' Two of the king's servants patrolled the compound shouting for silence – their master was about to eat his midday meal and could not be disturbed. In opposite directions they wove between the huts and eventually met outside the king's hut.

oNdini's busy routine came to an abrupt halt. In suspended animation, the residents waited for Cetshwayo to finish eating. No one moved. Or spoke. Apart from the lowing of the cattle waiting to return to the *isibaya* for their midday milking, silence reigned. No one questioned its purpose other than to assume it would help the king's digestion and put him in good humour. On this occasion, it clearly hadn't worked. Cetshwayo's irate voice resounded through the *umuZi*, 'My own flesh and blood!' The windowpanes of the residence shook with the violence of his rage.

Nomguqo and the other *isiGodlo* girls who had just served his lunch backed away while he ranted, 'Tell me it's not true!'

The messenger, object of his ire, stuttered, 'Ha… Ha… Ha…'

'Spit it out!'

'Hamu…' he blurted out, then completed the rest in a rush, 'has joined the *abelungu*.'

The king pounded his fist into the palm of his hand. 'Traitor! At Khambula, you say?'

The messenger nodded.

'When?'

'Yesterday, Ndabezitha.'

Picking up an earthenware pot of *amaSi*, the king hurled it against the wall. Shards of pottery and milk curds flew everywhere, showering the girls. They covered their faces protectively.

'Alone?'

'No, Ndabezitha. Many of his followers were with him.'

'Get out,' Cetshwayo snarled at the *isiGodlo* girls. 'I have no appetite.'

Nomguqo and the other girls fled into the adjoining room. As they left, they heard him shouting instructions, 'Bring Mnyamana here. Now!' His footsteps pounded on the floorboards as he paced furiously up and down.

Through the window, Nomguqo saw the chief minister arrive, answering the summons with as much speed as his rheumatic knees would allow. As a venerable gentleman of seventy he preferred to take things slowly, but the urgency in the messenger's voice had made him run. Through the partition wall, the conversation was as clear as if they were still in the room.

'This is catastrophic!' Cetshwayo bellowed. 'If Hamu has taken his people to the British, how many others will follow?'

Mnyamana struggled to regain his breath. 'With respect, Ndabezitha, it doesn't surprise me. Hamu has always been a law unto himself. His loyalty has been in question since he challenged you at the *umKhosi WokweShwama*.'

'Exactly! And I could have nipped it in the bud right then and there. But what did you tell me? *We can't afford to alienate the man who protects our northern borders.*'

'In my defence, circumstances are different now.'

'Not as far as my brother's concerned. Well, I want him punished. He must pay the price for betraying us.'

'What would you suggest?'

'Take his cattle. Burn his crops. Sack his grain stores. Turn his *umuZi* into a wasteland.'

Mnyamana nodded. 'Consider it done.'

Cetshwayo motioned him to sit. 'He's been negotiating with the British for some time.' He tapped the side of his nose. 'A servant in his household regularly reports to me, tells me Hamu's been sending messages to their command. I suspected it but never thought it would happen.'

'We must make sure the governors of other remote corners of the kingdom remain loyal,' warned Mnyamana. 'Right now, we need complete dependability.'

'I'll leave that to you. Right now, I'm thirsty…' He called, 'Bring *uTshwala*.'

Nomguqo ran in with a *khamba* and poured beer into two beakers. Cetshwayo studied her. 'Have you recovered from your ordeal, daughter?'

Lost for words, she placed the pitcher on the table.

'You have great courage, child. We must begin to think about choosing her a worthy husband, eh, Mnyamana?'

The chief minister's eyes twinkled. He too had the highest regard for Nomguqo and took an interest in seeing her well married.

Cetshwayo sized her up, a roguish look in his eye. 'I'm sure your suitors are queuing up. Anyone caught your eye yet?'

'Well, Ndabezitha…' she faltered.

'Who is this boy you've been seen with?' he teased. 'Is it serious?'

'I like him,' she said.

'A brave warrior in the making, Mehlokazulu tells me. Seems he is performing the drills like a veteran. Shikashika, is that his name?'

Nomguqo's cheeks burned with embarrassment. How did the king know so much about her? Was nothing private?

'Well, I have no doubt he will prove an attentive *iSoka*, but you'll do well to accept my advice. Don't confuse romance with the duties of marriage. Eh, Mnyamana?'

The minister inclined his head deferentially.

'Take a sweetheart, by all means; whisper sweet nothings to each other. But remember, marriage is a different proposition. A girl must marry a man of substance, a man rich in cattle. And your bride price will be substantial, I can assure you.'

'As Your Majesty wishes,' said Nomguqo.

'Go and enjoy your Shikashika.' He dismissed her with a wave of his hand.

As she left the room, she heard laughter.

'I wanted the ground to open and swallow me whole. Why do you think he wanted to make fun of me like that?'

Nomguqo and Shikashika lay side by side in their hideaway on Hlophekhulu Mountain.

'It means he likes you,' Shikashika said.

'And what do you think he means by a "substantial" bride price?' Turning on her side, she rested her head on his chest. 'I don't want to marry anyone but you.'

'And you won't. When the king allows my age group to take wives, you will be my bride.'

'Well, that's settled.' Reaching around her neck, she undid her bead necklace. 'You can wear this as a token.' She wrapped the rawhide thong around his neck and knotted it at the back. Putting her hands on his shoulders, she levered herself up, so their faces were level. Then set a seal on their union by rubbing her nose against his.

He responded by drawing her close. The playfulness of their contact was quickly replaced by a more urgent feeling. Their lips parted as they kissed. His hands ran down her back and she felt a delicious tingle as they reached the curve of her hips. His fingers began an exploration of the skin beneath the waistband of her kirtle, encouraged by the depth of her kisses. Then he used his purchase on the skirt to pull her up, so their groins were touching. Through the flimsy fabric of their garments, she felt his erection. Its size and stiffness surprised and, at the same time, excited her. It was the first time they'd been so intimate, and she was overcome with a melting need to be one with him. Tears started in her eyes. Her fingers caressed his face, and she covered his forehead and eyelids with tiny kisses.

He looked up at her with surprise, brushing away the tears on her cheeks. 'What is it?' he asked.

'I've never been so happy.'

'But you're crying.'

'Tears of happiness. Kiss me again.'

He obliged, and his arms went around her waist and over her shoulders rolling her over, so she lay on her back. His weight pressed her down into the grass.

Breaking away, he pushed himself into a kneeling position. She frowned, then understood as he leaned over her again. This time, he kissed her throat, all the way down to her breasts. He took one of her nipples into his mouth.

She giggled. 'Have you done this before?'

'No, why?'

'You seem very practised.'

He stopped. 'Don't you like it?'

'I do.'

'Shall I carry on?'

Her giggles got the better of her. Her shoulders heaved as her laughter became uncontrollable.

He looked shocked and a little hurt, but her giggles were so infectious he couldn't help joining in.

Breathless from laughing, she was suddenly in the throes of a full-blown asthma attack. She raised her shoulders to pull air into her lungs. His broad grin quickly faded.

'It's… all right,' she gulped, '…don't worry.'

'Don't worry! You can't breathe.'

'…I'll be fine…'

'What should I do? Shall I go and get help?'

'…Don't fuss.'

'I know. I'll get some water.' Jumping up, he ran to the stream.

Without him fretting, she found it easier to cope. She did what she always did when she had an attack. Forcing her shoulders down, she focused on breathing more deeply and slowly.

By the time he came back it had returned to normal. He bent to offer the water cupped in his hands, droplets dripping through his fingers. But when she came to drink, there was nothing left. She burst out laughing again.

'Don't start that again,' he said. 'I was really worried.'

She lay back on the grass and he flopped down beside her. They lay without speaking, the afternoon sunshine slanting across their bodies.

'Where were we?' Rolling onto her elbows, she traced the white vitiligo patches on his chest. But the urgency of their lovemaking had been replaced by an understanding that it could wait.

He collected her into the crook of his elbow and brought her close, his fingers caressing the top of her head.

She lay on his chest, moving with the rhythm of his breathing. 'When you go off to fight, you will come back to me, won't you?' she whispered, not daring to express the premonition she'd been feeling.

'Of course.'

'The *amabutho* must be recalled.'

The *isikhulu* sat in the shade of the acacia tree, paying close attention to their king. 'My brother's treachery has left a vacuum in the north and the British are already exploiting it. Their general at Khambula behaves as though Zululand has already fallen. He must be stopped.' Kicking out at a stone, he sent it skittering across the cattle pen. 'Mbilini has sent word his homesteads are being burned and his cattle run off. He's been forced to retreat to his *umuZi* on the top of Hlobane Mountain. It can't go on like this. Reinforcements must be sent. Immediately!'

Pulling his blanket tighter, Mnyamana answered, 'Ndabezitha, our warriors have fought like lions in the recent engagements, but they have suffered terrible casualties. They need time for their wounds to heal and their strength to return.'

'We're being attacked on all sides, Mnyamana,' Cetshwayo said. 'The situation on the coast is equally serious. Dabulamanzi may have them pinned down at Eshowe, but it won't be long before more soldiers are sent to relieve them. As it is, we're spread too thin.'

'Absolutely,' said Ntshingwayo. 'After their reverse at iSandlwana, the *abelungu* are weak. While their morale is low, we should strike and drive them to the sea.'

'And how would we provision our warriors?' Mynamana asked. 'The grain stores are empty. It will be weeks before the harvest is gathered. Do we send them to war with empty bellies?'

'The *amabutho* should do what they've always done – forage on the ground,' the king said. 'The abaQulusi are rich in cattle: Mbilini has over two thousand head on the top of Hlobane – more than enough to supply our warriors for the few days it will take to defeat the British.' Clearly in no frame of mind to be contradicted, he glared at the council members, challenging them to defy him.

Ntshingwayo conceded, 'Our spirits are high. We know we can succeed. We have already proved it.'

Reluctantly, the others muttered in agreement.

Cetshwayo drew the meeting to a close. 'Send messengers out. The *amabutho* are to reassemble here at oNdindi to receive their preparations before marching to Khambula. See to it.'

THIRTY-ONE

Hlobane

High on the slopes of Hlobane Mountain, a large male leopard licked moisture beads from his muzzle. His long canines flashed white in the rays of the early morning sun. He crouched, ready to attack, yellow eyes fixed on his prey.

The calf stayed close to its mother. From time to time, she lifted her head, alert to any potential risk. Others in the herd continued to graze, unaware of the danger above them.

The big cat sprang.

Hooves skittering on the loose shale, the calf reacted to the movement, but not quickly enough. Its neck was held fast in the leopard's jaws, its windpipe slowly crushed by the relentless pressure.

The mother mooed plaintively, but she was powerless to help. A short, spasmodic struggle and it was over.

The rest of the herd scattered over the hillside – a pointless waste of effort because the leopard had made his kill. Dropping the body onto the shale, he licked the blood seeping from the puncture wounds, a preliminary to the feast he'd enjoy later.

From a vantage point further up the mountain, Mbilini watched with frustration. This was another loss he could ill afford. Since the British northern column had invaded his territory, there had been too many instances of his cattle being driven off. He had made retaliatory raids. And with some successes. When the redcoats burned him out of his ebaQulusini stronghold, he mounted a counterattack on a community protected by the British garrison at Luneburg, slaughtering men, women, and children and driving off their cattle. Through two whole moons, the raids and counter raids had continued. Now, like the leopard, he waited to spring a trap he'd set for the current assault. Redcoated horsemen were already picking their way up the mountain.

Four hundred abaQulusi, armed with guns and traditional Zulu weapons, were concealed on either side of a track that led to the plateau where their cattle were pastured. These were the prize the soldiers were seeking. Over two thousand animals, captured from Boer farms in the Transvaal, grazed there, protected by the natural features of the mountain. Hlobane was a fortress, its steep slopes leading to a wall of cliffs two hundred feet high around the summit. Access was up narrow boulder-strewn tracks, the most clearly defined of which had been turned into an ambush site. Large stones had been rolled down the slope to form a barrier across the path.

The previous day, his scouts reported that two companies of redcoats had left the Khambula garrison en route for Hlobane. Their progress was carefully monitored; runners sent hourly reports, one of which informed Mbilini that a detachment was moving to the western flank. He dispatched a full *iviyo* to confront it. The larger force was making swift progress: it would not be long before it came within range.

He watched the leopard pick up the limp body of the calf and drag it out of sight.

Mehlokazulu rose early. The chill in the night air had precluded any possibility of sleep. Having shivered under his blanket for several hours, he decided to keep his limbs moving. He left the flat area by a waterfall where the iNgobamakhosi were bivouacked and followed the stream up to the iNyathi ridge. He stared out over the landscape. Behind him, the northern flank of Hlobane, deep in shadow, stretched into the night sky, but in the south towards the open country leading to Khambula, he could see the sky beginning to lighten.

As dawn broke, tipping the cliffs of Hlobane with golden light, he made his way down to his men, who were already awake, stretching their frozen limbs and groaning from lack of sleep.

Huddled under his blanket, Shikashika clung to the last remnants of sleep. Mehlokazulu prodded him with his foot, then tossed him a corncob. 'Breakfast.'

Bleary-eyed, Shikashika fumbled to catch it.

'On your feet,' Mehlokazulu ordered.

It was a general instruction. The warriors ran on the spot to restore their circulation. He walked among them, summoning his section commanders to a briefing meeting. Once they'd assembled, he outlined their part in the overall tactical plan. 'We'll keep our position on the right flank with the uKhandempemvu and uVe, and move north to Hlobane, circling around to cut off the *abelungu* being driven down from the mountain by the abaQulusi. They'll be caught in a pincer movement. I estimate we'll engage by mid-morning.'

The junior officers grinned. Not a moment too soon.

'Return to your men,' Mehlokazulu said. 'We'll move off immediately.'

The leading horseman – an officer by the braid on his red tunic – was thirty yards away, perfectly aligned in Mbilini's sights.

Reacting to the obstruction of boulders across the path, the cavalry slowed. The officer approached, looking for a way around.

Mbilini's finger tightened on the trigger.

The round caught the officer fair and square in the chest, knocking him out of the saddle. A fusillade from the concealed abaQulusi forced the others to take evasive action. Driving their horses into cover behind the rocks, they returned fire.

The abaQulusi's aim was random; many of their bullets ricochetted harmlessly off the rocks. But several horses were hit, throwing their riders to the ground.

The main force followed, under the command of an officer who was clearly mad, foolhardy, or extremely courageous – perhaps all three. Determined to prevent his men being mown down by the crossfire, he rode up to the barricade while bullets pinged off the rocks around him. Making a quick decision, he spurred his horse through a narrow gap between the boulders. Two hundred horsemen followed and rode hell-for-leather up to the mountaintop. The others took their chances and retreated the way they had come.

The abaQulusi blazed away. Several more horses went down, and another officer was shot through the head. But most of the redcoats avoided the ambush and continued up the mountain. It was a waste of ammunition to continue firing. Grabbing his *iklwa*, Mbilini ran to the fallen soldiers and slashed each across the stomach to release the *umnyama*. Others vented their anger in a frenzy of stabbing. The rocks soon ran with blood. Turning to the redcoats who were escaping down the track, Mbilini split his force, sending the majority after the troopers up to the summit, while he took fifty warriors obliquely down the mountain. On foot, they would easily outrun them.

In the distance beyond the retreating cavalry, the main Zulu army appeared, two distinct horns heading to either side of the mountain. It resembled the shadow of a huge thundercloud passing over the landscape. Even for someone as used to warfare as Mbilini, it was an awesome sight.

On the Hlobane summit, the British cavalry fanned out across the undulating grassland. Like practised cattle thieves, they rounded up the scattered groups of grazing cows and corralled them into a herd to drive back down the mountain.

Unwittingly, they were serving Mbilini's purpose. He had counted on the cattle being the lure to attract them up the mountain in the first place. Now he could spring the trap.

The troopers drove the herd towards the western end of the plateau, where the land appeared to drop away gently to the lower plateau of Ntendeka. The officer clearly assumed this was the exit route from the mountain.

By now the abaQulusi had reached the plateau and were streaming towards them.

The officer rode to the edge. Alarmed by what he saw, he brought his horse up short. Instead of a grassy incline, it was an almost vertical, two-hundred-foot-long, ten-foot-wide ramp. Large boulders lay along its length, making it virtually impassable on horseback. Precipices on either side were additional hazards.

Abandoning the cattle, they quickly dismounted and started the descent, scrambling over boulders and dragging their horses behind them. Bullets glanced harmlessly off the rocks until the abaQulusi found their range. Then the soldiers began to take casualties.

Sensing victory, the abaQulusi discarded their rifles so they could use their stabbing spears.

It was no place for cumbersome cavalry boots. To avoid breaking their ankles the soldiers were forced to concentrate on where they put their feet. The abaQulusi had no such problem, their bare feet allowing them to leap from one boulder to another. They bore down on the troopers, stabbing indiscriminately.

Racing down the mountain, Mbilini and his men reached a series of deep caves. From these they had a perfect line of sight to the track below. The cavalry would be completely exposed until they reached a deserted cattle pen. It was a perfect killing ground. He stationed his men in the caves, checking that their rifles were loaded and that each had sufficient ammunition.

The leading riders of the second cavalry company came around a bend in the track and approached the point where it started to climb up the cliff face. They had no idea that fifty looted Martini-Henrys were trained on them.

The first volley took down half a dozen. The survivors took evasive action, spurring their horses towards the cattle pen. Dismounting, they tried desperately to put themselves and their horses out of the line of fire. More casualties fell in the frantic dash. Ten troopers had their horses shot from under them and were picked off as they ran, the fusillade of high-velocity rounds blowing them to pieces.

Mbilini loaded, fired, and reloaded in quick succession, ducking instinctively as a bullet grazed his forehead and bounced off the rock behind him. Blood trickled into his eye. He checked the damage. Nothing serious – a flesh wound. Squinting through its sights, he tracked his rifle over the area in front of his hideout. A redcoated officer appeared in the opening. He fired. The shot took the top of the man's head off.

The troopers couldn't move, pinned down by the heavy barrage from above. They returned fire as and when they could, but their position was dangerously exposed. A few courageous souls tried to mount an attack on the caves – like the officer who had rushed Mbilini's position – but they all came to the same end.

Mbilini and his men had a field day, the muzzles of their rifles now too hot to touch. He wondered whether their ammunition would last at that rate of fire. It would be touch and go. Then the battle cry of two thousand warriors in full voice put his mind at rest. *uSuthu! uSuthu! uSuthu!*

Less than eight hundred yards away, wave upon wave of warriors came into view around the mountain flank and headed towards their position – the uKhandempemvu in the lead, closely followed by the iNgombamakhosi with Mehlokazulu at the front.

Up on the mountain-top, the British commanding officer ordered a retreat, aware of the pincer movement on their flank. As the troopers took to their heels, it became "every man for himself". Some tried to make a stand but were engulfed by the relentless tide of uKhandempemvu. They didn't last long, chopped down with stabbing spears or their brains dashed out with war clubs. The only chance of survival was on horseback, but the horses were so terrified it became a battle to control them. Mbilini and his men took full advantage, spearing both horses and men.

When it was obvious the day was theirs, the abaQulusi broke cover and joined the warriors in the cattle pen, who were disembowelling the dead. Shikashika, with no experience of the *qaqa* ritual, watched with appalled fascination.

Among the abaQulusi were men Mehlokazulu recognised from his exile in the ebaQulusini *umuZi*. He greeted close friends, then, catching sight of Mbilini, he held out his arms in greeting. Noticing the blood seeping from the head wound, he pointed with his *iklwa*, then feinted the blade into Mbilini's chest. 'One bullet you couldn't dodge, eh?'

THIRTY-TWO

oNdini

Sixhwethu struggled against the rawhide thongs that pinned her arms, the leather cutting into her flesh. Her face contorted in a silent scream as they dragged her towards the execution rock. Her heels carved deep tracks in the dusty soil. However hard she tried she couldn't break free: the hands gripping her were too strong.

A warrior waited, a polished war club in his hand. His expression was as hard as the execution rock itself.

Because she was dragged backwards, Sixhwethu hadn't seen him yet. Now, as she was flung at his feet, she saw his pitiless expression, and the reality of her fate became obvious. She whimpered with fear.

Her escort formed a circle around her so she couldn't escape. She scrabbled on hands and knees, desperately grabbing at their legs, hoping for some sign they'd take pity on her. They kicked her back towards the executioner.

He lifted the heavy club above his shoulders, the muscles in his powerful arms rippling. There was a blur of movement as the carved ball of the club head whistled through the air.

'Where's Sixhwethu?' Nomguqo sat upright, her eyes focused on the empty space where Sixhwethu normally slept.

Her anxious voice roused Nguyaze who peered from the recesses of the dark hut. 'Who cares?' she said.

'I'm worried something might have happened.'

'You're a strange one, Nomguqo – after what she did to you. She's probably peeing.'

Nomguqo was already on her way to the entrance, stepping carefully over the sleeping girls.

A light drizzle had started to fall, but the air retained some heat from the late summer sun. She had no idea where to search but an instinct led her towards the king's residence. Darkness shrouded the *isiGodlo* huts as she slipped noiselessly between them.

Passing the *eNkatheni*, she noticed a figure crumpled in the doorway. Sixhwethu was out cold, stretched on her side, a half-empty bottle beside her. Even from a distance, Nomguqo could smell the gin fumes. Her heart skipped a beat. Sixhwethu must have helped herself to the king's store. The bottle's label was the proof; it matched all the others stacked in the royal cupboard. The implications were terrifying. To be found in this condition with the damning evidence beside her would provoke the king's anger beyond all bounds. And this time there would be no saving her.

Once again, Nomguqo was forced to protect her hutmate from the consequences of her own stupidity. First, she had to wake her. A hard smack on Sixhwethu's cheek produced a single shocked snort. A bleary eye opened, then closed, and her snoring resumed. Slapping her again, Nomguqo hissed, 'Wake up. Wake up.'

This time, Sixhwethu remained awake. 'What is it,' she slurred.

'Have you lost your mind?'

'Leave me alone.'

'Get up.'

'But I want to sleep.'

Nomguqo slipped her arm under the other girl's shoulders and, though considerably slighter in build, heaved her into a sitting position.

'Get off me,' Sixhwethu said.

'Keep your voice down,' Nomguqo whispered, nervously scanning the compound. 'We need to get you back to the hut. If you're found here, you'll be sent to kwaNkatha.' Hauling a virtual dead weight, she manoeuvered her to her feet. Sixhwethu's knees threatened to buckle, and Nomguqo had to wedge her shoulder into her armpit to keep her upright. Half carrying and half frog-marching her, she manhandled her towards the hut. Much to her alarm, Sixhwethu sobered up enough to carry on a running commentary. 'It was naughty, I know, but one little bottle out of all those in his cupboard… he'll never miss one, surely?'

'Will you be quiet!'

By the time they reached the entrance, Sixhwethu lapsed into unconsciousness again. Nomguqo kept her upright by propping her against the doorpost. But her legs gave way, and she slid down, settling with her chin on her chest beside the doorway.

Nomguqo pushed aside the oxhide door covering. Then, grabbing Sixhwethu's ankles, dragged her dead weight into the hut, taking little care to prevent her head bouncing off the bumps and hollows of the uneven floor. Her hands were slick from the rain, which made the task doubly difficult.

With Sixhwethu out of harm's way, she ran back to the *eNkatheni* and collected the gin bottle, jamming the stopper she found lying close by into the neck. She couldn't return it to the cupboard half empty. The large gourd set to catch the rain off the *eNkatheni* roof provided the water to top it up.

Banking on the residence being empty, she pushed open the door, her heart in her mouth. What she was about to do would put her life literally on the line. The door of the drinks' cupboard was wide open, with the normally tidy bottles all jumbled up. She carefully rearranged them, putting the one she'd adulterated at the back. Fear of discovery made her jittery. Her trembling hands nudged a bottle in the front row, toppling it forwards. With lightening reaction, she caught it before it smashed on the floor.

Replacing it with the utmost care, she closed the cupboard door behind her.

Fifty miles away in the Zulu camp at Hlobane the mood was very different. The warriors celebrated their triumph. The British had been comprehensively beaten. The ruse to frustrate their cattle raid had been spectacularly successful. Not only had the soldiers been routed, with large numbers lying dead on the Hlobane hillsides, but the abaQulusi herd remained safe on the mountain top.

Across the White Mfolosi river plain cooking fires were alight, joints of freshly slaughtered beef sizzling in the embers. Retelling the story of the battle, warriors boasted of their part in it, a rehearsal for the tales they would tell when they returned home. It was also an opportunity to agree on the details before reporting back to the king. The accuracy of their account would determine whether they would wear the heroes' necklace.

Mehlokazulu picked his teeth with a thorn. 'Another triumph to add to iSandlwana, and more *abelungu* sent to their ancestors.'

'Over two hundred, I heard,' Shikashika said.

'And a dozen of them, officers. Today was a good day.'

'And tomorrow?' Shikashika asked.

'The same,' Mehlokazulu said, 'Their soldiers are no match for us. You saw them today, running away like scared children. If we find an opportunity to close with them, they won't stand a chance.'

Nomguqo's insomnia was rapidly turning into a habit. She tossed and turned until the early hours when she finally managed to drift off. Then a persistent shaking of her foot jolted her awake. Opening her eyes, she found herself staring into Sixhwethu's anxious face.

'I haven't dared leave the hut,' she wailed. 'I'm just waiting for the *iziMpisi* to come.'

'They won't come.'

'Yes, they will – after what I did last night.'

'Don't worry, I put the bottle back. Ndabezitha will be none the wiser.'

'You did?'

Nomguqo nodded.

'Oh, thank you, thank you.'

'Now, go back to bed. I've had no sleep, thanks to you.' Clicking her tongue irritably, Nomguqo wrapped the blanket around her shoulders. 'What possessed you to steal the king's gin?'

'I don't know. I've so many bad thoughts in my head. I wanted them to go away.'

'Did they?'

'I suppose so. For a while.'

'How do you feel now?'

'Horrible. My head hurts and I feel sick.'

Nomguqo turned her back. 'Well, don't be sick on me.'

'What you did is a mark of real friendship. I don't deserve it.'

'No, you don't.'

Sixhwethu's eyes filled with tears. 'Do you know why I spoke to Dlephu Ndlovu?' She supplied the answer. 'I was jealous. I watched you up on the mountain – when you lay with Shikashika – and it made me want Maweni's skin next to mine. I wanted him in my arms again. And I knew I never would.' She sobbed. 'He was the only one who really understood me. With him I never felt alone.'

Nomguqo propped herself on her elbows. 'Do you normally feel alone?'

Sixhwethu wiped her eyes. 'Don't you?'

'I did when I first came here.'

'And now?'

'I've got used to it.'

'That was my fault too, wasn't it?'

Nomguqo's silence was her answer.

'Do you hate me?'

The automatic answer should have been yes, but with her knowledge of her family background, she saw her in a different light.

'I've given you every reason,' Sixhwethu said. 'Calling you names and picking on you…'

'That's in the past now. Isn't it?'

Sixhwethu put her hand over Nomguqo's. 'I'd like to be your friend. If you'll have me.' Her eyes were full of sincerity.

A huge weight was released from Nomguqo's shoulders.

Ntshingwayo's voice cut through the clear morning air: '*Abaqawe*, every one of you. Heroes of iSandlwana!'

Fifteen thousand voices echoed, 'iSandlwana!'

The mood of optimism in the Zulu camp lasted through the night. The warriors were impatient to continue where they had left off. They paraded in full battle order on the riverbanks to receive their commanders' instructions.

Ntshingwayo shouted, 'Your achievements will be celebrated for many years to come. Our enemy quakes at the mention of your name. And yesterday's triumph served to confirm your invincibility.'

'iSandlwana!'

'Today we can increase that reputation still further. Our purpose is to draw the enemy out into the open. To that end we shall march to the enemy garrison at inqaba kaHawana. Our scouts tell us it's on high ground and heavily fortified. Artillery pieces have been set up and we know from our experience at iSandlwana what damage they can do. We'll deploy in our usual formation using five columns. Our initial advance will take us to the south-west of the camp. There we'll wait. Expect further instructions at that point. Understood?'

An answering shout went up. '*Usuthu!*'

'The commander-in-chief will address you. Pay careful heed to what he has to say.'

Ntshingwayo stood to one side as Mnyamana took his place, shivering in the cold. He pulled his oxhide cloak tight around his shoulders. 'The future of our nation lies on your shoulders,' he said. His voice was much weaker than Ntshingwayo's and warriors in the rear ranks struggled to hear him. 'Never before have we faced a greater challenge. If today is lost, perhaps there is no future for the amaZulu. Be steadfast and strong.' With nothing more to say, he stepped back.

The *amabutho* stood in shocked silence. Surely their general – the king's most senior counsellor – would have something more inspiring to offer, exhort them to lay down their lives for king and country. But nothing more was forthcoming.

Ntshingwayo was reluctant to leave on such a note, but his inferior rank forced him to remain silent.

Breaking out of the *umkhumbi*, the warriors regrouped into their battle formation. Mutters of discontent ran through the ranks. If their commander-in-chief had so little confidence in them, what hope was there?

Through the early part of the day, Mehlokazulu and the iNgombamkhosi in the right horn advanced until they reached a point about a mile from the Khambula garrison. They halted to await further orders. British soldiers were clearly visible behind a rampart of ox-wagons linked together by a network of chains. Twenty feet above that, earthworks had been raised as a platform for the gun battery. To one side a large herd of cattle was penned behind a palisade. The whole fortress looked impregnable.

Mehlokazulu scanned the area on both sides. To the right, the ground fell away sharply into a deep ravine. From what he could see, this was a definite weakness to exploit. If he and his men could get close enough, they would use it as protection from the guns. For the moment they would have to wait.

An hour later they were still waiting. When would they receive the order to attack? The iNgobamakhosi were completely isolated. Apart from the uVe on their left flank, they had no sight of the other *amabutho* and could only guess where they were.

Desperate to prove themselves, the younger warriors began to fidget. Having witnessed the horrors of iSandlwana, Shikashika had a good idea what to expect. He was nervous, wondering how he'd behave in battle, whether his courage would fail at the last minute.

Just when Mehlokazulu had given up hope, Shikashika pointed to movement at the camp entrance. A gap opened in the barricade and two squadrons of cavalry mustered outside, their white helmets and red tunics bright against the khaki hillside.

Shielding his eyes, Mehlokazulu counted the horsemen. The odds were overwhelmingly in their favour: less than a hundred against the combined force of iNgobamakhosi and uVe.

Wheeling, the horsemen moved forward at a collected canter, directly towards them.

The iNgobamakhosi shuffled nervously, on the point of breaking ranks to charge. They were like hunting dogs. Now they had scented their prey, there was no holding them back.

'Stay calm. Let them show their intentions,' Mehlokazulu said.

Maintaining their moderate pace, the cavalry continued in a direct line. 'What is their game?' Mehlokazulu wondered out loud. 'A charge against us would be suicide. We'd cut them to pieces.'

Within two hundred yards of the Zulu lines, the British halted and dismounted.

The temptation was too great. Breaking ranks, the iNgobamakhosi rushed forward, brandishing their weapons.

'Get back!' Mehlokazulu shouted. 'Stay in formation!' but he might as well have bayed at the moon. His orders were drowned by his warriors' war cries. With no alternative, he joined the rush.

Right at the back, Shikashika ran alongside Mehlokazulu. His shield felt light on his arm. The adrenaline gave him strength and the ferocity of his comrades inspired him. He was glad he wasn't on the receiving end.

The cavalrymen knelt, rifles up and ready. When the iNgobamakhosi came within range, they fired, and thirty front-runners went down. Not stopping to check their successes, the cavalry remounted and spurred their horses back to camp.

The iNgombamakhosi accelerated after them. Shikashika ran past the fallen warriors. The severity of their wounds made him falter. One gasped like a stranded fish, his shield arm blown away, the severed arm still clutching the shield. Another choked on his own blood, a ghastly red hole where his lower jaw had been.

Reining in again, the cavalry went through the same drill, discharging their carbines into the massed iNgobamakhosi. And with the same effect. More gaps appeared in the line.

Undeterred, the warriors came on. Then, just as before, when they reached the range of their throwing spears, the horsemen remounted and galloped away.

By now, Mehlokazulu had pieced together the strategy – to lure them within range of the artillery and massed rifles of the garrison. 'Stop! Stop!' he yelled. But either they couldn't hear or wouldn't listen. Their blood was up. Their sole purpose: to wash their spears.

The garrison gates opened to receive the galloping horsemen, then closed behind them.

The iNgobamakhosi front ranks reached a line of white-painted stones. Behind them, some twenty paces back, Mehlokazulu implored them to pull back.

His words were swallowed by the massive volley of rifle fire that cut a swathe through his men. Clearly the white stones were range finders because the fire was devastatingly accurate. Warriors fell like ninepins.

With a deafening roar, the artillery pieces mounted behind the palisade discharged rounds of case shot. Across the width of the iNgobamakhosi advance, the air was filled with razor-sharp shards of metal.

Seeing the puffs of smoke, Shikashika knew instinctively to drop to the ground. Lying prostrate, he watched horrified as those ahead of him were cut to pieces, the shrapnel ripping chunks of flesh from their bodies. The ground became a charnel house, blood from severed arteries spouting into the dust around him. Paralysed with fear, he turned, looking for somewhere to hide from the flying metal. Mehlokazulu, also flat on his belly, signalled towards an outcrop of rocks ahead. It was the only shelter close enough, but to reach it would mean exposing themselves to the guns again. Following Mehlokazulu's lead, he waited until the guns reloaded, then took off like a rocket.

Rifle bullets kicked up puffs of dust at his feet as he ran, crouched low, zigzagging across the open ground. Though it took only seconds, it seemed like an eternity. As he reached safety, the guns started firing again, a ferocious and deafening barrage.

Panting with relief that he'd survived, he rested against one of the large rocks. Not realising that part of his shield was still exposed, he received a forcible reminder of the danger when a bullet struck the tip of the wooden brace, breaking it off and showering him with splinters. He crouched into a ball to present as small a target as possible.

Mehlokazulu's brain worked overtime to figure out an escape from the desperate situation. He glanced back to the open spaces beside the white range finders. Hundreds of iNgobamakhosi bodies littered the ground, mangled by the cannon fire. If they retreated, they'd have their backs to the guns; going forward at least gave them the chance to see when they were being reloaded – they could advance during the lull. Checking on the men grouped around him, he was alarmed by their body language. Their sullen expressions and slumped shoulders confirmed his worst suspicions: they had the air of defeated men, their morale blown away by the horrifying fusillade. For the time being, any further assault was out of the question. They needed a breathing space, time to recover their spirits.

A warrior beside him muttered, 'Where are the others?'

As though in answer, a distant salvo of shots came from the far side.

'Sounds like the left horn is in position,' Mehlokazulu said, then stuck his head out. He retreated quickly as a rifle round pinged off the rock and onto his forehead, opening a gash two inches long. Blood poured down the side of his face. The sudden pain forced him back on his heels, but he had seen enough to know that both the left horn and the chest were in action.

From an elevated position on the western flank, Zulu sharpshooters used the Martini-Henrys looted at iSandlwana to fire on the British garrison.

The uThulwana had assembled in the ravine to the south out of sight of the camp. Now they came in waves, breaking over the ridge. But as each line of warriors came within range, they were exposed to withering fire. Like the iNgobamakhosi on the other side, they were mown down in droves. Despite their massive casualties, they pressed forward, successive companies clambering over their comrades' corpses in their blind faith they would survive.

After thirty minutes of battle raging on the far side, Mehlokazulu judged his men sufficiently recovered to make a further attack. He stood to his full height, raised his rifle high in the air and shouted the battle cry, *uSuthu!* He took off like a cheetah on its prey and was joined by the rest of the iNgobamakhosi. With a deep breath, Shikashika broke cover.

For at least fifty yards, they made rapid progress without loss, using the advantage that the British were concentrating their firepower on the southern and western boundaries.

Then the guns found them again. It was instant carnage. Case shot ploughed into the ranks, shredding the bodies of those in the way. Shikashika was drenched in his comrades' blood. Steeling himself, he redoubled his pace and matched Mehlokazulu stride for stride.

Half of the iNgobamakhosi died in the first hundred and fifty yards. The rest were forced by the relentless bombardment to seek whatever shelter they could. Some cowered behind large stones they carried for the purpose. All pressed themselves flat, while bullets tore through the air around them.

For three hours, Mehlokazulu and his men were pinned down. Then, when the sun was at its zenith, burning with pitiless intensity, he finally ordered the retreat. He had no alternative, even though it meant exposing them to further danger. As they retired to the ridge, the British gunners poured volley after volley into their backs.

Shikashika ran for his life. His nerves in shreds, he summoned his last reserves of energy, discarding his shield to increase his speed. If ever he needed justification, he had already seen how ineffective its protective qualities were. More than one warrior had been shot through his *isihlangu*, the oxhide easily punctured by the high velocity rounds.

Several paces behind, Mehlokazulu tripped over the abandoned shield and clicked his tongue with disapproval. If the boy survived, he would call him to account for his lack of discipline.

Shikashika reached a dip in the landscape. A sharply inclined slope stretched ahead. Pausing to force air into his lungs, he glanced over his shoulder and saw a squadron of cavalry emerging from the camp. They galloped in a direct line towards the fleeing warriors, their lances couched under their arms. Belly contracting with fear, he launched himself up the hill, and in his panic, failed to notice where he was treading. His foot disappeared in a rock rabbit burrow. The shooting pain from the snapped tendon took his breath away; he went over like a shot gazelle.

Seeing how much ground the horsemen had already covered, Mehlokazulu realised they were in trouble. Reaching down, he helped Shikashika to his feet. Whimpering in pain, the boy shifted his weight from his damaged leg. Mehlokazulu looked into his eyes. Both understood that for Shikashika there was no escape.

'Go,' Shikashika implored him. 'I'll take my chances.'

The horses' hooves pounded ever nearer. Though reluctant to abandon him, Mehlokazulu had no choice; it was his duty to fight another day. Unshouldering the Martini-Henry, he slid back the bolt and loaded a bullet into the breech. Helping Shikashika into a more comfortable sitting position, he placed the rifle in his hands. 'You're a brave boy. You will join your ancestors a true umZulu.'

Shikashika clenched his teeth against the pain. 'Tell Nomguqo I sold my life dearly.'

There was nothing more to say. Mehlokazulu ruffled the boy's hair and continued up the hill.

In the time it took him to reach the top, the horsemen reached Shikashika. A rifle shot echoed across the hillside. Looking back, Mehlokazulu saw the leading horseman tumble from his saddle.

For the boy the outcome was inevitable. Mehlokazulu stayed long enough to watch three horsemen thrusting their lances into his chest and belly. Shikashika writhed on the ground, the lances pinning him down. One hand clutched the spear in his belly while the other grasped the beaded love token round his neck. His mouth stretched wide in silent supplication.

The news Mehlokazulu would carry back to oNdini was dire. The death toll was in the thousands. After the warriors were routed from the battlefield, they were chased across three mountain ridges by the British cavalry. In retaliation for iSandlwana, the British were merciless; they took no prisoners and butchered every wounded warrior they found. The handful who escaped did so only because it was too late in the day for the British to track them down. For miles around, the ground was littered with Zulu corpses.

At dead of night Mehlokazulu crept back. His mission was threefold. He was desperate to retrieve his rifle, the instrument he would use to take his revenge. He felt obliged to show Nomguqo evidence of her *iSoka*'s bravery. And, most importantly, he was *inxweleha*, tainted with the enemy's blood. For several days, it was taboo for him to return to oNdini.

The battlefield was completely deserted. The light of a new moon guided his steps. The scale of British brutality was shocking. For hundreds of yards on either side of Shikashika's corpse the ground was covered with his iNgobamakhosi comrades.

He knelt beside the boy. His body was folded in on itself, knees drawn up in agony, his hand still clutching the love token. He gently prized the fingers away, one by one, slipped the necklace over the boy's head and wrapped it around his wrist. It would be safe there until he returned it to Nomguqo.

Then he set about digging a grave. He hadn't time to honour all his comrades in the same way but burying Shikashika went some way to discharging his regimental duty. Fortunately, the ground was soft and already riddled with holes dug by rock rabbits. Using his *iklwa*, it didn't take him long to excavate a hole of sufficient depth. He laid the body reverently in the grave and covered it with the spoil, rolling several large boulders on top.

Shouldering his rifle, he headed south.

Nomguqo stood ankle-deep in the stream filling the calabash. She tipped the lip of the container into the flowing water. As it filled, a shadow passed over her. She looked up, but the sun's glare was such that she didn't immediately identify him. His voice was unmistakable though: 'Nomguqo.' Her heart skipped a beat. Shielding her eyes with her hand, she stared into Mehlokazulu's face. His expression and the trail of crusted blood running from the cut in his forehead made her shiver with apprehension. Her gaze travelled past him to the other side of the river, checking if Shikashika was with him. He was alone.

Untying the bead necklace from his wrist, he handed it to her. There was no need for words. She knew she would never see Shikashika again.

The scream rising in her throat was cut short as she fainted and fell towards him. Discarding his heavy war shield and weapons, he caught her and carried her to the riverbank. He laid her on the grass, returning to retrieve his shield and Nomguqo's calabash.

The other *isiGodlo* girls clustered around her, clucking in alarm. Nguyaze dipped a cloth in the stream and applied a cold compress to her forehead. Sixhwethu assumed the reason for Nomguqo's distress and commented philosophically, 'We're destined to finish up old maids, she, and I. How did he die? A hero's death or a horrible accident like my Maweni?'

'Stop prattling, girl,' Mehlokazulu said. 'Attend to your friend.'

'No need to be rude,' she retorted. 'But you can't help yourself, can you, Mehlokazulu nGobese? You were born an ignorant pig and you will die one.'

He was too exhausted and demoralised to argue further. Picking up his shield, he marched off to the *umuZi*.

Nomguqo's eyes fluttered open. Four anxious faces peered down at her. Her consciousness restored, she felt again the pang of her loss. Despair threatened to choke her. Fighting to control her breathing, her eyes filled with tears.

'She needs water.' Cupping her hands in the stream, Sixhwethu raised a dripping handful to her mouth. Nomguqo shook her head mutely, sobbing with the effort of breathing – a full-blown asthma attack to add to her woes.

'We're crowding her,' Sixhwethu said. 'Give her some space.'

Their kind solicitations were too much. As they stood back, she hugged her knees and howled.

THIRTY-THREE

Cetshwayo strode down the path between the *isiGodlo* huts. A pace behind him, a slim young white man in his mid-twenties struggled to keep up. He carried a leather bag over his shoulder. A Dutch trader stranded by the war, Cornelius Vijn had accepted the king's offer of sanctuary and, in return for his hospitality, was acting as his secretary, helping him write conciliatory letters to the British authorities in Pietermaritzburg.

Royal children playing alongside the path stared as their father headed to the servants' dwellings. The king's shoulders were hunched as though carrying a great burden. The scale of the defeat at Khambula had physically diminished him.

Pausing outside Nomguqo's hut, Cetshwayo turned to Vijn. 'You are sure your medicine will be effective?'

'Quite sure, Your Majesty.'

Stooping, Cetshwayo entered the hut.

Nomguqo lay on her bedroll propped against the inner wall. She was barely conscious, her breathing shallow and laboured. Her companions were gathered around her, Sixhwethu the most attentive, holding a beaker to Nomguqo's lips, entreating her to drink. At the king's appearance, she backed away deferentially.

'Nomguqo,' Cetshwayo called.

Her throat whistled, and her lungs wheezed like leaky bellows. The whites of her eyes showed as she implored him – anyone – to bring her relief.

'I've brought someone to help you.' The king beckoned the young man forward. 'This is Cornelius Vijn. He has medicine to ease your breathing.'

Reaching into his bag, Vijn produced a handful of powder, grabbed the beaker from Sixhwethu, dropped the powder into it, and swirled it around to mix a potion. Then placed the lip of the beaker against Nomguqo's lips. 'Sip,' he said, tipping it gently.

Registering the sensation of liquid on her lips, her eyes came into focus.

'And swallow,' he said.

Still gasping like a fish out of water, Nomguqo opened her lips and allowed the medicine into her mouth.

'Good girl,' said Vijn as she swallowed. 'Soon you'll be breathing normally. If it works for me, it will work for you.'

Already the calm reassurance of his voice had an effect. She sipped steadily until the beaker was empty.

'What is it?' the king asked, intrigued at the effect.

'Dried leaves of the ephedra plant. A Chinese herbalist on the coast supplies me,' Vijn said. 'I don't know what I'd do without it. If I have an attack, I make an infusion and I'm breathing normally within minutes.'

'Better stockpile it, then.' Cetshwayo nodded with satisfaction as Nomguqo's breathing slowly resumed its usual rhythm.

She burst into tears of relief. 'Thank you.' She curled into a ball on her bedroll; her eyes closed and within seconds she was fast asleep. Reassured that the crisis had passed, the king made his exit.

She slept like a baby – through the day and the following night. By the time she woke, the tightness in her chest had lifted, and over the following days, the sharp pangs of grief subsided into a dull ache.

Indulgent at first, Nomvimbi soon expected her to resume her duties. 'The prince and princess won't look after themselves,' she said tartly on the second day. 'Look lively. I can't have you moping about like this. You're not the only one to lose a loved one, you know.'

'Of course not,' Nomguqo agreed.

The princess's piercing scream reinforced Nomvimbi's argument. Dinuzulu wore a guilty expression. The toddler was too young to explain what happened but howled fit to burst. Nomguqo picked her up and wiped away the tears.

'Not my fault,' Dinuzulu protested. 'She started it.'

Used to the spats between her offspring, Nomvimbi left Nomguqo to it.

'Started what?' Nomguqo asked.

Dinuzulu pointed to the carved figure in his sister's hand. 'She stole my warrior. I can't play my game without him,' indicating the make-believe battle he'd set up in a corner.

'And what did you do?'

'Hit her of course.'

'She's a baby. You don't hit babies. Besides, you can share, surely?'

'She doesn't share with me.'

Besiyile frowned at him from the safety of Nomguqo's arms, large tears rolling down her cheeks; at least she'd stopped howling. Gently prizing the toy warrior from her fingers, Nomguqo handed it to the boy. 'Promise me, you'll never hit your sister again.'

Satisfied he had won the real battle, Dinuzulu ran back to his pretend version.

'What shall we do, *inkosazana*?' Nomguqo set the princess back on her feet. 'I know, you can help me with *Umama's* beadwork, sort out the colours for me. How does that sound?' Beaming, Besiyile dragged Nomguqo to where Nomvimbi was working on a chest ornament. Peace was restored.

Over the days, the routine of looking after the children became her solace. More accurately, her distraction. Absorbed in their own needs, Dinuzulu and Besiyile were unaware she was quieter than usual. They made their normal demands and were impatient when she failed to attend to them quickly enough.

More surprisingly, Sixhwethu became another source of consolation. The girl who had bullied her for so long was sympathy personified. She assumed all Nomguqo's physical duties and prepared tasty food to tempt her non-existent appetite.

The girls were not alone in their sorrow. A pall enveloped the whole Zulu nation; the Khambula defeat hung over them like a funeral shroud. The losses of individual households were serious enough, but a greater and more damaging consequence was the acceptance that the *amabutho* were not strong enough to protect the kingdom. It was treason to speak of it, but those who had lost their menfolk wondered whether it had been worth the sacrifice. Further resistance seemed futile, merely delaying the inevitable surrender. The widespread disillusion was increased still further by news that Dabulamanzi's army had suffered massive losses in a catastrophic defeat at Gingindlovu. Would sufficient warriors be available to defend oNdini?

The people needed reassurance. A public appearance from the king might have set their minds at rest, but he chose to closet himself away with his advisors. Outside his trusted inner circle, no one caught so much as a glimpse of him for over ten days. The rumour mill ground away.

Cetshwayo exploded with rage: 'Damn him! May he suffer a thousand hideous and painful deaths!'

An *udibi*, barely twelve years old, ducked as the king flailed the air with his flywhisk. 'Tell me it isn't so.'

'I… I saw him with my own eyes,' the boy stammered. 'Pluck out my tongue if I lie.'

There was a long pause while Cetshwayo collected himself. 'What is your name?' he asked.

'Bhekisiza, Ndabezitha.'

'"Watchful", eh? You're well named, Bhekisiza. Those observations of yours are very important. Now, tell us exactly what you saw. The detail is important. Start at the beginning.'

The royal council members sitting under the *isibaya* acacia listened attentively.

'I was with the cattle that supplied the white men's army. Nobody noticed me because I was a boy. I wanted to gain information for you, Ndabezitha…'

The king smiled indulgently.

'I saw some men I recognised: kinsmen of yours, Ndabezitha. Also, sons of Jantoni. They carried guns and marched beside the redcoat soldiers. I saw Jantoni himself riding with the redcoat officers…'

Sihayo made a remark to Mehlokazulu inaudible to the king.

'Sihayo,' the king interrupted, 'if you've something to say, share it with the *ibandla*.'

'Jantoni's treachery was entirely predictable, Ndabezitha. We were wrong to trust him as long as we did,' Sihayo replied.

'I was wrong, you mean?'

The lack of response was eloquent. The other courtiers shifted in their seats, waiting for the predictable explosion of anger. To their surprise, Cetshwayo remained silent. He seemed to accept the implicit criticism.

Mehlokazulu spoke, 'My father means no disrespect, Ndabezitha. As events have shown us, white men are not to be trusted.'

Attention turned to Cornelius Vijn, who was sitting to one side of the king. The Dutchman defended himself, 'I make no common cause with the British. A conflict of interest has always existed between them and my countrymen. And, regarding the relationship between the amaZulu and Afrikaners, I'm in no position to apologise for my countrymen's past behaviour. What I will say is that my interests and the amaZulu's run completely in parallel. You have nothing to fear from me.'

Cetshwayo tutted impatiently. 'Thank you, Vijn. Let's hear Bhekisiza out…' He flicked his flywhisk at the boy.

'Two days ago, the redcoats entered the valley of the kings,' Bhekisiza said. 'Jantoni was in charge. He ordered ten of his men to take picks and shovels to each of the graves of your ancestors. They started with your father's…' He hesitated.

The council members gasped at the blatant sacrilege.

'Go on.' Cetshwayo's jaws were clenched with anger.

'They levered off the big stones and started digging. Jantoni encouraged them. Soon there was a large pile of earth beside the grave. Jantoni sent two men to pick up the body. One of them asked why, and Jantoni replied, "We're doing it to catch the king; for, once we have dug up his father, we shall soon catch him."'

Mehlokazulu seethed. 'If I'd been there, I'd have carved his traitor's heart from his chest.'

Mnyamana waved his hand airily. 'Yes, yes, Mehlokazulu. Act first and think later, that's always been your approach to problem-solving. And we all know how successful that is.'

'Enough. Let the boy finish,' Cetshwayo said.

Bhekisiza faltered, terrified of the king's anger.

'Go on, get on with it!'

'You'll punish me if I describe what they did next.'

'I'll punish you if you don't,' said the king.

Bhekisiza took a deep breath. 'While Jantoni's warriors dug up the graves, the redcoat soldiers ransacked the *imiZi* of Shaka and Dingaan. The valley was filled with smoke from the burning huts.'

Cetshwayo flinched as if he'd been punched. 'Ransacked?'

'Burned to the ground, every single hut.'

'Including Shaka's *eNkatheni*?'

Bhekisiza blinked, unaware of the implications of Cetshwayo's question.

The king's strength seemed visibly to drain away. 'That means Shaka's *inkatha* has been destroyed,' he said, his voice barely audible.

The other *ibandla* members sat in shocked silence. Shaka's sacred coil contained a mystical power that far exceeded any other. Not only did it embody the soul of the present Zulu nation but also those of all previous generations. It was literally the most sacred object in the kingdom. Cetshwayo's failure to protect it was directly related to his powers as a monarch. In that moment, everything changed. The *ibandla* members – the king's closest advisers – stopped believing the war could be won.

THIRTY-FOUR

Late afternoon sun behind the Hlophekhulu heights slanted across the Mahlabathini plain.

At the oNdini main entrance Nomguqo and the other *isiGodlo* girls waited for the guards to lift the heavy pole securing the gate. Balancing an empty gourd on her head, she eyed the warriors assigned to protect them on the last water-collecting detail of the day. Since the Khambula defeat, the relentless progress of the British forces through the kingdom had made the whole population jittery. Nobody left the *umuZi* without an armed guard. The three redcoat columns camped only fourteen miles away on the other side of the Mfolosi River were too close for comfort.

She found herself thinking of Shikashika. Since his death her memory of his features had started to blur; she had even stopped dreaming about him. Concentrating on the nearest warrior's face, she tried, as an experiment, to superimpose Shikashika's face. He was similar in many respects. Same age, same slim build. Similar facial characteristics: clear intelligent eyes and a wide generous mouth.

She looked away, frustrated. Try as she might, she couldn't

summon up her beloved's face. How could such precious features be so easily and quickly forgotten? Were her feelings so shallow she could stop mourning so soon? The thought struck her that she was not grieving Shikashika's loss as an individual, but more the senseless waste of life, the interruption of a natural order.

The girls, flanked by their warrior escorts, filed through the gate. Toiling up the slope towards them was a team of Zulu porters, steam rising from their sweating bodies despite the chill in the winter air. They were loaded down with two enormous elephant tusks, three men to each tusk. Stepping to one side, Nomguqo watched until the gate closed behind them. Sixhwethu's impatient whistle reminded her of her duty, and she followed the water detail along the path to the Mbilane stream.

Safe within the sanctuary of the *umuZi*, the porters set down their load and stretched their aching backs. Starting well before dawn, their day had been long and gruelling. Accompanied by three elderly envoys to whom Cetshwayo had entrusted his latest entreaty for peace, they had manhandled their heavy load all the way to the British camp on the Mthonjaneni Heights. Their mission was unsuccessful, and now they had to report the unwelcome news to the king. The *isiGodlo* guards escorted them to his quarters, where he was in conference with Cornelius Vijn. He beckoned them in. 'Well?'

The most senior replied, 'Your gift was refused, Ndabezitha.' He handed over a letter in a cleft stick.

Cetshwayo scanned it, hoping, despite his illiteracy, to derive a comfort from its contents.

Cornelius Vijn offered, 'May I, Your Majesty?'

The king listened with growing dismay as the Dutchman translated, *'From Lord Chelmsford, commanding Her Majesty's forces in South Africa. Your three messengers, Mgcewelo, Mtshibela* and Mpokitwayo have delivered your message, and the paper signed by C. Vijn, Trader. All I have to say in answer is: You have not complied with all the conditions I laid down…'

Cetshwayo protested, 'That is not true. I agreed to everything he asked for.'

Vijn continued, *'I shall therefore continue to advance, as I told you I should. But as you have sent me some of the cattle and state that the two cannons are on their way, I consent not to cross the Mfolosi River today to give you time to fulfil the remainder of the conditions. Unless all my conditions are complied with by tomorrow evening, you must take the consequence–'*

Cetshwayo interrupted again, increasingly more desperate, 'I don't know what else to do.'

Vijn completed the message, *'I return the tusks you send to show you I still advance. I will keep the cattle for a few days to show I am willing to make peace if you comply with the conditions laid down. I am willing that the men collected now at oNdini, whom I have seen, to the number of a regiment – 1000 men – come to me and lay down their arms as a sign of submission. They can do so at a distance of 500 yards and then retire; their lives are safe; the word of an English gentleman is sufficient to ensure it…'* Vijn snorted at the self-evident oxymoron. *'The arms in possession of the men around you now, taken at iSandlwana, must be given up by them. Chelmsford.'*

The king punched the wall. Dust and fragments of plaster, dislodged from the ceiling, showered the envoys.

Beside the Mbilane stream, the warriors leaned on their spears and peered towards the broad channel of the river Mfolosi, the expected route of the imminent offensive. Beyond, they could see smoke from redcoat cooking fires curling into the sky above Mthonjaneni. They clicked their tongues, urging the girls to hurry.

Filling their calabashes in the stream, Sixhwethu whispered to Nomguqo, 'I saw you looking at him earlier,' pointing to the guard nearby. 'Your type exactly. Shikashika without the white patches, don't you think?'

Nomguqo shook her head. How could anyone be so insensitive? But she realised Sixhwethu would never change; she would have to accept her as she was. A perfect nickname popped into her mind: *iwisa* (war club) – it had the same blunt bludgeoning qualities. Nomguqo smiled, which Sixhwethu misinterpreted. 'You *were* thinking about him, weren't you?' Then gave a sly wink. 'And I can guess which part.'

'You can think what you like.' Hoisting her full calabash onto her head, Nomguqo picked her way across the rocks.

Sixhwethu shouted after her, 'It's time you stopped moping and got on with the rest of your life.

Nomguqo noticed a faint light flickering in the far distance. She stopped.

Sixhwethu came up behind her. 'Did you see that?'

Nomguqo stared towards Mthonjaneni. A light flashed. Then another. They watched as the lights twinkled in a regular pattern.

'What do you think it is?'

'Too regular to be lightning,' Nomguqo said.

'The redcoat soldiers are signalling to each other,' the guard said. 'I saw it before Gingindlovu. It means they're preparing to attack.' He stamped the butt of his spear on the ground. 'Will you girls stir yourselves? I'm not risking my life waiting for you.'

Spooked, Sixhwethu took to her heels, and with water spilling over the sides of her calabash, rushed towards oNdini. Nomguqo and the others hurried after her.

The king paced in a state of high anxiety. He and Ntshingwayo were alone in his private quarters. 'Our cause is just, our impi still strong, but they still desert us. My brothers, I can understand. Dabulamanzi hasn't forgiven me for condemning his disastrous attack on kwaJim. But what else did he expect? It was sheer folly and cost us dear…'

Ntshingwayo agreed: 'No question.'

'And Makwendu is a silly airhead who changes with the wind; I never counted on his support. However, two members of the royal family defecting to the *abelungu* is a disaster for morale. How can I expect my peoples' support if my family don't set an example?' He thought for a moment. 'At least I can rely on the *amabutho*'s loyalty.'

Ntshingwayo reached for his *uTshwala*, thereby avoiding a direct reply.

'Can't I?'

The general drained the beaker. 'There is no easy way to tell you this, Ndabezitha. Mavumengwana hasn't been seen at any of the *ikhanda* for several days…'

'Meaning?'

'Draw your own conclusions.'

Cetshwayo leaned on the table. 'You're sure?'

'Have you used him as an envoy to the British?'

'Of course not.'

'Well, he was seen yesterday riding to their lines.'

The king pushed his chair so violently that it skittered across the floor. 'The regiments must be recalled immediately,' he ordered. 'I want them in their barracks within two days. The kingdom is in the gravest danger!'

At dead of night, long before the *imbongo* made his rounds, Mnukwa appeared at the *isiGodlo* girls' hut. 'Raise yourselves!' he called. 'Orders from the king,'

Bleary-eyed, they emerged one by one. Last to appear,

Nomguqo whispered to Nguyaze, 'What's the emergency?'

Once they were assembled, Mnukwa announced in a whisper, 'What I'm about to say must go no further. No one must know of this. Understood?'

They nodded.

'We're going to pack all the king's valuables and remove them from the *umuZi*.'

'Why?' said Sixhwethu.

'That shouldn't concern you,' the servant replied. 'Your job is to make sure they're safe.'

'Where shall we take them?'

'You'll find out when we get there. Now, stop asking questions and follow me.'

Out of the *inceku*'s earshot, Sixhwethu muttered: 'If the king wants his precious things removed, it means he expects the *abelungu* to steal them. I reckon the war is lost.'

'Sshh,' Nguyaze warned. 'That's treason.'

'Only saying what everyone is thinking.'

Inside the king's private quarters, Mnukwa had already assembled the royal goods and chattels. Piles of animal hides – big cat skins: serval, cheetah, leopard, and lion – lay next to his ceremonial regalia, and the personal body adornments of his wives.

'All this,' he said, 'has to be packed in these.' He pointed to another pile of oxhides. 'Now, get a move on. I want everything out of here before dawn.'

The long line of girls, heavy bundles perched on their heads, snaked up the steep slope beside a spectacular waterfall. They were climbing to a part of the Hlophekhulu hills they'd never visited. Here an underground stream had scoured out a system of caves, hidden from view except for where the fast-running current emerged from the rock and tumbled over a precipice.

Sixhwethu struggled up the last few feet. Her other hutmates and the *inceku* had already arrived and were standing beside a huge hole in the ground. Ropes ran over the lip and disappeared into the darkness. Adding her burden to the others piled up beside the chasm, she said, 'Where are we?'

'You'll see.' Mnukwa shouted into the hole, 'Ready?'

'When you are,' a voice echoed.

Attaching the first bundle to a rope, Mnukwa lowered it hand over hand. 'We've been using these caves since Mpande's time,' he said. 'Only we know they're here, so they're perfect hiding places.'

One bundle at a time, the royal valuables were lowered into the pit. Nomguqo watched, wondering whether Sixhwethu was right, that the war was lost.

From a long ridge that ran between two crossing points, Mehlokazulu looked across the White Mfolosi. British troops had started to assemble on the far side. Advance parties had prepared a camp a mile or so from the riverbank. In the distance, he saw a long line of ox-drawn wagons moving forward, laden with supplies. He turned to Zibhebhu who was standing beside him. 'It won't be long now.'

Zibhebhu's replied: 'This time we'll be fighting on our terms.' He spoke as the commander of the uKhandempemvu, directed to give warning of imminent attack. The regiment had suffered badly in the Khambula and Gingindlovu defeats; less than half of those who marched to iSandlwana had survived. Mehlokazulu had volunteered from a sense of comradeship.

Throughout the morning, they watched the British consolidate their position. Supply wagons were dragged into a circle around the camp to form a fortified laager. Platoons of engineers collected stones to build a temporary fort. Army quartermasters supervised the erection of mess tents and pickets for the horses. Squadrons of cavalry exercised up and down the riverbanks, circling each other in mock charges. The strategy was unmistakable – to remind the defenders of the Khambula defeat.

By midday, their nerves were shredded, and their tempers were at boiling point. Zibhebhu ordered marksmen up to the highest point on the ridge to teach the arrogant redcoats a lesson. The gunfire produced the desired effect. Any soldier bold enough to reach the water's edge retreated in short order. Volleys of return fire spattered into the rampart that served as the uKhandempemvu's defensive position.

'What's this?' Mehlokazulu drew attention to a herd of pure-white cattle being driven towards them.

Zibhebhu stared. 'Those are the king's prize animals.' He shouted to the herdboys prodding them forward with their sticks, 'What are you doing?'

'King's orders,' said an *udibi* bolder than his companions. 'We're to take them across the river to the *abelungu*.'

'Not on my watch.' Zibhebhu stood in the way, arms outstretched.

The herdboys kept coming.

'Take them back,' Zibhebhu shouted. 'They have no place here.'

Mehlokazulu joined him to shoo the cattle back. By now the beasts had scented water and were reluctant to be diverted. He called to the uKhandempemvu, 'We need help here.'

Fifty warriors ran forward and formed a line.

'What are we to tell the king?' the *udibi* asked.

'You can tell him what you like,' Zibhebhu replied, 'but

these animals are going no further.'

The cattle tossed their heads, uncertain which way to go.

'I take full responsibility,' Zibhebhu said.'

Reluctantly, the *iziNdibi* ran to the front and turned the cattle, driving them back to the *umuZi*.

Mehlokazulu wondered, *if the king has such little faith, where does that leave us?*

In a fury, Cetshwayo shouted, 'Our last chance to prevent our nation's destruction and you've thrown it away!' Spittle flying, he marched down the uKhandempemvu front rank. 'Don't come to me when the *abelungu* rape and butcher your wives and daughters!'

The warriors hung their heads, unwilling to meet his gaze.

The rant continued: 'Khambula taught us we are no match for British artillery. The only chance we have is to avoid conflict. But you, in your stupidity, have done everything you can to provoke it. Who countermanded my orders? Which of you thinks his judgment is better than mine? Which?'

The question was aimed directly at Zibhebhu. The king towered over him, but Zibhebhu stood his ground. They squared off against each other – cockerels with their hackles up.

Then Cetshwayo broke away to harangue the rank and file. 'This much I know – when you face the British again, you will need every ounce of your skill and courage. If you lose, your king will die.'

They shouted back, 'Never!'

He pressed home the point, 'You will need to fight until the last man stands.'

Their response was the battle cry: *Bhayede! Bhayede!*

'These are my orders…' He chose his words carefully, determined that his message should contain no ambiguity. 'You must not engage if the enemy is stationary and entrenched – under any circumstances! Bitter experience has taught us the consequences of attacking a prepared position. Our strength lies in attacking them in the open. Furthermore, we have the advantage of fighting on home ground – although I understand they've built a fortified camp on the far bank. When we win the day, do not be tempted to pursue them across the river. It would be suicide to attack that position. Do I make myself clear?'

The reply came thundering back: *Bhayede!*

Brandishing the sacred spear, he received the acclamation. Maybe his determination was born of necessity, but renewed hope shone in his eyes.

That night the warriors bivouacked on the Mahlabathini plain. Their campfires blazed as they cooked their last meal before the coming battle.

Waiting until the men had eaten, the *iziNyanga*, supervised by Dlephu Ndlovu, administered protective *muthi*. Each warrior was required to run past the vats of steaming medicine where he was sprayed from head to foot. Having seen how shrapnel from their enemy's weaponry shredded their comrades' bodies, many had doubts about the medicine's efficacy, but that was beside the point. The purpose was to bind the warriors to a common purpose – reinforced still further by their war chants. These continued late into the night, their voices filling the still air, basses and tenors combining in perfect harmony.

The singing reached the *isiGodlo* girls as they prepared to leave. Having addressed the *amabutho* in the afternoon, Cetshwayo had sent orders to evacuate the royal household. The proximity of the British put his family in great danger, particularly Dinuzulu his son and heir.

As well as her own possessions, Nomguqo was expected to carry the prince's. She chose what she thought he needed, keeping it to the bare minimum. Unwilling to sacrifice anything, Dinuzulu dug his heels in. Only when she was agreed to take everything that he considered essential, did he agree to leave.

The royal family – the king, his wives, and his children – assembled by the king's private entrance. They huddled together against the bitter winter winds blowing from the river. Around them, servants scurried backwards and forwards, loading pack animals with the few possessions they were allowed to take. Cattle were driven up from the pens to provide food for the journey. Mothers soothed babies protesting the disturbance to their sleep routine. Despite the activity, they were full of foreboding. No one knew what the future held.

Cetshwayo offered words of reassurance. Pointing to the thin sliver of moon that hung low over the distant hills, he said, 'Look, *inyanga entsha* – a new moon to watch over us. Have no fear, my children. When the battle is won, we will return home.'

Dinuzulu, standing beside Nomguqo, expressed the concern everyone was feeling: 'Where are we going, *Ubaba*?'

'Up into the mountains. We'll be safe there until we receive word the fighting is done. But we should make a start; I want to reach uMlambongwenya before morning.' Mounting his horse, he spurred it through the gate. The warriors recruited as bodyguards trotted alongside him, and the rest of the party followed.

Nomguqo could see campfires burning down on the plain. Though the *impi* were several miles away, their chanting carried through the night air, making them seem very close. Several paces ahead, Dinuzulu scolded her: 'You heard my father. Pick up your feet.'

Eleven years old and he thinks he's a man, she thought, following the long line marching towards the distant hills.

Climbing steeply now, she paused to catch her breath and looked back. In plan, the homestead – her home for over five years – seemed like a child's drawing. The perfect circle of individual huts, over a thousand, enclosed the vast space of the cattle pen. Distance diminished the scale, so the animals penned there appeared as so many dots on a canvas. There, she had known the depths of despair, the anguish of missing her family and the torments of being bullied. But she had also experienced the exquisite pleasures of love. Would she ever see it again?

A blanket over his shoulders, Mehlokazulu brooded beside the fire. The events of the previous six months crowded into his mind. Had he been able to see into the future would he have acted differently when he crossed the Mzinyathi to punish MaMtshali? The deaths of so many and the threat to the Zulu kingdom were high prices to pay for the restoration of his family's honour. And he had received precious little thanks. His father appeared indifferent; indeed, they had hardly spoken since.

In the bigger picture – he rationalised to himself – Zulu interests had long been threatened by the British imperialists. Had there been no resistance to the settlers overrunning Zulu grazing land, robbing their cattle of their pasture, the Zulu herds would have been destroyed, and the amaZulu would have starved. His part in the escalating hostility was neither here nor there. The war was as inevitable as a bush fire consuming everything in its path.

The *udibi* boy's death preyed most on his mind. Why Shikashika? Of all his dead comrades, the boy had the fewest attributes of a warrior. Why was he affected? Was it Nomguqo's affection for him? If so, why would he care whether she loved him or not? He admitted to himself he had found her reaction to his death strangely moving. He shook his head to banish all feelings of sympathy and tenderness because he needed every bit of resolution and willpower to face the coming battle.

THIRTY-FIVE

On the high ground above kwaNodwengu, Mehlokazulu kept vigil, waiting for the invasion to begin. As day broke, soldiers mustered at the crossing point on the far bank of the Mfolosi. Fog hung over the river, but weak sunlight intermittently broke through, and reflected off the white helmets of the soldiers trudging through the shallow water. They were followed by horses dragging gun carriages on which twelve artillery pieces were mounted. Squadrons of cavalry flanked the five thousand strong infantry battalions.

The ox-drawn wagons had been withdrawn at the end of the previous day, which indicated to the Zulu command that the British did not intend to establish a fortified laager and could therefore be engaged in the open. It seemed they had a chance to follow the king's advice after all.

During the night, warriors crept into hiding places across the plain, leaving the main body out of sight in the hills around kwaNodwengu and oNdini.

Though two miles distant, Mehlokazulu could see water splashes as cavalry galloped across the river to secure the ridge immediately above them. The foot soldiers then formed into a square formation around the artillery pieces and headed from the river towards the space between the two *imiZi*. His pulse quickened.

The square advanced steadily across the plain. Here and there it was forced to manoeuvre around thickets of scrub and thorn bush but, even so, it made rapid progress. Soon it reached an area of slightly elevated ground a mile and a half from the river. Now it was close enough for Mehlokazulu to identify individuals.

Still, the *amabutho* remained concealed, although wisps of smoke from their many campfires showed where they had bivouacked. The river mist partially obscured his view, but he saw the square come to a halt where the Zulu command had planned – on high ground midway between the *imiZi*, enclosed on three sides by hills from where the *amabutho* would launch their attack.

An order from a distant redcoat NCO floated on the breeze. The formation made a quarter turn to the right; the front ranks now faced oNdini. Sappers carrying spades ran forward and quickly dug defensive trenches on all four sides. Gunners manoeuvered their artillery pieces into position, protecting each of the four flanks. The rank and file fixed their bayonets. They were ready.

On cue, the amaZulu attacked. They came from all directions at once. The *amabutho* in the hills, including Mehlokazulu's iNgobamakhosi, rushed headlong down the slopes and joined those arriving from the east. To the British soldiers in their hollow square formation, they must have seemed like ghosts, running through the mist with the sun at their backs.

The warriors formed into a crescent, standing beyond the range of the guns. The *iziNduna* of each regiment paced in front of their men encouraging them to courageous deeds. *Who will be the first to strike the invaders? Who will come back a hero?*

Mehlokazulu addressed the iNgobamakhosi: 'I can't tell you not to be afraid. Our many experiences on the battlefield teach us that death hovers over us even now. It is certain that some of us will die today. But all men must die, sooner or later. The ancestors are waiting to greet us all. Fear of death should not deflect us from our purpose, only the fear of living as cowards. If we must die, let us be remembered as *abaqawe*. *Usuthu!*

Turning to face the enemy, the iNgobamakhosi took up the battle cry: *Usuthu! Usuthu!*

Far away to their right, a dense cloud of smoke rose from the kwaNodwengu *umuZi*. The warriors watched as flames licked the hut roofs. Then saw redcoated horsemen with torches riding back to the British formation. This destruction of King Mpande's "great place", where they'd received their battle orders, was a direct provocation. The warriors showed their anger by stamping their feet and shouting. The officers attempted to impose order, but there was no holding them back. Desperate for revenge, they broke ranks and rushed towards the British lines.

The front and rear ranks of the British formation wheeled outwards to enclose the horsemen who had set the fire and reformed as soon as they were inside.

A synchronised artillery salvo roared from all four sides, sending shells into the path of the oncoming warriors. At first, the shell-bursts had little effect on the widely spaced *amabutho*, but further salvoes at a closer range created huge gaps in their lines.

Soon, the breeze sweeping across the battleground carried the smoke from the burning homestead into the gunners' eyes. Smoke from their own guns compounded their difficulties by obscuring their targets. Their range finding became erratic, which the amaZulu exploited, advancing ever closer to the British square.

Now they were within rifle range. Warriors with guns looted at iSandlwana dropped to their knees and took aim. Mehlokazulu watched with satisfaction as his first shot dropped a soldier in the first rank. Exploiting the waist high grass to hide their positions, the iNgobamakhosi crawled to within a hundred yards. However, the naturally elevated position of the British trenches gave them the advantage. The closer the warriors moved towards the square, the more casualties they suffered.

The air filled with choking white smoke through which the warriors moved, desperate to close with the redcoats. Leaving his men in a natural hollow where they were protected from the guns, Mehlokazulu climbed behind the ridge trenches and, out of the firing line, took stock of the situation.

On the other three sides the *amabutho* were making very little impression and sustaining heavy losses. As far as he could see, the only possibility of victory was to break the British formation. If they could penetrate the front ranks on one side, they could outflank the other three sides. It was a question of numbers. Five thousand redcoats were no match for twenty thousand amaZulu.

Bugles sounded and, miraculously, the fusillade stopped. The impenetrable smoke was carried away by the breeze. Mehlokazulu exploited the lull to move his men even closer.

When the smoke cleared, the guns started up again, salvo after salvo. The rate of fire was bewildering, the noise deafening.

The bugles blew again, and the firing stopped. Mehlokazulu mounted his attack. Three thousand iNgobamakhosi and Uve charged towards the square. They were in close order, bunched together to increase their impact. Discarding their rifles, they raised their stabbing spears.

The British gunners responded by releasing a devastating

volley. They reloaded and fired again. Like spearing fish in a barrel, they couldn't miss. The two salvoes had the required effect. The momentum in the Zulu charge faltered. It became immediately apparent that the day was lost.

Lying among the piles of newly dead and dying men, Mehlokazulu realised that any further attack was hopeless. He himself only just avoided being one of the casualties. Having spotted the muzzle-flashes of the first salvo, he hurled himself flat and, from that position, watched his comrades-in-arms fleeing from the guns, their faces showing the measure of their defeat.

Orderly at the start, the retreat quickly degenerated into a rout as the British cavalry were ordered into the open. The warriors took to their heels, running for their lives. Hundreds were ridden down, their bodies pierced by the lances of the pursuing cavalry. Those fast enough to outrun the horses reached the high ground above the royal *imiZi*, where the rocky, sloping terrain gave them an advantage over their mounted pursuers. Some, still resisting, took up position behind rocks and returned fire. They had some success, managing to shoot the horses out from under several riders. But these pockets of resistance were few and far between.

From a raised position behind a rocky outcrop, Mehlokazulu used his rifle to good effect. Until he ran out of ammunition. Finally, outflanked by dismounted blue coated auxiliaries and unable to defend himself, he laid down his rifle.

Across the battlefield, the Natal Native Contingent took their revenge. Mustered from the amaZulu's arch enemies, they exploited their opportunity to pay back old scores. They butchered the wounded, sparing no one.

Like hyenas cornering their quarry, four amaSwazi surrounded Mehlokazulu. Expecting the same treatment as his comrades, he stared into his enemies' faces and wondered who would strike the first blow. Was this how it would end? Having rehearsed in his mind the circumstances of his last moments, he had never imagined it would be like this, slaughtered like a bull in the cattle pen.

'Wait a minute,' one of them said, on the point of plunging his spear into Mehlokazulu's chest. 'I know this man. He's *inkosi* Sihayo's son.'

'Are you?' said another, prodding him with his spear.

Mehlokazulu spat in his face.

'That's all the proof we need,' said the first. Reaching for a rope, he tethered his hands behind his back and passed the free end around his neck. 'Lord Chelmsford will be glad to meet you.'

A massive plume of smoke hung on the ridgeline as he was dragged to the British command post. Reaching the highest point, he looked down to what remained of Cetshwayo's "Great Place". oNdini was now an inferno, burning with ferocious intensity. Flames and sparks were carried high into the air. Even from half a mile away, he could feel the heat.

Observing with evident satisfaction was a group of British officers. One of them, tall and ascetic, and by his bearing the commander-in-chief, turned as the amaSwazi threw Mehlokazulu to the ground. 'Who is this murderous-looking fellow?'

The Swazi spokesman replied, 'Mehlokazulu kaSihayo nGobese.'

Chelmsford brushed his moustaches. 'The one who caused all the trouble, eh? Not much of a specimen, is he? Hardly lives up to his reputation.' As he took a couple of paces forward, Mehlokazulu glared balefully. 'Well, my fine fellow, you'd better prepare yourself for the hangman's noose.' Then, to his fellow officers, 'Prepare an ox cart to take him to Pietermaritzburg.'

The deserted kwaMbonambi military barracks provided a refuge for the royal family. After their long journey through the mountains, the wives and children were glad to have somewhere to rest. Cetshwayo enjoyed no such relief. Alone in a hut, guarded by his close attendants, his mind restlessly revolved around the same questions. What could he have done differently? Would compliance with the British demands have made any difference? Had he surrendered Mehlokazulu and paid the cattle fine within the timeframe demanded by the British, would that have prevented the invasion?

He had underestimated the persistence of the British authorities, that was certain. He had been naïve in assuming Zulu warriors were superior to British army soldiers, although the victory at iSandlwana had initially confirmed that assumption.

He accepted that he had made errors of judgment. High on his list was his choice of John Dunn as a confidant. The man who had shared his most intimate thoughts had proved to be a viper in his breast. It was axiomatic that all men were motivated by self-interest, by the desire to gain advantage over others. He recognised it in himself – after all, he had killed his own brother Mbuyazi to accede to the throne. Even so, self-interest usually contained the reciprocal element of *quid pro quo*. But this compensatory factor was entirely missing from his "friendship" with Dunn. He, Cetshwayo, had lifted Jantoni from obscurity and placed him in a position of influence and power within his kingdom. And his reward for that trust and friendship? A deep wound of betrayal from which his power was starting to ebb. Was his ability to read into the hearts of men so flawed that it compromised his competence to lead his nation? Exhausted by self-laceration, Cetshwayo finally fell asleep in the early hours.

The warriors guarding the kwaMbonambi main gate watched as a distant dust-trail materialised into a horseman arriving from the direction of oNdini. They stood back as he galloped through the entrance and headed for the king's hut.

The royal wives were gathered around the doorway waiting for Cetshwayo to emerge; it was already late in the day and there was no sign of him. They shifted their attention to the rider. Zibhebhu reined in and dismounted. From the way his mount was lathered he had ridden hard. The women surrounded him, demanding news of the battle. Sweeping them aside, he marched to the door. Though he had said nothing, his stern expression told them all they needed to know.

The *inceku* Mnukwa stood in his way. 'Ndabezitha is not to be disturbed.'

'He'll be disturbed soon enough if the *abelungu* capture him. Get out of my way.'

Cetshwayo scrambled to his feet as Zibhebhu pushed his way into the hut. 'Ndabezitha–'

The king interrupted, 'Is it over?' But he already knew the answer.

'You mustn't wait a moment longer,' Zibhebhu urged. 'The British soldiers are not far behind. Right now, they're spread across Mahlabathini, scattering our people, and setting fire to your *imiZi*. That will keep them occupied for the rest of the day. If you leave now, you should have at least a day's head start.'

Cetshwayo sagged as the enormity of the defeat sank in. There would be no way back from this. It represented the collapse of his kingdom and the loss of his power. The military might of the amaZulu was lost forever. 'And the *amabutho*?' he whispered.

'They gave a good account of themselves, but they were no

match for the British guns and, if I'm honest, they didn't fight with the same spirit as at iSandlwana or Khambula.'

'There were many casualties?'

'Yes.'

Cetshwayo's imposing frame collapsed in on itself. He sat back on his sleeping mat, his head in his hands.

Zibhebhu crouched beside him. 'Ndabezitha, it is imperative you make a start now. I cannot vouch for your safety if you delay any longer.'

'Where shall I go?' he asked. Any trace of self-reliance and authority had disappeared. The king seemed helpless.

Zibhebhu helped him to his feet. 'Mynamana instructed me to offer you refuge at his ekuShumayeleni *umuZi*. That is far enough away. I doubt the British will find you there.'

'The whole of my household?'

'With respect, it would be easier to guarantee the royal children's safety if they were lodged separately from you. I can house them with my family. My wives would be honoured to receive them at Banganomo. I guarantee they will come to no harm there.'

'Why are we the last to be told?' Nomvimbi demanded. 'Do we count for so little?'

Mnukwa stood among a group of frightened women, who were clamouring to know what contingency plans had been set in place. 'You'll know as soon as we know,' he said.

'Where will we live?' Usixipe asked.

'More importantly, *how*?'

'What about the children? Who will protect them?'

Mnukwa had no answers. Hysteria mounted as the wives surrendered to their fears. Some burst into tears, unable to control their emotions. They needed reassurance.

The king appeared, Zibhebhu by his side. With his bullhide cloak over his shoulders, Cetshwayo seemed more himself; some of his self-possession had returned. He held up his hand to calm them. 'We must accept a heavy burden, my children,' he said. 'Zibhebhu brings news that our brave warriors have been defeated…'

Sobs broke out again.

'…We no longer have the resources to stand against the British invader. Thus, we must make provision for the future. Terms of surrender will be negotiated, but right now we must take steps to maintain our immediate security. I have decided to accept Mynamana's offer of sanctuary. As for you, my family – my children, their mothers, and their attendants – my good friend and cousin Zibhebhu has generously volunteered the hospitality of his own household. I have every confidence we will be reunited eventually. I cannot tell when that time will come, but until then my comfort in my solitude will be the knowledge that you are safe and well.'

His children ran to embrace him.

He gently patted each on the head. 'We have a long journey ahead of us. Let us make a start with our hearts strong and resolute.' Gathering the smallest into his arms, he led the way through the gate and towards the mountain ridge on the skyline. The entourage, including a small herd of cattle, followed.

Their march continued through the rest of the day and into the night. His sense of purpose restored, the king pushed forward, relentless in his desire to make ground as quickly as possible.

Nomguqo walked beside the great wife. Nomvimbi made heavy weather of the climb, the continual rubbing of one thigh against the other evidently causing her pain. She stopped and rested against a rock. 'I can't walk another step,' she said. 'My legs are raw.'

Warriors leading riderless horses filed past.

'Why don't you ride?' Nomguqo suggested. It seemed obvious. What was the point in suffering if a horse could take the strain?

'My husband would never allow it,' said Nomvimbi. 'The wives must set an example.'

'Would there be any harm in asking?' said Nomguqo. 'He's on horseback after all.' She pointed to the head of the line where Cetshwayo rode a large thoroughbred.

'You can try.' Her tone suggested it would be a hopeless task.

Nomguqo ran to the front.

Cetshwayo was surprised to see her. 'Glad to see you're keeping up. I know it's hard, but we must keep going.'

'Ndabezitha…?' She took her courage in her hands, 'Would you allow the Great Wife to have a horse?'

'Has she asked for one?'

'No.'

'So, it's your request, then. Why do you think she needs a horse?'

'Well…' Nomguqo had already chanced her arm; she might as well go the whole way. 'We'll all move faster if she's on horseback.'

The king laughed. 'In which case, Nomvimbi must ride.' He whistled to one of the warriors. 'Take a horse to the Great Wife. Make sure it's a strong one!'

The weaker members of the party struggled up the steep mountain slopes. Even though her horse was doing the hard work, Nomvimbi kept complaining. 'Every muscle in my body is aching… this horse is too bony… when can we stop?… will this misery never end?'

Nomguqo stopped listening. She had done her best, but it seemed that still wasn't good enough. She wasn't prepared to risk the king's anger by suggesting he order a halt. In any case he and Zibhebhu were out of sight, on their way to a pass through the Ntabankhulu Mountains. Barring accidents, there would be no reason to stop until they were on the other side.

Nomvimbi finally reached the end of her tether. 'That's it, I'm going no further. I'm tired, hungry, and need to sleep. We all do.' Sliding off her horse's back, she collapsed by the side of the path. A large boulder provided a convenient backrest. 'If the king insists on continuing, you can just leave me here,' she said. 'I'll follow once I've slept.' Propped up against the rock, she shut her eyes.

Nomguqo, the sleeping Besiyile in a sling on her back, saw that Cetshwayo and Zibhebhu had stopped a hundred or so yards further up the track. They had reached the highest point, where the path divided, one track heading down towards the distant Khwebezi River, the other climbing higher up the mountain.

Referring to the lower of the two tracks, Cetshwayo said, 'You say Mnyamana is expecting me?'

Zibhebhu nodded. 'His ekuShumayeleni homestead is five hours march. You'll be there before sunrise.'

The king examined the other more perilous route that snaked further into the hills. 'I'm counting on you to look after them, Zibhebhu.' He looked back at his family gathered around Nomvimbi. 'They've already travelled far and are exhausted.'

'Ndabezitha, your family's comfort is one thing. Their security another. I would not be discharging my responsibility if I didn't insist that they keep moving. We still have a great distance to cover before we reach the safety of my *umuZi*. Then they can rest for as long they like.'

Retracing his steps, Cetshwayo squatted and took Nomvimbi's hand. 'Wife, you must continue your journey. I know you're tired, but I won't sleep easily until I know you and my children are protected. You can rely on Zibhebhu. He's a resourceful leader and, of all my *izinduna*, the one on whom I would stake my life.' He scanned his children's faces. 'We've reached the point where we must go our separate ways…'

Dinuzulu pleaded, 'Let me come with you, *Ubaba*.'

Cetshwayo smiled sadly. 'You have a man's job to do, Dinuzulu. You must look after your mother and sister.'

'How should I do that?'

'Be strong for them. Remember whose son you are.'

THIRTY-SIX

Ntabankhulu Mountain

Zibhebhu waited until the king and his retinue were out of sight, then adopted a radically different tone. He snarled at Nomvimbi, 'Get up, you fat lump. Either you start walking, or I leave you here for the jackals and hyenas.' He used the flat of his hand to beat the horse Nomvimbi had been riding. It took off and disappeared into the darkness. 'I'm not waiting all night,' he warned, aiming a kick at her.

The great wife spluttered but was too shocked to speak. And equally powerless to move.

Zibhebhu grabbed her arm and hauled her violently to her feet. Prodding her with a cattle switch, he drove her up the higher path. Her weary legs could barely sustain the pace and she soon stumbled.

'Stupid, lazy bitch.' The stick whistled through the air and cut her across the shoulders. Whimpering with fear, she had no choice but to put one foot in front of the other.

The other women in the party exchanged glances. This brutal treatment of the most important of Cetshwayo's wives demonstrated that Zibhebhu had lost all respect for the king and was unconcerned that his arrogance might be punished. Each began to worry about her own future.

To avoid the British patrols combing the area, they travelled only during the hours of darkness. It took two nights to reach Zibhebhu's *umuZi*, every moment filled with bullying and intimidation. On the second night, with no footpath to guide them, they had to force their way through open bush. Scratched by thorn bushes and parched with thirst, they finally arrived at kwaBabanango, where their hopes for an end to their ordeal were dashed. Instead, Zibhebhu revealed his true purpose. The cattle meant as food for the royal party were immediately confiscated and added to Zibhebhu's herd. He claimed they were a gift from Cetshwayo as repayment for the shelter he was offering them.

'Things will be different now,' he scowled, marching up and down the line of dispirited women and children assembled in his cattle pen.

Behind them, Zibhebhu's herdboys tended to the royal cattle, setting out water and fodder in liberal quantities. By the rules of Zulu hospitality, Cetshwayo's family should have received similar refreshment, but it wasn't forthcoming. They stood bewildered and disoriented by Zibhebhu's hostility.

'You can forget your previous lives, sitting on your fat arses while others jump to your whims.' He directed this remark towards Nomvimbi, but she was too exhausted to protest. 'From now on you will earn your keep. Any of you assuming you'll continue living your idle oNdini life is in for a shock. You'd better get used to it.'

His own womenfolk surrounded the new arrivals jeering and whistling at their shocked faces.

'You'll develop skills you never knew you had,' he added. 'Building, for one. I don't have Cetshwayo's advantage of exploiting able-bodied young volunteers, so if you want huts to sleep in, you'll have to build them yourselves.'

Nomvimbi finally found her voice. 'We've been walking for two days and nights. We're hungry and thirsty. For pity's sake, give us food and water.'

Though cowed and demoralised, Cetshwayo's junior wives echoed her.

He cut them off. 'You'll eat when the work is complete. Your hunger will motivate you to finish more quickly.' As he strode out of the cattle pen, his wives' catcalling intensified.

Sixhwethu took charge, 'Come on, the sooner we start, the sooner we'll finish.'

By the flickering light of rushes dipped in animal fat they worked into the night. Only when the four huts were thatched and protected from the weather did they allow themselves to rest. Ravenous from twelve solid hours of toil, they sat around a cooking fire and gobbled down a meal. It consisted of leftovers from Zibhebhu's household. There was hardly enough to go around, and it left them wanting more, but there was no point in complaining. Their bellies still grumbling, they checked their handiwork. It was by no means complete. More daub needed to be mixed to fill chinks in the lath walls, and more rushes collected to complete the thatching. But at least the wives and children had somewhere to lay their heads. Quarters for the *isiGodlo* girls would have to wait for another day.

From the start, Sixhwethu assumed the role of site manager, organising everyone into teams responsible for specific tasks – collecting the structural timbers, the roofing materials, the mud, and cow dung – and allocating construction jobs. Everyone mucked in, wives with the highest status working alongside girls who until recently had been their servants.

Throughout the day, Zibhebhu was a constant presence. Every time Nomguqo looked, she found him watching them. His hooded, predatory eyes made her flesh crawl. As night fell, he sauntered towards Sixhwethu, drew her to one side and spoke to her out of earshot of the others.

When he left, Nomguqo quizzed her, 'Well, what was that about?'

'He's invited me to eat with him this evening,' Sixhwethu replied.

'And you're going?'

'Do I have a choice?'

'All he wants is…' Nomguqo left the rest unsaid.

'I know what he wants.' Sixhwethu lifted an eyebrow. 'Who knows, maybe he wants to make me his wife.'

'Remember what happened to Umafutha,' Nomguqo warned.

'Don't be silly, Zibhebhu's not like that.'

'What, like Qhude? I wouldn't be so sure. Look at the way he treated Nomvimbi.'

'He speaks gently to me. Maybe I can offer him something she couldn't.'

'You've decided then?'

'It may be my only chance to find a man.'

When she finally got to sleep, Nomguqo was haunted by dreams of Sixhwethu being pawed by Zibhebhu. It wasn't that she felt morally superior to her hutmate. She just knew she would rather die than satisfy his lust.

Up to their ankles in water, Nomguqo and Nomvimbi dipped their calabashes into the fastest running part of the stream.

They shivered as the water filled the containers. The sun hadn't yet risen to warm the air. It wasn't so much the cold that chilled them. More the realisation that this was the first of a dozen trips they would have to make during the day. Zibhebhu's women seemed to have an inexhaustible need for water. Or was it that they needed to drive home the truth that the royal wives were their chattels, obliged to perform the most menial of tasks?

Nomvimbi tipped the heavy water vessel upright. Nomguqo helped her hoist it onto her head and she tottered off towards the settlement.

Heaving up her own calabash, Nomguqo followed. In the weeks since their arrival, the great wife's health had become a matter of concern. She was a pale shadow of herself. Dietary deficiencies showed on her face and body. Her cheeks had developed hollows and her skin hung in folds. Her energies were so far depleted she had difficulty walking in a straight line. But what worried Nomguqo most was her mental wellbeing. She was listless, devoid of interest in anything, least of all her children. Had it not been for Nomguqo, Dinuzulu and Besiyile would have been completely abandoned.

Staggering under the weight of the calabash, with water slopping over the lip, Nomvimbi approached the large communal drinking trough outside Zibhebhu's hut. She emptied the contents into it. Without thinking – because she was thirsty – she scooped water into her hand and drank.

One of the wives watched the doorway of from her hut. 'Did anyone give you permission to do that?' she asked. 'Polluting our water with your filthy mouth. I don't think so.'

Nomvimbi clenched her fists. If she had had the energy, she would have flown at the woman.

Nomguqo whispered, 'Let it go, she's not worth it.'

Movement from Zibhebhu's hut caught her eye. Sixhwethu scuttled through the door and disappeared into the shadows.

Nomvimbi also noticed. 'Treacherous bitch,' she muttered. 'May her womb dry up and leave her childless.'

'She's doing what she can to survive,' Nomguqo said. 'We all are.'

'Cetshwayo will make them pay, you can be sure of that.'

As though reading her mind, the wife called out, 'Zibhebhu has news of your husband...'

Nomvimbi's head shot around.

Like a cat toying with a mouse, the wife continued, 'The Dutchman Vijn betrayed him to the British. Paid him handsomely, I should imagine.'

Another wife joined in. 'Never trust an *umlungu* – we all know that.' She sauntered towards Nomvimbi. 'Your husband must have very poor judgment. Imagine. You'd never find Zibhebhu relying on a white man.'

Their husband emerged from his hut, smoothed down his *beshu*, and ambled to the water trough where he dunked his head. Shaking off the droplets, he drenched Nomvimbi.

It was the final straw. Months of deprivation and pent-up frustration boiled over. Nomvimbi shouted, 'When my husband hears of the way you're treating us, you'll pay–'

Zibhebhu cut across her, 'Don't waste your breath, woman. Your husband has no authority here or anywhere else. It ended when the redcoats dragged him from his hiding place. Like a rock rabbit pulled from his burrow.'

The irreverent simile struck him as funny. He threw back his head and laughed. The wives joined in, mocking, and pointing fingers.

Nomvimbi's face was a mask of misery.

'I doubt we'll be seeing Cetshwayo again,' Zibhebhu said.

'If he survives it'll be a miracle. Now more than ever, you'll be relying on my hospitality, so I don't expect any more complaints. Do I make myself clear?'

'Wake up,' a man's voice whispered.

Nomguqo was suddenly alert, her heart thudding. Had Zibhebhu come to take her, too? Only two days ago, as well as Sixhwethu, he'd abducted another *isiGodlo* girl. In a split second, she decided to kill herself rather than submit. She opened her mouth to scream, but a hand clamped it shut. She fought against the pressure, throwing her head from side to side.

'Shush, you'll wake the others.'

She stopped struggling when she realised the voice was familiar. With a surge of joy, she recognised her father. She relaxed, and the hand released its pressure.

The light of a full moon shining through the open doorway spilled across the hut floor. She scanned Sikhunyane's face, trying to understand how, after an absence of nearly five years, he could be with her now. It seemed barely credible. Was it one of her dreams, an illusory consolation for her present misery? The touch of his hand seemed real enough.

'It's me,' Sikhunyane reassured her.

'But how…'

'I'll explain later. I've come to take you home.'

Her eyes flooded with tears. She stifled the sob rising in her throat. Then a complication struck her. 'I can't leave Besiyile and Dinuzulu.'

Stirring at the sound of the conversation, several of the other girls started to wake.

Sikhunyane considered the options. He hadn't expected to rescue the royal children as well. 'It's too risky. They'll slow us down.'

'I'm not leaving without them. They won't survive if they stay here.'

Remembering how obstinate his daughter was, Sikhunyane sighed. 'Where are they?'

'Next door.'

Sticking her head outside the hut, she peered around the compound. Apart from distant snoring coming from Zibhebhu's hut, it was as silent as the grave. Where were the guards? Then she remembered that their captor had taken no precautions against his captives escaping, relying on his assumption that their spirits were broken. *More fool him*, she thought.

Keeping to the shadows, she tiptoed the short distance to Nomvimbi's hut and paused in the doorway. In the moonlight she could see the children's shapes next to their mother. She was on her back, mouth agape, her heavy breathing vibrating her lips.

Besiyile was so sound asleep she didn't move as Nomguqo gathered her into her arms. Dinuzulu woke to a gentle shaking and, suddenly alert, followed her beckoning finger. Outside the hut, she guided him to where her father waited, together with her four hutmates.

Sikhunyane offered his back to the boy. Still half asleep, he climbed up and threw his arms around Sikhunyane's neck. Nomguqo ruffled his hair to show she appreciated his trust in her.

Soundlessly, the girls followed Sikhunyane in single file through the compound. They held their breath as they drew opposite Zibhebhu's hut. They needn't have worried. The rhythm of his snoring continued unbroken. At the next hut, however, Nomguqo's heart skipped a beat as a figure stepped out of the shadows.

'You're leaving.' Sixhwethu said.

She couldn't deny it. Why else were the royal children there? Could she trust Zibhebhu's new concubine not to betray them? Previous form suggested she wasn't exactly trustworthy.

'I wish I could come with you,' Sixhwethu said.

'You can.'

Sixhwethu shook her head. 'My place is here now. It's not so bad. Zibhebhu's wives have finally accepted me. And when he visits me, it's over with very quickly.'

Nomguqo reached out, but Sixhwethu wouldn't respond. 'Wait a moment,' she said, and disappeared into the hut.

Sikhunyane clicked his tongue, impatient to leave.

Sixhwethu returned with the snakeskin amulet Maweni made for her and thrust it into Nomguqo's hands. 'This is my dearest possession. I want you to have it, to keep you safe.'

Nomguqo swallowed. This was a big gesture. The wristband was a token of what Maweni had meant to her; it was all she had left of him. She tried to express her gratitude, but the words stuck in her throat.

Sikhunyane's whistle reminded her of her purpose. She gave Sixhwethu's hand a farewell squeeze and rejoined him.

The gate was unbarred, and as expected, unguarded. Sikhunyane sent the girls ahead, scanning the huts to make sure they weren't observed. With Besiyile asleep in her arms, Nomguqo ran as though pursued by demons and hunkered down in the long grass outside the perimeter fence. She was joined by the other girls, then her father.

Clinging to Sikhunyane's neck, Dinuzulu asked, 'Won't my mother worry that we're not there?'

Nomguqo swallowed. Sikhunyane's appearance had been so unexpected she hadn't had time to consider the consequences of taking the children. She improvised, 'Of course, she will, but all she wants is you to be safe.'

'Will she be safe?'

Sikhunyane patted the prince's foot to reassure him. 'Nobody's going to hurt her. Or you once we're away from here. But we've a long way to go; we must make a start.'

Dinuzulu remained unconvinced. He had seen how badly his mother had been treated and had no confidence it would change. Indeed, it might become worse when Zibhebhu discovered he and his sister were missing. 'Where are we going?'

Sikhunyane hadn't thought that far ahead; his original plan hadn't involved the rescue of the royal children.

Nomguqo suggested, 'What about your uncle Ndabuko? You like him, don't you?'

Dinuzulu shrugged.

Sikhunyane added, 'Most importantly, he's still loyal to your father. And his *umuZi* is only six hours away. Once you're safe with him, we'll come back for Nomvimbi. How's that? Now, am I going to carry you, or are you going to walk like a grownup?'

Dinuzulu jumped down. 'Walk.' Squaring his shoulders, he put his best foot forward.

'That's more like it.' Charting a path from the position of the stars, Sikhunyane led his party across the mountain.

The full moon guided their steps through the night. They kept up a good pace, despite the rough ground. After three punishing hours. Sikhunyane felt secure enough to take a break. Resting beside a stream, they quenched their thirst in the water.

Nomguqo finally asked the question that had been bothering her: 'How did you know that Zibhebhu was keeping us prisoner?'

Sikhunyane smiled. 'Well, he's married to a Buthelezi daughter, and she boasted of it to her brothers – who are friends of mine.'

Nomguqo laughed. 'Not as clever as he makes out, then. And how did you know it was safe to come to our hut?'

'I hid in the long grass and watched. When I saw there were no guards, it was easy.'

'We'd begun to give up hope,' she admitted.

He gripped her hand. 'I'd never let you down.'

Tears pricked her eyes.

He scanned the horizon. The profile of the mountain range they'd just crossed stood out in relief against the starlit sky. Tapping Dinuzulu on the shoulder, he said, 'Better get a move on; they'll pick up our trail soon enough. You can lead if you like. See that notch in the mountains?' He pointed with his stick to the distant skyline. 'Once we reach that, we'll be home and dry.'

'How long?' Dinuzulu asked.

'If we don't dawdle, we'll be there by sunrise.'

Besiyile started to grizzle, missing her mother's breast. Through the long months of their enforced stay at kwaBabanango, she had been weaned onto solid food, but still exploited every opportunity to suckle. It was the one comfort Nomguqo couldn't provide, but she remembered a piece of dried meat she had tucked into her waistband. She gave it to the little girl to suck and the grizzling stopped.

When they resumed their journey, Dinuzulu matched Sikhunyane stride for stride.

Nomguqo fretted about her decision to take the baby from her mother. She had always considered Nomvimbi to be a negligent parent, but she knew there would be inevitable consequences in separating her from her daughter. Would she ever be able to look her mistress in the face again? On the other hand, Zibhebhu had made his intentions plain. The future of the royal children was in jeopardy, and it was her responsibility to keep them safe.

Dinuzulu led the way through the rest of the night. Not once did he flag. As dawn broke, the party reached the notch in the mountains and looked down into a fertile valley. Far below, a circle of huts surrounded a cattle pen. He pointed to the tiny figures busy around the cooking fires. 'Are those my uncle's people?'

Sikhunyane reassured him, 'You and your sister are safe now.'

'I hope he can feed us,' Dinuzulu said. 'I'm starving.'

Nomguqo laughed. 'Is it any wonder?' We haven't stopped all night. I promise you this. I'm not taking another step once we get there. Every muscle in my body's aching.' She tousled Dinuzulu's hair. 'Thank you for guiding us here.'

Sikhunyane added, 'Already halfway to being a great leader.'

The prince pushed out his chest with pride. *A great leader indeed.*

Ndabuko was overjoyed to see his brother's children. He immediately put them at ease, reassuring them that he would make it his priority to reunite them with their mother.

Nomguqo was sure they were in good hands. Though she had looked after their everyday needs for over two years, she handed over her responsibility with an easy conscience.

When it came to leave-taking, she softened the blow by presenting gifts. She gave the little princess a doll she had decorated with beadwork, and Dinuzulu a war club her father had carved from ironwood. Sikhunyane told him, 'I made it full-size because a boy big enough to lead us to safety is big enough to carry a man's *iwisa*.'

It took three weeks for Nomguqo and her father to reach the family homestead up on the Swazi borders. During their journey through Zululand, they witnessed the consequences of war. Long after the catastrophic defeat, the aftershocks continued to reverberate. Every homestead mourned its dead. Fields lay untended and uncultivated and would remain so for many months. Rumours abounded as to the king's whereabouts. Some said he had been taken down to the Cape Colony and was in prison. Others that he had been killed. It was hard to know where the truth lay.

Finally, Nomguqo and Sikhunyane limped into Mkhuze. From the high ground above the homestead, they saw Meliyam and Diboli working in the fields. Nomguqo forgot how tired she was and ran towards them, shouting their names.

They threw down their hoes, and received her in their arms, weeping uncontrollably.

It had been five long years since she had lived at Mkhuze. Much had changed: additions to the family, new wives for her brothers, new babies born. Her heifer Naledi was now a matriarch, with calves of her own.

Sikhunyane was overjoyed to have her home. In conversations during the journey, they had already filled in some of the gaps. She told him about life in the *isiGodlo*, editing out details that would invite his disapproval. She made no mention of Shikashika, beyond including him in a list of warriors who had not returned. Her account of the "smelling out" episode made him shudder with horror. 'But for Mehlokazulu, you might never have seen me again,' she admitted.

He talked about her mother – the first time she had heard him mention her name. Nomhlwathi had died bringing their daughter into the world, and though he had married again, the memory of her beauty still haunted him. 'You're the image of her,' he said. 'Like you, she was tall and slim. She had the same high cheekbones, which set off the beautiful dark pools of her eyes. Every time I look at you, I see Nomhlwathi.'

She quickly readjusted to life with her family, helping to look after the children of her half siblings – her brothers and sisters by Sikhunyane's other wives. They in turn adored her, insisting that she tell them stories of life at oNdini. They were enthralled by the intimate details of the king's daily routine, laughing out loud when she described the frockcoat he wore to visit the latrine. As she listed his eccentricities, she was reminded of great privilege she'd enjoyed, and, happy as she was to be amongst her nearest and dearest, she was nostalgic for her previous life.

She remembered the king's many kindnesses and showed her father the special herb Cornelius Vijn gave her to calm the asthma attacks. Only a few shreds of it remained, but now she was restored to her family, she felt sure she would have no further need of it. Indeed, the symptoms that plagued her childhood had become progressively less severe as time went by. She could hardly remember her last attack.

Though overjoyed by her homecoming and the warm welcome of her relatives, Nomguqo's spirit was troubled. Her sleep was disturbed by recurrent nightmares. One was so vivid it haunted her waking thoughts.

She was in a desert, parched and devoid of vegetation. The rains had failed so often that any tree in the landscape had been reduced to its essence, skeletal branches stretching to the pitiless sun. The bones of animals lay bleaching in the shimmering heat.

In the shade of a giant baobab tree, two lion cubs lay panting, abandoned by their mother as she searched for prey to feed them. The cubs hissed and bared their teeth as a huge wing-shaped shadow passed over them. A vulture circled, waiting patiently. The shadow became blacker as it planed down in ever tighter loops. The outcome seemed inevitable.

Nomguqo felt a constriction in her chest. The closer the vulture came to the lion cubs, the more she realised she was powerless to help them.

The vulture flapped its wings to slow itself in its final glide down to the ground. Nomguqo's breathing became tighter as both cubs broke cover and ran towards her, aware of the danger they were in. The vulture swooped, its sharp talons raised, its tail feathers spread. It landed in a flurry of movement, outstretched wings covering the cubs. Extending its scrawny featherless neck, it drove its curved beak at their heads. They screamed in pain as the terrible hook tore into them. The vulture folded back its wings to reveal the cubs, bloodied by its relentless pecking.

The nightmare lasted no longer than this – she always woke just as the vulture delivered the coup-de-grâce. She remembered every detail. But her own impotence troubled her most, her inability to stop the cubs being butchered. As with all her visions, she knew there was a deeper meaning. The vulture was Zibhebhu and the danger he represented to Cetshwayo's "cubs" remained. If it came to it, she had to be more effective in protecting the royal children.

THIRTY-SEVEN

Mkhuze

Nomguqo bent over Meliyam's head, tying beads of different colours into her braided hair. The three sisters sat in the shade of their shared hut, protected from the heat of the midday sun. Nomguqo took a step back to admire her handiwork. 'What do you think – red next?'

'Yellow would be better,' the youngest sister said. Had Nomguqo suggested yellow, Diboli would have chosen red – a contrariness that was her way of drawing attention to herself.

Nomguqo frowned. 'Red's prettier.'

'Definitely yellow,' said Diboli. 'But it's not my hair; you'd better ask Meliyam.'

It wasn't worth quarreling over. 'Yellow, then,' Meliyam agreed.

A small victory won, Diboli picked out the yellow beads from the bowl and handed them to her big sister. The girls were so absorbed in decorating Meliyam's hair they failed to register the arrival of two elderly gentlemen.

'*Sawubona, amadodakazi* (Good morning, daughters).'

Nomguqo instantly recognised the older of the two men. Maboya kaMbundulwane of the Buthelezi clan had been a familiar figure throughout her childhood. In King Dingaan's campaign against the amaSwazi, Maboya was her father's captor. He was a powerful warlord with a reputation as a ruthless warrior, but Nomguqo remembered him as a kindly avuncular figure who had given Sikhunyane his freedom and the opportunity to prosper under his patronage. Sikhunyane and his family had many reasons to be grateful to Maboya, but she was tongue-tied in his presence. It had been Maboya's suggestion that she be sent away to join the royal *isiGodlo*, so she associated him with an unhappier time in her life.

Diboli greeted their visitors. '*Inkosi*, you honour us with your presence.'

Leaning on his walking stick, Maboya smiled graciously. 'Where might we find Sikhunyane?'

'It's milking time, so he'll be in the *isibaya*.' Shielding her eyes against the light, Meliyam pointed out their father, clutching a parasol he'd improvised from a tree branch.

Nodding in appreciation, Maboya and his companion made their way to the cattle pen.

The three girls watched, curious to know the reason for the visit.

Sikhunyane threw down his parasol to embrace the visitors. 'Girls, bring *uTshwala* for our guests,' he called. 'And something to eat. They have travelled a long way.' He conducted his guests to his hut, where they sat in the shade of a large mopane tree.

The girls carried the refreshments and set them out.

'You remember Maboya?' Sikhunyane said.

'Yes, of course, *Ubaba*,' Diboli answered.

Maboya introduced his companion: 'This is my kinsman, Dazukile Sibiya.'

Meliyam offered them beakers of beer. '*Wamukelekile* (You are welcome),' she said.

Maboya turned to his host. 'Your daughters do you great credit, Sikhunyane. They are graciously hospitable. Beautiful, too.'

Diboli looked at Meliyam and giggled. Embarrassed, Nomguqo tried to make herself scarce.

'No, stay,' her father said. 'You must hear the news that our friends have brought. Only two moons ago they were with His Majesty at oNdini.'

Nomguqo overcame her reserve to ask, 'You saw him? How is he? Did you speak to him?'

'I saw him from a distance. The British kept us all back,' Maboya replied.

'Why was he at oNdini?' Sikhunyane asked. 'We were told it burned down.'

'When the British captured him, their general insisted he was taken there.' Maboya drained his beaker. 'It was so sad to see him among the ruins.'

Sikhunyane gestured to Diboli to refill it. 'He was alone?'

'Mnukwa and the two youngest wives were with him. Just them. He looked exhausted. Apparently, he was made to walk from Ngome forest – where he was found – all the way to oNdini – as though he was a common criminal.'

'How was he captured?' asked Sikhunyane.

'Considering how many redcoats were searching for him, it's a miracle he kept his freedom for as long as he did. They threatened, cajoled, offered bribes to the locals, but no one would reveal where he was. Says something about our people's loyalty, doesn't it?'

They nodded.

'Never slept in the same place more than twice. Moved from

umuZi to *umuZi* at night and laid up during the day. His last hiding place was at kwaDwasa, *inkosi* Mkhosana kaSangqana's homestead. You know where I mean?'

They shook their heads.

'At the bottom of a two-thousand-foot precipice, inaccessible apart from a dangerous path down the cliff face. He must have felt completely safe there. But the British captured two brothers and tricked them into revealing his escape route and this inevitably led them to kwaDwasa. No guards were posted, so he was completely unprotected. He gave up without a struggle, according to Mnukwa. The march to oNdini took three days. Because he wasn't used to walking, the flesh on the inside of his thighs was rubbed raw. By the time they arrived, blood was running down his legs.'

Nomguqo wiped away tears. 'Why were you there, *inkosi*?'

'I was summoned. We all were – the *iziNduna* from the whole kingdom. The British wanted us to hear the surrender terms. I must say Ndabezitha looked every inch a king, walking down the line of redcoats, head held high, taller than the tallest man among them. They announced that he was no longer king, and his kingdom was to be divided among the *iziNduna*.' He let the enormity of the revelation sink in. 'They said he would be a prisoner of the great Queen overseas. Then led him away. That was the last we saw of him.'

They were shocked into silence. Sikhunyane finally found the words to speak for them all: 'This is a terrible injustice.'

'There's worse. The following day we were summoned to the general's tent again. The traitors were also there: Hamu, Zibhebhu, Jantoni.' He spat as though the mention of their names had polluted his mouth. 'They are the ones who have benefitted most.'

'How so?' Sikhunyane said.

'The kingdom has been partitioned into thirteen provinces and those who deserted our cause have been given authority over the largest. Hamu has been given the northwest from the Pongolo to the Black Mfolosi; Zibhebhu, an area stretching right down to the White Mfolosi; and Jantoni, the biggest portion of all, from the Mzinyathi all the way down to the coast.'

'This is intolerable.' Sikhunyane said.

'And... the royal children are to be removed from the protection of Cetshwayo's brothers and handed to Zibhebhu. The whole family has been placed under his jurisdiction,' Maboya said.

It was as though a giant hand had reached down Nomguqo's throat and squeezed her heart. Her blood ran cold. Having witnessed first-hand Zibhebhu's brutal treatment of Cetshwayo's wives and servants, she knew what would happen to Dinuzulu and Besiyile. Without a thought for her own safety she announced, 'They will need someone to keep them safe. I must go to them right away.'

'You will do no such thing.' The vehemence of her father's response and angry set of his mouth told her it would be fruitless to pursue the matter. She realised he had risked his own life to rescue her. In any case, what could a mere servant girl do to protect the children from such a powerful man?

Maboya levered himself upright on his walking stick. 'The *abelungu* have miscalculated badly and this will end badly for all of us. More blood will be spilt.'

Isolated on the northern frontier, Sikhunyane and his family were unaffected by events in the rest of the kingdom. Until, six months after Maboya's visit, they received their first visit from Zibhebhu's warriors. Asleep in the sisters' hut, Nomguqo was woken by the bellowing of cattle. Instantly alert, she knew something was wrong. She ran outside to find the gate to the cattle pen wide open and marauders with guns and firebrands stampeding twenty of their best steers through the *umuZi*.

Her father and two brothers tried to turn their heads, but they were hopelessly outnumbered. The raiders – whom she recognised from her enforced stay at kwaBabanango – whooped and whistled as they drove the cattle.

Bravely, her brothers stood in their path, but Zibhebhu's men surrounded them, three to each boy, beating them with their rifle butts. They rolled trying to protect their heads but couldn't avoid the repeated blows. Like ragdolls, they lay unconscious in the dust. Sikhunyane had no choice but to stand aside and let his beloved beasts to be taken.

Closing the gate of the cattle pen, the last of the raiders followed his comrades. He ran past Sikhunyane crouching beside his sons and shouted, 'This is just the start; we'll be back for more.'

It was no idle threat. Over the months that followed, they returned again and again. Each time they took only a small number of beasts, using violence to enforce their demands. The effect was cumulative. The herd was reduced from nearly a thousand beasts to scarcely a hundred. They stole most of the breeding stock – the best of the herd – leaving only the weakest animals.

Nomguqo and her sisters worried about their father's state of mind. His fighting spirit deserted him. He spent his days sunk in apathy, or in a haze of *gwai*.

She was also anxious about the fate of the royal children. Word had reached them that the king's brother Ndabuko, to whom she had entrusted their care, had become Zibhebhu's vassal, relegated to the status of a servant. He was constantly humiliated, forced to perform the most menial tasks – tilling crops, and milking the stolen cattle – with little opportunity to fulfil his responsibilities as Dinuzulu and Besiyile's guardian.

By the end of the second year, the family's fortunes reached a critical point. They stared starvation in the face. Sikhunyane seemed resigned to their fate. Something had to be done. His children gathered to discuss what they could do to resist Zibhebhu. For the brothers, it was personal. They were determined to meet force with force.

Josia brandished Sikhunyane's antiquated muzzle-loader. 'Next time they come, they'll be facing this. At least one of them will die.'

'One perhaps,' said Nomguqo. 'Then what? They are many and we are few. And they're better armed. Put the gun away. All you'll do is get yourself killed.'

'And you have a better plan?' said Josia.

'We must persuade *Ubaba* to talk to the British authorities.'

'To achieve what exactly? It was the British who created the problem in the first place. In any case, how will you get our father off his backside? All he wants to do these days is drink *uTshwala* and snort *gwai*.'

'Leave it to me.' She smiled conspiratorially at her sisters. 'Girls have a way with their fathers.'

When Sikhunyane returned from Pietermaritzburg a week later, he brought news that cheered them all.

'Zibhebhu's power is broken,' he announced. 'The *abelungu* have removed his jurisdiction over the royal family. Ndabuko and the wives are free.'

'And Dinuzulu and Besiyile?' said Nomguqo.

'Them too. In Dinuzulu's case it was quite an adventure. While under Zibhebhu's authority, Ndabuko engineered the prince's escape and somehow, he found his way to Mnyamana's *umuZi*. He's a very resourceful boy – as you know, Nomguqo.'

'Zibhebhu must be furious.' She allowed herself a smile.

'Apparently, patrols were sent to hunt him down. But he dodged them all, hiding with families loyal to the king.' He chuckled. 'This will make you laugh – while he was on the run, he even visited kwaBabanango.'

'What?'

'And Zibhebhu didn't recognise him when he saw him.'

'He went to kwaBabanango?' Josia said. 'Why would he do that?'

Nomguqo answered, 'Devilment. Dinuzulu's always been full of mischief.' On tenterhooks, she urged, 'Go on, *Ubaba*, what happened?'

'He passed himself off as Dabulmanzi's son. Told Zibhebhu he'd come to pay his respects.'

'Ha!' Meliyam and Diboli chorused.

'Zibhebhu was so flattered he presented him with a choice piece of meat to help him on his way…' Sikhunyane paused for dramatic effect. '…this is the best bit. On continuing his journey, he met one of Zibhebhu's men going the other way. Giving him the meat, he asked that it be returned to Zibhebhu with Dinuzulu's compliments!'

The family exploded with laughter.

'Sounds just like him,' said Nomguqo.

'If Zibhebhu isn't our overlord,' said Josia, 'who is?'

'Jantoni,' Sikhunyane said.

'The whiteman?'

Sikhunyane nodded. 'I don't know whether it's a good or a bad thing. He says he will support the interests of the royal family.'

The pleasure of hearing about Dinuzulu's exploits curdled in

Nomguqo's stomach. 'Jantoni will always put his own interests first,' she said.

'How so?'

She remembered how her skin crawled when Dunn looked at her during his private meetings with Cetshwayo. 'He has no scruples in stealing other people's property.'

'How do you know?' Josia said.

'I've seen it with my own eyes.'

Sikhunyane remained optimistic. 'I'm sure the British administrators know best. They know their own man. They'll keep him in check.'

It didn't take long for Sikhunyane's assumption to be contradicted. Nomguqo's assessment proved accurate in every detail.

With the early arrival of the spring rains, new growth flourished in the pastures around the *umuZi*. The cattle that remained after Zibhebhu's raids took full advantage of the fresh grass. In a matter of days, their coats developed a healthy sheen and the milking cows' udders were filled with nourishing milk. Nomguqo felt a new sense of optimism as she and her brothers watched them suckling their newborn calves. A young bull kicked up his heels at the sheer joy of being alive. The normal routine of their pastoral lives was restored.

Until, early one morning, the peaceful sounds of the grazing cattle were interrupted by thudding hooves. A large body of mounted men appeared from the south, riding at speed towards them. The leader was a white man with a brick-red complexion – John Dunn.

The riders spread out on both sides, forming an arc to corral the cattle. Dunn came straight on and pulled up in front of them. Tipping his hat brim, he peered at Nomguqo, who was hidden behind the protective wall of her brothers. 'I know you. You were at oNdini. One of the girls in Cetshwayo's *isiGodlo*.'

Josia spoke up, 'How can we help?'

'You can direct me to the head man.'

'Our father?'

'If your father is Sikhunyane.'

'What's your business with him?' said Josia.

'My business?' Dunn nodded to where his men were rounding up the cattle. 'That's between him and me. Now, stop wasting my time and tell me where he is.'

Josia pointed to the homestead.

Dunn gave Nomguqo the once-over. 'Yes, I remember you. You were Cetshwayo's favourite. And I can see why.' The intention behind his leer was unmistakable. Pulling on the bridle, he kicked his horse towards the huts.

'You know him?' Josia asked.

'I know he's a thief,' she replied.

Dunn's men had enclosed the cattle in a tight circle and were cutting out those in good condition.

'I don't make the rules; I'm here to enforce them.' Dunn sat opposite Sikhunyane under the mopane tree. 'I've been directed to collect a hut tax from every homestead under my jurisdiction – ten shillings from every household. If, as you say, you have no money, I shall have to take your cattle as payment.'

'I have few enough as it is,' Sikhunyane protested. 'If you take those, what will be left to feed my family?'

Nomguqo and her brothers watched their father slump in despair.

'We have a dilemma, then,' said Dunn. 'The law demands you pay the tax, yet you don't have the means. What are we to do?'

Sikhunyane stared helplessly at the ground.

'What about your other assets?' Dunn's eyes ranged across the semi-circle of anxious faces, past Sikhunyane's wives and sons and older married daughters, past Meliyam and Diboli, finally coming to rest on Nomguqo. 'For a start, you have three unmarried daughters. Each would command a good bride price. That one for example…' he pointed at Nomguqo, '… would fetch fifteen milking cows at the very least.'

With every fibre of her being, Nomguqo willed her father to dismiss the idea.

'I'm only suggesting it as a solution to your problem,' Dunn continued. 'You don't need to decide now; the payment isn't due for another week.' Replacing his hat on his head, he stood. 'In the meantime, I'll take twenty of your beasts now as a down payment.'

Sikhunyane gritted his teeth. What could he say?

'…and return in six days for the rest.'

Nomguqo knew beyond a shadow of a doubt that "the rest" meant her.

Untethering his horse from the *isibaya* fence, Dunn pulled himself into the saddle.

Sikhunyane followed his beloved cattle as they were driven away, then stopped and stamped the ground in impotent rage. He turned back to the family. 'Hut tax be damned! It's just another pretext to steal from us. He might take my beasts, but he will never take my children!'

They'd never seen him so angry.

'What are we to do?' one of the wives asked. 'We have to give him something when he returns in a week.'

No one spoke while they searched for a solution, then Meliyam piped up, 'He will have to find us first.'

Sikhunyane frowned. 'What do you mean?'

'If he can't find us, he won't be able to steal from us.'

'You mean hide?'

She smirked mischievously.

'Where?'

'It would need to be very secure,' the wife said.

Meliyam grinned, prolonging the suspense. Then one by one, the other children realised what she had in mind. They chuckled at the audacity of the idea.

'It's perfect,' Diboli said.

'Why didn't we think of it before?' said Nomguqo.

'Also, it's big enough to contain the cattle.' Josia added.

Sikhunyane sucked his teeth impatiently. 'Well, are you going to share your secret?'

Only a short distance from the homestead, the Ingwenya mountain range rose above the river Mkhuze. Under the summit of Ngwibi , the highest, lay the hidden entrance to a system of caves. Nomguqo and her siblings had used them as hiding places when they were little and, as far as they knew, nobody else knew about them. The entrance was so well concealed that, unless a pursuer knew what he was looking for, he would never find it.

It took the family the rest of the day to collect and pack their necessary belongings. Eventually a line of animals – goats and the few remaining cattle – trailed towards Ingwenya. Sikhunyane and his family carried their possessions on their heads. The two brothers brought up the rear, dragging branches across the path to obliterate their tracks. It was slow going and the light was already fading when they reached the cave entrance.

Lighting torches, the boys headed down the narrow passage in the rocks. The others waited, then heard their distant voices announcing it was safe to proceed.

Driving the cattle ahead of them, the family picked its way between rocks dislodged from the roof, the torches' flickering light casting shadows on the immense cavern walls. Having played hide-and-seek there with her sisters, Nomguqo knew every detail. She felt an overwhelming sense of relief. Given sufficient food, they could live there indefinitely, knowing they would never be discovered.

Over the next few days, they set up a new routine, venturing into the open only at night to forage for food and fodder for the animals, taking care to keep the cave entrance hidden under fresh tree branches. They eked out their supplies, existing on tightly controlled rations. Their hunger was never satisfied, but at least they were safe.

Six days passed, and on the seventh, they heard men shouting and dogs barking on the hillside outside. They retreated further into the caves, as far from the entrance as they could. For over three hours they sat in the dark, in complete silence. They heard John Dunn's voice. 'I know you're here somewhere. Give yourselves up and I promise you'll come to no harm.'

They sat tight, waiting it out. Eventually Dunn's voice stopped, and the dogs' barking grew fainter. Peeping from the cavern's entrance, they watched them retreat down the mountainside.

They were not to know that their isolation would last a whole year. During that time, they suffered enormous privation, wasting away until they became just skin and bone. Once the livestock had been slaughtered, they had literally nothing left to eat. At that point Sikhuyane decided they would have to take their chances in the open. He could not watch his children waste away any longer – their gaunt bodies and hollow eyes pricked his conscience and were a reminder of his paternal duty.

The homestead at Mkhuze was in ruins, the huts burned to the ground. All that remained were the charred ends of the supporting timbers. Even the thorn fences surrounding the cattle pen had been pulled apart and scattered. They inspected the damage, hearts heavy with the huge rebuilding task ahead of them.

The shock of finding their home destroyed was suddenly mitigated by the sight of friendly faces. Maboya and fellow members of the Buthelezi clan picked their way through the ruins towards them.

'We thought you were dead!' Maboya clasped Sikhunyane to his chest. 'But somehow you survived. The ancestors be praised.' He held him at arms' length, dismayed at his friend's emaciated state.

Sikhunyane gestured with mute despair at the damage.

'It was Jantoni,' said Maboya. 'After you disappeared, he came here with his men.'

'To destroy what he couldn't take,' Sikhunyane said. 'That man's wickedness knows no bounds.' He pointed to the cattle-pen with its torn-down fences. 'Maboya, you must excuse us if our hospitality falls short of what you would expect.'

'No need to apologise for the malice of others, old friend,' said Maboya. 'In any case we have enough food to share with you.' He pointed out a small herd of goats being tended by one of his kinsmen. 'Come sit and tell us your news.'

The family members and their guests gathered in a circle on the ground.

'News?' Sikhunyane folded his arms. 'What news? Stuck in those caves, our world has been very small. You must tell us.'

'Well…' Maboya began. 'It's a small comfort, I know, but you're not alone. Across the kingdom, our countrymen have been oppressed by the traitors. But amaZulu can always be relied on to fight back. Pockets of resistance formed and coalesced into a faction loyal to the king. Tensions mounted. To the extent that the king had to lobby the authorities to let him return as the only way of preventing war between us and the traitors. The British believed it would have the opposite effect, so kept him in exile on a farm in the Cape Colony. However, the sheer number of complaints was overwhelming. They had no choice but to let him come back. We're just returning from Mthonjaneni where he was installed.'

'Installed?' Nomguqo said. 'You mean he's king again?'

'As I live and breathe,' Maboya replied.

Each family member absorbed the implications of this wonderful news. It meant there would be no more persecution from the likes of John Dunn, no more fear of starvation.

'Are you sure?' Sikhunyane asked. Given what they had suffered, his scepticism was understandable.

'As sure as I'm sitting here,' said Maboya. 'I saw it with my own eyes.'

The emotion they'd suppressed for so long poured out of them. Jumping up, the boys improvised a dance and sang victory songs at the top of their voices.

Nomguqo burst into tears.

Meliyam put a consolatory arm around her shoulders. 'Why are you crying, silly? This is the best news ever.'

'I know,' Nomguqo sobbed. 'Ndabezitha will be so happy to be among his people again.'

'And that's a reason to cry?'

'Just remembering how happy I felt when I came home.'

The next hour or so was spent preparing a celebratory feast.

Using the broken fencing material, Nomguqo's brothers built a cooking fire, and Maboya's kinsmen slaughtered and butchered a couple of their goats.

'Tomorrow we'll start the rebuild,' Maboya said. 'But, right now, we must celebrate your survival.'

His men threw steaks and ribs onto the fire. They provided the rest of the meal, mealies and pumpkins and large quantities of *uTshwala*.

Full of optimism for the future, the two families sat cross-legged in the ruins of the homestead. For Sikhunyane's family, it was their first proper meal in over eleven months. Their spirits soared.

'Now Ndabezitha is back,' Nomguqo said, 'all our troubles are over.'

'Not quite, *sthandwa* (darling),' her father corrected her. 'Maybe when we have a roof over our heads.'

'Don't you worry about that.' Maboya pointed to his kinsmen. 'My boys will help. With us all working it will be done before you know it. But that's tomorrow's task. Tonight, we drink.' He held up his beaker to be filled.

'Well, well...' Sikhunyane mused. 'That's one over on the land grabbers. Their day of reckoning is coming at last.'

The feast continued long into the afternoon, during which large quantities of *uTshwala* were consumed. While she attended the guests, a single thought possessed Nomguqo – how to serve the king. Her vision of the vulture killing the lion cubs was still fresh. She would do everything in her power to protect the royal children. If offered the opportunity, she would ask the king to take her back into his *isiGodlo*.

Her family's ordeal had brought them together as never before, but she realised how much she missed her life at oNdini. The responsibilities within the royal household gave her a sense of purpose she had not felt since her return. She missed her status as an *umndlunkulu* (handmaiden).

When Sikhunyane left the company to use the latrine, she followed. It was the perfect opportunity to speak to him in private.

'*Ubaba*? Would it displease you if I were to rejoin the *isiGodlo*?'

He frowned. 'You wish to leave us, child?'

His sad expression struck home. 'No, No. Please don't misunderstand me. It's just that Ndabezitha needs the services of those he trusts right now. If you forbid me to go, of course I shall obey you, but I hope you'll grant me your permission.' Kneeling at his feet, she inclined her head submissively.

He placed his hand gently on her head. 'You're a strange child, Nomguqo, conscientious to a fault. Just like your mother.' Then he pressed his forehead against hers. 'Go, with my blessing.'

PART FIVE

RESTORATION

THIRTY-EIGHT

oNdini

Nomguqo was footsore. She had been walking for three days and nights, and now her journey's end was in sight, she was desperate to rest.

Familiar landmarks began to appear. She plodded forward, one exhausted step after another, a small bundle of personal possessions balanced precariously on her head. As the river Mfolosi came into view, her spirits rose. Memories from the past came flooding back.

So much had happened since she had been away. Her experiences had torn away the veil of innocence and trust. She had seen into the darkest recesses of the human soul and witnessed first-hand the full extent of the human potential for deceit and treachery.

As she crossed the river, her excitement overcame her fatigue. She wondered how many of her old hutmates would be there, whether she would be able to resume her old duties caring for the royal children. Above all, she was anxious to discover what had happened to Mehlokazulu.

During nearly four years of enforced absence, Nomguqo had often thought of the people who had shared her life at oNdini. Her most vivid image was of Mehlokazulu. During her time in the royal household, he had been present at all the significant moments. He had helped her more than once, had spoken out against the *iziNyanga* who would have "smelt her out" and condemned her as a witch. She literally owed him her life.

Cresting the rise, she looked across the Mahlabathini plain. Where she expected to see the royal settlement on the skyline there was nothing, no sign of the thousand huts that once comprised oNdini's "Great Place". All the familiar landmarks had been obliterated. Except one.

On the path leading to the burned-out settlement, the mission station still stood, its whitewashed walls bright in the summer sun. Its once well-tended gardens, however, had been sadly neglected. Self-seeded tambookie grass overwhelmed the fruit trees and creepers invaded the thorn hedge. The station had been abandoned.

Shading her eyes against the light, she watched lines of people making their way over the horizon, carrying their belongings. They seemed to have a common destination, but she couldn't make out where they were going since the lines extended beyond the skyline. As though on automatic pilot, she let her weary feet carry her in the same direction.

Nearing the mission station fence, Nomguqo had a sudden recollection of the last time she had been there. It was the day Pastor Gundersen's wife was buried. She stopped at the corner of the orchard. The place was as she remembered it, except that weeds and uncut grass now concealed the grave. All that marked its existence was a white-painted wooden cross. Beside it, and enjoying the shade afforded by the peach tree, was the figure of a nine-year old Zulu girl wearing a dress of sprigged cotton.

She stopped and stared closely at the girl. Though her childish features had been replaced with more angular lines, there was no mistaking her. It was Pastor Gundersen's adopted daughter. Intent on the grave, Gunhild Christine had not registered Nomguqo's presence.

Nomguqo walked along the perimeter fence until they were level. Gunhild looked up. 'Hello,' she said, as though they had seen each other only yesterday.

Behind her the front door opened, and a woman appeared in the doorway. She called in a language Nomguqo remembered as Norwegian.

Gunhild Christine shouted back and ran to greet her friend properly. The two girls stared at each other over the fence. Gunhild reached to grasp Nomguqo's hands. 'You came back.'

'So did you.'

'You're so thin,' Gunhild said. 'You need to eat. Come inside and tell us your news.' She ran towards the gate.

The exhaustion of three days' walking disappeared as Nomguqo raced her. Reaching the gate, they fell into each other's arms and embraced.

Nomguqo held her at arms' length. 'Look how you've grown. Nearly as big as me.'

'So much to tell you,' Gunhild gabbled. 'But what about you? Where have you been? How is your family?' Her questions tumbled over each other.

The Norwegian woman shouted again from the house.

Gunhild shouted back, '*Vi kommer* (We're coming),' then translated, 'she says the food is on the table. Come on, I'm starving.' Grabbing Nomguqo's hand, she dragged her up the path to the house.

As they reached the verandah, the familiar figure of Pastor Gundersen appeared. His blue eyes crinkled in recognition.

'Nomguqo.' He helped her up the steps. 'Come into the shade.' He gestured at the wilderness of weeds and unruly growth on either side of the house. 'Not as tidy as when you last saw it; I have lots to do. But after lunch, we'll see if there are any ripe peaches to pick.'

Nomguqo smiled at the reminder of happier times.

He turned to the strange woman. 'May I present my wife Marthe?'

Nomguqo was unable to hide her shock.

'Gundvall told me all about you,' Marthe said, inviting her in.

Nomguqo's mind worked overtime. The idea of the pastor re-marrying made her feel uneasy. But why? It wasn't as though the idea of a man taking a second wife was foreign to her. She had grown up with polygamy: Zulu men could marry as many wives as they could afford. Somehow, she felt, it must be different for the *abelungu*. She imagined that, like the hoopoe bird, white people had one partner and mated for life.

Another thought struck her. Perhaps the pastor's haste to take another wife had less to do with his own personal needs than the responsibility of parenthood. From her own experience, she knew every child needed a mother. Also, the woman's appearance gave her reason to think that passion was low on his priorities. She was short and dumpy and the way she had dragged her prematurely grey hair into a severe bun made her seem so much older than him.

Her voice was friendly enough and her isiZulu fluent. 'Come sit, child,' she said. 'I hope you have a good appetite. I've made Gunhild's favourite – mealie porridge with molasses. And the ribs roasting in the oven won't take long. Are you thirsty?' Pouring milk from a jug into a beaker, she set it in front of her. 'Fresh this morning. I milked the goats myself.'

Nomguqo drained it in one draft, the residue creating a

creamy line round her lips. Without thinking, she reached across to help herself to the food, but paused when the pastor cleared his throat.

Closing his eyes, he invited them to join hands. 'Almighty and most merciful Father, you have seen fit to bless our fellowship. We thank you for restoring Nomguqo to us. We pray that she, too, may walk in your footsteps and feel the joy of your presence. For this and your many other bounties we thank you. In Jesus's name, amen.'

As he finished, Marthe started to talk. And didn't draw breath. Piling a plate high with food, she handed it to her guest then, nodding towards the half-unpacked chests of china and linen that lined the walls, she said, 'Please forgive the chaos. We arrived only yesterday. There's so much to do. Still, with the good Lord's help, we'll have it stowed away in no time. Gunhild is helping, aren't you, dear?'

Gunhild's eye-rolling suggested she hadn't much choice.

'My sister is also married to a pastor,' Marthe continued. 'They're on a mission station down on the Mhlatuze in John Dunn's territory. Now, there is an evil man. How he can live with himself, I don't know.' She crossed herself, the mention of his name invoking a malign spirit. 'They've only just been allowed back themselves...'

Nomguqo blinked at the barrage of new information.

Gundersen explained, 'Dunn is no friend to the missionaries. The king's exile forced pastors like me to leave our missions. Our church at Eshowe was burned down.'

'He burned my father's *umuZi* too,' Nomguqo volunteered. 'All because we wouldn't surrender our cattle.'

'Now that Cetshwayo has been reinstalled, Dunn has been forced to change his policy and welcome back the missionaries,' the pastor said. 'I imagine he is none too pleased.'

'Help yourself to more, dear,' Marthe urged.

Nomguqo spooned another helping onto her plate. 'I am happy to see you, Guniseni. And I'm sure Ndabezitha is too. You were always welcome.'

Gunhild Christine piped up, 'There were pictures of Jesus on the walls in his house, remember.'

Nomguqo was puzzled. Either Gunhild had misremembered, or her own memory was faulty; she couldn't recall any pictures on the walls. She also wondered on what occasion Gunhild would have entered the king's private quarters.

Gundersen changed the subject. 'We've returned to serve the Zulu people again. The king has agreed to allow us to hold services here. We shall be preaching the word of God in the mission. We hope you'll join us.'

'How is Ndabezitha?' Nomguqo asked.

Marthe replied, 'Gundvall says he is much changed. I've never met him, of course, but apparently, he's much fatter. A life of idleness in Cape Town, I suppose.'

Gundersen patted her hand. 'Everything is back to normal. Praise be to God, we've all survived. And your family, where are they?'

'Rebuilding the homestead at Mkhuze.'

'And yet you left them to return to oNdini,' said Marthe. 'Why?'

'My father has my sisters to look after him. Though Ndabezitha has far more servants than he could ever need, it is my duty to help him in whatever way he requires.'

Her energies restored by the Gundersen family's hospitality, Nomguqo clambered up the slope towards the new construction. Her life at oNdini had turned almost full circle. She had arrived as a girl of thirteen while the *umuZi* was in the process of construction. Now, seven years later, on a site several miles to the east of the original "Great Place", a new homestead was being built.

Nomguqo was thrilled to see how many people were involved. The king's restoration had attracted a lot of support. Ox-drawn carts, piled high with building materials, lumbered up a newly built track to the main gate. The general shape of the *umuZi* was already defined, with the *isibaya* fenceposts and perimeter fence already in place. It was on a smaller scale – half the number of huts with a greatly reduced cattle pen, reflecting the diminished size of the royal herd.

The hut walls were mostly complete. Mud mixed with cow dung was daubed on the wooden frames, then smoothed over to bake dry in the sun. Teams of women prepared bundles of thatch to apply to the roofs.

High on the brow of the hill, the king's compound was taking shape. The brick walls of a facsimile European house were well under way and the huts housing his wives and children were nearly finished. Of all the buildings in the *isiGodlo*, the *eNkatheni* stood out as complete. The *inkatha*, embodiment of the spirit of the Zulu nation, was already in place, inspiring the king's subjects to greater effort in re-establishing his power and status.

Nomguqo wandered past the construction gangs. Here and there she recognised faces from the past. Then, through all the activity, she saw Mehlokazulu standing in the middle of the stockade organising the distribution of materials. She felt the muscles in her stomach tighten and the palms of her hands become clammy – a reaction she had experienced before, but in relation to Shikashika. When she registered that he wore his hair long and hadn't formed it into a married man's head ring, the sensation changed to one of relief. It appeared that he was still single.

During her time in the royal household, she had been constantly aware of him. For three years, right up to the outbreak of war, they had seen each other every day. Even so, his sex and age prevented him from associating with her. Older men were forbidden to enter the *umndlunkulu* (handmaidens') huts, or indeed address them by name. Mehlokazulu was as remote to her as the man in the moon.

Observing the confidence with which he coordinated the work gangs, she remembered how thrilling she found his natural authority, his obvious physical prowess. At the time, she had suppressed her feelings because he was inaccessible. Now, she realised, his remoteness merely increased his allure. As she passed into adolescence, he assumed the significance of a phantom lover, the object of forbidden desire, the epitome of Zulu manhood. Shikashika, sweet boy that he was, had been a poor substitute for her real passion. Heart thumping, she walked towards him and called, 'Mehlokazulu nGobese.'

Turning, he acknowledged her presence. Nothing more. No sense of being glad to see her or relief she had survived. 'When did you get here?' he asked.

'Just now.'

He looked her over. 'You're…' searching for a suitable epithet, '…older.'

'So are you.'

'You survived.'

'As you see.'

'I'm glad.'

I'm glad. Her heart skipped a beat. It was the closest she'd heard him come to expressing emotion of any kind.

A whistle from a cart driver wanting to know where to deliver his load interrupted them. He pointed to where it was needed, then turned back.

She prompted, 'You were saying?'

'What?' Having lost his train of thought, he opened his arms to encompass the scale of the work being undertaken. Over four thousand people were working on the rebuild. 'It's been like this for over a week. So much to do and so little time. Timber must be imported from the Nkandla Forest because there's nothing left around here. Thatching materials, too. The British burned everything.'

'When will it be finished?'

He shrugged. 'In the time it takes.'

'Where is Ndabezitha?'

'In a meeting with the council. I should be there, but he thought this was more important.'

'You're a member of the *ibandla* now?'

'I've taken my father's place. He's semi-retired…'

His body language told her he had more important duties to attend to. She made her excuses, 'I'd better announce myself, make myself busy. I'll–'

But before she completed the sentence, he had moved away, shouting instructions to a team of warriors carrying a large container of cow dung for the hut floors.

THIRTY-NINE

oNdini

The new oNdini *isibaya* offered no tree cover, so the royal council members were exposed to the full glare of the midday sun. Tempers, already frayed by the subject being discussed, were further irritated by the flies and the incessant noise from the adjacent building site. It was a measure of the urgency of their agenda that Cetshwayo had summoned the meeting in the first place.

The king flapped his hands at the insects buzzing around him. He surveyed the semi-circle of his most intimate advisors. Using a blanket and a pair of walking sticks, Ndabuko had improvised some shade over the elderly prime minster Mnyamana. Next to them, the minister of state Vumandaba fidgeted uncomfortably. More accustomed to discomfort, the generals Ntshingwayo and Mavumengwana wafted their flywhisks stoically. The first official *ibandla* since Cetshwayo's restoration, it was a much-reduced gathering. Those who had defected from the royal cause – Zibhebhu and Hamu – were notable by their absence. Sihayo, sunk into a deep depression by the loss of his homestead and so many of his sons, sat next to Cetshwayo, his presence on the council a mark of the king's continued friendship.

Now the official representative of Qungebeni interests, Mehlokazulu spoke with a newfound authority. 'We must mount a pre-emptive strike, act before they have time to collect their forces. Zibhebhu's insult to the royal family is an outrage. It's intolerable that you, Ndabuko, were forced to swear allegiance to him.'

Ndabuko nodded. 'Give me the *amabutho*, Ndabezitha, and I will avenge our honour. I will teach that strutting whoreson a lesson. He has plundered our herds and our lands. The security of my own lands is compromised, surrounded as they are by his territory. It's time to make a stand.'

'The same is true in the north,' said Ntshingwayo. 'Hamu is also threatening us.'

'The white locust too.' Vumandaba added. 'Jantoni.'

Cetshwayo spat. 'Don't pollute the air with that man's name. He should die the coward's death – a thousand times over. I trusted him, sent him as our emissary to the British. But he took my words and twisted their meaning. Did the same to me with the government's words. He's directly responsible for where we are now.'

The mention of Dunn brought Sihayo out of his self-absorption. 'Never trusted him in the first place,' he muttered.

'You were right, old friend,' said the king. 'Even now, when my people expressed their wish for my return, he showed his true colours by seizing their cattle…'

'…And constantly claimed to the government that the people rejoiced in your absence,' Ndabuko echoed.

Mehlokazulu broke in, 'Do we have a consensus? Shall we send a force against all three traitors?'

Cetshwayo considered the possibilities. 'Who is the greatest threat?'

'Zibhebhu has the largest force and has been the loudest in arguing against you,' Mnyamana said. 'Make him an example.'

'I agree,' said Ndabuko.

'A show of hands then,' Cetshwayo said. 'Objections to an *ibutho* being sent to punish Zibhebhu.'

No-one moved a muscle.

'Let us show the traitor who the true king is.' Cetshwayo nodded to Ndabuko. 'Call up the *amabutho*.' With a weary sigh, he pushed himself upright and strode to his private quarters.

The *izikhulu* mopped their brows, relieved that the business had been concluded so swiftly.

Mehlokazulu helped his father to his feet. He waited until the others were out of earshot, then whispered, 'Is it my imagination or has Ndabezitha lost some of his vitality?'

'If he has, he's not the only one,' Sihayo replied.

During the first few days after her return, Nomguqo's main concern was to be reunited with the royal children but, as far as she could discover, they hadn't yet arrived. On her third morning, she found Usixipe in the Mfolosi bathing pool washing her baby son. The child's sturdy legs kicked and splashed water in every direction. She commented, 'He's lively.'

'A real handful,' Usixipe agreed.

'How old is he?'

'Eighteen months, born while we were at the Oude Moulen farm...' She explained, '... where they sent the wives while Ndabezitha was in prison.'

'Prison?'

'Yes. A grim place called The Castle in Cape Town. He wasn't there for very long, then joined the four wives on the farm.'

'Four? Why only four?'

'That's all they would allow.'

'Well, I know Nomvimbi wasn't there because she was at kwaBabanango with us.'

'Still moaning about it, apparently. They say she'll never get over it.' Pulling her son from the water, Usixipe waded to the bank. 'Well, well. Look who we have here.'

Nomguqo turned. Sure enough, Nomvimbi was making her way up the track from Mthonjaneni. A baggage train followed her, accompanied by a retinue of servants. Striding ahead was a youth she recognised as Dinuzulu. He had grown in the four years since she had last seen him – tall, with his father's heavily muscled legs. Her natural impulse was to run to greet him, but she felt inhibited. What if he rejected her? What if he had outgrown their intimacy? Since the path passed close to the bathing-pool she let matters take their own course.

As the party approached, she took the opportunity to study them. The privations of Nomvimbi's time with Zibhebhu were only too apparent. She had aged appreciably. Deep creases lined her face, and her hair was streaked with grey. Princess Besiyile had grown too, but out rather than up. Unfortunate to have inherited Nomvimbi's genes, she had developed the maternal tendency to corpulence.

As he passed, Dinuzulu glanced towards Nomguqo. She hesitated, on the point of greeting him, but when he stared through her and carried on walking, she kept her mouth firmly shut. She searched for a reason for the snub. What had she done to offend him? Maybe it wasn't personal. Maybe, like all Zulu boys his age, he had cut the apron strings and was preparing for life as a warrior.

The answer came, indirectly, from Nomvimbi. Spotting Nomguqo, she walked straight up to her. 'You took my children. I will never forgive you.'

The accusation hit home: it was true.

Usixipe came to her defence, 'That's unfair, Nomvimbi. Tell the whole story. She took your children to save them from our enemy. The fact they're with you today is entirely because of Nomguqo.'

'Keep your nose out of it. A servant's loyalty is to her mistress and that girl,' pointing at Nomguqo, 'is the definition of disloyalty. You have no idea how painful it is to lose your children. My daughter wasn't even weaned.'

Usixipe was shocked into silence. How could Nomvimbi say such a thing? Surely, she'd remember that her baby twins had been murdered. But what was the point in dragging up the past? Swaddling her baby on her back, Usixipe marched up the path towards the settlement.

Nomguqo turned to Besiyile, whom she had nurtured as a baby. Would she show her some affection? But again, the princess looked at her with complete indifference, her eyes cold and expressionless.

Nomvimbi waved imperiously and her retinue proceeded towards the settlement.

Nomguqo stared across the river, trying to process what had happened. She could understand Nomvimbi's hostility, but the children? Why had they rejected her? It was obvious they'd been turned against her. Her sadness made her cheeks ache with unshed tears.

True to form, Nomvimbi resumed the idle life she'd enjoyed before the war and ran her servants ragged. The way she treated them made Nomguqo glad she had been rejected.

Anxious to remain of service to the king, she volunteered to be directly involved in his welfare. Mnukwa recruited her to help prepare his meals. To begin with, he used her as a skivvy to scrub the cooking pots, but gradually trusted her with more creative jobs. Working side by side, they chatted about every subject under the sun. One afternoon, as they chopped meat for a stew, he recounted the details of the king's exile. 'When we sailed to Cape Town, Ndabezitha was limited to the number in his party. He chose me as his only *inceku*. What an honour that was. His choice of wives was even easier: he picked the youngest.'

She laughed. 'That explains Nomvimbi's bitterness – in part anyway. She had a bad time at kwaBabanango. We all did. You wouldn't treat a dog the way they treated us.'

'But you got away...'

'I was lucky.'

'...And rescued the royal children. Ndabezitha told me how grateful he is.'

'Nomvimbi not so much.' Nomguqo shook her head ruefully. 'I miss Dinuzulu. We had such fun when he was a little boy.'

'Well, that little boy has big responsibilities now. He is spending a lot more time with his father, learning what's expected of him. The country he will inherit is very different from the one we knew.'

'Oh, I wouldn't worry about Dinuzulu,' Nomguqo said. 'He has an old head on young shoulders. He will learn fast.' As she scraped the diced meat into a cooking pan, she noticed the amulet around her wrist. It reminded her of its previous owner. 'I wonder what happened to Sixhwethu: my old hutmate, remember?'

Mnukwa's expression hardened. 'If you value your life, you will never mention that girl's name in Ndabezitha's presence.'

The warning shocked her. 'What do you mean?'

'He has put her on a par with all the other traitors.'

'Because Zibhebhu took her as a concubine?'

'Exactly.' He lowered his voice confidentially. 'Between you and me, the real reason is the *lobola*.'

'Oh?'

'As an orphan, Sixhwethu fell under his protection, so if she married, she would attract a very large price. Now that she's Zibhebhu's property, he has lost that potential income.'

That didn't seem right. She knew the king was capricious, but surely the loss of Sixhwethu's bride price would be his last concern, knowing how much she had suffered. She wondered whether she would ever see her again.

The *umuZi* was now complete, the building tools stowed, and the paths swept clean of any debris. The huts looked bright and clean with their fresh grass thatches. Mnukwa and Nomguqo gathered a group of porters and led them to the Hlophekulu mountain. The king had requested that his personal possessions be retrieved from their hiding place so he could use them in his new house.

As the lightest in the party, Nomguqo was lowered on a rope into the cave. When her eyes became accustomed to the dark, she could see it was empty. She shouted up, 'Are you sure this is the right cave?'

'Why?' called Mnukwa.

'There's nothing here.'

'There must be. Have another look,' he insisted.

The place had been plundered, stripped bare. There was only one possible explanation: someone from the party that had stowed the king's belongings had returned to remove them.

They pulled her back to the surface.

'What are we going to tell the king?' she asked.

Assuming Cetshwayo's wrath would fall on his head, Mnukwa looked for a scapegoat. 'Well, it wasn't one of the *izinceku*; I'd stake my life on it. Must have been one of you *umndlunkulu* shooting off her mouth. Someone must have heard where we'd hidden them and helped themselves.'

'You have no proof it was one of the handmaidens,' said Nomguqo.

'We have to find someone to blame, otherwise he'll end up blaming us.'

'I know.' Her eyes sparkled with mischief. 'Who's the person he blames for everything, the one he hates so much he'll never question it?'

'Jantoni?' Cetshwayo was still coming to terms with the shock of his loss. 'What makes you think it was him?'

'Well,' Mnukwa replied, 'he's taken everything else belonging to Your Majesty.'

'Nothing left, you say?'

'Nothing, Ndabezitha,' Nomguqo replied. 'I went down into the cave and saw with my own eyes.'

She waited for the explosion of rage. Cetshwayo strode up and down, brows furrowed, and then, to the surprise of everyone in the room, burst out laughing. He pointed his finger at Mnukwa, shoulders heaving.

'That's funny – "everything else",' you said. It's true, Jantoni is a thief, the biggest thief I've ever known.'

The *inceku* was unsure whether it would be appropriate to join in, but he couldn't help himself. Nor could Nomguqo.

The king's laughter finally subsided. 'We'll have to make do with what we have. It's not as though we're destitute. I'll take my meal now. Mnukwa, go and announce it in the *umuZi*. You girls can go and prepare it.'

Nomguqo remembered how all activity in the homestead stopped when the king sat down to eat. Nothing was allowed to interrupt mealtimes, lest the royal digestion should suffer. The *inceku* gestured that the household should go about its duties. As Nomguqo moved towards the kitchen area, the king stopped her.

'Nomguqo, stay. I have something to discuss with you.' He indicated the chair next to his at the table. 'Come sit, *inkosazana.*'

The familiar address *inkosazana* (princess), once used ironically by the *isiGodlo* girls, produced a familiar twinge in the pit of her stomach, yet the king's tone was gentle, without a trace of sarcasm. As she waited for him to speak, she could see the other girls listening through the kitchen door.

'Are you ready to take a husband?' he began.

The unexpectedness of the question took her by surprise.

He smiled. 'I know it's early for your age-group to marry, but I've decided to make an exception in your case. You have given me, my wife and children, great service. I wish to reward you with a husband who will appreciate and care for you. In return, you will bear him many sons and be a credit to your family. If you approve of my choice, I will send messengers to your father. I know he'll agree that the man I've chosen is the perfect match.'

Nomguqo's stomach flipped. There was only one name she wanted to hear. She stammered, 'Ndabezitha, I don't know what to say.'

'Then say nothing. Just listen to your suitor's virtues. I've thought long and hard about this. As an *inkosazana* you deserve a husband with status and power. I would never marry you to someone beneath you.'

He watched for her reaction, but she said nothing.

'Though my choice may not be descended from kings, and though he may not be in the first flush of youth, he is one of my closest advisors and friends. He is wealthy in land and cattle and as his youngest wife you will have many privileges. Can you guess who?'

Her heart sank. The description didn't square with the name she wanted to hear. She concentrated on concealing her disappointment.

'Sihayo,' he said triumphantly.

She searched desperately for a response that wouldn't offend him.

'Why the long face?' he asked. 'Are you not pleased with my choice?'

'On the contrary, Ndabezitha...' Her voice faltered. 'I'm honoured...'

'Honoured?' he snorted. 'That hardly describes the feelings of a bride-to-be.'

This was a defining moment in her life, she realised. She had been brought up to be respectful and accept the advice of those older and wiser. The king was the ultimate authority; she automatically deferred to him. Also, her father had taught her that service in the royal household had conferred status on her whole family. The king had singled her out by making her the keeper of the *eNkatheni*. She was one of his special favourites. Despite all this, his proposal was completely unacceptable. How could she marry a man old enough to be her grandfather?

As though intuiting her inner thoughts, the king spoke, 'In the matter of marriage, physical attraction is of low priority. What is important is mutual respect and understanding. Sihayo's experience gives him wisdom and compassion. Which is what I admire in him and why I think he will be the perfect husband for you.'

'Ndabezitha...' She collected herself. If she yielded now, she would regret it for the rest of her life. 'I'm grateful you should show such concern for my happiness. I have always known you have my interests at heart, but in this case…' Her nerve failed her, and her legs turned to jelly.

'Yes, child. Finish what you were going to say.'

'If you want me to be happy, please don't marry me to an old man,' she blurted out, the words tumbling over each other.

Cetshwayo's genial expression changed. 'Your happiness is immaterial. What I require is your obedience. I suggest you reflect on how you've displeased me and come to me when you've decided to follow my wishes.'

Terrified by his sudden coldness, Nomguqo backed away. Tears welling, she waited for him to dismiss her.

'Get out of my sight.'

The other *isiGodlo* girls watched goggle-eyed as she slunk from the room.

Throughout the night she wrestled with the problem. How could she come to terms with his wishes? How could she accept Sihayo as a husband? She considered the positive aspects. His age for a start: the marriage would inevitably be short-lived. Would it be so bad? She had tolerated worse than accepting the duties of the marriage bed. But would yielding to the king's wishes reinstate her in his favour? Maybe she had already been banished to outer darkness.

Also, she realised, living in Sihayo's *umuZi* would mean being close to Mehlokazulu. That prospect in different circumstances would have filled her with joy, but if union with him was impossible, it would be a knife twisting in the wound.

By the time dawn broke she concluded that her initial reaction was correct. Though it would involve displeasing the king, she would continue to refuse Sihayo.

Placing a pre-breakfast pitcher of whey before him, she took a deep breath and delivered the speech she'd prepared. 'Ndabezitha, I haven't slept for fear I've offended you. I would rather have cut out my tongue.' She glanced sideways to gauge his reaction. 'I beg you to think again. If you insist, I shall obey you of course, but...' she took another deep breath, '...I must tell you my affections lie elsewhere...'

The king's laugh stopped her. '*Inkosazana*, you're either very brave or very foolish. Not only do you persist in defying me, but you say you want to choose your own husband. No Zulu girl dares to do that.' He smiled indulgently. 'But then you amaSwazi have always trodden your own path.'

The tension she felt began to subside; he didn't seem angry any longer.

'Where do your affections lie, then? Who is this man? Describe his qualities to me. If you convince me he's suitable, you shall have my blessing.'

Relief flooded through her. She even risked a smile as she enumerated Mehlokazulu's virtues: 'He's a great warrior; he's distinguished himself in many battles and earned the right to wear the willow beads many times over. He's recently come into his father's fortune and has been made *inkosi* of his people. He now sits among the council of your advisers.' Cetshwayo gave nothing away as she continued: 'He has over two thousand head of cattle and, thus far, has chosen not to marry.'

'I have no idea who you're talking about,' he teased. 'Tell me his name.'

'Mehlokazulu,' she whispered.

He roared with laughter. 'Mehlokazulu? Are you sure he's worthy of you?'

Her face shone with happiness. 'Am I worthy of him, Ndabezitha?'

'Well, well, the son, not the father. My wives will never let me hear the last of it.' Gesturing that she should kneel before him, he placed his hand on her head. 'Mehlokazulu kaSihayo nGobese, eh? He's a very lucky young man.' He tipped her chin up and looked into her eyes. 'If I speak to him, are you sure he'll be in favour?'

'What do you think?' she asked.

'He'll have no choice in the matter. And he's much more obedient than you.'

The playful rebuke brought a smile to her lips. 'Ndabezitha, all I can say is, my heart beats faster whenever I see him.'

'That's settled, then. I will agree a bride price and we'll arrange the ceremony.'

The *isiGodlo* girls filed in carrying the royal breakfast and laid out plates of food on the table. They had heard every word and wanted to congratulate Nomguqo, but protocol demanded they use their discretion. They withdrew but not before noticing the tears of joy coursing down her cheeks.

'Dry your eyes, girl, and hand me some meat.'

Choosing the juiciest rib, she laid it beside him.

He shook his head in disbelief. 'Allowing girls to choose their own husbands – whatever next? I hope I won't regret it. You know, I didn't sleep so well myself last night. I couldn't stop thinking about Jantoni. I've always prided myself on being a good judge of character. But I don't mind saying, his treachery has shaken me. What a scoundrel.' He became more reflective. 'You know how I met him?'

'No,' she said, astounded he should take her into his confidence.

He stared into the middle distance. 'One stormy winter night I was sat before a large fire in my hut. My attendants announced that a white man in a miserable state had just arrived claiming my hospitality. I ordered them to bring him in. Jantoni was dressed in rags and shivering with fever. I drew my cloak aside and asked him to sit by the fire, told the servants to bring food and clothing. I loved him as a brother. As you know, I made him one of my *iziNduna*, giving him lands and wives, the daughters of my chiefs.' He paused as he considered the depth of the betrayal. 'Now the sun has gone down. John Dunn is sitting by the fire, but he doesn't draw his cloak aside for me.'

FORTY

While waiting for the king to make a formal announcement, she used every available opportunity to watch her future husband training on the Mahlabathini plain. He had become less remote. Though they had exchanged fewer than a dozen sentences in all the time they had known each other, she felt they were more intimately connected.

He had been promoted to a senior *iNduna* rank and now commanded five *amaviyo* of the iNgobamakhosi – some two hundred and fifty men. She loved watching their drills, wheeling this way and that, and was totally absorbed by the patterns they created. She was fascinated by their reaction to his orders, clearly inspired by his leadership to outdo each other in feats of skill, courage, and endurance. His reputation was clearly deserved. He seemed so much in command, not just of his men, but also of himself. Would the intimacy of marriage ever relax his apparent inflexibility? She looked forward to the challenge.

After spending one fine winter's day in the fields hoeing between the rows of ripening pumpkins, instead of returning to the *umuZi*, she chose to head towards the level ground where she knew he would be exercising. Head down and absorbed in her thoughts, she didn't notice the warriors streaming towards her, until they were almost upon her. Stepping aside to avoid them, she saw they were Mehlokazulu's men. And their commander wasn't far behind.

'Are you following me?' he said.

The blood rushed to her cheeks. 'No.'

'Well, that's strange; must be a coincidence…' He paused. 'But you know what's even stranger: it's been the same coincidence for the last five days… While you've been watching our drills.'

Had she been that obvious? Covered in confusion, she said, 'What if I have? Is that so wrong?'

'Did I say it was wrong? I was merely asking whether you were following me.'

'Well, I wasn't exactly following you. I was just hoping to see you.'

'Well, that's cleared that up.' He smiled. 'And I was hoping to see you.'

He took her hand in his, entwining their fingers together.

She looked up at him. 'Anyway, why shouldn't I want to see the man I'm going to marry?'

'My thoughts exactly.'

'I know it's not seemly for a maiden to be alone with her *iSoka*, but I don't care.'

'Seemly? That's a funny word, but you're a funny girl.' His other hand stroked her cheek.

'What did the king say?' she asked. 'Did he order you to ask for my hand?'

'No. Why?'

'I wasn't sure you wanted me, that's all.'

He threw his head back and laughed. 'Of course, I want you. I've wanted you ever since I found you in the mud with your bundle of hoes. Remember?'

How could she not? His broad back and the interplay of his muscles was fresh in her memory. 'Yes,' she said. 'You were very kind.'

He nuzzled the top of her head. 'Have you finished for today?'

She nodded.

'So, you can spend some time with me?'

She nodded again.

'Good. I've something to show you.'

He led her up the path to the distant hills. They both knew the track from their many trips to collect drinking water for the royal family: Mehlokazulu, in his capacity as Cetshwayo's bath attendant, and Nomguqo as one of the *isiGodlo* girls responsible for bringing sweet water to his wives.

Hlophekhulu Mountain had other memories for her. Only four short years previously, she had nursed Shikashika back to health there. The bittersweet memories of a boy she had adored, with whom she hoped, and expected, to spend her life, started to surface. Now she was walking over the same ground with another man, one who, in a very short time, would be her husband.

They followed the stream as it coursed down the hillside. With every step her misgivings grew. As the path narrowed, they were forced to walk in single file, with him taking the lead. She stared at the back of his head trying to fathom his intention. Her composure and sense of security slipped so that, by the time they reached level ground, tears were welling up. The very hollow where she had lain with Shikashika was covered with a bower of branches thatched with freshly collected grass.

He turned, stretching out his hand to lead her to it, and was shocked to see tears running down her cheeks.

'What is it? Why are you crying?' He wiped them away with his thumb.

'Why here?' she sobbed.

'What do you mean?'

'Of all places you chose this. It's very cruel of you.'

'Cruel? I thought you'd be pleased. I wanted us to have a place to share, somewhere special.'

'You must have known.'

'Known what?' He was completely mystified.

Now she had a dilemma. Could she tell him the whole truth? Could she admit she still had feelings for Shikashika? It was a test of her confidence in him. She took a deep breath. 'When Shikashika came back from iSandlwana, I brought him here. It was a special place where he could forget the horrors he'd seen.'

His features softened with understanding. 'It's peaceful here, and that's why I chose it for us.' Drawing her close, he laid her head on his chest. 'Mourning him is completely natural, even after all these years, but because you were happy here with him doesn't mean you can't be happy with me.'

The barrier between them had broken. She wrapped her arms around his waist.

'We'll call our first son after him,' he said. 'Shikashika is a good name. It will remind me of a comrade-in-arms who died a hero's death.'

Whenever they could, they spent time together in the bower. Its solitude and beauty inspired them to confide in each other. Soon there were no secrets, no barriers, nothing to intrude on their union.

They made plans. Looking across the Mahlabathini plain

where the royal herds grazed, he described the cattle his father owned, the pedigree animals from which his own stock was bred. The herd, which had been depleted by the war and the theft of the British occupying forces, was almost back to full strength. He was now a man of considerable wealth, easily capable of paying the bride price of twenty-five animals negotiated by the king. He teased her, 'I hope you're worth it.'

He described kwaSogekle, its rich grazing land and its fine position overlooking the Mzinyathi. With sadness, he recounted how the British, in their settlement after the war, had awarded Qungebeni land to a rival *inkosi*. Sihayo's family was displaced and forced to settle elsewhere. He was determined to reclaim kwaSogekle and install her there in her new status as wife of the rightful *inkosi*.

They discussed endlessly the names they would choose for their children. She was determined to maintain the link with her Swazi heritage by selecting Swazi names.

'I agree – for the girls,' he conceded, 'but the boys need Zulu names if they're to be warriors. Anyway, I thought we'd agreed on Shikashika.'

'I don't want any sons of mine going to war,' she said. 'Too many Zulu homes have only women in them. The world our children will inherit will have no war. Neighbours will live in peace side by side.'

He stared towards the burned out remains of the original oNdini settlement. 'No one can live with the British,' he said. 'They take and take until there's nothing left.'

He told her about his trial in Pietermaritzburg, how the prosecution's case had been dismissed by the judge because no crime had been committed on territory under British jurisdiction, adding bitterly: 'Yet enough crimes have been committed by the British on Zulu land.'

As each learned more about the other, their trust and reliance on each other grew. Though social taboos inhibited the full expression of any physical intimacy, they became adept in finding ways to release the sexual tensions that developed. In all ways but one, they were man and wife.

Nomguqo's dream of a world without war was frustrated by the ever-present threat of Zibhebhu and his Mandhlakazi. It took a month before Cetshwayo's mobilisation order reached the warriors still loyal to him. Five thousand finally assembled, received their *muthi* and, armed with their regimental shields, marched to confront Zibhebhu at his Nkungwini *umuZi*. As they left, the autumn storms began. It rained for two solid days, turning streams into torrents and dust into mud. At daybreak on the third day, the clouds lifted, and the sun broke through. It seemed that fortune was on their side. Expectations rose.

At midday a messenger arrived. He had ridden hard to deliver the news that the Mandhlakazi had been routed and driven back. Zibhebhu's *umuZi* was in ruins, burned and razed to the ground. Though it gave reason for optimism, the news was not conclusive; victory could not be assumed.

Cetshwayo gave orders for extra sentries to be posted in the event the outcome went the other way. Through the rest of the day and into the night he paced in his private quarters. After midnight, the guards on the main gate saw a lone horseman riding at speed towards the *umuZi*. Blood poured down his horse's flank from the wound in his thigh. He was conscious, but weak, his hands gripping the horse's mane to stay on its back. They let him through, and he set the horse between the rows of huts in the direction of the royal enclosure.

Alerted by the hoofbeats, Nomguqo joined the throng,

anxious to hear the news. Elbowing her way to the front, she stood in the open space in front of the king's front door.

When they saw the gash in the man's leg, the residents flinched. It was not a good sign; messengers from victorious battlefields usually appeared without wounds.

With Mehlokazulu and his *izinceku* at his side, Cetshwayo stepped forward to receive the report.

Sliding from the horse's back, the warrior collapsed to the ground.

As the crowd pressed forward, Nomguqo looked for comfort in Mehlokazulu's expression. There was none.

Mnukwa bound up the wound with bandages he'd collected. Everyone waited for the warrior to speak but, aware of the king's tendency to visit his wrath on the bearers of bad news, he kept his lips tightly shut.

Mehlokazulu encouraged him. 'Sakhile, we can see from your wound you fought well. Tell us how it fared with the *amabutho*. Speak the truth. You have nothing to fear.'

Sakhile turned to the king. 'We had them on the run, Ndabezitha. But…'

'But?'

'Their retreat was tactical. They had set up an ambush in a narrow valley. It had steep banks on either side.'

'uMsebe,' Mehlokazulu murmured. He recognised the description from his time with Mbilini.

'We should have sent scouts ahead, but we went in, a full-scale advance, the whole army.'

Cetshwayo stiffened. 'Who gave the order?'

'Ndabuko, Your Majesty.'

The king shut his eyes. How could anyone, let alone his brother, have made such a simple tactical error?

'Then Zibhebhu sprang his trap. Hidden behind bushes and

trees high above us, the Mandhlakazi cut off all the paths in and out of the valley. They surrounded us, hacking and stabbing. In the confusion we panicked and, instead of holding our ground and using our superior numbers, we broke ranks and fled. They cut us to pieces.'

Mehlokazulu broke the stunned silence. 'How did you get away?'

'Sheer luck. A gap opened in the middle of the fighting. A riderless horse appeared, and I grabbed hold of the reins. I was speared as I vaulted onto his back but managed to pull it out. The horse did the rest.'

'And what of the *amabutho*? My brother?' Cetshwayo asked.

'Ndabezitha, I fear the worst.'

Mehlokazulu turned to Nomguqo, but there was a space where she had been.

The next few days passed in a whirl. There was no time for the lovers to meet, no time for him to allay her fears, no time for anything but prepare for Zibhebhu's inevitable attack. The uMsebe defeat had devastated the numbers of available fighting men. Of the five thousand men who had started the battle, only one in five had survived. Among the Mandhlakazi, they learned, there were only a dozen casualties. Mehlokazulu was permanently engaged in council, debating the best course of action. Reports from other sectors did nothing to raise their spirits. Hamu was raiding with impunity in the northern territory and Zibhebhu continued to pillage homesteads still loyal to the king, driving away their cattle, raping their women, and burning their huts.

'Preemptive strikes are the answer,' Ntshingwayo advised. 'While the traitor is raiding, his homesteads are unprotected. We should burn them like he burned ours.'

'There must be a diplomatic solution,' said the ever-cautious Vumandaba. 'I'm happy to lead a delegation to Pietermaritzburg. Surely the commission will step in to stop these incessant attacks. It's not in the British interests to have Zulu fighting Zulu.'

'On the contrary,' said Cetshwayo, 'It's their policy to divide and rule. Has been for as long as they've been in Africa. Suits them to have us at each other's throats.'

Ntshingwayo spoke, 'After uMsebe, morale is low. We need successes on the battlefield to build it back up. Our men must wash their spears with blood.'

Mehlokazulu jumped in, 'You count the blood of women and children as successes?'

The king turned his flywhisk over in his hand. 'What do you suggest?'

'By ourselves we have less than a thousand men,' Mehlokazulu replied, 'but combined with Mnyamana's *amabutho* in the north, we could easily destroy the Mandhlakazi in the open field.'

'Whatever we do, we must settle this once and for all.' Cetshwayo struck his palm with the flywhisk. 'There can be only ruler in Zululand.' He gestured to Ntshingwayo. 'Inform Mnymana we're marching against Zibhebhu and he should join us.'

Lying in Mehlokazulu's arms, Nomguqo stared into the night sky. The heavens were studded with bright pinpoints of light. Low on the horizon, the moon appeared as the faintest of outlines. 'Do you see,' she said, 'The moon is alive and will keep you safe.'

He kissed the top of her head. 'Don't worry, *umntwana*. I'll be back before you know it.'

She gazed into his eyes, 'And then we'll be married?'

'The bride-price is already set aside,' he said, 'My best milking cows.'

Brushing his lips with hers, she said, 'I promise to be the best wife I can. But I have no one to teach me. Sikhunyane is a man and I have no mother. You will have to do it. What do you expect in a wife?'

Without thinking, he answered, 'Obedience. That's what my father would say. One virtue my mother lacked...' He tailed off, aware the reference to MaMtshali was insensitive and inappropriate.

Tidying the remains of their picnic from the floor of their bower, she threw the rib-bones and half-eaten mealie cobs into the fire, sending sparks up into the sky.

'That came out wrong,' he said, anxious to restore their intimacy. 'I wouldn't compare you to my mother for all the world.' Resting his hands on her shoulders, he pulled her back and stroked the frown from her brow. 'You are who you are and that is why I love you.' Taking her in his arms, he squeezed her tightly. She responded, reaching under his *isiNene*.

His breath caught in his throat. 'What are you doing?'

'Isn't this what wives do?' She held his cock in her hand, feeling it fill with blood. Rolling her over, he pinned her down, his mouth reaching for hers. Her body reacted instinctively as he pressed against her pubic bone. With no thought of the consequence, she allowed her thighs to roll outwards, opening herself to him.

A distant sound reached them. They froze.

'What is that?' she said.

Every muscle tense now, they listened. Amplified in the still mountain air, the faint but definite rhythm of men on the march floated towards them. They scrambled on hands and knees to identify the source. He drew her attention to movement on the ridgeline to the north. Lines of warriors were moving into position.

'Who are they?' she whispered.

Without replying, he took off and sprinted down the path to oNdini. Then paused so she could catch up. 'The *umuZi*'s about to be attacked,' he said. 'Zibhebhu's up to his old tricks. He must have seen our *amabutho* leave. It will be a bloodbath unless we warn them.'

They ran without stopping until they reached the main entrance. 'Head to the *isiGodlo*; I'll find you there,' he said, hammering on the gate, 'open up.'

Creaking on its hinges, the gate swung open. Armed guards appeared in the opening. 'The Mandhlakazi are up there,' Mehlokazulu pointed to the distant ridgeline, 'and will be down here before we know it. Sound the alarm.'

The guards stared at him. 'But there's no one here. The fighting men are in the field.'

'I know. But the king must be protected at all costs. You,' Mehlokazulu pointed to the guard who had spoken, 'wake the *iziNdibi*. Get them to bring the cattle from the pen and corral them here.'

'In the entrance?'

'Yes, in the entrance. Quickly. We don't have long.'

The guard immediately took off towards the *isibaya* while the others slammed the gate shut and propped heavy logs against it.

Side by side, Mehlokazulu and Nomguqo ran through the sleeping settlement until he stopped beside the *iziNduna*'s huts. She stood, uncertain whether to go or stay.

Cradling her face in his hands, he said, 'Go, wake the wives and children.' He kissed her, then ducked through the entrance of the nearest hut.

Continuing through the *isiGodlo*, she arrived outside Nomvimbi's place. Throwing aside the entrance curtain, she called, '*Umfazi Omkhulu*. Wake up. There's no time to lose.

'How dare you disturb me?' Nomvimbi muttered from the depths of the hut.

'We're about to be attacked. I haven't time to explain. I must wake the others.'

Her raised voice brought the other wives from their huts. They gathered, clucking and cackling like frightened guinea fowl.

Cetshwayo emerged from Usixipe's hut still groggy from sleep. But when he saw his bodyguard running past, carrying shields and stabbing spears, he was instantly alert. He grabbed Sihayo and Ntshingwayo at the rear. 'What's happening?'

'The Mandhlakazi are about to attack.' Sihayo replied. 'My son saw them massing on the north-eastern ridge.'

'Numbers?'

'We don't know yet,' said Ntshingwayo. 'Ndabezitha, we must get you out of here. They'll be coming from the front, so we must use the rear gate. You still have time to escape.'

Drawing himself to his full height, Cetshwayo snarled, 'Am I to run from a cur?'

Against the tide of people desperately seeking refuge, Nomguqo saw Mehlokazulu push his way through to the cattle-pen, a dozen armed warriors at his side.

Chaos overwhelmed the area around the gates. The cattle driven down from the *isibaya* created a bottleneck, their heads tossing nervously as the herdboys ran around them. Their heavy bodies jostled against each other making access through the main entrance impossible. Mehlokazulu's plan was proving effective.

The remaining *amabutho* gathered in the cattle pen. The younger, fitter regiments were already in the field, leaving only the oldest men. Though Mehlokazulu was considerably younger, the veterans acknowledged his outstanding record in feats of arms. He had fought in all the recent battles against the invaders and distinguished himself as a worthy leader. He ran up and down the lines of the grizzled warriors to make sure they were in good heart, stopping occasionally to give specific words of encouragement. He had no time to form them into an *umkhumbi* to receive the *iNyanga*'s doctoring; instead, relied on each man for his courage and fighting skills.

Ntshingwayo and Sihayo arrived, armed and ready for battle. As senior officer, Ntshingwayo took charge. He shouted, 'We'll fight in our usual formation. The iNgobamakhosi under Mehlokazulu will take the left flank, the uMbonambi the right. Sihayo and I will be with the uKhandempemvu in the chest.' He raised his shield high in the air. 'Are you prepared to defend your king against the usurpers?'

uSuthu! reverberated back at him and spears were held aloft, blades flashing as they caught the rays of the rising sun.

Terrified residents, women, and children, stood aside as the warriors, in formation, ran down to the gate, using their shields to push through the tangle of horns and heaving bodies.

Advancing from their holding position on the ridge, the Mandhlakazi were now only six hundred yards from the gate. They checked their progress to a walk as the defenders streamed from the *umuZi* and settled into the characteristic crescent formation.

The two forces advanced towards each other, the gap between them narrowing with every footfall.

Mandhlakazi warriors taunted the veterans. Brandishing his *iklwa*, one shouted, 'Prepare to die, old men. Soon you'll feel the sharpness of our spears.'

Ntshingwayo and Sihayo stood shoulder to shoulder in the front line of the uSuthu "chest".

'I recognise that man,' Sihayo said, 'Son of Qethuka, who *kleza'ed* with Hamu. That explains why there are so many. Zibhebhu must have persuaded Hamu to join him.'

'And Jantoni,' said Ntshingwayo grimly.

They stared at the oncoming regiments, outnumbering them many times over.

'I promise you this,' Sihayo said, 'When they find my body at the end of the day, it will be surrounded by twenty of their corpses.'

Ntshingwayo shifted his grip on his shield. 'Remember how you felt the first time you washed your spear?'

'I never felt so alive,' Sihayo replied. He stood ramrod straight, the torpor and depression of recent years now forgotten.

They advanced across the plain towards the Mandhlakazi. When they were a hundred yards off, Ntshingwayo signalled a halt.

The *uSuthu* battle cry started as a hum, spears rattling against shields in the ritual challenge, growing louder and louder until the ground shook with the stamping feet. When Ntshingwayo gave the signal, they rushed forward. Many men in opposing ranks were messmates. They had been in the same regiments and had fought alongside each other against the British. Now they were pitted against each other.

Out on the left flank, Mehlokazulu led his men to complete the encircling manoeuvre; the uMbonambi reciprocated from the right. The thunderous battle cries sounded as the opposing "chests" came together. He watched Ntshingwayo and his father in the front rank cutting and thrusting like warriors in their prime. They seemed to be holding their own, despite the enemy's youth and superior numbers. Then, his confidence drained as he saw Qhude kaKuhlekonke step up to his father. Separated by a hundred yards and preoccupied with his own mission, Mehlokazulu was powerless to help. Sihayo's resistance was nominal, swept aside by Qhude's powerful spear thrusts. He was trampled under Mandhlakazi feet as they surged forward. At exactly that point, Mehlokazulu had his own, more immediate problem, to manage. A Mandhlakazi barely out of his teens lunged at him. Battle-hardened and quick on his feet, Mehlokazulu easily avoided the thrust and used the boy's forward momentum to trip him with the point of his shield. As the boy went down, Mehlokazulu ripped upwards with his spear and opened his belly. The boy sank to his knees, intestines spilling onto the ground. Mehlokazulu looked back to the "chest", but Sihayo's body had disappeared in the dust raised by the fighting men.

Some distance from the *umuZi*, beside a tributary of the Mfolosi, Cetshwayo was hidden in a clump of trees. Mnukwa and the other *izinceku* had arranged to lead a decoy in the opposite direction, but it had not gone according to plan. A group of young Mandhlakazi found the king crouching in the long grass. They called on him to stand. And, when he showed himself, they launched three spears at him. One missed, but the other two struck him in the right thigh.

Cetshwayo bellowed, 'I am your king!'

Recognising his voice, the youths froze. For them, the king's person — even though they were attacking his followers — was sacrosanct. 'Ndabezitha, please forgive us,' said one. 'We didn't recognise you.'

'Well, I recognise you. Each one of you. And when this business is concluded, you will answer for this.' He sank back onto the grass, paralysed with pain.

They approached, horrified by what they had done. 'Your Majesty, let us to tend your wounds.'

Teeth gritted, Cetshwayo let them make amends. They pulled out the spears and irrigated the gashes with water drawn from the stream, then bound up his thigh with tight bandages. They helped him to his feet. 'Are you able to walk, Ndabezitha?'

'What do you think?' He wouldn't give them the satisfaction of showing how badly he was hurt. 'Now, which is the best way out of here?'

When the main gates were breached, Nomguqo was still with the royal wives. Because the defenders were outside the perimeter fence, they had no protection. The slaughter began immediately. The Mandhlakazi rampaged through the *umuZi*, stabbing, and cutting down the defenceless women, ignoring their pleas for mercy. They systematically set fire to the huts, the tinder-dry thatches immediately catching fire and wind carrying the smoke across the settlement.

Bunched together in fear, the women ran from the advance. Some with babies had them snatched from their arms and thrown into the flames. Qhude was particularly brutal, surrendering completely to his sadistic nature. His torso was stained red; blood ran down his arms. The whites of his eyes showed, and his limbs trembled in the fury of his blood lust.

The billowing smoke obscured much of the horror from Nomguqo. Like everyone else, she searched desperately for an escape route, or at least a safe place to hide. The exit behind the king's hut seemed an obvious way out, but the route was clogged with women with the same idea. Qhude and the Mandhlakazi were still some distance away, their progress slowing as they found increasing numbers of victims. Bodies piled up, some of them still writhing in their death throes. The screams were deafening.

Carried by the relentless press of women, she found herself in the dead centre of the *isiGodlo,* right outside the *eNkatheni.* Stepping from the crowd, she realised where she could hide. No one would think to desecrate this sacred place, the holiest site in Zululand.

She opened the door. There, in the middle of the polished floor, lay the *inkatha,* the symbol of royal power and repository of the amaZulu collective spirit.

During her time at oNdini, only four individuals had access to the *eNkatheni*: King Cetshwayo, his chief *iNgoma* Delphu Ndlovu, Nobathwa the guardian of the coil, and Nomguqo herself, accorded the honour of cleaning it. Under pain of death, all others were excluded. She closed the door behind her.

On the plain, Mehlokazulu was swept up in the rush to the main gate, pursuing Mandhlakazi who were desperate to join the rape and bloodletting.

The bodies of his father and Ntshingwayo stopped him in his tracks. He sank to his knees beside Sihayo. The rents in the old man's shield showed how stoutly he had defended himself. All his wounds were on his front, on his chest and belly. To the end he had stayed faithful to the Zulu code. Mehlokazulu made a silent vow. He would take the old man's body back to the ruins of kwaSogekle and bury it with due ceremony in the middle of the cattle pen. It would be a fitting memorial to a true *iqawe.*

The battle around him continued. The iNgombamakhosi circled around the Mandhlakazi, cutting them off from the oNdini gates. The less fleet of foot were run down and tripped from the rear, spears finishing them on the ground. No quarter was given.

Ahead of them, the gates were smashed to pieces, and the paths through the *umuZi* were choked with bodies. Mehlokazulu peered intently through the smoke from the burning roofs. He had a specific target, one man he was seeking above all others. A sudden breeze blew a hole in the smoke, and he caught sight of Qhude high up on the slope leading to the *isiGodlo*. He quickened his pace.

Nomguqo crouched in her hiding place, the sounds of continuing violence reaching her from beyond the door. She felt protected by the ancestral veneration of the holy place. However, she was concerned for Mehlokazulu. She trusted his warrior's skills; he knew how to defend himself. But with the king's forces so heavily outnumbered, how would he survive? And how would she survive without him? She had dedicated her life to him. She thought about their intimate moments in the Hlophekhulu bower, how he had kissed and caressed her. So tender, so caring.

A sound outside the *eNkatheni* made her blood freeze. It was the gutteral, heavy rasping of a man's breath. The door opened slowly, deliberately. Sunlight spilled across the threshold. The shadow of a man's lower half appeared – heavily muscled calves decorated with cows' tails. The outline of a spear followed. She swallowed as blood dripped from the blade onto the doorstep. Her eyes travelled up the figure moving forward into the entrance. Because he was silhouetted against the light, she couldn't identify him. His voice, however, was unmistakable. 'What have we here?' Qhude said.

Her body contracted instinctively. Umafutha's description of this monstrous man's brutality – the rapes, and beatings

– came flooding back. She knew instantly she was in great danger.

'Don't you dare come in here.' The determination in her voice belied her terror. 'You're violating a sacred place.'

He laughed. 'Sacred? Not to me.' He moved forward, his thickset build blotting out the light.

Her eyes darted this way and that. How could she get past him? Could she use speed to surprise him?

She had no choice. Edging along the shadows on the walls, she made a sudden dash, dropping low as she reached him. With shield in one hand and spear in the other, he very nearly missed her, but just as she passed under his arm, he dropped the spear and grabbed her neck. With a single movement, he pulled her off her feet and threw her to the ground. The back of her head struck the floor, and she lost consciousness for a second.

The sharp pain of his teeth in her neck restored her senses. An innate defence response kicked in. She twisted and turned, beating him with her fists. But it made no difference. Using his knees, he forced open her thighs and pinned her down with the heavy bulk of his body. She could nothing to prevent the violation. She whimpered as he thrust deep into her, rupturing the delicate membranes, bursting open the flesh. The scream she was desperate to release stuck in her throat. This was more than a violation of her body. Her soul was being ripped apart. Every fibre of her being rebelled. Every muscle contracted in reaction to the loathsome intrusion.

Mercifully, it ended almost as soon as it began. Qhude's eyes rolled upward as he finished, his convulsive thrusts dying away almost at once. The livid scar pulled his lips back into a horrific leer.

Withdrawing, he reached for his *iklwa*, holding her down by the throat. She would not live to testify against him. Pressing the blade against her throat, he leaned his weight on it. She felt it biting into her skin. She resigned herself, accepting that this was how she would die.

Then unexpectedly, his body convulsed with a sudden shock, and the pressure on the blade lifted. Qhude's grunting was replaced by Mehlokazulu's shout: 'Animal!'

As Qhude rolled away, she saw blood pouring from a wound in his shoulder. For a heavy man, he was surprisingly agile. Howling with rage, he used his momentum to spring to his feet. His right arm hung by his side, the nerves controlling its movement severed by the spear thrust. Glaring balefully, he rushed forward. The impact took Mehlokazulu off his feet and they both crashed into the wall.

She drew her knees to her chest, and wrapped her arms around them, her torn and bruised flesh making her shiver with pain.

The two men wrestled on the ground. Their flailing feet kicked over the wooden platform on which the *inkatha* rested. Skittering across the polished floor, the python skin casing broke open and the contents of grass and body essences collected from the whole Zulu nation spilled out.

With only one effective arm, Qhude was at a disadvantage. He used the one weapon available to him, his teeth. He bit deeply into Mehlokazulu's shoulder muscle.

Struggling to shake free, Mehlokazulu used his feet to gain purchase, but there was no traction on the slippery surface. Locked in a ghastly embrace, they rolled over and over. Managing to wrench away his spear arm, Mehlokazulu planted the blade in the plaster daub and levered their bodies apart. On his knees above Qhude, he lifted the spear and, with a single downward motion, plunged it into his throat. Blood from the severed artery arced across the room. Fingers desperately clutching at the wound, Qhude tried to sit up, but it was too late. His blood pressure dropped, and the flow slackened until it was a trickle through his fingers. He slumped back, sliding into the pool of his own blood. He twitched spasmodically and his eyes rolled back. Then he was still.

Breathing hard, Mehlokazulu turned to Nomguqo. He offered his hand, but she recoiled, every inch of her flesh shuddering in reaction to the violation. She couldn't look at him. She longed to be held, to be enveloped into the comfort of his arms. But she knew that, if he touched her, she would start to scream and never stop. With absolute clarity she knew she would never be his bride. The words he had spoken when describing Sixhwethu's parentage sounded in her ears: *A woman who accepts another man's seed deserves to die. It's the Zulu way.* Henceforward it would always be between them. Now she was "spoilt", polluted by another man's seed, she would always feel unworthy of him. She pulled her knees even more tightly to her chest, retreating into her pain and sorrow.

She watched him walk to the door, his expression confirming Sixhwethu's prophesy that she would die an old maid. Her eyes fluttered and she lapsed mercifully into unconsciousness.

Outside the *eNkatheni*, the Mandhlakazi continued to run amok, torching the huts. The air was thick with smoke. Watching the destruction from the shelter of the doorway, Mehlokazulu realised it was only a matter of time before it reached the *eNkatheni*. He had minutes to save Nomguqo from a painful death.

Running back, he scooped her inert body into his arms. Doing so, he noticed the pool of blood on the floor where she had been lying. Blood dripped onto his arms from between her thighs. Holding her and seeing the evidence of her violation, he felt suddenly alienated. He considered her with no more attachment than he would any wounded creature. Nomguqo was right. She was now *ukuzila*, taboo.

With her dead weight in his arms, he peered from the doorway. Then, choosing a moment when the Mandhlakazi marauders' attention was directed elsewhere, he zigzagged from one hut to another and headed to the rear exit. The screaming of dying women and shouts of triumphant warriors remained a constant background noise.

A horse was tethered outside the king's quarters. It had been brought up in readiness for the king's escape but abandoned in the panic of the moment. Levering her body onto its back, he twisted her hands into its mane, wrapped the trailing halter around her shoulders, and guided it to the gate.

Her whispered voice, scarcely audible in the din that surrounded them, made him stop and listen. She pushed herself up from the horse's withers. Her lips formed the syllables of his name and her eyes gazed imploringly, but no sound came. He bent towards her, trying to hear what she was saying.

A movement in his peripheral vision made him turn just in time to avoid a spear thrust. The Mandhlakazi lunged again, but Mehlokazulu swivelled on the balls of his feet and seized his wrist. Twisting as the man's weight came forward, he used the momentum to disarm him, driving the *iklwa* into his chest. The Mandhlakazi slumped to the ground, the weight of his body driving the point of the blade through his back. Thus impaled, his eyes glazed over in death.

Spooked by the fight, the horse bolted. With Nomguqo barely conscious on its back, it careered through the open gate.

Mehlokazulu watched it climb the short slope towards Mthonjaneni. Then she was gone, the woman who was to have been his bride.

FORTY-ONE

Nkandla

Cetshwayo limped the last few feet to the highest point of the ridge, panting with the effort. Rivulets of sweat ran down his chest. A thick crust had formed over the wounds in his thigh, but a trickle of fluid leaked from a corner where the tissues had reopened. His teeth were clamped against the pain.

He had been on the run for over eighteen days, one step ahead of the warriors Zibhebhu had sent to track him down. His powers of endurance had served him well, but he was exhausted. If it had meant the end to his suffering, he would have surrendered there and then. As it was, his journey was almost complete. He had reached his destination.

He stared into the gorge. Far below was somewhere he could hide and allow his body to heal. He turned to his *izinceku*. 'Here we'll be safe.'

The gorge was a massive mile-long ravine within the remote and impenetrable Nkandla Forest. Walls on either side rose almost perpendicularly to the top of a three-thousand-foot mountain. On the right a razor-edged spur dropped vertically down to the river Mome to form the exit at the extreme end of the gorge. Beyond this lay the "stronghold", a series of caves behind a waterfall at the end of a steep and dangerous path through the forest. It offered a perfect refuge for the king – particularly since it fell under the jurisdiction of Sigananda, chief of the amaCube people, prominent members of the uSuthu faction that remained loyal to him.

Cetshwayo began his descent, frowning with pain as he placed his weight onto the injured leg. He steadied himself on the shoulder of one of his servants and continued step by step down the slope.

Nomguqo's recollection of her flight from oNdini was blurred. She presumed that instinct alone had guided the horse away from the burning *umuZi* and towards her family home. She had no idea how long it had taken, or by what route, but her first clear memory was of her father Sikhunyane holding out his arms and her tumbling into them.

In the ensuing weeks, she felt dead inside. Nothing seemed to justify her continued existence. If only she had died there and then. Had Qhude slit her throat, it would have been over quickly instead of the prolonged agony of self-loathing. He had not just violated her flesh. He had ripped out the humanity that connected her with others. She felt alienated, incapable of reaching out. Her self-worth destroyed, she convinced herself that no one else valued her either.

Unaware of what she had suffered, her father and sisters watched helplessly as she withdrew further and further into her own silent world.

'Cetshwayo, we know you're in there,' the redcoat officer shouted into Sigananda's cave, 'Come out now and no harm will come to you. I have orders to bring you to Eshowe. You're to meet with government officials there.'

A platoon of soldiers stood behind him, their rifles cocked and aimed, along with Mandhlakazi warriors sent by Zibhebhu to witness his rival's capture.

Sigananda, surrounded by his own people, stood some thirty yards away, outnumbering the redcoats by ten to one, but the soldiers' superior weaponry counterbalanced the threat. Sigananda shouted a warning, 'Stay put, Ndabezitha. Zibhebhu's jackals–'

The redcoat officer interrupted. 'I'm running out of patience. If you won't come out, we'll be forced to smoke you out.' It was an empty threat because his orders were to bring the king in peacefully.

After a long pause Cetshwayo responded. 'I cannot move. The wound is infected, and my leg is swollen. If the officials wish to meet me, they will have to come here. If your promise to safeguard me is sincere, you must return without the Mandhlakazi. I do not trust them.'

The officer stepped back, realising he was stalemated. He couldn't force the issue. His priority was to deliver Cetshwayo safely and the bad blood between the factions put that under threat. With bad grace he marched to his horse, climbed into the saddle, and dug his heels into its flanks.

Gradually, the routine of family life restored Nomguqo to some form of normality. It acted as a balm to heal her physical and emotional wounds. The initial pain receded but she developed a passivity that allowed her to accept the ups and downs of life with complete indifference. She felt no sorrow, but by the same token, she felt no joy. Nurtured by her family she gradually regained her sense of purpose and, reassured by the constancy of their affection, slowly recovered her reasons for living.

Five months later, news that would shock all those loyal to Cetshwayo reached them. The king was dead. Cornelius Vijn made the announcement, sitting in the Mkhuze *isibaya*.

'Poisoned?' said Sikhunyane with disbelief. Nomguqo and her sisters were mute with shock.

'That is one theory. The official version is, he died of a heart attack.' Vijn drank *uTshwala* from his beaker. 'Yet only two hours before they found him dead, he'd taken his usual morning walk and seemed in perfect health. Poisoning can be the only possible explanation. Anyway, I heard that his body has been prepared in the traditional way and is to be taken to lie in the Nkandla Forest.'

The Dutchman's casual description of the last moments of someone who had had such an influence over their lives seemed almost sacrilegious. Nomguqo turned away, the heavy weight of grief pressing on her chest. For the first time in years, indeed since she'd exhausted her supply of Vijn's Chinese herbal medicine, she felt the symptoms of her asthma returning. She started to wheeze.

Vijn's reaction was immediate. 'Get me some water,' he ordered.

Diboli ran to the water container while Vijn delved into his satchel and produced a tin. He showed it to Nomguqo. 'Recognise this?

Tears streaming down her cheeks, she nodded.

'We'll have you breathing normally again in no time.' Throwing powdered leaves into the beaker Diboli brought him, he swirled them around to create the infusion. Handing it to her, he encouraged her to drink, 'All of it, down to the last drop.'

Though the medicine calmed the symptoms of Nomguqo's distress, it had no effect on the root cause. Vijn's careless announcement of Cetshwayo's death tapped into the limitless well of misery over which she had managed to place a lid. Now it overflowed, wave after wave of agonising grief. There was no consoling her. She wept uncontrollably, in mourning for her loss – the future she would never have, the husband she would never love, the children she would never bear.

PART SIX

THE DAY THAT I DIE

FORTY-TWO

Malakata

Mehlokazulu waded into the stream. Bare feet slipping on the smooth pebbles, he chose his steps carefully. He picked a spot where the water ran fastest, knelt, and with arms stretched wide to steady himself, plunged his head and shoulders into the icy water.

He re-emerged, gasping with shock. Water streamed from his shoulders. Shaking his head, he released a shimmering shower of droplets caught in his *isicoco*, the ring of hair and gum that denoted his married status.

The action of the cold raised goose bumps on his arms. Running his hands over them, he sluiced away the remaining beads of water. Within seconds the remaining heat from the setting sun dried his skin.

His muscles and joints ached as he levered himself into a standing position. The strength and suppleness of his body had long since deserted him. Now in his fifties, the years had taken their toll. The pads of fat softening his jaw and waistline showed the effect of a life of enforced idleness. Peering down at his paunch, he reflected on the arrogance of his youth when he had scorned the *izilomo* – the "soft old men", favourites of the king, who sat around the eating mat, their pudgy hands resting on their bellies. The realisation he was one of them made him shudder with disgust.

Clambering from the water, he swung his arms around his torso to restore some warmth to his extremities. The exertion made him breathless. He tested for stiffness in his shoulder muscles and concluded that the cold water had had a restorative effect. The blood coursing through his veins had brought a new vitality to his body and, with it, to his spirit.

A sudden cool breeze ruffled the leaves of the low-lying bushes beside the stream. His horse's soft snicker reminded him of its presence. Running his hand over its muzzle, he reached for his clothes, pulled a shirt over his head, and stepped into a pair of canvas trousers, tightening the belt over his belly. He still felt uncomfortable wearing European dress, but it was expedient. These days, the wearing of traditional Zulu garb attracted too much attention and begged too many questions. There were far more important issues to fight.

Inhaling deeply, he looked down to where his followers were camped. He had left them earlier in the day and climbed up to the high ground. He needed a clear head, free of the distractions of domestic life. Too much of his energy was expended in resolving petty squabbles between his wives. How much simpler life would be with only one wife, but was there a woman capable of satisfying all his needs? There had been one over twenty years ago, but she had been denied him. Ever since, not a day passed when he didn't regret it.

Ten days earlier, redcoat soldiers had driven him and his family into the hills and, for the second time, destroyed the kwaSogekle homestead. He was determined to stay ahead of them.

To the west the great red disk sank over the mountain range, its ridges and gullies offering sharp contrasts. Shading his eyes, he scanned the horizon. His eyesight had always been needle-sharp. Now, the "Eyes of the Zulu" found it increasingly difficult to make out distant objects. Faculties he had taken for granted had lost their power, and this waning potency had extended as far as his marriage bed. Recently, he had taken to sleeping alone to avoid the barbed comments of his wives – better a celibate life than the reproaches of disappointed women. Yet it did nothing to relieve his own contempt for his dwindling prowess. Every action was a painful reminder of what he had lost. His body mocked him for the carelessness of youth.

His mortality had preoccupied him for some time. After the sacking of kwaSogekle he had known that a day of reckoning with the *abelungu* was inevitable, but his resources in manpower and arms were pitifully inadequate. His thousand warriors armed with muzzle-loaders and spears were no match for the artillery and machine-guns of his enemy. The consequence of military action was inevitable. And he would be leading his men to certain death.

The tension had been building for over a year, since the British authorities imposed a poll tax in Zululand to pay for their war against the Boers, making it clear that extreme sanctions would be applied to anyone who refused to pay. As the Qungebeni *inkosi*, Mehlokazulu knew it would place an intolerable burden on his people. An epidemic of cattle disease in the country had decimated the herds, forcing them to slaughter their breeding stock to survive. Any additional financial strain would tip the balance towards starvation.

The amaQungebeni were not alone. Throughout Zululand, tribes felt the pinch and opposed the unjust tax. They had their own issues with the Boer *izikhonyane* (locusts) and derived no benefit from the British wars with them. They saw no reason why they should be forced to pay for the consequences of British greed.

Already armed insurrection had broken out. Warriors of the amaZondi, a tribe living on the British side of the Zulu border, had attacked and killed a British police patrol and fled across the River Thukela beyond British jurisdiction. Their *inkosi*, Bambatha kaMancinza, and his adherents, growing in number as they moved through Zululand, had taken refuge in the Nkandla Forest, and were arming themselves for an inevitable confrontation.

Bambatha's insurrection had put Mehlokazulu firmly on the spot. Already young Qungebeni hotheads demanded action, insisting their chief follow Bambatha's example. Mehlokazulu was reminded of his younger self, contemptuous of the caution shown by the old men who sat on the king's council. The irony that the position was now reversed had not escaped him.

He watched the top edge of the moon emerge on the horizon. He had spent too long away from his people. Climbing onto the horse's back, he allowed it to pick its way down the mountain track. There was no going back. He would fight until the last drop of his blood was shed to drive the hated white man from Zululand.

A jagged blue flash split the night sky, followed seconds later by a deafening thunderclap.

Torrents of water came in pulses, gusting across the bleak mountain landscape. A solitary tree stood firm against the howling wind, its branches stripped of their leaves by bitter winter frosts.

Another lightning strike. The short burst of light illuminated a huge black ox standing close to the tree.

He rolled his eyes in fear as a crack of thunder shook the ground beneath him, rolling away into the distance. Water poured off his head and thick neck. The muscles in his massive shoulders shivered.

The storm was now directly overhead. A vivid flash found its way to earth through the heartwood of the tree. Split in the impact, one half was hurled in the direction of the black ox. The remaining section burst into flame and burned like a roman candle.

The ox pawed the ground, his hooves ripping up clods of earth. The burning branches gave off a flickering yellow light, reflected in the gleaming flanks of the terrified beast.

Then, out of nowhere, dark shapes appeared, running towards him. They kept low to the ground, almost skimming the surface. Converging from all sides, the shapes seemed propelled by supernatural speed.

The force of the driving rain weakened. The wind dropped. Unaware of the shapes racing towards him, the ox relaxed. His muscles stopped twitching as he waited for the storm to pass.

Then the shapes were upon him. Bellowing, he dug his hooves into the soft earth and drove forward.

The light from the burning tree made every detail of the ox visible. Not so the shapes. Their features were harder to identify; men or animals, it was impossible to say. Matching the ox stride for stride, they crisscrossed behind and in front of him. Some passed under his belly, just managing to avoid the flailing hooves.

Light flashed on a metal blade. Other blades appeared.

The ox faltered. The blade flashed again, severing the tendons in his leading leg. He went down, his forward momentum pitching him over and over. He came to rest on his side, his massive chest heaving with the effort of the flight.

He bellowed in fear and pain as the shapes overwhelmed him, blotting out the firelight.

The blades flashed again, slicing into his hide – razor-sharp spears that severed the thread of life deep inside him.

His mouth opened in silent protest. A deep sigh escaped his punctured lungs and his eyes bulged in his death throes.

A trick of the flickering light perhaps, but the bulging eyes were becoming human. The beast was becoming a man.

The mouth opened. The death rattle sounded. The head slumping forward was unmistakably Mehlokazulu's.

Nomguqo sat bolt upright, heart thumping and sweat beading her forehead. She attempted to swallow but her saliva had dried.

She tried to find her bearings in the darkened room. When she realised she had been dreaming, her breathing gradually resumed its normal rhythm.

Throwing her legs over the side of the bed, she padded to the open window, lent on the rough frame, and inhaled drafts of fresh night air. The panic of the nightmare subsided.

'Nomguqo?'

She turned in the direction of her younger sister Diboli, who sat up in the bed they shared, eyes wide from being woken unexpectedly.

'Go back to sleep. It's nothing,' Nomguqo said. 'Just a bad dream.'

Pulling the blanket off the bed, Diboli draped it over her shoulders as she joined her sister at the window. 'Again?'

Nomguqo nodded. Considering what she had witnessed during her time in Cetshwayo's *isiGodlo* it was hardly surprising. Death had become commonplace in the war against the British. She had seen with her own eyes the terrible wounds the guns had inflicted: warriors returning from the battlefields with missing limbs or gaping holes in their chests, men who had marched off so full of courage and optimism reduced to cripples. She had come to dread the nighttime. In the dark the images bubbled up from her subconscious: never the same but always with a common theme, animals and anonymous humans suffering agonising deaths.

This morning's dream had been different. The victim had an identity. She had not seen or heard from Mehlokazulu for over twenty years and here he was appearing in her nightmare. What did it mean? With a deep sigh she released her pent-up tension.

Diboli stretched the blanket over her sister's shoulders. They perched on the windowsill together. Stroking her hair, Diboli made soothing sounds.

Both women were now in their forties, Nomguqo the older by three years. They wore identical cotton nightshifts, which covered them from neck to knee but were made semi-transparent by the half-light of dawn. Long hours toiling on the farm where they lived had kept their bodies trim, and the flat stomachs of their girlhood had remained undistorted by pregnancy. Their facial characteristics, however, were altered – Nomguqo's most dramatically. The deep lines etched into her brow and around her eyes conveyed a deep sadness.

Bracing her shoulders, she shook her head impatiently. It was just a silly dream and meant nothing. She threw off the blanket and her sister's warm embrace.

FORTY-THREE

Mome Gorge

Bambatha, Mehlokazulu and Sigananda watched the *iNyanga* Malaza stirring the concoction. The herbalist wore his full war regalia. The monkey tails around his waist swayed in rhythm with the movements of his arm.

Steam from the cauldron mingled with the smoke of the wood fire and swirled into the mist. Twelve hundred men, standing in the traditional *umkhumbi* circle, watched Malaza make his final preparations. In the early morning light their faces were tense, each showing his nerves in his own way. Ricked ankles and pulled muscles showed how hard the night march through the mountains had been. They were impatient to get started; they had waited long enough. For over four months the colonial forces had been pressing at their heels, burning them out of their homesteads and hounding them from pillar to post.

Satisfied his medicine was ready, Malaza announced, 'This *muthi* is very strong, guaranteed to repel the bullets of the *abelungu*. It has extra-special ingredients.'

Mehlokazulu sucked his teeth. A veteran of four major battles against the British, he had seen too many bodies mangled by Gatling guns and rapid-firing Martini-Henrys to accept the *iNyanga*'s claims. However, if it helped the men to believe the medicine made them invincible, who was he to contradict him?

Besides which, the ground they were standing on gave them an unassailable advantage. Sigananda, the *inkosi* who had offered Cetshwayo refuge in his final flight from oNdini, was now an old man of ninety-one, but he still bitterly resented the British invaders; early in the rebellion he had allied his amaCube to the cause and made available a thousand fighting men, inviting Bambatha to make a stand in his home territory of Mome Gorge. The steepness of the surrounding hillsides and impenetrability of the vegetation made access virtually impossible. And for anyone loyal to the memory of the last great Zulu king, it provided an added spiritual dimension. It was only half a mile from where Cetshwayo had been brought after his death. He lay there still, buried in a secluded stand of trees.

Mehlokazulu peered into the cauldron bubbling over the wood fire. The stench from the seething mixture was overpowering. He wrinkled his nose in disgust. On the surface of the liquid floated a mixture of herbs and animal parts, but among them was an ingredient he found hard to identify. He studied the strange object, gelatinous on one side and, as the bubbles rising from the bottom of the iron pot turned it over, long matted whiskers on the other. He realised it was a human upper lip sporting a thick moustache.

Bambatha grinned. 'From the officer at Mpanza.' He added, 'We also took his cock and balls. They're in there, too.'

Closing the door to their sleeping quarters, Diboli joined her sister. The rising sun streaked the sky with ribbons of orange and gold. Nomguqo yawned. The nightmare featuring Mehlokazulu and the bull continued to haunt her. She was exhausted by the interruptions to her sleep, and by Diboli's continual attempts to explain its significance. She didn't need her sister's interpretation of the hidden meaning. She knew only too well what it meant.

The sisters had a routine of rising earlier than anyone else on van Rooyen's farm, so they had the place to themselves. They headed for the main farmhouse, a single-story whitewashed building with a veranda around it. A well-tended vegetable garden lay to one side, stocked with squashes, beets, and mealies, with a large orchard of pomegranates, naartjies, and bananas beyond. The farmstead was laid out in typical Boer fashion. Its fresh paint and the good order of its buildings indicated it had been recently built. In fact, Gert van Rooyen had settled the land only ten years earlier. The annexation of Zululand had allowed him to claim it, since when he had developed it extensively, introducing breeds of cattle resistant to the diseases that decimated the Zulu herds.

Van Rooyen lived according to strict Christian ethics. He acted as a Good Samaritan, helping his Zulu neighbours and offering advice in European farming methods. He had been particularly generous to Nomguqo's family, offering them accommodation in his compound and employment on his farm when Zibhebhu drove them from Mkhuze and lung disease destroyed their herds. They honoured him with a Zulu name: Shede Foloyi.

Diboli marched ahead, determined to seek guidance in her sister's spiritual welfare. 'God wants to tell you something through your dream,' she said. 'Shede Foloyi will explain its meaning.'

'Diboli, I forbid you to talk about this,' said Nomguqo

sternly. 'I do not want him thinking I have *ufufunyane*, that I'm a crazy woman. I do not have evil spirits.'

'Your dreams are not normal, Nomguqo. They will make you sick in your soul. Shede Foloyi will help.' She quickened her pace, scattering the chickens foraging for insects in the grass. Diboli had absolute faith in van Rooyen. His support for the family had a spiritual as well as a material dimension. Through van Rooyen's teaching and the ministry of the local Lutheran mission, the family – apart from Nomguqo – had accepted Christ as their saviour. Liberated from superstitions and pagan rituals, they believed they had been saved to dedicate themselves to the service of the Lord.

Nomguqo took the opposite view. After everything she had suffered, the notion of a merciful god was impossible to accept. The Bible's teachings were irreconcilable with what she had experienced first-hand. A god who sanctioned, perhaps even devised, the misery and pain of His people was, in her opinion, manifestly lacking in grace, compassion and mercy.

Diboli tapped on the open door.

The Zulu cook busy preparing breakfast replied, 'He's in the barn, delivering a calf.'

Diboli set off in that direction.

Nomguqo caught up with her. 'Please, Diboli, he will only laugh at me.' She had no wish to share her private thoughts; she wanted to leave the painful feelings from the past where they belonged – in the past.

Reluctantly she followed Diboli through the barn door. It took a while for their eyes to adjust to the reduced light level, but they could hear the bellowing of a cow in pain. The orange glow of a paraffin light showed the farmer leaning against the cow's hindquarters, his arm deep inside the birth canal. He made soothing noises, '*Schatzi*, gently does it…' Sweat beading his freckled brow, he looked up as the two sisters appeared at the stall. 'I've been with her all night. She's having a tough time, poor girl. Twins in her first calving.'

The cow's flanks shuddered as a new contraction took hold. He withdrew his arm and watched with concern as the distressed beast moved from side to side.

'One is presenting normally. I'm not sure about the other.'

Nomguqo shivered involuntarily. Thirty years were condensed into a split second as she recalled Uxisipe's newborn "*umnyama*" twin boys being snatched from her. The memory was as clear as yesterday. She saw Dlephu Ndlovu's pitiless expression and Uxisipe's agony. Then her own horror at discovering the tiny skulls above the execution rock.

Under her tail, the cow's vulva contracted. Fluid ran down her hind legs, pooling in the straw bedding on the mud floor. An involuntary kick sent a bucket full of water flying.

Van Rooyen grabbed it. 'Make yourself useful. One of you, fill this.'

Realising that if she volunteered, Diboli would use her absence to share her nightmare with the farmer, Nomguqo stared her sister down.

'Make up your minds.'

Giving ground, Diboli took the bucket and disappeared outside. Nomguqo pulled handfuls of straw from a nearby bale and laid them over the sopping floor, treading them down to absorb the spill.

The cow started to breathe heavily, indicating she was about to deliver. The first calf's forefeet appeared. Taking them in his large hands, Van Rooyen gently pulled. The heifer blinked as her jet-black calf was delivered. He laid it on the straw, massaging its chest until it spluttered and took its first breath. 'A strong, healthy bull calf,' he announced.

Nomguqo took over the post-natal care while he delivered the second. She dried off the little bull with a handful of straw and put him beside the mother. Bending her head, the heifer nuzzled her newborn. Nomguqo watched with eyes full of tenderness. The birth of an animal was an everyday occurrence on a farm. But every time she was overwhelmed with loss for the children she would never have. Tears blurred her vision.

'Shede Foloyi…?'

He looked over.

'Diboli wants to talk to you, but since it concerns me, you should hear it from me first. My sleep has been troubled recently by dreams.'

He stroked the heifer's flanks as the second calf's hooves appeared.

'I say "dreams", but it's always the same one. Diboli says I have the gift, that my dreams have meaning. If that is so, I fear the meaning in this one.'

'What do you mean?'

The second calf slipped effortlessly into his hands. He handed it to her to clean.

'I see a black bull,' she continued, 'the biggest and fiercest in the herd. Then a thunderstorm. Lightning splits a huge tree in half. It burns brightly. The bull is stampeded by the storm and is attacked by black shapes.'

'Shapes?'

'Yes, lots of them.'

He listened intently, using straw to clean the blood and amniotic fluid off his hands.

'The shapes kill the bull. Butcher it. And… and… then I wake up.' She laid the second calf beside its mother's head, and carried its older brother to the cow's udder, placing its mouth over a teat.

He dried his hands on his trousers. 'Shapes, you say. What kind of shapes?'

'I don't know, they're just shapes. Black. I can't see what they are. Human or… I can't tell.'

He prompted, 'And you fear the meaning in this dream?'

'I'm afraid it's a portent of someone's death.'

'Someone you know?'

'Someone I knew.' She watched the older calf noisily suckling and the heifer cleaning his brother with long strokes of her tongue and was surprised that, after so many years, thoughts of Mehlokazulu awakened such strong emotions. She had erased so much of that day, the day she had last seen him. It didn't seem real any longer. The facts, however, were undeniable. She had been violated, her rapist killed in front of her, and she had rejected her deliverer. But any emotions she had a right to feel weren't present. She felt nothing – no fear, no anger, no disgust. A total void.

Returning with the water pail, Diboli placed it at Van Rooyen's feet. 'If you were wondering what took so long,' she said, 'she had kicked a big dent in it. I had to knock back into shape.' She stood back, aware she was interrupting, 'What are you talking about?'

'My dream,' Nomguqo answered.

'Oh.'

Van Rooyen patted Nomguqo's shoulder 'I'll tell you what I think it means. Diboli is right: you do have the "gift". You have been blessed by our Heavenly Father. Your dream is directly from Him, and what he is telling you is as clear as day. The lightning of your dream is the Holy Ghost splitting the tree of ignorance and bringing the light of the Christ's teaching to the heathen.'

Diboli interrupted, 'And the black bull?'

'…is Satan himself, the personification of evil. Satan is the tempter who offered Jesus the world if he would bow down and worship him. It's in the scriptures. Your black shapes are the angels of the Lord, led by the archangel Michael, casting Satan into the pit of hell.'

Mehlokazulu the "personification of evil"? That made absolutely no sense to Nomguqo. Her one certainty was that the man who should have been her husband had a pure heart. He may have had a distorted sense of honour; he may have followed the Zulu code too rigorously. But, in his own way, he had loved her.

Diboli turned to her sister. 'What did I tell you? I knew Shede Foloyi would have the answer.'

He clasped his hands earnestly. 'This is a sign. Nomguqo, receive Jesus as your saviour, I beg you. You have been blessed as his messenger. Pray with me now.'

He knelt on the straw in front of the two sisters. Diboli pulled Nomguqo down. Offering his hands to the women, he closed his eyes in prayer.

'Our Father, which art in Heaven,
Hallowed be thy name,
Thy Kingdom come,
Thy will be done
On earth as it is in Heaven.
Give us this day our daily bread
And forgive us our trespasses,
As we forgive them that trespass against us,
And deliver us from evil.
For, thine is the Kingdom, the Power, and the Glory
For ever and ever.
Amen.'

Neither Diboli nor Van Rooyen noticed that Nomquqo's voice was silent in the response.

Visibility in the valley was poor. The earlier mist had turned to heavy rain, which drenched Mehlokazulu's men as they took up position. They didn't have long to wait. A shot from an artillery piece shattered the early morning peace and reverberated around the hills. The shell exploded in the front ranks, sending body parts into the air. In the time it took to reload, another shell whistled into the rebels. Rather than take further casualties by holding their ground, Mehlokazulu ordered a retreat along the Mome stream. The ground climbed more steeply here, exposing the warriors even further. Another shell burst, scattering shrapnel across a wide area. Half a dozen more were cut down.

Down on the valley floor, soldiers on horseback dismounted and levelled their rifles. A volley of shots rang out. Mehlokazulu turned as four of his men went down, their lungs and hearts literally exploding from their chests. As they fell, he registered the tiny entry holes in their backs. The soldiers were using exploding bullets. Already aware the odds were stacked against a successful outcome, he now understood they were insuperable. This understanding came not with regret that his life was ending – his warrior's training and experience precluded fear for his own safety. His overwhelming feeling was one of disappointment that they had failed, that their cause was defeated.

As they climbed, they came under fire from above. Picked off from the rear and from both sides, they were fish in a barrel. Now it was every man for himself. They swarmed up the course of the stream, tripping over the rocks, using the only escape route available: the waterfall at the rear of the cliff. Water cascaded down the steep slopes, turning the stream into a torrent. They fought against the power of the water.

Mehlokazulu's age and lack of fitness took its toll. His lungs wheezed and whistled as he waded through the deluge. All the time bullets ricochetted off the rocks around him, sending sharp splinters into his arms and chest. A clump of trees gave him a brief respite. Resting his elbows on his knees, he gasped for breath, then checked to see how his men were faring. Bullets spattered around them. They were in desperate need of cover. A hundred yards behind, Bambatha struggled through the water, then disappeared. Mehlokazulu waited for him to reemerge; it was hard to know whether he had tripped or been shot. With no further sign, he concluded he must have been killed outright.

His own situation was desperate. If he left the shelter of the trees, he would expose himself to sharpshooters on three sides. But he had no choice. He ran forward.

He heard the shot that killed him. In the split second before the bullet struck, he had the strongest sense of the rightness of his actions. He had bent his knee to no one except his king.

Time stretched as he fell. He counted each millisecond as if it was limitless, but he knew this was the end; the damage to his internal organs was too great. Blood from his punctured lungs filled his chest and windpipe and choked him. As his consciousness ebbed, he thought of the unborn son he would never see. He had asked that the boy be named Mhlawosuku, "The Day that I Die". Even as the light dimmed, he smiled. What a prescient choice. He had only one regret. He knew he had lived the life of a true umZulu, but would his son have any sense of those values? Would future generations understand what he had lived and died for?

He remembered Shaka's words: "You will not rule when I am gone, for the land will see the white locusts come". How accurate the great king's prophecy had been, how apt his analogy. Like insects, the white men had overrun the country, devouring everything in their path. He had done all he could to confront them, to stop the spread of their contaminating influence but, as he surrendered to death, he realised that even he, an *iqawe* to the end, had been unequal to the task. A calm and serenity descended on him with the recognition that at least he had tried.

A couple of flies settled tentatively on his eyes, which stared sightlessly into the clear blue sky. Emboldened by the absence of any discernible life, they sent out their exploratory tongues to collect the moisture. Before long they were joined by others, and Mehlokazulu, the "Eyes of the Zulu", disappeared in a black cloud of buzzing insects.

AFTERWORD

NOMGUQO never married. During her time at van Rooyen's farm, she had a vision that she interpreted as a visitation from Jesus Christ. She was baptised a Christian and given the name Paulina. She dedicated the rest of her life to spreading the Gospels' teaching throughout Zululand. One of her co-missionaries was a German Lutheran, Heinrich Filter, who was intrigued by her story and wrote it down. Following Paulina's death on 12 December 1942, the memoir was lodged in the Killie Campbell Africana Library. The Zulu scholar Sighart "SB" Bourquin translated it into English and published it in 1986 under the title *Paulina Dlamini: Servant of Two Kings*.

After the defeat of the *amabutho* at oNdini, MEHLOKAZULU was put on trial in Pietermaritzburg for the murder of his mother. The judge released him with no more than a reprimand because he had committed no crime under Natal law. The detailed answers he gave to the prosecution counsel are a matter of public record, contained in The James Stuart Archive of Recorded Oral Evidence Relating to the History of the Zulu and Neighbouring Peoples, edited by Webb C. de B. and Wright,

John, 5 volumes (University of Natal Press, Pietermaritzburg and Durban, 1976, 1979, 1982, 1986, 2001)

JOHN DUNN's fortunes reached their zenith after Cetshwayo was deposed. His reward for the service he gave to the British forces during the war was the largest section of the former kingdom. After Cetshwayo's restoration, his territory was drastically reduced but he retained considerable land in the Mangete district. This became known as Dunn's Land and is occupied, to this day, by his descendants. John Dunn published a memoir entitled *John Dunn, Cetywayo, and the Three Generals in 1886*. He died aged sixty-one on 5 August 1895.

Within the European population of Natal, support for the invasion of Zululand and the deposition of Cetshwayo was not universal. Many voices were raised in protest. One particularly eloquent dissenter was the bishop of Natal, JOHN COLENSO.

On Wednesday 12 March 1879 after the battles of iSandlwana and Rorke's Drift, he preached a sermon at St Peter's Church, Pietermaritzburg, in which he systematically listed the injustices of British policy:

Wherein in our invasion of Zululand have we shown that we are men "who love mercy"? Did we not lay upon the people heavily, from the very moment we crossed the border, the terrible scourge of war? Have we not killed already, it is said, 5,000 human beings, and plundered 10,000 head of cattle? It is true that, in that dreadful disaster, on account of which we are this day humbling ourselves before God, we ourselves have lost many lives, and widows and orphans, parents, brothers, sisters, friends, are mourning bitterly their sad bereavements. But are there no griefs – no relatives that mourn the dead in Zululand? Have we not heard how the wail has gone up in all parts of the country for those who have bravely died — no gallant soldier, no generous colonist will deny this — have bravely and nobly died in repelling the invader and fighting for their King and fatherland? And shall we kill 10,000 more to avenge the losses of that dreadful day? Will that restore to us those we have lost? Will that endear their memories more to us? Will that please the spirits of any true men, any true sons of God, among the dead? Above all, will that please God who "requires of us" that we "do justly" and "love mercy"?

ACKNOWLEDGEMENTS

Thank you to Simon Clegg for his enthusiastic support at the start of this project.

Also, to Sadie Mayne for her sound editorial advice.

Robert Dinsdale read an early draft and gave helpful and supportive notes.

Lindizwe nGobese, resident historian and guide at iSandlwana Lodge, kwaZulu-Natal, provided personal insights into the life of his ancestor, Mehlokazulu kaSihayo nGobese.

Members of the Rattray Family from Fugitives' Drift Lodge were generous with their observations about the battle of iSandlwana.

Lastly, but most importantly, I'm endlessly grateful to my wife Lizzy Ashard for her design for the front cover and for her loving support. In the journey to write this book she has been with me every step of the way.

GLOSSARY OF isiZULU WORDS

abaqawe heroes
abelungu white men, Europeans
amabutho army regiments organised by age of members
amaDlozi spirits of ancestors
amadodakazi daughters
amakhanda military barracks
amaQhikiza older, menstruating women who act as advisors to younger girls
amakhosi chiefs or kings
amaklwa short-hafted stabbing spears used in close combat
amaSi milk curds
amaZulu Zulu people/nation
beshu a square of hide worn over male buttocks
eNkatheni royal hut containing the *inkatha*, the sacred coil of the Zulu nation
dongas deep ravines
hlomula practice by which the group takes collective responsibility for the death of a hunted animal or an enemy, each man stabbing the quarry after death
giya war dance performed by a warrior to demonstrate and

enhance his reputation
gwai dried cannabis leaves ground into snuff
ibandla royal council of senior advisers to the king
ibutho army regiment organised by age of members
iDlozi spirit of an ancestor
ikhanda military barracks
iklwa short-hafted stabbing spear used in close combat
imBongo praise singer
imikhonto throwing spears
imiZi homesteads, settlements
impi army
impondo zankhomo horns of the buffalo: Zulu military tactic
inceku male servant in the royal household
iNduna state official or officer of an *ibutho*
iNgoma witchdoctor, believed to be able to commune with the spirits of the ancestors
iNgoma a royal anthem, or dance-song associated with the first fruits festival
iNgomane challenge or celebration signalled by drumming shields with spears or sticks
ingulele cheetah
ingulube pig
inhlendla crescent-shaped spear carried by the king in the form of a sceptre
inkatha the sacred coil of the Zulu nation, a grass coil thought to contain mystical substances embodying the strength and unity of the nation
inkosi chief or king
inkosazana princess
inqina hunt
insila body dirt in which is contained powerful soul essences
intelezi invincibility medicine

intulo salamander
inxweleha literally "wet with yesterday's blood", a warrior not yet ritually cleansed of the taint caused by killing
iNyanga herbalist
inyanga entsha new moon
iqawe renowned warrior, a hero
iQhikiza woman who acts as advisor to younger girls
isibaya cattle enclosure
isicoco hair twisted into a ring and stuck down with gum denoting married status
isiGodlo the private quarters of the king, containing the huts of his wives and concubines, also used to denote the unmarried female servants of the royal household
isihlangu large war shield protecting a warrior from chin to knees, property of the king
isikhulu Zulu aristocrat or great man
isiNene the square of hide worn over a man's genitals
isiZulu the language of the Zulu people
iShoba wand consisting of a wildebeest tail used by iziNgoma in "smelling out" ceremonies
iSoka official lover or recognised friend
ithonya superhuman powers instilled into warriors with the application of *muthi*
iviyo company of warriors
iwisa war club, sometimes known as knobkerrie
izibongo praise songs commemorating the deeds of a great man recited by an *iMbongo* (praise singer)
izikhonyane locusts
izikhulu Zulu aristocrats or great men
izilomo men of influence, favourites of the king
izimpi armies
iziMpisi hyena men

izinceku male servants in the royal household
iziNdibi herdboys, carriers of adult warriors' sleeping mats
iziNduna state officials or officers of an *ibutho*
iziNgoma witchdoctors, believed to be able to commune with the spirits of the ancestors
izinxweleha literally "wet with yesterday's blood", warriors not yet ritually cleansed of the taint caused by killing
iziNyanga herbalists
Ji! shout of exultation used in battle
ka son of, as in Cetshwayo kaMpande
khafula outcast (literally 'spat out')
kleza to drink milk direct from the cow's udder, an invitation from the king that marked an adolescent boy as old enough to join an *ibutho* (army regiment)
kwaNkatha the execution rock
lobola bride price
muthi medicine thought to contain spiritual properties used for preparing warriors for battle
Ndabezitha Majesty (honorific title relating to the king)
ngiyabonga thankyou
qaqa to slit the belly of a fallen enemy to free the spirit of the dead man and prevent it from haunting the killer
phakela draft, mobilisation of the amabutho
sawubona "I see you" greeting
sthandwa darling
ubaba father
udibi herdboy
ufufunyane spirit possession
uhlalankhosi "tree of kings", a thornbush whose thorns were reputed to hold the spirits of royal ancestors
uKhamba drinking bowl
ukuhlanza ritual vomiting

ukuHlobonga sex without penetration
ukukleza an invitation to drink milk from a cow's udder
ukunuka umThakathi smelling out of a witch
ukuxoxa ritual challenge offered by competing regiments
ukuzila taboo
umama mummy
umfazi omkhulu great wife
umkhonto throwing spear
umKhosi Wokweshwama annual festival of the first fruits held in December or January to invite the ancestors to bless the new harvest
umkhumbi circle formed for warriors to receive their *muthi* and battle orders
umlungu white man or European
umndlunkulu handmaiden/concubine
umntwana little one, baby
umnyama literally "blackness", a bad omen
umThakathi witch
umutsha leopard skin apron
umuZi homestead, settlement
uMvelinqangi the first of the ancestors
umZulu Zulu person
ungathinti "Do not disturb", an instruction for total silence at the king's mealtimes
untinginono secretary bird
unwabu chameleon
uSuthu! the royalist battle cry, used by the supporters of King Cetshwayo
uTshwala millet beer

BIBLIOGRAPHY

The following is a list of works I consulted during the research for *Black Sun*. I am sure there will be scholarly objections that I have overlooked essential studies. I would say in justification that I set out to create a fiction, not a definitive history. My intention was to tell a story about characters drawn into events with consequences beyond their control, and through them evoke an impression of how the amaZulu reacted to the unwarranted and unprovoked invasion of their country.

A Zulu King Speaks: statements made by Cetshwayo kaMpande on the history and customs of his people (Killie Campbell Africana Library, 1978)

Binns, C.T., *The Last Zulu King: the life and death of Cetshwayo* (Longmans, 1963)

Binns, C.T., *Dinuzulu: the death of the House of Shaka* (Longmans, 1968)

Binns, C.T., *The Warrior People* (Robert Hale, 1975)

Colenso, Frances E., and Durnford, Edward, *Colenso and Durnford's Zulu War* (Leonaur, 2008)

David, Saul, *Zulu* (Penguin, 2005)

Dlamini, Paulina, *Servant of Two Kings*, compiled by H. Filter, translated and edited by S.G. Bourquin (Killie Campbell Africana Library, 1986)

Haggard, H.R., *Cetywayo and his White Neighbours: Remarks on Recent Events in Zululand, Natal, and the Transvaal* (Trubner & Co., London, 1882)

Hale, Frederick, (ed.) *Norwegian Missionaries in Natal and Zululand: selected correspondence 1844-1900* (Van Riebeeck Society Second Series no. 27, 1997)

Knight, Ian, *Zulu Rising: the epic story of Isandlwana and Rorke's Drift* (Sidgwick and Jackson, 2010)

Knight, Ian, *Great Zulu Commanders* (Arms and Armour, 1999)

Knight, Ian, *The Anatomy of the Zulu Army: from Shaka to Cetshwayo 1818-1879* (Greenhill Books, 1995)

Laband, John, *Kingdom in Crisis: the Zulu response to the British invasion of 1879* (Pen and Sword Military, 2007)

Lock, Ron, *The Anglo-Zulu War – Isandlwana: The Revelation of a Disaster* (Pen and Sword Military, 2017)

Lock, Ron & Quantrill, Peter, *Zulu Victory, The Epic of Isandlwana and the Cover-up*, Greenhill Books, 2002

Mitford, Bertram, *Through the Zulu Country, its Battlefields and People* (Greenhill Books, 1992)

Moodie, D.C.F., *John Dunn, Cetywayo, and the Three Generals* (Natal Printing & Publishing Company, 1886)

Morris, Donald R., *The Washing of the Spears* (Pimlico, 1994)

Morrissey, D. Caellagh, *Fugitive Queens: Amakhosikazi and the Continuous Evolution of Gender and Power in KwaZulu-Natal (1816-1889)*, thesis presented to the Department of History and International Studies and the Robert D. Clark Honors College, University of Oregon, December 2015

Norris-Newman, Charles L., *In Zululand: with the British throughout the War of 1879* (Greenhill Books, 1988)

Turner, Noleen, *Scatalogical License: The case of ribald references and sexual insults in the amaculo omgonqo (puberty songs)*, (South African Journal of African Languages, vol. 31 no.2 2011)

Vijn, Cornelius and Colenso, John William, *Cetshwayo's Dutchman: being the private journal of a white trader in Zululand during the British invasion* (Bibliolife, 2009)

The James Stuart Archive of Recorded Oral Evidence Relating to the History of the Zulu and Neighbouring Peoples, edited by Webb C. de B. and Wright, John, 5 volumes (University of Natal Press, Pietermaritzburg and Durban, 1976, 1979, 1982, 1986, 2001)

The South African Military History Society has published a series of articles that are of particular interest. http://samilitaryhistory.org/